STRANGERS ON THE SHORE

STRANGERS ON THE SHORE

RANDHIR KHARE

NIYOGI
BOOKS

Published by
NIYOGI BOOKS
D-78, Okhla Industrial Area, Phase-I
New Delhi-110 020, INDIA
Tel: 91-11-26816301, 49327000
Fax: 91-11-26810483, 26813830
email: niyogibooks@gmail.com
website: www.niyogibooksindia.com

Editor: Gita Rajan
Cover design: Dsgn Unplugged
Layout: Shashi Bhushan Prasad

ISBN: 978-93-83098-61-3
Publication: 2015

Printed at: Niyogi Offset Pvt. Ltd., New Delhi, India

For Susan

Contents

1 WAITING

Dark

After a walk along the beach, I sit down on a boulder and look out at the sea change colour and the sky turn from a flat impersonal blue to a shredded orange blistered with yellow and red. Boats with their sails on fire move across the shimmering waters and dissolve out of view. The sea hardens to dark steel, the sky is powdered with rust and a flock of sandpipers swirls in and settles on the water's edge, only to be ruffled into flight as a buffalo with sweeping horns staggers down the beach along with two young men chatting loudly. Their words are tossed into the air by a wind that swims through the gathering dusk. I can smell the breath of the night as it crawls in on its belly over the hump of the hill. It reeks of dead fish, seaweed and salt-drenched sand.

It's dark now and time to go home but home isn't the house I once was so scared to live in, the house so crowded with memories and bits and pieces of the past, pieces that didn't belong to me. But then the house isn't far away from where I live now, it stands right there a few yards outside my door and constantly reminds me of all the baggage that I am trying hard to get rid of. Through the sun, wind, rain, night and grumble and roar of the sea it stands, with its enormous tiled roof resting on weather-beaten walls, windows with blue paint flaking off their wooden ribs, cracked panes and geckos scurrying along the roof of the veranda. My armchair still rests out there in the open. I had decided to leave that behind because it would be out of place in my new abode. It was my ancestor the Great Mathew's prize possession, given to him by a Portuguese sailor somewhere in the past.

Not sure when the tenants are going to start renovating the house. They are supposed to be turning it into some sort of a boutique resort with a rock garden and lily pond and an outdoor restaurant. Honestly I don't care what the hell they would like to do with the place so long as they keep doing up my place and fit it with whatever I want. And of course so long as they keep giving me a tidy rent.

My place is small, sure, but who cares? Once a storage shed in our compound, now my new home. They did a good job of the place. I mean who'd ever guess that it was once a shed? But I'm not rid of the house and the memories it holds within its walls. They stay with me. In fact, every inch of the place has a story. Walking back through the compound is like crossing a minefield. I am not sure when I'll step on something that will blow me into the past. That's what's so strange about the past and the present, that's what's so strange about time. It has a way of slipping through the fingers or is it that we slip through time? I can't tell the difference anymore. Maybe I never could tell the difference. I remember as a child getting confused. One moment I was playing out on the sand and the next I was sleeping in the shade of coconut palms and then again when I opened my eyes I was eating mashed dal, rice and crispy pieces of fish from my mother's hands. I slipped in and out of dreams so quickly that I sometimes couldn't tell whether I was awake or asleep.

Are you awake or asleep? Mother would ask, shaking me. *I can't tell because your eyes are open. You scare me. Cedric, Cedric, maybe we should show this boy to a doctor.*

Ah, that's a family habit, Monica; it's in our blood, the Great Mathew, did just that. My father didn't sound like he was joking. He sounded dead serious.

This is not about your great grandfather, it's about Arnie, I don't want him to see anything more than what you and I can see, Mother said emphatically. There's enough to see in the real world. He needs to see a doctor to put him right.

And so we did the rounds of doctors, Father staying home most of the time. When he was home, he loved staying home. When he was away at sea, we never saw him for months. Mother became obsessed about not being able to tell whether I was awake or asleep. She started slipping pellets of opium into my mouth, knocking me out and I was pushed into a haze of timelessness. One day I fell asleep with my eyes open in class. The teacher was scared out of her mind and didn't know what to do. The Principal summoned Mother and she took me home.

Finally, half way up a coconut palm one day I lost my footing and slammed on to the mud below. They found me an hour or so later, blood trickling from a gash on the back of my head. Three stitches and all was well. In fact, I stopped sleeping with my eyes open. *Thank God, you are normal now,* said Mother, *who knows, the next time you have a fall, you'll probably wake up a genius.*

But there was nothing prophetic about that statement of hers. There was no hope of me becoming a genius. I was just an ordinary fellow who lived in a world of his own, who had no friends, who was so self-conscious about talking to girls that he would sometimes even wet his pants with fright.

Time plays with memory. Memory plays with time. Time and memory dissolve into the dark and wake up with the light. Often I would be awake and just lie there in bed, allowing time and memory to play hide and seek. That kept me awake at night.

Mother always slept well. She would sink into such a deep stupor that nothing could shake her out of it. Her snore would start softly and steadily get louder, changing as it went along from a hiss to a croak. At night it seemed as if her bedroom was a pool filled with frogs. Probably that's why Father couldn't sleep in the same room whenever he was home and decided to sleep on the couch in the sitting room instead. And when he started rolling off the couch, he moved to the veranda and slept on a camp cot with a mosquito net hung over it. He slept so quietly that I sometimes wondered whether he was there or not. Actually on some occasions he wasn't.

I remember getting up one morning early because I wanted to see a new fishing boat go out to sea. *Jesus My Saviour* was bright blue with a large red metal cross on the prow. It was Mendes Babu's vessel and he had made it with his own hands and the hands of half a dozen brothers and cousins. When it was ready, the entire family had a drunken feast which resulted in Savio, his younger brother, walking into the sea like a zombie. They found him far down on the beach in a state of disrepair.

Now where was I? Why am I talking about Savio? Where did I start from? Yes, Mother croaking in her sleep like a frog and Father under the mosquito net outside in the veranda. That was the time I went to see Mendes Babu's boat *Jesus My Saviour* go out on to the Arabian Sea so her crew could cast their nets. It was *surmai* time–when the sea offered up a harvest that blessed whole families in the village. And mackerel time too … and crabs the size of dinner plates … so I went out to see *Jesus My Saviour* go to sea. Since Father had said he wanted to be there too I lifted the mosquito net to wake him up but he wasn't there. It looked like he hadn't even used the bed. So I walked on to the beach with my torchlight picking up the sand ahead of me and headed for the row of boats a little way down the beach. Everyone who was anyone was there, except my parents of course, to cheer the boat out to sea. Savio and his men sang like nut cases as they headed out. The dark sea air smelled of wet salt, weeds and dead fish. When I got back home I lifted the mosquito net again and he still wasn't there. I couldn't blame him for running off somewhere to sleep considering the way Mother snored.

I had become so used to her snoring that when I packed her off to the old folk's home I couldn't sleep at night. All I could hear was the sound of the sea, the wind, the rustle of the palms, distant dog yaps and voices floating through the dark from the village. It made me feel so alone, so bereft, so isolated. I started imagining that Mother was asleep in her room, snoring. I became obsessed with the need to have Mother in the house. She was the house, the house was her. Father and I had been visitors, outsiders, people who lived on the fringes. Maybe that's what chased him away. Anyway, he didn't really mean that much to me. She did. And yet I was so scared to get near her because every time I did, she'd envelop me, take over my life. I was helplessly dependent on her. She wanted to know everything I was doing, all the time. I never brought kids home from school because she'd constantly question them … they thought her strange.

Most kids look forward to a birthday. I was scared of mine. I was scared because ever since I could remember, my birthdays were an embarrassment. Mother would dress me up and rub rouge into my cheeks, pomade my hair, give me a little puff and make me wear a frilly shirt. Kids thought I looked very funny. Some of them called me pansy behind my back, others called me Annie. The name stuck. With every birthday, I had fewer kids over. And finally at eleven, no one came. There was just Mother and me ... and more food than we knew what to do with. After that I never had a birthday party. Instead, we went off to a cinema show in Bombay and after that an ice cream 'cram'. I would wallop as many as four different types of ice creams and she managed six.

Back home I'd stay away from school for a couple of days because I was down with either a tummy upset or a sore throat. Mother survived the eating binges and would get inspired to start playing around with all sorts of dessert recipes. She was awful at it. Her gulab jamuns were like mini golf balls and her cakes turned out like rock or were still sticky or sank in the middle. But she soldiered on and forced the results of her experiments down my throat. By sixteen I took to falling ill on my birthday to avoid the unpleasantness but that didn't stop her. *This is the only time I can show you how much I love you*, she'd say, clutching me to her chest in such a way that my face would get smothered between her enormous breasts. I'd have to wiggle my way out of the embrace.

At eighteen I found myself a girlfriend. Brenda. Actually the truth is that she found me. I didn't have too much of a choice. A big tough girl. Mother wouldn't let her into the house because she was a Convert. A Catholic Convert. *I won't have a CC in this house*, she said, *they're outcasts where I'm concerned.*

Mother, she's just a friend, I said, trying to halt her in her tracks. *What do you have against CCs?*

Now don't you 'mother' me. I don't need to give you an explanation. A CC is a CC. That's all there is to it. I'm not having you shack up with a CC. You are a PC, a Pure Catholic. And Pure Catholics go with Pure Catholics. So PCs with PCs and CCs with CCs.

If you don't want me to bring her home, I won't. But don't tell me that she can't be my friend. She's just a person. I'm not interested in her religion. I'm interested in her.

What does she have that interests you? Eh? Speak up boy.

She's a friend, isn't that enough? Why should I give you a reason?

She doesn't even look like a girl or a woman or that sort. She has a moustache. Have you noticed her moustache?

How can you be so rude?

I'm just telling you about what I can see. As it is I hear that they call you Annie. It'll be a joke. Annie and Brian.

Her name is Brenda, Mother, Brenda.

Looks more like a Brian to me.

I walked out of the house and stayed away the whole day, roaming the beach. When I got back, she was sitting in the veranda in tears and jumped up when she saw me and hugged me so hard that my ribs nearly cracked. *Don't do that ever again. You are all that I have. Don't do that again.*

Then you don't behave like that again, Mother. I'm eighteen and I have my own mind. Why don't you let me make my own choices?

What mind? What choices?

There's nothing more to talk about. I went into my room and slammed the door. Then opened my window, jumped out and sneaked off. *Let the woman bang on my door and suffer a bit.*

I rambled off along the beach and bumped into Brenda and her mother and little sister Jacinta. *Where are you off to in this heat?* her mother asked.

Going for a walk Aunty Golda.

A walk? I can see your mother coming down the beach. She's waving her hands like a windmill. Something the matter? Shouldn't you stop and wait for her?

It's none of your business Mother, Brenda snapped. *It's between them. No one asked you for your opinion.*

What are you butting in for? Aunty Golda turned on her. *What's going on between you two? Something surely is.*

By then Mother had reached us. *Think I'm a bloody fool eh? Shut the door and jump out through the window? And it's all because of you,* she glared at Brenda.

Why is it because of her? Aunty Golda reacted.

Because they are a pair these two.

What did you say? Aunty Golda looked like she was ready for a fight.

Ask this daughter of yours and she'll tell you. Mother was sarcastic.

Come on, Brenda clutched and tugged at her mother's arm. The woman shrugged her off.

You really imagine that my daughter would want to be seen with that pansy of a son of yours?

If my son's a pansy your daughter's a dyke.

Mother, no more. I pleaded. But neither of the women would listen and went for each other's throat. Jacinta fled screaming down the beach whilst both of us fell into each other's arms, shivering.

When the two women finished with shaking and slapping each other, they turned and looked at us, disbelievingly and started crying. The two of us joined them. *I think we should go back to my place and have a nice cup of Assam Tea and jam sandwiches,* announced Mother. And that's what we did.

It was a little awkward at first but then Aunty Golda and Mother settled down in the kitchen for a chat whilst they made tea and sandwiches. Just when a nice cosy warmth was settling over the house as if a giant hen had sat on her eggs, Uncle Alex, Brenda's dad, turned up with a sobbing Jacinta. *What's happening here?* He barked aggressively. *Where's your mother?*

Inside, Brenda looked uneasy.

Golda, Golda, he yelled and went into the house, dragging the weeping girl behind him. A huge argument broke out and we could hear the two women shouting at the fellow. He scrambled out of the house, stumbled down the steps and started walking away across the beach. Jacinta stood at the head of the steps, bawling her head off.

A little later we all sat down at the dining table and had tea and sandwiches. *I've asked them to come for dinner on Saturday,* Mother announced.

I nodded, not knowing what to say.

When they were gone, Mother sat me down and said flatly, *we've struck a deal. You two can see each other, you can be friends or whatever. But no knocking around the place. You are welcome to visit her in their house and she can visit you in this house. No knocking around the place together anywhere else, you hear me? Her parents and Alex's parents aren't CCs but PCs. So we've decided that it's okay you two are around with each other because she doesn't have friends because of the way she looks and you don't have friends because of the way you look.*

I wasn't particularly looking forward to the Saturday dinner. Anything could happen once everyone was inebriated. They would either continue to be friends or turn hostile. Gorai has always been an unpredictable place. Nothing has ever been constant. But Mother threw herself into the preparations and didn't stop until an hour before the arrival of our guests.

The dinner was a crazy affair with the three adults getting so drunk that they sat around dazed. Jacinta fell asleep on the sofa with her head in her mother's lap. Brenda and I slipped off into the yard and she gave me a lesson or two in deep kissing. I tried to imagine that I was a real he-guy kissing a real she-girl and it was enjoyable until she started feeling me up. I squirmed but she persisted and she grabbed my hand and made me feel her up. Then we staggered back.

That was the nearest I ever came to Brenda because Mother regulated her every move when she visited and her mother did the same when I went over. Outside, we seemed to have been watched by everyone as if we were up to some hanky panky. That's the problem with growing up in a village. A bunch of hypocrites. The lot of them. Everyone was up to their own tricks behind closed doors or among the rocks on the beach or in the bloody bushes but outside they were damned saints. Real damned saints. There were the CCs, PCs and a horde of others, all praying to their gods and worshipping on holy days and yet they'd live their lives like hypocrites.

Brenda and I were so desperate to find ourselves a secluded spot that we finally managed to slip off one evening, far beyond the rocks to a tiny cove and she quickly undressed and told me to do the same. I was halfway through getting out of my clothes when we realised we had company. Three guys turned up, couldn't make out their faces in the shadows. They punched and kicked me till I was dropped to the wet sand, then they grabbed Brenda and slapped her silly. When she fell, they were on her and I could hear her moaning *don't, please don't.*

We walked back slowly, blood trickling down her thighs. *I don't know what I am going to tell my folks,* she sobbed, *you go on to your own place, I'll manage.*

No, I'm coming with you, I insisted.

When we reached her place, Aunty Golda opened the door to us then collapsed in a heap. Uncle Alex shouted obscenities at me and punched me in the face then pushed me out, slamming the door. I crawled to the gate and walked home unsteadily, expecting to face Mother's wrath. But to my utter surprise she behaved in just the opposite manner. She became hysterical, swabbing my bloody face. *My son, my child, my little Annie. Who did this? Who did this to you?* She looked more worried than angry. She blamed no one. She didn't even want to know how it had happened. All she was worried about was that I was injured.

She fussed over me, calling me Annie but I didn't stop her. If she was comfortable saying it I was happy to let her say it. God only knows–maybe she had always wished for a daughter instead of a son.

I was worried, really worried about Brenda. What would happen to her? I desperately wanted to tell Mother everything before someone else did. But my brain was a mess. I tried to sleep but couldn't because Mother's bedroom had become a pool of frogs that serenaded the night.

The next day Mother was at my bedside.

Alex and Golda were here. I am so proud of you. So very proud of you. Brenda told her parents all about how you got those goons off her. You saved her. You are my child. My own flesh and blood. You saved her.

Where are they?

The goons?

No Mother, Aunty Golda and Uncle Alex.

They've gone.

The days that followed were a blur; Mother tended to me like she was a hospital nurse and loved every bit of it. I had become her little Annie. Then one afternoon, we got the news, Brenda had taken her own life.

Half and Half

With Brenda gone, there was little hope of finding female company. I didn't have much of a reputation in Gorai so I tried my luck in Manori. There were a few I thought I'd be able to hit it off with but other young guys got to them first and pulled the rug from under my feet. And with a mother like the one I had there wasn't much of a chance for me to spread my wings and go hunting in Bombay. College was a disaster with her shadowing me and controlling me and purposely giving me a meagre allowance so that I couldn't get anywhere with it. There were a few occasions when I did manage a small fling or two but that was it. Prospects improved a little when I became a Librarian at a convent school. Not a very big library but the teachers were interesting. Got to start something up with one of them but then it fizzled out when we were caught in each other's arms in the library store. The teacher handed in her papers out of embarrassment but I shamelessly hung on to my job after apologising profusely. Mother Superior was severe, *another something like this and I'll have to ask you to leave Arnold. This is the house of purity and wisdom, keep it this way, don't defile it.*

I wondered if things would have been different if Father had been around. Would he have allowed me to grow naturally into a man the way other young fellows had had the opportunity. He obviously had no time for me because he wasn't in the least bit interested in what happened to me. *You've probably got brothers and sisters at every port*, said Mother sarcastically. *So careful who you fall in love with.*

Sure enough, Mother wasn't far from wrong. A half-sister showed up one day. It was Sunday morning and Mother was busy in the kitchen cleaning a duck for the curry she had in mind. Two Sundays a month we had duck curry, one Sunday we had pork and on the other we had crispy masala fried mackerel. That Sunday we were going to have duck. The chubby black and white duck that had learnt how to do all sorts of tricks–it could jump up into the air and snap up a morsel of food thrown its way. He was a bully, the fellow, and used his weight to shove aside the others. Mother picked him because she said that that way the others could live in peace and be equal. I didn't fancy the idea of eating a bird that was such an original performer. I mean he was quite a character. I had named him Houdini, of course not the whole name but just the first three letters–HOU. Mother thought that it was idiotic. *What sort of a name is that? Hou. Just imagine a duck called Hou. More like a name for a Chinaman.*

Hou is short for Houdini, Mother, Houdini.

You mean the fellow who tried to fly like an angel and dropped like bird's shit on the earth and popped it?

That was Icarus.

There we go, another name to deal with. Was your Houdini fellow a Chinaman?

What's this Chinaman fixation that you have Mother?

Just that they have slit eyes like a duck and they cook it well with all sorts of oriental sauces.

Anyway, it was a Sunday morning and Mother was in the kitchen getting Hou ready for the pot. I was in the courtyard mooching around, doing nothing of any consequence when suddenly two characters turned up at the gate. The woman was small built but rather good looking in a strange sort of way. Looked a bit younger than me and the guy looked a bit older. *Hello, hello, I'm looking for Arnold,* she said.

Holy Mother of God, I said to myself, *who is this?*

You Arnold?

I had to think up a reply so I did a bit of quick thinking and came up with one. *I can give you a bit of info if you tell me why you are looking for him.*

She neared. *Now listen, honey, we're not the cops as you can see.*

Who are you?

I'm looking for Arnold. She persisted. *Are you the guy?*

What if I say yes?

Then I'll say, 'hello brother.'

Brother?

Yes, brother.

Hang on there, are you one of those Bible thumpers who turns up at people's homes unannounced and calls them brother or sister and tells them that they've had a dream where the Lord has told them to bear witness and pass on the message to the unfortunate inhabitant of the house and the Lord loves them and wants to save them?

You're a funny fellow.

I'm just talking from experience. I even had one guy pour water over my head and another babble in a strange language.

You are Arnold, aren't you, also known as Arnie? She stood there before me, beaming. She had familiar eyes. Really familiar. I was sure that I had seen her before. *Have we met?*

Not really. Just that we share the same Dad.

What are you talking about? Share the same Dad? That means you're my sister. I don't have a sister.

What's going on here? It was Mother. *What are you folks doing on my property? This place is not for sale.*

The woman who called herself my sister replied cheerily, *I haven't come to ask if the place is up for sale. I've come to visit my brother.*

Now wait a minute. Mother was down the steps in a jiffy and trundled over to us. *I don't have a daughter so how can you be his sister? Doesn't make sense.*

We share the same dad not the same mum.

Mother looked like she had been shot between the eyes. She stood there gaping, unable to close her mouth. When she was able, she dribbled, *then who did he bed to produce you?*

My mother.

Okay then, Mother tried to sound matter of fact, *I'm off the hook*. After a pause,

We didn't even know that you existed. What brings you here now?

Just visiting. Came to meet my only living relative, Arnie. And get his blessings. Jason and I are getting married.

Fair enough, but where exactly have you dropped from? Couldn't be down the beach.

Colva. Goa. Mother's interrogation didn't appear to bother her in the least and her answers flew back spontaneously.

Where's your father and mother? Came the next question.

With the Lord.

And you have no other living relative?

No.

Oh. Well, that means there's no one in the shadows. Come on in.

And so we all went in and the fellow with her was quite awkward because he hadn't been formally introduced. So I shook his hand, *Arnold.* He shook my hand but didn't reply. *What's her name?* Questions went round and round in my head but I didn't get any answers.

Sorry for barging in, Arnie, but I had to meet you. We had to meet you. We had to meet you. Jason and I.

That's when the fellow popped into the conversation. *But you haven't told him your name.*

Gosh, sorry. I'm Christine, Chrissie for short. I'm so sorry, I forgot to tell you my name.

It happens, Mother responded. *Particularly when there are more important things to discuss. So what's the real point of this visitation?*

Here's where I thought I should take hold of the situation and make Chrissie and the guy feel a little more welcome. *A cup of tea?*

Well, we'd love a cup of tea but it kind of smells like you folks are preparing for lunch so don't bother. We'll push off and drop in later on if that's more convenient. Chrissie tried to sound her accommodating best.

Mother cleared her throat then slowly got up. *Don't be silly* she forced herself to say, *I'll get you tea. After all you are Arnie's sis, since you say you are. You certainly have his father's eyes. That was his problem–his eyes. That got him into all the trouble. Arnie has them too but haven't seen him really use them yet.*

It's never too late, Chrissie responded.

Hmm, Mother walked off then stopping at the kitchen door, *please stay for lunch, there'll be enough of Hou to go around. He's a chubby fellow and I'm trying out a new recipe.* Then she turned and went into the kitchen.

Chrissie followed her, *what's a Hou?'*

Jason sat there looking at the palm of his right hand as if he was a palmist. *It's absurd I know, coming all this way to meet a stranger and ask for blessings. But then that's what Chrissie wants. I told her 'let's just go get married, we're both adults.' But she'd have none of it. She wants her family to be by her side … and you're the only family that she has.*

You mean you've come all this way because she wants my blessings so she can marry you?

That's it. She's old fashioned. That's the way she wants it. She's the love of my life. My first and only love and I don't want to lose her so I agreed. So we're here.

I wanted to start laughing but didn't want to offend the man. *What about you? Do you have a family?*

No. I grew up in an orphanage and was unofficially adopted by a priest. Father Paulo.

So you're asking him to bless the marriage too.

I'd have to go up there to do that.

Sorry.

That's okay. There was a pause then he tried to change the topic. *Nice traditional home you have here, very Goan in a different sort of way.*

Yes, but we aren't Goan. We're East Indian.

I did say 'Goan in a different sort of way' and not Goan. What's the fuss about? What's wrong with being Goan? Chrissie is Goan and she is your half-sister.

We sat in silence and then I decided to settle the matter once and for all. *So what does this business of blessing involve? What will I have to do?*

You'll have to give away the bride.

Mother will cause a riot. I don't think she'll want to have anything to do with this.

Jason had an unusually large Adam's apple that moved up and down as he swallowed hard, cleared his throat, paused, *this doesn't have anything to do with your mother, it's got to do with you.*

Of course it has to do with my mother too.

How? You aren't a minor. You're a working man.

Yes but I'm living in my mother's home.

Okay, have it your way. He looked a bit fed-up.

Let me put it this way. I was calm like I was sitting pretty in the eye of the storm. *Here we are, my mother and I, minding our own business and you two turn up and start organising us. I'm supposed to give away a sister I never knew existed. And you are behaving like I'm being uncooperative and insensitive.*

He looked at the palm of his hand again as if checking out whether the direction of the lines had changed. *So you don't want to bless your sister and give her away in marriage to me?*

I never said that. All I said was that Mother will have a reaction.

And I'm saying, he blustered, *don't be so flustered about your mother. She'll get used to the idea soon enough.*

I'm going for a walk. Here's today's newspaper.

Fat lot of a walk I'd be able to go for in all that heat but I got out of the house all the same. It was all getting too much for me. On a perfectly peaceful Sunday when it was a time to be lazy who should turn up but an unknown half-sister with her husband-to-be all the way from Goa. Why? To ask for my blessings so they could get married. My blessings. I find that suffocating because I know that it's not going to be as simple as it sounds. There'll be shoo sha and a wedding and the frockwallah will do a holy thingamy and that'll be a good opportunity for him to start giving me a lecture about going to Mass regularly and I'll blow my top.

Chrissie came out to get me. *Must apologise for turning up unannounced.*

What's done is done. Jason told me why you are here. Have you told Mother?

No, not as yet. Not sure what she's going to say. Anyway, do you have any objection?

Why would I object? I don't have to do anything other than bless your marriage. So long as there's no frockwallah involved. I tried to sound firm.

She giggled. *Frockwallah? What's a frockwallah?*

A priest.

Of course there'll be a priest involved.

Why?

Because a priest has to be there to make the ceremony happen.

That was too much for me. *You mean I'm going to be part of a wedding ceremony? I thought I was just blessing your marriage.*

I'm sorry to put you through this but you're the only family I have.

I walked out on to the beach, confused and annoyed. Why can't people just go off and get married and cut out all these frills? *Listen here Chrissie,* I said when she caught up with me, *have you checked out whether the man who was our father didn't sow some wild oats somewhere else too? Maybe if you search hard enough you'll find a couple of them who'll be willing to give you a group blessing.*

Her overly made-up face was smudged with tears. *Your father and my father is one and the same person, we are connected. Today I have no one I can call my family, except you. I don't even have a mother. You have a mother.*

You're welcome to borrow her.

I don't think this is funny. She grabbed my arm and squeezed it as hard as she could. *Please help.*

I really didn't know how to respond and take a decision for myself without thinking that I was doing something that Mother didn't want me to do. I was already in my early thirties and earning my own living but I was still inside her womb with only a slight inclination to get the hell out of there. Was I looking for excuses? Possibly I was. It's damned easy blaming someone else, particularly my parents and saying that they were to blame for the way I was and am. No one is right and no one is wrong. The only certainty is that the sea constantly grates the edges of my world, denuding it and it will eventually carry away my house and everything except my memory and my past. We are all strangers on the shore waiting for the sea to wash over us and ease out our memories and past.

I looked into Chrissie's eyes and found myself peering into a well, far below the disc of water shivered with life. Leaning over the wall, I looked harder and found myself drawn deeper into her past. The further I went, the closer I came to myself. We shared the same spirit. With one small shift of circumstances maybe she would have been in my position and I in hers. I wondered how she would have got on if she was mother's daughter. Would she be like I am or would she be different? Then I toppled over and went headlong into the trembling disc. *Ok, you can count on me. But don't tell her that you discussed this with me first. She likes to have the first and the last word.*

She let go of my hand and fell into my arms. *I don't know how I'm going to thank you for this.*

What's on with you two? Mother was out on the veranda.

Just trying to understand each other, I lied.

Maybe Chrissie will be able to figure you out but I don't think you'll be able to figure her out. You don't understand women Arnie, you never will. Few men can. Come in for lunch you two, Hou is waiting to be had and Jason already looks like he's ready to go back to Goa.

So there we were at the table, around a big bowl of Hou curry. Typically Hou. Each morsel played magic in the mouth. With fluffy steamed rice, smooth dal sprinkled with green coriander and fried brinjals on the side, we stuffed ourselves silly. Good food has a way of silencing everybody just like a camera. When the table was finally cleared and Jason had quite successfully broken a quarter plate and cracked a glass, we lounged around satiated. *I'm already drowsy,* Mother declared, *time for my nap. But first tell me what's your plan? Now that you've got your brother's blessings I suppose you'll be headed back. You're welcome to spend the day with us and the night and leave tomorrow whenever you want.*

Actually, said Chrissie quietly, *I haven't got my brother's blessings as yet. There are still the arrangements to be made and the ceremony.*

What arrangements? What ceremony?

Arrangements for my marriage. Chrissie kept her calm.

Mother looked flustered. She glanced at the three of us. *Is there something that you three know that I don't? Is there some conspiracy going on here?* Typical of her, wanting to know everything and be in control.

No, I said.

I'm not talking to you Arnie. Chrissie, tell me, what arrangements? What ceremony? Are you expecting us, I mean me, to get you married?

Not at all. But there will be a marriage ceremony and I really want Arnie, my only family member, to be there to give me away. So if there's going to be a marriage ceremony, we'll have to make arrangements. I was surprised at Chrissie's patience.

Mother didn't let up. *So where do we, I mean I, fit in?*

You don't have to do anything. We, Jason and I, will make all the arrangements, we'll pay for everything. We could have it at the church in Gorai if you are okay with that.

Mother looked suddenly lost. Everything had slipped out of her control. Then she appeared to gather all her strength and wits, put them together and let fly, *this is all happening too fast. This isn't fair. First you turn up and announce who you are without even letting us know in advance that you are coming … then this blessing business. All in a couple of hours. Your father who is also his father and I took our time to decide. We didn't just jump into it ...*

You are getting us wrong. Jason and I have been together for years. It took us time to decide to do this.

And it didn't strike you to consult us first?

Why? We're not marrying you and we're not marrying him, we're marrying each other.

Marriage. It's a big fat joke. Your father and I got married and see what happened to that dream. I'll give you one thousand and one examples. See where it has left me. See where it has left him. But we have managed. Why do you want to get married?

This time Jason stepped in, *because we want to have a family, a proper family.*

A proper family. She doesn't have a real mother and father and you have no one and you want to start a proper family, what do you know of a proper family? Mother's voice began to rise.

Mother, that's rude, this is their life. I joined the fray.

Oh you shut up, don't try your debating skills on me.

You don't want us to get married in this church because you don't want everyone to get to know the truth about your husband and my father. Chrissie was clearly losing her patience.

That's not true.

All we request is a small wedding ceremony and I'd like Arnie to give me away. Why are you fussing? He has already agreed.

Mother nearly levitated. She clenched her heavy jaws, squeezed her palms into fists and became rigid. It looked like she was about to die. But she didn't. She fainted, falling face first on the thick rug in an untidy heap. We carried her to her room and revived her. When she opened her eyes she asked, *are there any bruises on my face? I don't want to look like a victim at the wedding.*

The ceremony turned out to be a tame affair because it wasn't really a proper ceremony but more a blessing of sorts.

The Parish Priest was confused as to what was really happening and Jason used his unbelievable charm and the ability to drop other priestly names. All I had to do was stand beside a teary eyed Chrissie until Jason joined her. The Parish Priest rattled off all sorts of platitudes and ended up by giving me a lecture in the bargain.

After it was all over and Jason had plied the Parish Priest with a healthy looking envelope of notes as a 'small donation', we went back to the house. Mother got so carried away with the simplicity of the ceremony that she declared, *this is the way in which everyone should get married.*

We'll still need to register the marriage, Jason reminded her, *in Goa.*

We should have a proper wedding there. I'll contribute if needed. I'm not all black you know, I'm just a woman who has been badly hurt.

I'll contribute too, I added.

Chrissie was in tears and hugged Mother who looked embarrassed. A few moments later, she responded and held her close. Jason hugged me, his Adam's apple bobbing up and down. *This means you'll have to come to Goa too.*

Two days later, they were gone. *I really don't know what we've let ourselves into,* Mother sounded philosophical. *But I'm a woman and I wasn't going to send another woman away empty handed.*

Triangle

When the time neared to leave for Goa, Mother started getting cold feet and it took a lot of coaxing to get her to travel. Once there, she took to the place like fish to water. Her afternoon naps went out of the window and she joined in the preparations without a second thought. Years fell away from her and she became more jovial. In between all the rushing around, we even managed to do a bit of sight-seeing. She wanted to see the pickled body of Francis Xavier and spent ages staring up at it, *fat lot of good that will do for all these people who come and pray here and fat lot for the poor man himself.*

It was interesting to see how she quickly became Chrissie's pretend mother and took on the task of helping her out at every twist and turn. She mothered her friends too and a following gathered around her every evening at the small but comfortable house that Jason owned. Chrissie seemed to enjoy the good fortune of not only possessing a 'brother' but also a surrogate mother. I'm sure she would have loved to give me some of her time but the magic of the moment was far too heady for her to notice me. Jason, on the other hand had decided to enjoy the last few days of his freedom and would vanish on the pretext of work and return late night most definitely tipsy. I was at a bit of a loss because I found myself excluded and didn't know what to do. So one morning, I pushed off to the bus stand and caught a bus to nowhere in particular, got off on the way and walked through village after village. By evening I was drinking Feni in a wayside bar and got myself so smashed that I ended up sleeping on a mat, thanks to the hospitality of the owner. She woke me up at night and asked me at what time I wanted coffee in the morning. *Six*, I said, and slumped back to sleep.

I awoke when it was still dark and found myself sleeping inside her home, next to her. My trousers were lying neatly folded on a nearby chair. Scrambling up. I put them on, checked for my wallet and leaving a large note walked out on to the narrow lane between the rows of small cottages. The first bus got me to Colva Square at six and I reached the house before anyone was awake. A cold bath got me ready for the day.

No one asked me where I had been, they hadn't even noticed my absence.

So it was all a happy and cosy scene until two days before the wedding. Some of Chrissie's mother's friends turned up and tried to wrest control from Mother but she staved them off after a valiant struggle. It didn't end there. They dug out old stories about the loveliness of the departed one, her essential goodness and graciousness, her taste for elegant clothes and whatnot. Actually, it was quite comical to listen to them tugging stories out of midair and bandying them about under Mother's nose. She half ignored them first then started getting irritated and finally pitched in by cutting them short whenever they started their eulogies.

Finally, on the day of the wedding, everyone was too busy getting themselves to look good that they gave up on trying to get the better of each other. Mother had a field day, rushing around the place, controlling everyone and everything in sight. No one interfered with her–not even the Parish Priest and the two altar boys and of course when the bride had to be given away Mother managed to muscle her way almost up to the altar. I secretly laughed to myself imagining Mother racing to the altar before us and waiting for us to get there and the Parish Priest standing there confused. But that didn't happen and in the end there were tears and confetti and roses and everyone blessed the couple … and the wining and dining following and there was dancing too. Then we sent the couple off to Rocks End, a local hotel on the beach. Mother was all set to book herself a room in the same place and with the greatest of difficulty I managed to get her to return to Jason's place.

Once back, she collapsed in a couch and fell asleep with her feet up on the centre table and snored. I searched for liquor in the house and found half a pint of rum. Settling down in the small courtyard to swig it, I looked up at the sky burning with stars, trying desperately to shut out Mother's snores.

The next morning, she was restless and got herself together, had a quick breakfast and grabbing her handbag and hat headed out. *What's the rush,* I called out.

To check if all's okay with Chrissie.

Mother, I think you should leave them alone. They're married now. This is their special time.

What special time? Its morning and they'll be up and Chrissie may need things.

They are in a hotel, they'll get all the help they need. Please.

She stopped dead in her tracks. *Now don't you try and teach me how to suck eggs. I know the sort of help women need. What do you know? You are a man and only her half-brother.*

Control, control, control, damned control, that was her obsession. First she was cold to Chrissie then when she found that I was willing and happy to support her cause, she switched her responses and went full throttle to control Chrissie and to show that she was more responsible than I was. Damned. Why do relationships end up so complicated? Why?

Mother left Goa reluctantly and once she was home in her own territory, she focussed on letter writing. Letters rushed back and forth but as time moved on, they were fewer and far between. I got the brunt of it whenever I tried to explain to her that my sister (I dropped the half after the wedding) was probably busy setting up home. *No*, she insisted, *not as simple as that, not like Chrissie. There's something underneath it all.*

Come on, don't be so suspicious. Maybe she's pregnant.

If she was, I'd be the one she'd tell first.

When a letter finally arrived after a gap of months, Mother tore it open, read it quickly and smiled triumphantly, *see I told you. There was something. Jason started sailing again. Merchant Navy. Everyone thought he was done with it. Now he's gone off. First signs that the marriage is on the rocks.*

Stop sounding like the voice of Doom. It's to earn more money. Everyone knows that.

That's what your bloody idiot sleazy father told me Arnie.

Any news there about her being pregnant?

That's all you seem to be concerned with. Ok yes, if you want to know, yes, she's in her seventh month.

Mother replied hastily, writing a long letter and handing me a fat envelope to post. I did what she had asked, not without opening it carefully and reading it. Mother had stuffed a few big notes in too. What took me a bit by surprise was that she signed off as 'Mother.' This really bothered me. Mother was deliberately wiping out the natural relationship that had started with my new-found sister. She was shutting me out. I was now determined to find some of the letters that Chrissie had written her. When I did, the truth stared me in the face, Chrissie signed off as 'Your Daughter.'

I didn't like it, I didn't like it at all. Who the hell did Chrissie think she was? She never ever signed off a single letter of hers to me as 'Your Sister.' It was always just Chrissie. She had very cleverly invaded my space and my relationship with my mother. My mother had invaded my space and my relationship with my sister. I was so confused and hurt and irritated that I decided to shut them both out and get on with my own life. But what life did I have?

Until then, I had kept to myself and minded my own business, whether I was at home or at work. Now I decided to be different. And I was going to start being different at work. Actually it wasn't easy being different at work. Very little scope there. I was the Librarian in one of those staid old schools where you were not supposed to look at female teachers or students in the face. You had to talk to them without looking at them. So I used to get a look at them when they were not looking and that ended up as a bit of a joke.

A Librarian is a nameless, faceless, person. The books and the space he inhabits are more important. Once he gets into a library and eases into his chair and tends to his work, the world loses him and he loses the world. People come and go. He's something like one of those rocks out on the sand, sunk in deep, the tide rises and the tide ebbs. Birds shit on him, crabs crawl past him, waves slam him. The sun rises and sets, seasons change. He remains.

There was no scope for any excitement at work ... certainly not since the place was run mainly by nuns. I had messed up the only chance that had come my way.

So I started floating around after work hours, seeing a movie sometimes and at other times going to bars run by women. And occasionally going for a sexual massage. There's some fancy name for that sort of parlour but it all ends up the same. Mother at home got upset that I'd started returning at odd hours. *What's it with you Arnie? Don't you know you should be back by seven?* She came at me one day. *Seven means seven.*

I'm not a school boy, I'm an adult and you don't have to be worried, I can take care of myself.

I'm not worried. I've gone through it in my head and I've thought up everything that you could be up to and every possible thing that could happen to you. Even the worst. That's not my point.

Then what's your point?

When I tell you seven I mean seven.

Sure you mean seven Mother but I don't have to report to you as if you are a Hostel Matron. I'm a man and I'm earning my keep and contributing to the house. And …

But she didn't let me continue. *Sure, say what you want but this is my house. Mine and not yours. I could ask you to leave if I wanted.*

Mother, do you realise what you are saying?

She didn't respond.

When this sort of confrontation repeated itself, things started hotting up. So to challenge her I came home at ten. My defiant act was badly timed. Mother had decided to latch and bolt all the doors from the inside. I wouldn't have minded sleeping outside in the veranda but there was a thunder shower and rain and wind lashed the shoreline. Two coconut palms had come crashing down and it seemed as if Gorai was going to get washed off the face of the map.

I banged on the doors and windows. *Enough of this. You hear me? Enough of this. Mother, open the door. Open the door, you hear me? Please open the door. I'm drenched. I cannot understand your cruelty, your controlling ways, your spitefulness, your disgusting small mindedness. Just let me in and I'll pack my bags and leave in the morning so you can have the house to yourself and rent it or sell it or die in it for all I care. Open the door.*

Finding a dry space under the corner of the shed I sat down and waited for the morning. The sea roared and thrashed the shore and I crouched there listening to its complaints, unable to respond because I knew that my voice wouldn't have been heard above the awesome din.

When light finally broke through and the storm subsided, it was 8:00 am. I staggered towards the front door and found it open.

Here's a towel, Mother said, *keep your wet socks and shoes outside the door, take off your shirt and trouser, dry yourself. Don't come in here as you are or you'll mess up the place.*

I walked straight in past her, ignoring the towel that she offered and went into my room, without saying a word. I'd had enough and it was time to leave.

What do you think you are doing? She asked, as I packed my belongings.

Can't you see?

I can. But why are you packing?

I'm going to Australia.

How's that possible? You don't have a passport, you don't have a visa, you have nothing, how can you be going to Australia?

You know I'm not going to Australia, you know I'm leaving to go off to live by myself and do what I want to do. I'm going. You know that and yet you are busy asking me pointless questions. You purposely shut the doors and windows so I couldn't get in. You were trying to humiliate me.

That's not true Arnie. I bolted and latched the doors and windows because of the storm.

Then why didn't you open up when I banged on the doors and windows. You knew I was out there. You knew.

Okay, have it your way. If you leave, there's no coming back. I'm writing you off the Will.

I suppose you are writing in Chrissie. You're so predictable.

It wasn't going to be easy finding paying guest accommodation straight away so I checked into a small Guest House in Andheri and lived out of cases for a month. For the first time in my life I was out in the world alone, living my way. Everything seemed new except for the rain. It was heavy that year and I spent the nights lying in a large soft bed, listening to huge drops lash the streets and the wind rattle the water pipes and blow in puffs of water through the window that I had left open. I shut out images of the house by the sea and my bed by the window through which I could see heads of coconut palms and hear the whisper of their leaves as they rustled.

When the rain let up, as it usually does during the monsoons, I spent time flat hunting from Borivali to Tardeo. A widow offered me a room in her home in an ancient building which was propped up by makeshift wooden beams, bamboos and rusty metal girders. While we were talking a large slab of plaster fell on her daughter's shoulder and she had to carry her to the nearby hospital leaving me waiting in the house. I waited respectfully in the house, not wanting to leave it open. A neighbour returning from work saw me inside and peeped in and called out to the woman but when there was no response he asked, *who are you and what are you doing inside here?* I explained what had happened but he didn't believe me, *I have heard more imaginative stories before, come on out.*

Sure, if you are willing to take care of the place whilst she is at the hospital.

Making a fool of me eh? Making a fool of me? We'll see who will make a fool of whom. He knocked on the doors of the neighbours and in a moment had a crowd outside the door. *Come on out and let us see what you have in your sack.*

This isn't a sack, it's a sling bag. There's nothing special in it. Just a couple of books. You wouldn't understand their contents even if you tried. There's Crime And Punishment *by Dostoevsky and ...*

Don't give me that big talk. The sack, I want the sack. He tried to snatch it from me but I pushed the man away. Others came at me and tried to grab the sling bag. I punched and shoved at them, broke through the crowd and escaped down the rickety wooden staircase. I didn't turn back to look as I wound my way down a crooked lane strewn with crap and garbage.

But I didn't give up the search.

In the old quarters of West Bandra, I came across an old bungalow with a 'Rooms To Let' sign nailed on the trunk of a tree near the front gate. When I lifted the latch one section of the gate fell off but I didn't bother to put it back in place. The bungalow was large and sprawling but as I neared I noticed that the front door and windows were boarded up. I rattled the latch, *hullo, hullo. Anyone in there? Anyone in there?* But there was no response. So I walked around the side and kept calling *hullo, hullo.* When I had walked around the entire place and came to the front door a lanky but stooped buzzard of a man stood there staring over the rim of his spectacles.

Yes, what are you doing on my property? He had an unusually feminine voice.

I saw the To Let sign out there on the tree.

How many of you?

Just one. Me.

Come inside, I'll show you a couple of rooms that you can choose from. So I followed him in through room after room crowded with dusty furniture. *You pick the room and I'll clean it up for you.*

I suppose you could clear out a lot of the furniture because I'll need only a few bits and pieces.

These aren't bits and pieces, he trilled, *this is all antique furniture and all of it stays here. My mother wanted it this way.*

Where's your mother? Perhaps I could speak with her.

You'll have to go up there to speak with her, he said with a squeak.

Then that shouldn't be a problem at all. She's not going to know if you move the furniture.

I promised her.

Another controlling mother, I thought to myself. Looking at the man, *sorry, I'm not interested.*

He stopped me at the front door, *Listen, we can strike a deal. If you're willing to live with that furniture, I'll do the cleaning for you, breakfast free and the other two meals at rock bottom rate. How about that?*

You must really love your mother.

She was a bitch, he replied, *she was capable of having left a curse for me somewhere in this house.*

I trotted off, leaving him calling out after me.

The next place I checked out was in a colony of single bedroom apartments built for people supposedly from lower income groups in Mahim. A number were occupied by families of fisher folk who had bettered their lot. The local kingpin was a gent who went by the name of Bhakku Dada. He and his massive joint family occupied an entire block which was painted in bright pink. Balconies had been glassed in and the façade was posh. Any resident wanting to rent out his or her apartment had to take the prospective tenant to Bhakku Dada. So the owner of the apartment I intended to rent took me to the Big Mick.

There the man sat on an enormous settee carved from imitation rosewood, lungi drawn up above his knees and an unusually long cigarette dangling from his lips. After he had got my name and permanent address and place of work, he said, *you can't do business here.*

I am working, I have a job, I don't have any time for business.

But I am saying you can't do business here. Agree or no agree.

But what business would I do? I wanted to know.

Lending library. And porn books and all and all.

Agree.

Okay, you go. Put one thousand rupees in box near door.

I didn't argue but followed his instructions.

The block I had agreed to stay in was right next to his so I guessed that no one would bother me. The owner was a genial fellow who had provided basic furniture and a cooking range with a few pots and pans. It was good having my own space and I spent all my free time during the week doing it up. On the weekend I pottered around the place, putting finishing touches to everything. What I didn't know was that the days to come would be harrowing. First came an invasion of cockroaches of all sizes, followed by rats and then when I got them under control then wiped them out, a bunch of noisy, drunken and violent neighbours moved in and I was witness to a number of pretty sordid bang ups. The cops appeared and disappeared, two of them knocked on my door, searched the tiny apartment, asked for an ID and then vanished. One of them actually tried his luck in extortion but didn't get far. When life quietened, Bhakku Dada's block was raided and he was carried off along with a number of his cohorts. I joined the crowd downstairs and watched as the cops brought the lot out and shoved them into a caged van and carried them off. The next day, the water supply was cut off and we had to collect buckets of water from a common tap a little way from the block. The queue was long and it was no fun standing out there at five in the morning, assaulted by the stench blown in from the sea.

A month later I set out again in search of a place and ended up on Worli Sea Face. Guru Dev Apartments. It all looked quiet swank from the outside and I was almost certain that I wouldn't be able to afford it. But I could. Geeta Malkhani, the owner, agreed to let me have one of the bedrooms with an attached bath. The other was rented to a young couple, the Bhatanagars. We shared the kitchen and the sitting room.

Aarti and Mahesh Bhatanagar minded their own business. Every evening, she experimented with unusual recipes in the kitchen whilst he experimented with the magic of song by exercising his vocal chords. They had no visitors and kept each other company in more ways than one, particularly at night when they'd fill the air with passionate grunts and groans and whines. I had got really used to that and it became a sort of lullaby. When they vacated the place, they left me a bundle of handbooks inspired by the *Kamasutra.* Rather embarrassing stuff which I threw into the garbage bin on the street corner.

Ritu and Rituraj Rajhans came next. The latter had a penchant for omelettes of all kinds and had his wife whip them up whenever he fancied one, even if it was in the middle of the night. They vanished one day and were replaced by Savita and Anil, newly returned from East Africa. *We never went to the cinema or any sort of public show,* he said one day, *because we were surrounded by black faces. And a smell that was appalling.* That put me off them until they forced me into accepting a movie and dinner. It was some sort of a mystery movie and they ruined the suspense with constant cracking and crunching of peanuts. The dinner was a disaster because Anil got into an argument with the waiter and then the Manager and demanded to meet the owner and caused a real scene. I left them to their fate. I learnt later that the matter got complicated when Anil slapped the Manager and the police were brought in and they put him away because the owner had some underworld connections and the cops couldn't refuse his request. That was the last I saw of them. Geeta Malkhani informed me that the police had even visited her place to ask her a few questions about Anil. And that was that.

With all the excitement of being out in the world alone, I had pushed Mother into the background. Then quite unexpectedly, slowly out of somewhere from the recesses of my mind, Mother came back. I should say sort of leaked out just the way the yolk of an egg leaks out of a cracked shell, drip, drip, drip. She trickled into my dreams and something or the other everyday reminded me of her. Then she turned up one day at work. One of the nuns, Sister Nazareth, came over to my desk in the library and said, *she's there outside, your mother. At the reception. It's urgent, she says.*

Huh, everything was urgent for Mother. When she wanted something, she wanted something. I walked out to the reception and saw her sitting there on a wooden bench so contritely that it broke my heart. We hugged each other. The cold war was over.

We went over to the apartment and she was quite impressed by the neatness of my room and how I had looked after myself. Geeta Malkhani was a bit taken aback when I handed her the keys and told her that I was moving out and would come back later for the deposit. *That your mother?* She asked.

I nodded.

He's a gentleman, your son.

Mother smiled.

So then, back in the jug I went. The experience in the world outside had filled my life with people, many of whom I'd possibly never meet again but who had touched me with their spark of reality. After the initial flurry of excitement, Mother slid into her same old ways. Chrissie was in the doghouse because she had made promises of writing more often but never kept her word. *I'm not writing to her any more, never more.*

What about her baby?

She had a boy. Wanted a girl and got a boy. Few mothers get what they want.

It's difficult for parents, particularly mothers, to get it right with their children, true. But it's equally difficult for children to get it right with their parents, particularly their mothers. True, true, true.

It's a marvel how I can remember so many details considering it all happened so long ago. All I need is for a window to open, the curtain billow up and it's all there with its tiniest detail. All of it. But then I don't know when the breeze will stop billowing the curtain and the window will shut. And when it shuts it becomes dark and I slip into a sort of quicksand and get sucked in, deeper and deeper. Faces and places disappear and everything is a blur. And in that blur, I know that everything I was and saw and felt and thought and touched and loved and hated exists. The present, for me is all I was and am. Everything. And in that churning, stuff floats to the surface and is reborn. It becomes so real again that it seems like it's happening before my eyes. Then the window flips open again and the curtain billows in the breeze. Who decides when this is to happen?

I wish I could shut down like one of those power plants. When I say shut down I mean switch off completely. No power. Nothing happening. No thoughts. No feelings. No memory. Blank. And be suspended like that till my mind and body are ready to switch on. I don't mean being mummified. Mummies don't come back, they remain embalmed inside the heart of tombs swathed by the desert sands. And they get dug out and put in museums. I'm no use for a museum because I don't represent anything of significance.

Instead, I'd prefer to be frozen. Everything intact, but frozen. Put away for a year or two or maybe more and then be thawed … the heart pumping just like the heart of the earth pumps after winter in cold, ice-bound countries, ice dissolving, melting slowly, streams flowing, green pushing out of the sleeping soil, rocks shining and everything clear and blue and open and refreshing and life starts all over again. Why can't my life be made up of seasons? At least seasons are predictable and I know in winter I can rest, unheard, untouched, undisturbed. On the other hand, I need to know from myself whether this is in fact what I want or do I want to die?

I will never get a response I know.

If Mother was around, she'd have an answer. That's the way she wanted it to be. Nothing vague. No loose ends. Everything had to be tied up and finished with. She was a tough woman. I never loved her. I was frightened of her. She had tamed me. That was my security. A bond. Mistress and slave. Of course I challenged her now and then but at the back of mind there was always the secure truth that she'd be there. Just like the fig and the wasp. Each species of fig has its own species of wasp attached to it. Living inside the fruit. The wasp cannot live without the fig and the fig tree cannot produce seeds without the wasp.

Yes, she was a tough and confident woman. Always in control of things. Even her own death. I remember the last time I visited her in the old people's home that she insisted I'd put her into. She sat there in the wheelchair and said firmly, *I'm going tonight, better wish your mother a happy and safe journey.*

She's been saying that for the last month, dribbled the ninety-seven-year-old, sitting in a wheelchair near me. *She said she'd go peacefully.* He shut his eyes when he said the last word, chewed softly on it, opened his eyes and smiled His wrinkles moved like waves, dancing at the corners of his mouth. Then slowly moved back into place. His head slumped to one side and he slipped into sleep.

I've even told him when he's going, she said triumphantly. *Two years from now. Tenth March. First thing in the morning.*

How do you know that? I asked.

She ignored my question. *I hope you've been keeping the house clean,* she said.

I nodded.

And the pig, feeding it enough?

Yes, I replied.

You haven't started glugging the bottle again, have you?

Come on Mother, what do you think I am?

Someone has to keep an eye on you. Why don't you get married? No affairs. Straight to the altar first. Your wife should be everything to you ... your daughter, your mother, your sister, your wife, everything rolled into one. And don't go for the ones who flash their headlights at you because they wouldn't hesitate to beam them on any Tom, Dick and Harry. Beware of the ones who don't wear knickers. Even the bugs in the haystack get a chance.

It's unlikely I'll get married now.

No, now you listen to me. I'm going to have the last word.

But you've always had the last word.

So, just listen, listen. I've seen life.

I'm on the way to sixty, I said quietly.

She didn't listen. Just went on and on. Those were excruciating moments. I lived our whole relationship through once again. And in the end, like all ends, said nothing. *And if you stray, Arnie,* she said, *I'll haunt you. I'll scare the living daylights out of you.*

When she died, it was as if a terrible burden had been lifted from my chest. I felt like sleeping. Sleeping and never getting up till I was well and truly rested. It was the sleep of the dead. Deep. Dark. Dream-filled. Colours. Sounds. People. Places. I dreamed of my father. He had planted three rows of tomato plants on her grave. The leaves were thick and pale green. A red sap oozed from their stems, drop by drop, trickling down, soaking the mud. And the tomatoes were red and swollen. I watched him in the early morning sunlight. He plucked one, rubbed it on his palm to make it shine, then dug his teeth into its flesh, juice dripping down the sides of his mouth. He licked his lips. *These are fine tomatoes, son. You should try growing them and eating them raw. You see, they do better on graves. You shouldn't be afraid. Your mother's not around to collar you. She's gone. Out of your life. Don't wait till the pig gets fat. Pigs and tomatoes have nothing to do with each other.*

The light changed when he commenced working on the patch. Moonlight. A wind ran along the length and breadth of the graveyard. He threw down the shovel and walked in the silver light to a small shack. He waited outside the door. *Come,* he said, *don't you want to go in?*

Mother was dead. My mistress was dead. I was free.

A slave set free in the wilderness. But I wasn't free of the past. Mother was everywhere, around me. The house was cluttered by her presence. As if that wasn't enough, she had insisted that a cupboard full of her things be kept intact. It was a gigantic Burma teak cupboard. Like an outsized coffin. Often I'd lie awake at night and imagine that her body was inside it, swelling, swelling.

For months I lived in a daze. Half asleep. I couldn't tell what was real anymore. At the library I watched students and teachers come and go and nuns like penguins waddle in and out of my life. And nearby, the sea continued making sand. Peacefully. Ruthlessly.

One night I threw open the cupboard and emptied its contents. I burnt it all in the backyard. Then I slipped back into the old groove once again. The old waking and sleeping and tending the pig and the fowls and ducks. The sea nearby continued too in its usual sort of way. We had a few storms. The fishing village was badly hit. A few weddings, births and deaths followed. A murder. Someone caught a shark. I walked every morning at sunrise on the beach.

I wasn't accustomed to being alone, without Mother.

Storm

I'm in bed now, listening to the sea wash the rocks thinking about all those years of loneliness before Sarah the waif breezed into my life. Those were pretty desperate years when I was even willing to open my doors to the wives of drunken fishermen. Those were intoxicating moments whilst they lasted, cruel, painful, beautiful, delicious but in the end always the feeling of emptiness.

Then Sarah came into my life.

Beads of perspiration break loose across my forehead when I remember the day I asked Sarah why she hadn't buried the cat. She appeared much more relaxed. In fact, she even stopped burning herself on the palms of her hands with cigarette ends. She finished her morning cup of coffee and curled up on the couch and fell asleep.

In the bedroom, the carcass of the cat lay in state in a basket, its shrunken frame wrapped in polythene all sprinkled over with flowers. One week since it had departed into oblivion. One stinking week.

Yes, she had well and truly taken over my life. And it all started not so long before that.

She arrived at my gate one Sunday, looking lost, asked for a glass of water, ended up inside my house and remained. A day, two days, a week, a month. I don't remember how that happened, but it happened.

Then we lost control of time and she was there to stay. Not that she did very much at home. She'd lie around on the couch, on the rug, on the bed, wrapped in a sheet with a small soft pillow under her head. I rarely saw her awake during the day. The night was hers. She'd pad around the house, sit near the open window, swing the doors on their hinges and then just vanish into the night.

She said that her name was Sarah, that she was sixteen and an orphan.

I didn't know what to do with her. The neighbours would start talking. And in a small place like Gorai, that can be horrible. So, one night I caught her at the window. *Listen here, Sarah, we can't go on like this, you hear? We can't go on like this. People will start talking.*

And so? she asked.

So, it'll become embarrassing for me.

Just say I'm some distant cousin's daughter, Arnold.

Don't call me Arnold. I'm fit to be your grandfather.

So I can be your grand niece.

You must have lived somewhere before this. Why don't you just go back there?

Because there's nowhere to go back to.

I don't believe you.

You don't have to. Take it or leave it.

But why? Why did you pick on me?

Because you're so gullible. You look so faithful, so trusting and friendly. Like a Labrador.

The next day I decided to go to the police station. When I reached the Station House Officer's desk I chickened out and returned home. I felt angry with myself for giving in so easily, for being afraid, for not reacting to being trodden upon. I felt hopeless. I had to confront her. Sort her out. I had to put my foot down ... even if my leg went knee-deep into goo.

Why are you doing this to me? I asked her that night. *I don't care who you are or what your problem is–why can't you just go home? Go away, leave me.*

Where will I go? she asked.

Anywhere. Just anywhere. Leave me alone. Why are you doing this to me?

Why did you bring me here? she asked, smiling, *why did you? What did you have in mind?*

You looked lost and homeless and frightened and God knows what. I felt sorry for you.

You pitied me. That was it. Pitied me. And pity is stronger than love and compassion. It makes people do strange things.

You don't sound as if you're sixteen, I said.

I may not be. Want to take a look? Want to find out? I'm nice and seasoned. I won't give you any problems at all.

Before I could say a thing, she had taken off all her clothes and stood there naked in front of me. My mouth went dry. *What a beautiful creature. O God, dear God.* I almost wet my pants. *Why are you doing this to me?* I asked, my voice shaking.

I want to give you what you've been fantasising about, what you've been longing for. It'll save you the seduction. Don't stand there with your eyes falling out of your head and your tongue reaching your navel. Do something. Please. I want it.

God.

Is that all you can say? Say something raw. Something wicked. Whisper it. Stretch out your hands. Touch me.

Will you put on some clothes at once. Aren't you ashamed of yourself?

Or do you want me to wiggle my bums and do a little act for you? She jumped around singing some sort of a bawdy song.

Stood up on the chair. Hopped again. Sprawled on the floor. *Ladies and gentlemen, Lovely Lucy!* She bowed, then stood straight. Still. Without moving. Widened her eyes. Then she asked, *or do you want Sulky-Susie-pouting-in-one-corner-because-her-mummy-won't give her-milky-wilky sort of thing? Or do you want the Slug-on-the-tiger-rug thing?* She flung herself across the bed and posed.

I walked out of the house and slept on the beach that night. I awoke at dawn, my clothes soaked and my hair sandy. A grey light washed the morning.

And so life dragged on in the usual sort of way. I got up each morning, caught the bus and went into the city of Bombay, got swallowed up whole, churned around in its stomach and returned home each evening with a little of my soul digested.

Then something odd began happening. I actually started looking forward to the return home. It was not a disconcerting experience anymore. It was fascinating. I began to enjoy the mystery that was Sarah. I knew nothing about her and yet I suddenly couldn't do without her anymore. Her morbidity, her laziness, her abandon, her defencelessness.

She turned my house upside down, made it literally into a pig sty, broke most of my mother's precious crockery, damaged the refrigerator and stained the upholstery of the couch and I accepted all of it. Because that's the way she was–anarchic.

I even began to dream of a future with Sarah. Not a fresh, clean, well-mannered person as my mother would have liked her to be but an insolent, hard-headed whip of a woman who nearly blew me out of my own house and washed me out to sea. I loved the feeling. I was frightened by the feeling.

You should drink sometimes, she said one evening.

I used to drink a lot. I've stopped. I don't want to ruin myself.

That's what your mother would have said, I'm sure.

How do you know what my mother would have said?

One look at you and it would be obvious, she said sarcastically.

Now you sound like my mother.

For god's sake, don't compare me to your mother ... but would you be happy if I sounded like your mother? Drink, it'll relax you.

I don't think so.

You should relax.

You sound like a shrink.

I think I'm good for you, she said.

I don't know.

Have you ever had a woman?

No, I replied, *my mother believed in marriage.*

I'm not talking about your mother. I'm talking about you.

No.

Do you want it?

Want to 'what'?

Fuck.

I couldn't reply.

You won't regret it. And it's easy to do it. All you have to do is let yourself go. Just let go. It'll happen by itself. Listen, I've always wanted to have a virgin. Why don't you let yourself go?

I walked out of the house, sick and frightened.

It was near midnight and the tide was low. Far away in the dark I could hear the water hissing little wavelets across the sand. The sky was overcast and a cool wind filtered through the casuarinas. I lost a slipper and took off the other and flung it into the dark. I walked on till I reached a deserted corner of the beach, away from the neat rows of bungalows with their manicured gardens. A watchman's whistle sliced the silence into wedges. They fell apart as a flock of sandpipers rose in a gust and swept away down the shoreline. I sat on the wet rocks and looked out to sea, thinking of the little boy who tried to empty the sea into a hole in the sand.

Who was being stupid and unnatural and weird–Sarah or I? Why was I frightened? Was I going to treat all women just the way I had treated my mother? With repulsion, with attraction, with dislike, with passionate dependence? Whether Sarah was sixteen or twenty-six or thirty-five or whatever ... was I attracted to her or not? Was I afraid of her or myself?

The next day I bought a bottle of rum on my way home from work, locked myself in my room and drank half of it. Slept.

I did this almost every evening.

I didn't talk to Sarah for a week.

Can I join you? she asked me one evening, through the closed door.

I let her in.

We finished a bottle.

I passed out.

The next morning I found myself asleep with Sarah in my arms.

You were good, Arnie. Really good. You gave it your best, she whispered.

You're fit to be my granddaughter.

And so?

Well, it's not done. I got out of bed, my pyjamas slipping off as I stood up.

She started laughing.

Shut up, will you. I don't think this is funny.

You've got a cute backside.

That night, I locked myself in and drank alone.

She knocked on the door. *Can I join you? Just a small one.*

No. You're young. Too young.

But old enough to be had, is it? she asked, giggling, *Come on Arnie, be a sport.*

You're sixteen.

I'm twenty.

You're sixteen, I insisted.

I told you just now, I'm twenty. Going to be twenty-one. Taurus.

You can't drink, that's it, I snapped.

That's not it, she replied. *If you don't open the door, I'll get my own bottle tomorrow.*

Where'll you get the money from?

I've sold your mother's silver knives.

You did what? I shouted and opened the door. She was sitting on the ground outside the door. She looked at me innocently.

Yes, she said, *there're other things I've sold in the house.*

Thief.

So now you'll hand me over to the cops, right? I'll tell them what you've done.

I grabbed her by the arm and hauled her up on her feet.

When I let her go, she slipped down to the ground again. *Why don't you come down to earth for a change?* she asked.

I wanted to yell at her and walk out of the house in a rage but I didn't. I hauled her up and dragged her into my room and shut the door. *Now, sit down here Sarah,* I said to her, *here, on the bed. Right. You listen to me ... I don't think it's right that we are doing all this. I don't mind you staying here. But stay away from me. This isn't right.*

Okay. But what about the cutlery I sold?

Forget about the cutlery, that was a burden anyway. Just stay out of my way.

She got up. *Now I'm of no use, is it?*

Listen Sarah, we shouldn't be doing this.

Who says so?

It's not done.

According to whom?

People, society. The laws of nature.

You're talking rubbish. If you like someone and are attracted to the person, what's to stop you, eh? What's to stop you? You don't really want to stay away from me, Arnie. You like me.

I don't know what got hold of me. *Take your stuff and scram, get out.* I grabbed her arm and took her to the front door. *Get out and don't come back.*

She stood outside in the dark, swaying from side to side like a half-cut casuarina. *You don't really want to throw me out.*

I banged the door shut.

A strange feeling swept through me at that moment. It was as if I was outside the house and she was inside. I was drunk out of my mind and fell into bed. I dreamed of water. Water everywhere. Tables and chairs were floating away. The Burma teak cupboard creaked and shook as each wave slammed against it.

Fire in the Belly

It took me a week to realise that Sarah had actually left. First I stubbornly kept her out of my mind–then she seeped in. I began to feel stupid and childish. A hypocrite. Remorse stricken. I continued drinking.

I was not myself anymore. But did I have a self? I wonder.

One long, continuous, drunken dream.

Then someone was at the door. It wasn't a knock but a rattle and bang. *Sarah*, I shouted and opened the door.

A six-footer stood outside. Strapping chap. Jeans, sneakers and a T-shirt. His hands on his hips. He looked distinctly Middle Eastern.

I wanth the gurl, I wanth the gurl, he muttered. *Don'th sthare ath me like thath. I wanth the gurl. Thath Sasa one. I wanth the bloody gurl.* He gripped my shoulder and stared into my eyes. *I wanth the gurl you dick dick old man. I wanth the gurl.* He looked into the house, over my shoulder.

Thath Sasa, he yelled, and his breath smelled of stale meat.

She's gone, I stammered, *Gone.*

Gone? he asked. *Whath you mean thath she gone?*

Yes, just that, I replied, *the bird has fled the coop.*

Whath birdh? he looked confused.

The bird, meaning the girl.

Whath you calling my gurl a birdh, eh? You calling her a birdh?

Okay, I replied slowly, *your girl has left. She isn't here anymore.*

His hand slipped from my shoulder. *I'll search the house.* And he did just that. Turned the whole house upside down in the process. *I wanth the gurl. I wanth the gurl,* he kept shouting.

Will you damned well stop destroying my house, I yelled hoarsely. *This won't do. I'll call the bloody cops.*

He stopped, turned and walked towards me. *Call the cops eh, old man? Call the cops? I'll drive a thruck up you and do a u-turn inside and the cops won'th sthop me for speeding.*

He advanced menacingly. *Whath you did with the gurl? Thath Sasa eh?* He grabbed me by the collar and lifted me up. *How much you did with the gurl? Eh? How much you did with the gurl?*

For god's sake, put me down, I said softly. *I've done nothing with the girl or to the girl. I just let her stay here that's all, you idiot. She's fit to be my granddaughter.*

Buth she's noth. No? She's noth. He was furious. *I will thake your head from your shoulders and make a molothov cockthail from ith. Okay? Okay? Answer me, okay?*

Okay, I said, and he put me down.

Now go geth a glass of some drink, he said, then sat down amidst the wreckage and breathed heavily.

A sip later, *You have thoo. Come, come, have I say. Have. I wanth a loose thongue from you. A loose thongue.* I poured myself a drink and joined him.

Now thell me fellow, he said, *thell me where you hidden her.*

Hidden? She just walked out. I haven't seen her for days. Honestly. And I'm quite relieved, I lied. Then I went on to tell him how I had met her. He listened and appeared to believe my story. *And how did you meet her? How do you know her?* I asked.

Firsth ask me who I am, he said. *Since I ask on your behalf don'th bother to ask. I am Joseph. The Muslims would call me Yusuf. I am from Iran. You know Iran? Ha, yes, you musth know Iran. I was commando there. I can break your neck with my leethel finger.*

Then the Shah fell and I fell and losth my family and ran away. O, I thravelled and thravelled. I did drugging in Afghanisthan. Good business. Came to India, this counthry. Ho, I was pushing and jabbing and doing crazy things and even servicing rich ladies thoo. You know servicing, no? In Bombay here I meth one good soul. One fellow Alphonso. Man. He saved me. So good man thath chap Alphonso. Then I stharth tho work with thath man Alphonso. I thold him, 'Alfi, you goth the Ayatolla from my guth, I help you now.' So I help. I help and help.

His voice trailed off and he started brooding.

Then she, thath gurl Sasa came. Ho, Alfi thried and thried to make her okay buth no chance. Then she wenth away. Too many clinics thried but no chance.

You mean she was on drugs?

Yes, man, everything. Ho, Sasa was always so high in the air thath you could look up her skirth whenever you liked. Like that gud she was. Then I thell Alfi, 'Look here you geth the gurl in the clinic man, I cure her.' So Alfi said, 'Okay, okay' and her parenths said, 'Okay, okay.'

Parenths? I asked and suddenly realised I was imitating him. *Parents?* I asked again. *I thought that she was an orphan.*

Orphan? Ho, no chance. She's noth an orphan like you noth her grandfather. Okay? So her parenths say, 'Cure her, cure her, geth her off our hands.' But Alfi say, 'No, you're sthill responsible'. Then I pull Alfi aside in one corner and say, 'Alfi, when she is cured I shall damn well make sure she is their responsibilithy.' And so Sasa joined the clinic. Firsth thing I did, I thell her, 'I look afther you okay? You do naughthiness and I give you one with my ring finger. It will hurth so hard you will be straighth line again. One shoth and you'll see sthars.'

So threathmenth wenth on and on and on and I see my leethel flower growing up again. Small leethel flower. And I have looked afther this leethel flower ever since then. You see anyone thrample on the leethel flower and I geth angry. Angry.

And her parents, where are they now? Don't they want her back?

Ho, the parenths are here in Bombay. They are split up somethimes and somethimes thogether. And I look afther Sasa. Father gave me special pay packeth thoo.

And why did she run?

Ho, she geth the Ayatollah in the guth again maybe. I didn't fight with her. Just gave her one with my ring finger. Now where is she? he asked. *Where man? Where? I want the gurl now.*

She walked out and never came back.

Justh walked outh eh? Justh like thath? You thried something eh? You thried?

You make me sick, I said and got up to pour myself another drink. When I returned he had collapsed on the floor. I didn't touch him. Just sat there and looked at his body sprawled out in front of me. A pathetic refugee. I didn't know what to do with him. Was he going to stay on and take over my life just the way Sarah had? What if Sarah suddenly returned and they decided to stay on? The thought of it frightened me. Between them I'd probably end up in Alfi's clinic with the bloody Ayatollah in my gut, shouting hysterically, *careful of my ring finger, careful of my ring finger.*

I shut the front door and the windows and put off the light and went into my room. I didn't shut the adjoining door. I was afraid he'd break it down thinking I had locked him in.

I couldn't sleep. I waited. Then the noise began. I could hear him bumping into furniture, kicking and shouting in a language that I didn't understand. I opened my eyes and saw him standing over my bed, staring down at me. *I am going old man, okay? I will find her myself. If I don'th, I will come back again for sure.* And he left, battering down the front door and kicking open the gate. He cursed loudly.

Slowly, the sound of the sea drowned the noise and the sighs of casuarinas grew.

I thought of Sarah. Why had I thrown her out of the house when I actually needed her? I must have been rejecting myself, my own inadequacies, my own longings, my own confusion. Tried desperately to keep her out of my thoughts. But it didn't help.

I dreamed of her. I dreamed of her continuously. I even dreamed that we had settled down in the house. But there was always this hoarse broken voice which hung in the air above *I wanth the gurl, I wanth the gurl.*

But then, life dragged on in its usual sort of way. The pig was fat enough to be cut. Warren, promised to help. Strange fellow. He seemed to enjoy doing pigs in. He could handle goats pretty well too. And fowls and ducks. But pigs, he seemed game anytime.

Good to see you alone, he smiled. *We're all so used to seeing you alone.*

That's the problem.

What's that? he asked.

Nothing. Come on. The pig is waiting.

We tied the animal's legs and pinned him down. Warren did it quick and fast. I saw the startled look in the pig's eye. There was blood everywhere. Warren wiped his hands on the grass. *Another one bites the dust,* he muttered. He got up and stretched his legs while the animal lay kicking. *I'm not frightened of anything,* he said. *If you ever need me, just say so. If you want the chap thrown out, just call me. All the folks here respect you. You're an elder.*

Warren was the local fixer. Lived by himself way down the beach. Did odd jobs for anyone who needed him. And of course he was a caretaker at one of the flashy bungalows on the seafront. Everyone wondered what caretaking he was doing considering he was all over the place all the time. Want a fence repaired or a roof redone? Warren was there. A pig done? A goat done? A rabid dog disposed of? Party shopping from Bombay? It was Warren all the way. And strangely, even though people never failed to use the man they never failed to gossip about him. One time word went around that he had escaped from the court in Cuttack when he was being tried for a case of theft, another that he had abandoned a wife and a child in Darjeeling or someplace like that. Then there was the big one–that he was a drug peddler and a *charsi.* But through it all, the man never reacted. He went about doing his bit.

When he was a bit tipsy, which was a rare occasion, he'd land up in my place and babble his heart out. *You're an okay chap Arnie. I know you won't go off and tell the whole world what I'm saying here, I know that for sure. Everyone thinks that I turned my right ear into a cauliflower when I was into street fighting. But I never was a street fighter man, never.* He fiddled with the chewed up protrusion which stuck out from the side of his head. *A Doberman did this. It was decent enough to have left something behind after the bite. Long time back man. The House Master's dog. The fellow's name was John Kimberly. He set his dog on me for writing a love letter to his daughter. A possessive old son-of-a-bitch he was, that befuddled chap John Kimberly. But what a daughter. A nice, neat, sleek thing. Silky legs and eyes that could drive even the devil crazy. And she knew she had it all. Fifteen and a wow. I had danced with her just once at the social and she was soft as baby's skin. Sweet-smelling too. That Anglo fellow Clark claimed to have squeezed her well. Quite some bird. Got laid by a whitie then married him and produced a brood 'back home' somewhere, that's what they all said.*

Another time, he said, *Warren isn't my real name. It's Ricardo Gonsalves. When I was growing up, they called me Gonsie all because I'm a goner. A nobody who has always missed the bus.*

Gonsie, back in school where I tripped over my undone boot laces as I rushed towards an open goal, my hockey stick flying into the air and the spectators jeering. Gonsie, on the diving board, knocked cold when I bumped my head, then nearly drowned. Gonsie, booking film tickets in advance for the wrong day then spending the evening with my date on a dark wall in the park and getting picked up by the cops for indecent behaviour. Gonsie, in college, because I was neither arty nor sporty nor a bookworm.

Gonsie, looking for a job and not getting one because I was found to be under confident. Even my own family thought I was a simpleton. My sister, Paradise Gonsalves, affectionately known as Para, though like the back of a bus, was married off and settled in a job as a secretary and looked after my folks. But Gonsie? No such luck.

Not all Warren's ramblings interested me. I suppose mainly because it sounded as if he was making them all up. So I'd change the topic. *If your name is really Ricardo, why did you change your name? Running from someone? Hiding something? Or is it all just made up?*

Now, you look at me straight in the face Arnie, look at me, eye to eye. Does it look like I'm making all this up?

But that doesn't answer my question. I persisted. *Why did you change your name?*

He never answered me but drifted off into a babble only he understood. Sometimes, his babbling became coherent and I'd catch intimate stories that took my breath away.

Is all this true? Maybe you're just too tipsy to be able to separate fact from fiction. I patted him on the shoulder.

Stop being so bloody patronising Arnie. Fact and fiction … what's all this you're talking about. To me, this is real as I sit and speak to you. So it's real. Fact. I thought I could trust you.

Sorry Warren, I'm carrying around my own ghosts. There are too many to deal with. Don't think I can be of much help to you. That's what I told him so he looked at me with his wobbly eyes, and rambled on that he wasn't asking for help and that he felt comfortable enough in my place to speak about what was inside him.

You don't have to listen to me, you can go about whatever you are doing, just leave me to my talking. I don't want your help damn you. If I'm such a bother, I'll sit out there in your veranda and do my talking.

So while he'd babble on I'd sometimes nip off and get on with whatever else I wanted to do. Midway through one of his sessions, he got up and staggered off into the dark. I didn't see him for quite a while but I knew he was around somewhere doing his odd jobs and caretaking. I began to wonder how many people he had told these stories to. Was he really Ricardo Gonsalves? I'd never know because when he did visit again he started off another string of stories and never brought up the name bit again.

But that day when he had come to help me do the pig in, he was a different sort of person. He was focussed on the job on hand and only offered a few comments. He talked like a local. *So as I said Arnie, want me to help fix this Iranian guy, just let me know. We'll send him to where his Ayatollah is sitting … wherever that may be. And here's a piece of advice … don't trust this Sarah girl, she'll be your undoing. It's good you chucked that chick out. We were wondering how you kept her here. You want to know the truth about her?*

What's it?

She's here.

Before he could explain any further, Sarah turned up. *God, Arnold, you're hurt.*

It's the pig, I said. *We've cut it.* We stood and stared at each other. *Where were you?* I asked, almost like a child.

We? Who's the we?

Warren and I.

Warren? There's just you here.

Must have done the bunk.

She smiled. *See what I have here,* she said, *a Siamese kitten.*

Where did you get it?

A good friend gave it to me.

Huh, good friend my foot. And what's in those packages?

Oh, things to eat and all. For you.

Where were you?

Around, she said quickly, *nearby.*

In Gorai?

Yes. Along the beach. That's another story.

Along the beach? Along the beach? So you had been in one of those bungalows. You didn't tell me that you know someone here, I said.

It wasn't important then. Now it is.

I was scared to tell her about Joseph. It may have frightened her off. So I remained silent.

That night I barged into her room and slipped under the sheet next to her. *I'm not asleep, you know,* she said.

I know.

So I'm going to watch how you go about things.

What things?

Stop behaving like a child, Arnold. I'm not going to help you along. You have to get through the whole thing yourself. You want it again, you have to take it yourself.

I don't want anything, I *just want ...*

Do it Arnold.

I did.

Then later, much later, when she seemed asleep, I stood at the window, looking into the dark outside. I wondered how would I tell her about Joseph. The problem solved itself a few minutes later. *Something bothering you?* asked Sarah.

I thought you were asleep.

I asked you, is something bothering you?

Yes. Joseph ... the bloody ring finger Iranian bouncer friend of yours.

Who are you talking about?

Joseph, that's who.

Which Joseph?

Joseph, I repeated, *the one and only Joseph. Your Joseph. The Joseph who looked after you at the clinic. The leethel finger fellow. Remember? Or was that so long ago that you've forgotten?*

So, where is this Joseph?

Why don't you tell me the truth?

You've made all this up, she laughed. *I shouldn't have left you alone by yourself.*

I left the room.

I avoided her for the next few days. Often I'd come home and find her gone. She'd return late at night. I never asked her where she'd gone.

The house was now back to its old comfortable mess. The only change of course was that we now had a cat. Along with the cat was cat's pee and cat's shit. And the stench that went with it all.

My work began to suffer too. Everyone seemed to notice that there was something wrong with me. So I was sent on long leave. A convenient way of putting me out of my misery.

I needed a regular income.

I wasn't going to touch my savings. That was for a rainy day when I'd be too old and ill and weak to fend for myself. It was to protect me from the world. My last defence. My self respect.

So I decided to rent out part of the cottage to weekenders or people on short holidays.

You're doing this because you want me to leave, said Sarah.

No, I need the money.

But you're well-padded with notes.

That's for when I'm left alone to die.

It's time I left, she said.

I didn't reply, just kept drinking.

You heard what I said, didn't you? she asked.

Suit yourself, do what you like.

That means you're throwing me out.

I'm not throwing you out. All I'm saying is that I need a regular income–so I have to give part of the house out on rent.

Where will I stay? There'll only be your room and the hall.

You can share my room if you want. We'll put two beds there, or we could even put a couch in. I'll sleep on the couch.

That's if anyone would ever want to rent a place like this.

Strangely, some people did. A young couple. They didn't seem to mind the mess. That's because the rent was cheap.

One month, the woman said, *we'll be staying for a month. My ...*

He didn't let her finish her sentence, *husband*, he added.

Yes, my husband and I will be out almost all day. They shifted in a few days later.

Now, how should I describe them? Jillian must have been about thirty-six, slim, tall, dark wheat, quiet, self-assured. Sanjay looked a lot younger. A gaunt, intense face. Pale. Sarah started changing. She actually began bathing regularly, wore clean clothes and seemed quite preoccupied with getting to know the couple. She appeared civil, polite and unusually aloof with me. In fact, she started behaving as if she too was a tenant and was paying rent. I found myself doing most of the work. Even the cooking. It was an odd feeling–becoming a servant in one's own house. Jillian helped whenever she was home. Sanjay tried washing dishes and ended up breaking two. He stopped and didn't try again.

I knew I had lost Sarah. So had the fellow in the bungalow down the beach. But the young man, Sanjay, was now the centre of interest. He didn't seem the sort. He was hardly interested.

One night, *Sanjay is a teacher you know,* Sarah said.

How do you know that?

He told me. Such a clever fellow. Works with handicapped children in a school in Bombay and so gentle.

And Jillian?

Oh, she's the clever, clever sort. Thinks she knows everything. And she bullies the fellow.

What does she do?

Secretary to some French fellow. But there's one thing I don't like about this Sanjay chap. A little too fast for my liking.

Fast?

Hmm. Already started touching me up.

What do you mean?

What do you think touching up means? Touching up. That's what. Feeling up. But I don't think he should be doing these things. He's married.

Where did you do all this?

At the back. In the dark when we went to look for Kitty.

I turned away from her and tried to sleep. She got out of bed and sat on the couch near me. *Listen, you have to help me, I'm scared.*

I sat up and stared at her in the dark. *Cut out your bloody games, Sarah. I know you well enough by now, don't I? Either you're making the whole damned thing up or you're just trying to get him. Why don't you stop playing these games with me and with yourself?*

What games?

I was wide awake by now. *About this Joseph chap. That Iranian.*

What about him?

You know him, don't you? Answer me straight.

No.

He said you were on drugs. Is that true?

Why are you treating me like a criminal, Arnold?

Don't you dare call me Arnold, show some bloody respect for your elders.

What are you talking about? Elder? You? You're a tiger in bed.

Stop making fun of me. You are not human. I don't know what you are.

She burst into tears and threw herself into my arms. *Maybe I'm not human. I don't know what I am. I don't know who I am. Maybe I'm not me. Maybe I'm somebody else.*

She slept on the couch with me for a while. Huddled close. Sobbing sometimes. Often murmuring words I couldn't understand. Then she got up, and opening the door, walked out of the room. I didn't ask her where she was going.

It was one of those quiet nights. Even the grating of the sea was soft. I stood at the open window, looking out. The milky sky was washed with tiny stars and a low breeze was blowing through the trees. Palm fronds scraped against each other. An owl called and somewhere far away a lone gull cried. How the hell could I ever have complicated my life to such an extent? I was so upset that I couldn't even think anymore.

Then I started sweating. I felt cold. I was suffocating. I felt imprisoned in the house. Everything outside the window seemed far away. Almost unreachable. My entire life lay scattered inside me like the shattered bits of an old-fashioned bone china plate. Even if I had managed to paste each piece together again–what purpose would it serve? Suicide. Would that make any sense? Maybe. All I would have to do is take a decision. Yes, a decision. It would be my decision. I was deciding. I was taking my own life. My life, my death, my decision. My will. My choice. For once–mine and mine alone. Only mine. I felt a power surge through me. A confidence I had never felt before. I emptied the contents of a bottle of pesticide concentrate and collapsed.

Lazarus

After all the heartache and confusion, it is amazing how easy it is to decide to take one's own life. Whoosh. One moment you are there and the next you aren't (that is–if you are lucky). You shut out the world and fall into an endless whirlpool which takes you to a place from where you cannot return. I nearly reached that place. Actually it isn't a place really but a feeling. An overwhelming feeling of peace, of letting go, of flowing with the tide. But the feeling didn't go on. I was torn out of it like Lazarus was torn out of his tomb still swaddled in death-cloth and smeared in balm and the hand of Jesus yanking him out of the peaceful dark and back into the blinding world of fret and worry and heartache and doubt and loss ... into a world he had turned away from.

I didn't succeed in taking my own life.

What a mess. What an awful mess.

They carted me off to the local hospital and pumped the stuff out from my stomach. They took death away. They took peace away. And it wasn't just that ... everybody knew what I had done. I was the sad old man of Gorai. The one who once had a mother who was a tyrant. The one who was a cradle snatcher. The one who had opened the doors of his home to an insane Iranian and a strange couple.

You have to drink more liquids, said a voice. I opened my eyes and found myself looking into Jillian's face.

How long have I been like this?

A week, maybe a little more. You need to drink more liquids and you need to sleep. Come on, I'm going to make you sit up and drink this ...

She sounded like my bloody mother so I closed my eyes and stopped responding. I didn't want to have anything to do with a person who was trying to be my mother. One mother was enough, even though she was physically not present. Couldn't manage another.

Come on, please, sit up, Jillian said softly. Her tone irritated me. I wanted to sit up and tell her to stop bothering me. But I didn't. I let her continue to play Florence Nightingale. I ignored the tone, ignored my irritation, sat up and drank the soup. I remained seated upright after I had finished the soup but avoided looking at her.

She left the room and I sat there, overwhelmed by a once familiar space. I was sitting in the bed in which I had been born. Though the sheets and covers and pillow cases and mattress had been changed and the woodwork of the bed had been repaired many times over, it was still the same bed on to which I had landed as a newborn, yelling my head off. My life had come full circle. I had arrived at the place from where I had started out. I was trapped. Would I ever break free?

Out on the veranda I heard voices. Sarah and the young man were chatting. I couldn't hear Jillian. She'd probably pushed off for a walk because she couldn't stand being indoors.

What do you teach kids with no arms and legs? I heard her ask.

Of course, they have arms and legs. The problem is their limbs don't listen to them, he replied.

How can limbs listen?

Not listen, in that sense of the word. Okay. You know, all of us 'move' that way. When you decide to pick up a stone, say–with your left hand, your brain sends a message to your left hand to pick up the stone and the left hand obeys. But in a spastic child, since the brain is damaged, messages sent to the hand are all confused.

So the child can't pick up the stone.

Yes.

It's only with the hand, is it?

No, it can even be with the legs and mouth and eyes and all parts of the body that move.

So they are trapped in a jungle of mixed-up messages. Can't some people be spastic in their thoughts? I mean, think one thing and do something else?

There was an awkward silence. My senses were wide awake by then. I listened carefully for his response but it didn't come. Instead, a little later, he asked, *something the matter? You are drenched. What's the matter? You're perspiring. Are you okay?*

Nothing. I've told you everything. What do you want to do? Start teaching me like you teach your spastic children?

What's the matter, Sarah?

I want to be alone. Alone for a while. Why don't you go for a walk with your wife, there, she's out there, go on. I want to be by myself. Okay, if you're not going, I am.

Sarah, where are you going? Sarah?

She's taking you for a ride, let her go young man, I shouted.

There was silence. A small shrivelled coconut shell came flying into the room in response to my suggestion.

I'm serious, I said loudly, *she's not a patch on your wife. Jillian's a good woman. You're lucky to have her. This one is dangerous.*

A string of footsteps later he appeared at the door. *You said something?*

Yes I did.

This may be your house but we're paying you a rent … and anyway what I do or say is none of your business. He stood there, resting against the door and staring down at me.

I am just trying to help.

Don't need your help you old shit. You're just an unreliable drunk. A lecherous one at that. You're keeping Sarah. Taking advantage of her now that her parents are in Australia.

For god's sake, what are you talking about? I cut him short.

Now you are playing innocent. Suffering from amnesia? You brought Sarah here, drugged her, had her and she was too frightened and embarrassed to say anything. It's sickening. Can't you see how you've hardened her? I came here because I'm exhausted and need to recover … and you are ruining the little time I have.

You are so full of yourself young man that I feel sorry for you. You don't know the truth.

I do. You talk to invisible people. I know that. Sarah told me. You're a crackpot.

Before you go on, I think I should tell you that Sarah said that you've been taking a try.

What? He advanced menacingly, reached my bedside, bent down and grabbing me by the nightshirt yanked me up, shouting into my face, *you'll burn in hell.*

What do you know of hell?

Everything. I know what hell is, idiot. You've broken her, twisted her, his voice dropped to a loud whisper and he sat down on the edge of my bed and said softly … *you will never know what I feel for her. Every time I see her I want to touch her, comfort her, hold her close, stroke her hair, her arms, her body, soothe the anger, the hurt, the screaming need.*

You fool, was all I could say.

I'm no fool, his voice was almost inaudible. *Do you know why I am here?*

No.

Because one of my students choked on a sandwich and died. He deserved more than what he had got from life. Since both his parents worked they had to get special permission to leave office early to get back home and be there when the school bus arrived. When they didn't get there on time, Sunit would have to sit on the front steps of the building and wait for them. Everyone avoided him. Children were not allowed to play with him because he scared them with his crab-like body. His life was full of waiting. Waiting. He died waiting for his parents to turn home. On the steps, outside the building. He choked on a piece of stale sandwich. I saw so much of myself in him.

I felt sorry for the young fellow but couldn't fathom why he had told me that story. Don't know what got into me, I reached out and patted his hand. He didn't flinch. Just sat there with his eyes closed. *You don't have to be so angry with me,* I said, *I'm telling you the truth.*

I don't know what's the truth anymore.

You're destroying yourself, Jillian was at the door. *What's there between you two? Tell me now. Now. I want to know now. There'll be no tomorrows. This once. Now. You have to tell me now.*

What do you know? He asked.

Just that she's a junky and has virtually destroyed the old man. And you're having a scene with her.

She says that this old bugger raped her and has blackmailed her into staying here.

How could you believe that? It's a lie.

What do you or I know of what is true and what is false? He asked. *Besides that, I'm not having a scene with her.*

Sarah walked in. her face was white. She held the body of the dead cat in her hands. *Dead, dead. Strangled.*

Sarah, what happened? I asked, dragging myself out of bed. *Where did you find it?*

Hanging on the gate post. Arnold, Joseph is here, I think.

Joseph? So, you know Joseph, is it?

Oh damned you judge. Damned you and you and you, all of you judges. Look inside your bloody selves. You don't even know me and you're sitting in judgement. Aren't you ashamed of yourselves? She looked at Jill, *I'm sure this old chap did it to you good and proper because you finally played the mother image. And your husband spent his time mooning on the beach with that divorcee in the bungalow next door.*

Which divorcee? Jill asked Sanjay.

Sanjay started stammering, *I don't know what she's talking about. She's making up the story. How can you tell such a blatant lie?*

There were footsteps outside. The front door was smashed open. Everyone stopped talking. Joseph walked in and stood behind Sarah.

Ah, my leethel flower, he said and rested his hand on her shoulder. *Where have you been, eh? I came looking for you and you weren'th here. Lasth thime only. Won'th you inthroduce me tho your friends? Old man I know. Naughthy, naughthy,* he said, wagging his finger with a laugh. *You?* he said looking at Sanjay.

A tenant.

Ah, nice, nice. And this belongs tho you? He asked, pointing to Jill. When he got no response, he shouted, *this belongs tho you?*

Her husband nodded.

Then he patted Sarah on the shoulder. *This flower is mine. Why we all sthanding? Leth's sith down. Puth the kithy down Sasa dear,* he said gently–as if it was a tray of dirty dishes. *We'll thake care of ith lather.*

His politeness was almost sinister. He drummed on his right knee, smiled occasionally. *I'll justh have a small dhrink,* he announced. *Come here my flower, sith on my knee.* Sarah smiled coyly and did as he ordered. *Well, I have come here to thell you good news. The UN is finally sending me tho Canada. Good eh? Very good. before I go I thake Sasa back tho her father. Maybe,* he said pinching her cheeks, *a leethel threathmenth eh? You like threathmenth, no?*

He pinched her cheek again and this time left a welt. No one said a word. The silence was oppressive. Something was going to happen soon. No one knew what.

Jill produced a meal which we ate quietly. Only Joseph continued babbling. He filled the room with his presence. He filled the house. He invaded us.

Finally, long after dinner, he stood up and announced, *I'm sleepy eh, where do I sleep? Where do you sleep?* he asked Sarah.

She pointed to my room. And before I could respond, *Come, leth's go,* he said and walked into the room shutting the door behind him.

Two hours or so later, we were still sitting huddled in the veranda.

Are we going to leave the cat there? asked Jill. She got no answer. *I mean how can we just keep sitting here like idiots,* she asked exasperated. *Don't know what the hell is happening in there. We should inform the police.*

The police? I asked, *she'll implicate all of us.*

Jill reacted, *If no one is going to do anything, I am.*

Don't, I was worried, *I'll get into trouble.*

Why should you get into trouble? Of course–if you've done something ... then it's a different story.

What if she's a minor? Sanjay almost shouted.

God, you're sick, really sick. You two supposedly care for this girl. And what are you doing about it? Nothing. Sitting here whilst that lunatic is locked inside with her. Jill went into the house then returned quickly when a loud sobbing broke loose from the bedroom. Sarah screamed. Window panes shattered. Furniture was thrown about the room. The door crashed open and Sarah came flying out. Banged into the wall and slid down, collapsing in a heap. Clothes hung in shreds from her body. Joseph stepped out. He was bare to the waist, a large gash oozed blood from his forehead.

She, she, she thried tho kill me, he said, then he moved towards her.

Sanjay picked up an old brass lamp stand. *You son of a bitch you touch her and I'll knock your brains out of your head.*

Joseph turned towards Sanjay and advanced. *See this leethel finger. One shoth from this and your neck will snap like a thwig.* He closed in.

Come closer and I'll finish you, he shouted.

For god's sake, stop it, shouted Jill. But no one listened.

Come on, come on, the young fellow called to the bare-chested brute. *Come and get it.* When the man was close enough he was hit on the shoulder and he crashed into the sideboard.

I picked up an iron rod and rushed at the fallen man. Jill snatched the rod from me.

A young fellow from the village stood at the open door. *We'll take care of him.*

I looked out and a huge crowd had collected. People shoved their way into the house and dragged Joseph out. They kicked and slapped him.

No one breaks into our homes here and goes scot free, someone said. *When we've finished with him and handed him over to the cops,* he said, *there'll be so many cases against him that no one will trust this refugee anymore.*

Then he looked at Sanjay, *Get out. Take the bus and shove off with your wife.*

And that's just what they did–left the next morning.

I wish you'd listen to me, Sarah said finally, when we were alone again.

To your lies?

I'll tell you everything. Why this happened. Why I am what I am.

What good will that be? It's too late.

It was too late for you when I came here Arnold. I began to mean something to you. I nearly saved you.

Saved me? Bullshit.

Arnold, I want you to help me now. Just listen to me, that's all.

I had nothing to say. I was tired and couldn't fight anymore. I needed to rest.

But she persisted. *Do you want me to leave Arnold? Do You?*

Do whatever you want. Jump into the sea for all I care. Go on.

So you are throwing me out? Is that it Arnold?

Okay, yes, I am throwing you out. Go on, get out, out, I whispered tiredly, sure that she wouldn't take me seriously.

A few days later she left, taking her bundle of clothing. Must have slipped off early in the morning and caught the first bus to Bombay. Or maybe she went over to one of the bungalows down the beach where she had someone tucked away. A strange feeling swept over me and I began to perspire and breathe heavily. I walked up and down the stretch of beach, hoping to catch a glimpse of her and by the evening gave up and sat out on the veranda, waiting. Now that she had left, the tiredness seemed to have seeped out of me and got replaced by a sadness instead.

It was a misty winter that year and the seagulls and terns had arrived in great flocks, wheeling and crying over the wide expanses of water, over the stretches of beach and the rooftop of houses. When the weather became clearer, they'd leave and the beaches would be quiet again. But, for that time, they were there, filling the air with their cries, one more mysterious than the other. But I'd never want to know their secrets.

The Aftermath

After the Sarah fiasco, I was given centre stage in the life of the village. Everyone was obviously curious as to whether something 'sinful' had happened between Sarah and me or not. And obviously there were three camps–those who were sure that some hanky panky had happened, others who felt that there was no *kala* in the *dal* ... and then the fence sitters who couldn't make up their minds. I tried not to take any notice of them and went about my life, pretending that nothing had happened. And who did they send as a snooper? Princey, Jacinta's son.

Though Princey was an okay fellow he was also capable of being a smart ass. *Arnie, I never know what's going on inside you. You are deeper than the Arabian Sea. Honestly tell me, do you know what's inside there?*

No, I replied, *I don't.* All set to humour him.

There you are then, what's the point of thinking so much when you can't even see what's inside you? I'm different. I think a little and live a lot. Try it and you'll see the difference pretty soon. Now don't turn around and tell me that you are too old. You are as old as you think you are. So shake a leg and get out there and be who you are.

Well, well, Princey, you seem to have seen the light.

What's that mean? he asked, taken off-guard.

It means you've suddenly got wise. Fasting a lot? Novenas?

Come on Arnie, I thought I could be myself with you. Obviously not. You don't know how much I respect you. You know why? You are the only elder in the village who allows any and everyone to call him by his first name.

Oh come on Princey. I'm not exactly an elder, I'm an outsider, that's more like it, an outsider. So everyone thinks that they can treat me anyway they like. Now everyone suspects I was up to some hanky panky with Sarah.

Not everyone.

See, there you are. So they've sent you to snoop around.

No, just chatting. Ever had a girlfriend? He tried to change the topic. *Now I wouldn't put Sarah in that category. But have you had a real girlfriend?*

I think you should leave Sarah out of it, that's a very delicate topic. But yes, I have had women, if that's what you want to know. Looking for advice? I was interested in finding out where the conversation was leading to.

I want to know if you've had a real girlfriend, I don't want to know if you've had a woman.

Aren't you prying?

Not at all, I'm just having a man to man talk Arnie.

A number, I lied, waiting to see what he'd come up with next.

I'm sure the girls went for you with your height and those eyes.

Where's this conversation headed? I ambushed him.

Aunty Rosie keeps asking about you. You know Aunty Rosie, the lady who lives at the foot of the hill far down the beach?

I know who Aunty Rosie is. You're forgetting that I've been here a lot longer than you have.

Now you're sounding your age. She's a good woman. Forty-five and no family.

Are you trying to play matchmaker Princey?

No. But you two will make such a good match.

Do you have a girlfriend? I asked.

I've had many girlfriends but still haven't found the perfect one. Mum will find a wife for me just the way she found a husband for Flora and my seven cousins. She has a knack of finding the right life partners. Actually it's her idea–this getting you and Aunty Rosie together.

So I'm with someone older, right? So I'm kept out of mischief?

Come one Arnie, be a sport.

I could see that Jacinta had done a lot of work on her son. Primed the fellow. Yes, she had come a long way from the girl bawling her head off on the beach. She was anything but a wallflower. A tough nut, determined and focussed. Dumped by her man, she took on the task of bringing up two kids, tending to her mother and running a small but successful Bombay duck and shrimp pickling unit. Even though the pickling unit, hardly a stone's throw away from the house, stank to the high heavens, the house smelled of lilies. Don't know how the woman managed it. Everything was in its place … and clean, so clean, it seemed unreal. You could eat off the floor in the toilet if you wanted, it was that clean. Even their dog was not allowed into the house. *He'll bring fleas and ticks and worms into the house. And I don't want any of us getting infected.*

I got all this straight from the horse's mouth. I mean Princey when he was a little fellow. He'd get so tense about being regimented by his mother that he'd end up spilling it all out to me. I remember him saying at Christmas time, *my mother broke her backside making the plum cake.* Or another time when he told the Parish Priest during moral instruction class, *I know all about Adam and Eve … they were not married but living in sin.* That damned self-righteous frockwallah made those lines legendary.

When Princey and Flora returned from school they weren't allowed into the house in case they carried in the muck from outside. They'd have to bathe at the well, change into 'house clothes' which she had hung up on the line for them and then enter the house. Their school bags were kept in the 'study room' which was at the corner of the house, just off the veranda. *Cleanliness comes first and then there's Godliness. And then everything else. So the most important thing in life is to keep yourself clean. Short nails, clean ears, no smelly bum, well brushed teeth and a pink tongue.*

Princey knew these lines by heart and imitated his mother to perfection. Golda, his Granny, always found it funny the way the little fellow sent his mum up in smoke. He'd wave his hands and roll his eyes and end up looking heavenwards. She'd never stop him because she had learnt that the best way to survive was to mind her own business. *The Almighty knows best and if this is what he has planned for me–so be it.* It was her slogan and she'd repeat it like a prayer.

When my mother heard her one day, she snorted, *what's it with you Golda? You need to put your girl across your knee and give her a few quick slaps on the butt.*

She's not a girl anymore but a woman of substance who has done so much to keep her home together. Remember, she started her little business all by herself and she's done well with it, thank God. Richie dumped her good and proper … she had no choice but to take control.

There must have been a reason why Richie dumped her. Mother egged Golda on.

I don't know nor want to know what happened between them. I've left my life in the hands of the Almighty and the Almighty knows best and if this is what he has planned for me–so be it.

Come on Golda, Mother chided her, *where's your spunk?*

My spunk? I don't have any left. I gave it all to my beloved Alex and he made good use of it. Pity the sea got him. He was a hero. A real hero. I invested all my spunk in him so he'd continue to be my hero.

That means your spunk got wasted. What was the point?

You can't challenge the sea dear, she'd finally say, *you can't challenge the sea. In the end she has the last laugh.*

If the sea's that sort, Mother went on, *how come you call it a she? Shouldn't it be a he? Only a he would keep doing something like that.*

No, that's wrong, a she is capable of more cruelty than a he. Then she'd turn to me and ask, *what are you doing hanging around here? On your way, on your way. You shouldn't be listening to this prattle between women. You're not wise enough to really understand what we are talking about.*

Let him be Golda, Mother would say in her typical irritating way, talking from the corner of her mouth and curling her lips once the words had been released, *he's not capable of understanding these subtleties. Isn't that so Arnie?*

But that didn't scare me away and I stubbornly remained.

Then one day I returned to find the two women locked in Mother's room. Golda was crying, *what's the point? What's the point of it all? She's so damned bossy that I can't even lift a finger and say a word until she allows me to. She, SHE, has to give me permission. And those kids are like puppets. I refuse to go back.*

Now listen to me Golda, Mother said firmly but reassuringly, *you are welcome to stay here for as long as you want, I repeat–as long as you want. You can sleep wherever you want in this house, eat whatever you want, do whatever you want, you don't have to ask my permission. But what's your daughter going to say eh? What's your daughter going to say? Not that I'm scared of her. I can handle her if she comes barging into my house. But do you think you can manage to handle her once you return home?*

Home? Squeaked Golda, *home?* I could imagine her screwing up her eyes piggy-size as she spoke. *That's not home anymore, it's a halfway house, bossed over by a woman who was once my daughter.* Then I heard her melt into tears again and babble, I've *left my life in the hands of the Almighty and the Almighty knows best and if this is what he has planned for me–so be it.*

So what has he planned for you? Mother's voice took on a practical tone.

To stay right here.

So be it, Mother's voice softened and I could imagine her stroking Golda's head like a pet dog then kissing her on the forehead. *Now you lie down here for a bit,* she said, *and I'll make some hot chicken soup for you. That should be nourishing.*

Before I could move away from the door, Mother opened it. *Poor woman's at her wits end. That daughter of hers is driving her crazy. Why don't you shift over there as a fair exchange? Maybe she needs a man,* she muttered sarcastically.

Maybe her Almighty is the sea, I said.

I'm not talking about this woman. I'm talking about her daughter.

You must be crazy.

Crazy, my foot. That's what happens when some women lose their men. A woman's man dying is one thing … but running off with another woman? Now that is not right. She shuffled off to the kitchen saying, *but then you wouldn't understand what I'm saying.*

By late evening Golda was up and about, helping Mother in the kitchen. The next morning she was sweeping the house and dusting the furniture and making breakfast for us, singing some hymn or the other softly to herself as she went along with her chores. Mother didn't know what to do. She tried stopping her but Golda wouldn't listen and emphatically shrugged her off. *You don't expect me to live off your charity,* she said, *if I'm going to stay here, I'm going to contribute. In fact, I'm going out to the boats today to get some fish from the catch.*

You wouldn't dare do that, Mother was firm.

You bet I will. What's the worst that will happen? My daughter will see me there? What else?

Golda don't cause a scene. Anyway, sooner than later, Jacinta is going to turn up here and take you home.

How do you know that? How will she know that I am here? Have you gone ahead and told her?

This is Gorai Golda not Bombay. Everyone knows that you are here.

But Golda wouldn't listen. The next morning she went out to meet the boats to buy fish from the fresh catch and when she returned Jacinta trailed her back. I wasn't there to see what happened but I heard it from Mother.

And there was this Golda who wouldn't listen to me even a pinch. She went off out of the gate and down the beach to meet the boats. I went rushing after her but gave up and said to myself damned stupid woman let her go and meet her Almighty for all I care. And when she came back there was Jacinta following her. She came in, handed me the fish and rushed into my room and bolted the door from the inside. Jacinta strode right in as if this was her property and went up to the door and started banging on it, 'come on out Mother, I don't have all day on my hands, I have other things to do, come on out and let's go home.'

Would you believe it? Golda didn't say a word.

Jacinta raised her voice so loud that I was sure all of Gorai would come pouring in to watch the fun. 'Mother, I'm counting ten and I want you out by then.' By the time she reached seven, the door whooshed open and Golda stood there with her hands on her hips. 'Listen here pipsqueak, I'm not one of your puppet children. Counting to ten are you? Counting to ten? Count to ten thousand for all I care.'

'Mother please come home, what will people say?' Jacinta suddenly whined.

'People? People? So you are more worried about what people will say than what I feel.'

'What do you want from me?'

'To treat me like your Mother.'

'As God is my witness, I will, just come home now and don't create a scene.'

Mother had got so involved in recounting the episode that she didn't realise that she had been swirling the ladle in the air and was splashing a spray of fish curry everywhere.

So then finally she went home, I attempted a conclusion.

Not on your life, I heard Golda's voice behind me. *I told her I'd return when I am ready.*

The good thing about having Golda with us for the next week was that she kept Mother busy and out of my hair. The only uncomfortable bit was when both the women kept suggesting that I visit Jacinta's place now and then. It seemed like some sort of cruel joke to me considering all that had happened. It's far too painful to remember that now, far too painful. But then, that was so long ago. Shouldn't have mattered anymore ... shouldn't have, but it did.

Coming back to Jacinta's idea of bringing Rosie over to my place. The two women turned up with a small hamper of homemade snacks. *This place needs a lot of cleaning,* Jacinta went from room to room. *It's falling apart. There's dust everywhere.* After a few exaggerated sneezes, *if you can't do it, you should get someone to come in and clean up. Better still, you need a woman's touch here to put it back the way your mother left it.*

That was a bad start. I was already irritated with the woman but I suffered her because she had brought along the plump Rosie who had a lovely pair of lips, amazingly slender fingers and a throat that left me a little weak. She had potential. Of course, all those thoughts went spinning around in my head but when it came to speaking–I was tongue-tied. So I watched the two women explore the innermost secrets of the house and I followed them around, wondering what to say.

They got tea ready, laid out some of the snacks and we sat down supposedly to chat.

You've changed so much, Jacinta played her first card.

Don't get you, I played mine.

I mean, you've become so quiet. Quite a recluse. You used to like walking along the beach early in the morning and late evening. I know that. I remember you sometimes did that with my sister. But that was long long ago. But even later on, you were quite an active fellow. Rosie here likes walking. So that's one thing you have in common. I'm sure there's a lot else. Why don't I just leave you two to find out what you have in common. I'll take a walk around your courtyard while you are at it.

When she left the room, Rosie looked at me, *you are really embarrassed. Sorry about this. This was her idea.*

That means you didn't want to visit.

It's not that. But I didn't fancy just landing up here. Thank you for not being hostile.

Why would I be hostile? Then I quickly changed the topic. *All this stuff. You cooked it?*

Yes. I enjoy cooking. I'd be happy to come over whenever you like and cook. I could even share my recipes with you.

That's nice, my throat went dry.

You're getting wasted, she said suddenly. *You need a woman. Didn't you ever think of getting married?*

Thinking is one thing and doing quite another.

Are you scared of women?

No.

The conversation was becoming far too loaded for my liking. Maybe she was coming on too fast. Fools rush in where angels fear to tread, they say. That's what I did. *Is there someone in your life?* O God what a ridiculous question.

Obviously not. Why do you think I'm here? I've watched you over the years Arnie and I always found you interesting. Of course I realised that you'd be a challenge. But I found you interesting all the same. Mind you, even when my man was alive and kicking and by my side, you floated around nearby. And now after all these years here I am and here you are and I am sitting in the same room, across the same table and talking to you. I don't want to rush you Arnie … actually I would have landed up here much earlier if it wasn't for that waif of a girl who got here before me. And all those rumours about you and her … rumours … mere rumours …

I wanted to reply, *rumours? You must be joking.* But I didn't. Instead I smiled and looked into her eyes.

By the way you are looking at me, anyone would imagine that you wear your heart on your sleeve. But you don't, I know you don't …

How sure are you?

Very.

Jacinta came in and swept her friend away like she was cleaning up the room. At the door I asked Rosie, *will you come again?*

Yes.

The Trap

Rosie kept her word and dropped in a number of times, unobtrusively putting the house together again and giving it some semblance of order. She even took me out to get new curtains stitched from one of the shops in Malad. That's the time we ended up going to a movie and having a meal and returning late. She slept over, locking herself into one of the rooms.

The next morning she made breakfast and left. Her parting shot, *I wouldn't have shut the door on you if I was absolutely sure that those were only rumours about that girl.*

She let the issue dangle in midair and walked off. When she visited again, a few evenings later, she cooked a delicious meal which we sat down and ate. I felt like a goose that was getting fattened for the table. I knew the question would visit again, this time more aggressively.

Shall we talk about the girl Arnie?

Which girl?

O for Christ's sake, don't start that ignorant act again. You jolly-well know who I am talking about–Sarah, that girl with loose morals. The one who'd drop her pants and spread her legs if she knew it would get her somewhere. How did you let her in here? People are still talking. She left the table and walked out on to the veranda.

Let them talk Rosie. They don't seem to have anything better to do. This is my business. I can do whatever I want with whoever I want. What's tickling them?

She still didn't look at me. Her body tensed, losing its soft tenderness. I walked up to her and put my hand on her shoulder. *Rosie, listen, why are you getting carried away by what other people are saying? That was long ago. Why do you want to hold on to something that has passed. It's gone. She was a lost girl …*

So then it was you who took advantage of her. You are a sick old man. Sick.

I put my arms around her and drew her close. *Listen, Rosie, you are a good woman, I don't want to argue with you or insult you because you have come here out of affection.*

No, not out of affection. I came here with the hope that you would turn out to be a decent fellow, someone who is just plain and simply misunderstood. But I don't find that. I pity you, Arnie, I pity you. She didn't respond to my embrace nor did she try to pull herself out of it. Beads of perspiration trickled down from the back of her ears along her neck. It had a faint whiff of garlic mingled with talcum powder and the mild fragrance of some perfume she must have picked up from some backstreet of Bandra. I kissed her gently on the neck and she sighed, almost painfully. Then she went on, *you shock me. You should be ashamed of yourself. Your mother's heart would have cracked into pieces if she were alive.*

This is my business. And I've done nothing wrong, Rosie. You're a good woman, can't you learn to enjoy just this moment?

And forget what's happened? You expect me to be a bloody ostrich and stick my head in the sand imagining …

Why are you judging me Rosie? Why? We all make our own mistakes, no one is perfect.

She yanked herself away from my embrace and turned around to face me. *This isn't just a mistake, it's something twisted.* She pushed me backwards. *Don't you touch me, you hear me? Don't you touch me.* I stood there looking into her eyes … they were pools, dark and smouldering. *What a fool I've made of myself, what a fool. I was stupid to imagine that you were innocent. Stupid to imagine that you would tell me that nothing happened between you and that wretched girl.*

It was a mistake. What's wrong with a mistake or two?

What's wrong? Dear God, you were fit to be her grandfather and you didn't think there was anything wrong? You should be ashamed of yourself. You men ...

What's there to be ashamed about? And what do you mean by saying 'you men'? That's all I heard from my mother when she was alive. And I'm sick of that phrase. Sick of it. I could be very well saying 'you women'.

Then say it, will you. Say it. I dare you to.

Wouldn't waste my time. I'm here in my own house, minding my own business, yes–my own business, and you come in here and invade my space and start pointing fingers at me and judging me as if it's your right.

The problem with you Arnie is that you don't like to be told the truth about yourself, you don't like being confronted.

But can't you understand that it's none of your business or anyone else's business. I could feel bile burning its way up my throat and into my mouth like lava. My palms became damp, my forehead burned, I felt dizzy. I staggered forward and stretched out my hands for support, she propped me up. *I think you should go and lie down. Come on Arnie.*

I pulled myself away from her and stood there swaying. *Don't lecture me, you hear? I know what's best for me, I know. I don't need you to tell me what to do.* She stepped forward to steady me and I pushed her away, *leave me alone, I don't want your pity.*

She turned away and stood with her back to me, resting her hands on the wooden railings of the veranda. *What a mess, what a mess. I swore to myself that I'd never have anything to do with a man … and here I am again … making a fool of myself. What a stupid mess.*

When the bile had retreated and the burning and dizziness had subsided, I embraced her, *Don't go away, please don't go away …*

Rosie swung around and slapped me, *Just keep your hands off me, you hear? Keep your hands off me, go and find little girls to cheer you up. Go on. Damn you, damn you Arnie. The sad thing about all this is that I came here with Jacinta because they wanted me to find out what really happened between you and that girl ... and also because secretly in my heart of hearts I hoped to prove them wrong and get you for myself. What a mess. What a horrible mess.*

She walked away on to the beach and then towards the hill shrouded in shadows. I watched her go until she had dissolved into the dusk. When she was out of sight I was overwhelmed by the need to be with her. She had offered herself to me on a platter and I had messed it all up. My big fat mouth did it. *Will she visit again, will she?* I wondered, walking up and down along the fence most of the night.

The next morning I went down to the market to meet Princey at his favourite tea shop and send a word to her through him. Half way there I met Golda wheezing along down the dusty path.

You're a sick man Arnold, a sick man.

Why do you say that?

Rosie came over and told us what happened and what you said to her. Not sure if your mother really knew the sort of person that she had given birth to.

Why are you bringing my mother into it?

She walked up to me, curled her lips into a sneer and jabbed me in the stomach with her right forefinger. *The problem with you is that you don't want to admit that you have a problem. If only you can get yourself to admit that you have a problem, it would be the first step towards sorting it out.*

I'm too old to sort anything out Golda, least of all my own problem. Anyway, since you and your daughter seem to be such authorities on other people's affairs, tell me–what's my problem?

Isn't it obvious Arnold?

What?

You are a hundred and one people rolled into one. How do you know which one is thinking, which one is feeling, which one is speaking and which one is doing? You don't! Everyone remembers that you slept with your eyes open and didn't even know for yourself whether you were in the unreal or real world.

How does my private life affect you people?

Because you are living amongst people. And you have to be sane if you want to live peacefully amongst people. And if you are not sane you should be put away.

I'm minding my own business Golda.

Minding your own business is not enough here. You have to live right. You have to live according to the values that all of us believe in. We are a community. You are living in a community not like a bloody Robinson Crusoe on an island. So when you bed someone who is fit to be your grand-daughter it worries us. No one is safe anymore with a fellow like you running loose.

What's going on Granny? It was Princey.

Nothing, the woman snapped.

What are you getting hot about? He persisted.

I'm not getting hot, I'm just telling Arnold his fortune.

It doesn't concern us. The man did it, the man did it. That's it. Let it be.

Now you don't start lecturing me you squirt. Pah. But it was done nevertheless. Enough is enough. If your father was around he would have thrashed the living daylights out of you if he had heard you talking to an elder like this.

But he's not around. Pushed off with someone else's wife. He'd hardly be in a position to talk.

Don't talk about your father like that, you hear me?

I hear you Granny, but I still have my own opinion.

Sounds like you're on his side. She pushed past me and went staggering and wheezing down the path.

Princey looked at me, expressionless. *It's over pal, everyone's talking. I'm opting out. Don't expect any support from me.*

I don't know what got into me and I heard myself saying, *okay, fair enough, but can you take Rosie a message from me? Tell her I would really want her to visit again.*

Holy ghost. You've scared the woman out of her wits and now you want her back. Make up your mind, what do you want?

Rosie.

He threw his hands up in the air. *Okay, let me try. I don't promise you anything, let me try. Just this once then don't even look at me again. I'm off your radar and you are off my radar.* He walked off.

I can't believe I was so bloody naive and stupid to ask him for such a favour considering that he belonged to the other side. But the flesh is weak and I nevertheless spent the rest of the next day lying in bed and staring at the ceiling, watching a gecko catch flies, wondering whether Rosie would turn up. By five in the evening I had more or less given up and set about fixing myself a meal. I hadn't eaten since morning and could feel the mice in my stomach scurrying about like crazy. So I put some rice and dal to soak and cut up a few potatoes, onions and tomatoes for a curry.

Nice to see you at work in the kitchen. It was Rosie in a soft blue dress which emphasised her fullness.

Oh, was all I could say.

She walked over to me and stood there smiling, obviously waiting to be hugged. I did and felt the soft silkiness of her skin and the fragrance of talcum powder. *I've brought you something special for dinner. It's on the table.*

What will I do with what I'm about to cook?

I'll cook it up for you and when it cools you can put it in the fridge. You can go and relax while I do it. Then we'll eat together.

Don't be silly, I'll cook that later. Might as well put the stuff in the fridge right away.

Stop trying to be so self sufficient Arnold. Start depending on others a little more.

I don't want any more mothers around me Rosie. Can't we just be equal? I drained out the water from the raw rice and dal and put the stuff in the fridge along with the chopped veggies. *There now, how about a little walk?*

Outside, the sun had already set and dusk gently smothered the sand, sea and sky. The beach was unusually empty and flocks of sandpipers skated along the water's edge tittering. A few gulls came in low over our heads, then swerved back and trailed low over the sand till they vanished from sight.

I won't speak of that Sarah girl anymore Arnie.

That's kind of you, not sure if she heard me.

So what do you want me to do for you? She went on.

Oh nothing really, I lied, *nothing at all.*

No, seriously, what can I do for you?

I don't want you to do anything for me Rosie. Just be a friend.

That will take time. Before that–do you want me Arnold?

I felt goose bumps all along my arms when she said that and couldn't understand why. Was she laying some kind of trap? Or, was I just getting suspicious for no rhyme or reason?

Anyway, we walked on down the beach, holding hands. When it was dark, we returned to the house and sat down for a meal. It was delicious. There was fluffy steamed rice, sorpotel, crisply fried shrimps, salad and a dal with spinach. We ate in silence and after the meal we sat out on the veranda. *What do you want to do now?* She asked.

I honestly didn't know what to say or what to do. I had waited for her the whole day wondering if she'd turn up and then when she did I didn't know what to do. Finally she got up and walked over to me and holding me by the hands hauled me out of my chair. *Now you look at me in the face Arnie. Look at me, eye to eye. Yes, that's it. Now Arnie, are you listening to me?*

I nodded.

Now Arnie, I don't have a man and you don't have a woman. I think I could make you happy if you gave me a chance. Here, feel me. She placed my hands on her breasts. *I am real Arnold, real. I am not a figment of your imagination. Do you understand what I am saying? Loneliness does strange things to the heart and to the mind. I know a lot has happened to you and I know that you find it difficult to trust people, even yourself. But try trusting me. Just a little. Should we give it a try? Should we Arnie?*

Why are you constantly using my name? I wanted to know.

Because I want you to know that I am talking to you and not anyone else. She hugged me and didn't let go. I felt the warmth of her body and her heart against my heart. *Do you want me now?* She asked and before I could answer she guided me into the bedroom and began stripping me. I didn't stop her. She laid me out on the bed and began massaging my feet, her fingers working their way upwards. When she finally reached my head and gently massaged the roots of my hair my body had become so warm that I could feel droplets of perspiration oozing from my pores. Her hands were all over me, kneading me till I was so limp that I stopped resisting and slipped inwards. It was dark in there, so dark that I couldn't see anything. Only the sounds of my body keeping itself alive, pulsed around me. Rosie was saying something but I couldn't understand her. Her words had become distant blurs. Then there was only silence.

Princey's voice brought me out. I surfaced and opened my eyes. He was standing beside my bed and looking down at me. *Are you okay Arnie?*

Yes, never felt better. Thanks.

Don't have very good news for you Arnie, Princey said quietly.

What do you mean?

Just that. Not good news. Aunt Rosie said she doesn't think she can get herself to visit you again.

When did she tell you this?

Last evening when I went over to visit her.

But she was here last evening.

Arnie, you need help.

He left hurriedly.

I went back into the kitchen and checked the fridge … the vessel of rice and dal wasn't there … nor was the bowl of chopped veggies. There was no evidence of the dinner that Rosie and I had eaten. The dustbin was empty.

I was suddenly so afraid of the house that I stumbled straight out of the front door, across the yard, scrambled to the water's edge and waded out. When I was waist deep, I stood there and let the water slam the fear out of me.

When I was calm again, I waded out of the water and squelched my way back home, stripped and showered …

I don't remember exactly what happened after that. It's all so blurred.

The Showdown

All Gorai was abuzz with the story of the dirty old man who had brought the village disrepute. And it didn't stop there. People took it on themselves to start bothering me because they probably felt that they had every right to do so. And among them there were vultures waiting for me to pop off so that they could lay their hands on the property. Stupid people, as if I was going to pop off so easily.

Anyway everyone kept up the heat. Caught some of them the other day walking into the hall. The cheek of it all, just imagine, just walked in and stood there and called out, *Arnie, hey Arnie, are you there?* Rascals, calling me 'Arnie'. So I decided to teach them a lesson and kept quiet and waited for them to go into the kitchen. When they were in, I rushed out of the store room and slammed the door shut and bolted it from the outside.

Hey old man, open the door. Open the door. Open it. Open it or we'll smash everything in your kitchen.

Little turds. Smash everything in my kitchen, my big fat toe. *Go ahead smash all you want,* I yelled at the top of my voice, *smash all you want.*

They began throwing around pots and pans and opening and closing the fridge door. They smashed a glass on the wall. *I'm going for a walk fellows, I'm going for a walk.*

You can't leave us like this, you can't.

Who says so?

We say so.

Who is 'we'?

Arnie don't do this to us.

Bye, I'm off for a walk. I went out on to the veranda and then into the yard then kept on going and looked out at the cluster of bare rocks covered with gulls. They stared back at me almost defiantly. After a while I walked slowly back to the house to find a larger group throwing stones in through the open door. They obviously thought I was in there somewhere and were trying to scare me off so they could rescue their friends. When they realised that I was behind them, they scattered. Once in, the stones started again and my prisoners pleaded loudly to be released. I let them out and watched them scamper away. At a safe distance, they shouted obscenities at me and joined by their friends, started stoning the house.

That wasn't the end of it. Sometimes they would come around at night and rattle tin cans, stand outside the house and howl like stray dogs and shake me out of sleep by singing loudly outside my bedroom window. Diwali was the worst time of the year with strings of firecrackers exploding around my property and rockets racing through the house, entering from one window and out of the next. I had become the right sort of bogeyman who all the local kids could take pot shots at. They had made me into the village crackpot.

Fed up, I went down to the police station to report the harassment but they brushed it aside saying that it was my imagination, adding that there were reports that I was becoming a public nuisance. Public nuisance? My big fat toe. How could I be a public nuisance? I was minding my own business, keeping out of everyone's way and instead it was I who was being harassed by a bunch of hooligans who were a public nuisance. But would anyone listen to the truth? No chance. They turned me away saying I was imagining all of it.

Princey rarely visited me and whenever he did, stood at the wicket gate that opened on to the beach. He wasn't the same chatty fellow anymore and seemed more interested in whether I was planning to sell out and go away. Why would I want to sell out and go away? Why? And if it was so–where would I go? Every time this happened, I became more and more convinced that they were trying to hound me out. They wanted to force me to sell out cheaply or bump me off and just snatch my property, I was sure of it. I had heard intruders in the yard at night but was too scared to go out and have a look. When I finally plucked up a little courage, I rushed with a stick and a torch onto the veranda and then the yard. I didn't catch anyone. Another time when I went into the yard, the lights inside the house went off. Someone had cut the wires, I was sure of it. The next day, even the phone went dead. I yelled out to Princey when I saw him walk past on the beach that evening. *Hey, Hey Princey, I need to talk to you. You have a minute?*

What are you so het up about Arnie?

No lights, no phone.

What am I supposed to do about it? He wanted to know.

I'm not asking you to do anything about it, just asking your advice. What should I do about it?

How would I know? Go complain.

What's the use? You know they chase me away don't you?

That's your problem. No one can help it if you've made a mess of your life.

Don't you lecture me. You've become like the rest of them. Sitting in judgment over me. You have no clue …

Now don't you lecture me, he snapped and stepped closer, staring at me so hard that it seemed as if he was going to hit me in the face. Then he turned and started walking away.

Princey, wait, what's happened to you? You've changed so much. I went out, after him. A little way down the beach I grabbed him by the arm, *listen, you're behaving as if I am some sort of a criminal. I don't understand what's going on. Still fretting about me being a devil?*

You scare me. Now take your hands off me.

What's wrong with you Princey?

Then he stopped. *Take your hands off me. I just told you–take your hands off me.*

Okay, I've taken my hands off you. Now tell me what do you mean by saying that I scare you?

You are a sick man Arnie. Sick. And being with you makes everyone think I'm sick too. I don't want people to think I'm sick.

Sick? What do you mean by that? Sick?

Loony, he said almost defiantly, *loony.*

I'm not loony, I corrected him.

If you aren't loony then you are possessed.

What's this rubbish you are talking about? I was scared and confused. I didn't feel that I was possessed. Anyway, what does it feel like when one is possessed? I was afraid to look him in the face because I didn't know what sort of expression he'd have. I wanted to run. My heart beat so hard against my chest that I felt it was about to break through my ribcage and hit him and burst like a water balloon.

He continued slowly with a deliberate edge to his voice. *So don't be surprised if you find Father Rozario turning up at your doorstep.*

I don't have anything to do with him and he has nothing to do with me. I haven't been inside that church for ages.

Precisely, Arnie, now do you see what I mean?

Because I haven't been to church I'm either loony or possessed?

That's just one part of it all. I'm off. He started walking away.

I grabbed his shirt. *Wait. Please wait.*

He swung around and started pushing me. *You don't touch me, you hear? Don't touch me.* Before I could say a word, he rushed off down the beach.

I staggered home to darkness. Rummaged around in the storeroom and found a lantern with a lot of kerosene oil still in it. Lit it and placed it beside me where I sat out in the veranda.

I must have fallen asleep in the chair because I was still in the same place the next morning. Father Rozario stood there looking almost pitifully down at me. *I have come here in peace,* he said, quickly turning on a beatific smile.

So?

You've neither slept nor eaten properly. You're looking quite a wreck. Maybe you should have a good bath and shave and wake up. I'm happy to wait. Don't even mind making you tea and if you have anything in the kitchen, I can rustle up some breakfast for you. I don't suppose you have anything in the kitchen.

Thanks and no thanks.

If there was any strength in me at that moment I would have stood up and hit him so hard that he'd go flying off the veranda and land in the sand under the palms. Bloody idiot. Walking into my house and telling me what I should do. A good bath. A shave. Have something to eat. I was so surprised I didn't exactly know what to say. So I collected my wits, held on to the handles of the chair and stood up, facing him, almost nose to nose. His ferret-like eyes seemed to be burning. They bored a hole through my head, bounced off the wall behind me then returned through my head to him and set off once again. *You smell, old man, you smell. There's a lot in there that I must get out. But I can't do it without your help.*

That's when I snapped. *I smell, do I? If I smell, you stink. You stink of goodness. Goodness that makes no sense at all, that's not of any use to anyone. You probably imagine that it will take you to heaven. Isn't that a joke?*

Don't make fun of me.

Why shouldn't I? If you can enter my house without even my permission then I have every right to defend myself.

But don't insult me.

You are insulting me. What right have you to say all the things that you've been saying?

It is my right. I'm your Parish Priest.

I'm not part of your parish. I don't even go to church.

But you are a Catholic.

I may have been baptised a Catholic but I'm not a practising one.

Then what religion do you follow? He raised his voice.

None of your bloody business. Get the hell out of here. Out. You hear me? Out.

He put his hand on my shoulder trying to calm me down. That set me off like a cracker and I threw myself at him with such force that the both of us went toppling down the veranda stairs and landed on the sand outside. I was on top of him and he struggled to get up. *The next time you come into my property uninvited I'll bury you alive.*

Get off me, get off me, he yelled. When I rolled off him, he scrambled up, lifted his skirts and bolted across the beach. *Run, run,* I shouted after him. He didn't look back.

Late afternoon, the electricity still hadn't come back on. The phone line remained dead. I was too overwhelmed to get myself together and go out to get in touch with the electric people and the phone people. Maybe someone just cut the lines and if I went out they'd all be laughing behind my back. *Ha haa. Trying to get his electricity and phone on again.* I was sure that word had already spread that I had roughed up Father Rozario and someone would catch me and beat me up. Actually I didn't really attack him, I threw myself at him. I could have broken my neck doing that. Fortunately I didn't. Imagine breaking my neck. I'd have probably lain there for ages before anyone cared to even help. I wouldn't have put it past the local dogs to try and feed off me … or the locals ransack my house whilst I lay there or Father Rozario would come and deliver one of his sermons whilst all the bloody locals stood around and crossed themselves … that too even before I was dead. And they'd take me away and give me a cheap burial even though I was not even dead and I'd lie there in the coffin suffocating. God, I'm scared of the thought of being buried. Just imagine being buried. Shut inside the earth, locked in, mud preventing me from getting out. And above, dogs sniffing and trying to dig up the grave and civet cats, mongoose and snakes joining them. But then if I survived and some kind soul, I'm sure there'd be one or two out there, decided I was good enough to take home and care for, I'd lie here, useless, not wanting to live, not wanting to go on and when I was fed up of living, there'd be no one who would allow me to die … except of course those who wanted to take over my property. But I hadn't broken my neck so I just rattled around in the house waiting for the dark, hoping that no one would come to harass me.

No one came but all night I kept the lantern burning low and listened to the sound of the sea, the sandpipers on the beach, the restless rustle of the palm fronds, voices floating from the village … and dog barks, plenty of them. Early morning when the smell of fish and seaweed wafted into the house and seeped into every nook and cranny, the kerosene ran out.

Determined to do something, I bathed, shaved, looked my smartest and set out. A few yards outside my front gate I was stopped by half a dozen village seniors and a group of young bucks, Princey was amongst them. Up front, strode Father Rozario. *Where do you think you are off to?* One of them barked.

To complain that I have no electricity and my phone's dead.

We want to talk to you, another butted in.

Turn around and walk back Arnie, said Princey.

This is a free country, I'll go where I please, I shot back and tried to move forward.

They hemmed me in and then started pushing me, shouting, *after what you did to our man of God, you should be ashamed of yourself.*

What right had he to come into my home and give me his holy nonsense?

He has every right to go where he pleases. Father Rozario is our Parish Priest, our shepherd, we are his flock. He does what he knows is best for us. It is his right.

What right? I persisted.

His holy right.

And who gave him that right? I yelled.

The Church, Arnie the Catholic Church. Rome.

So someone sitting in Rome has the right to allow someone here to walk into our homes? Don't you think that's stupid? That's my private property.

But you are Catholic.

Was.

You are Catholic, Father Rozario said softly, trying to sound compassionate.

He's got the dark one in him for sure, someone said, *get him back to his house.*

They were treating me like a criminal, a thief of some sort, a perverted man and began pushing and shoving me. Someone punched me in the ribs, I tried to push him away but he kept coming at me so I turned away sharply, dodged and banged into another person who grabbed me by the hair and yanked my head up. We stared into each other's eyes. His were heavily hooded and smouldering with a rage that I couldn't understand. I couldn't figure out who those eyes belonged to. I couldn't put a face to them. Then he spat in my face and banged his forehead hard against mine, toppling me backwards. When I fell, the group stepped back. That was my chance to get away and I used all the energy that was hidden inside my punched up body and rapidly crawled forward and lurched away from them. They were taken by surprise and by the time they could figure out what was happening I scrambled into a nearby clump of shrubbery and stormed into D'Costa's backyard. Guinea Fowl and chickens scattered in disarray and a clothesline snapped as I collided into it and pulled it past breaking point.

Bleddy hell what's going on? Old man Arnold's gone mad, screeched Lilly D'Costa.

She had hardly finished her sentence when I ran straight into her and bowled her over, sending her sprawling onto pickle jars that stood like an army of commandos. I fell on top of her.

Get off me, you madcap.

Her brother Joseph came charging out of the house and was about to descend on me when the crowd arrived, rampaging through his property. That diverted his attention and gave me those few seconds more to stagger up, trample over the plump prone body of Lilly and fly out of the gate, heading for a patch of mangrove thicket. It's suicidal trying to run through a mangrove thicket but I plunged on all the same. I was so desperate that I was willing to do anything, absolutely anything.

Scraped and bruised, I battered my way through. Exhausted and out of breath, I stopped suddenly and crouched down, trying to be as still as I could. That foxed them.

Can you hear him? A voice yelled.

No, another answered, *but he's there somewhere in that mangrove. Hey you scum, you can't run far. We're coming in to get you.*

Then I heard other voices and recognised Warren's. An argument had broken out and he was shouting at them like a maniac, *leave the man alone, just leave him alone. He hasn't harmed anyone.*

Wait till I get my hands on him, it was Joseph D'Costa. *He has taken my house apart, he's going to pay for it.*

Listen, we can sort this all out, Warren tried to explain but no one seemed to be listening.

I felt drained. I couldn't run anymore. My heart lurched. I started vomiting.

There's he there, there's he there, shouted voices and people came at me from all sides, surrounding me like jackals. I sat crouched, vomit all over my shirt and trousers which were already muddied and ripped. I could feel them close in around me … and then I was there, trapped. *Look at the mess he's in.*

Haul him up and take him home, someone said.

I'm not going to touch the man, he's stinking.

To save them the trouble I stood up and staggered homewards, accompanied by the crowd. I couldn't see Warren anywhere.

Once in my courtyard, I felt relieved and safe. Stupid of me to feel that since I was surrounded by people who had nothing but dislike for me. They pushed and shoved and jabbed me in the ribs till they got me to my feet and forced me into the house. Once inside, they sat me down in a chair. *Don't you move, stay there or we'll tie you to that chair.*

People filled the house, opening cupboards, riffling through drawers. They were searching for something, I couldn't tell what. Some of them were in the bedrooms, yanking off mattresses and ripping pillows whilst others were in the kitchen clattering among the pots and pans, opening and slamming the fridge door and clattering cutlery. *What are you looking for?* The question struggled out of my mouth.

Where do you keep your stuff Arnie? Princey called out.

What stuff?

Your black stuff.

What black stuff? I asked almost in tears.

You've got Satan inside you, Father Rozario declared. Then he signalled for all of them to leave. When they were gone, he asked, *do you know what I am planning to do?*

No.

Remove the darkness from inside you.

What darkness are you talking about? Speaking was painful for me, my lip was cut and jaw seemed out of place.

Evil.

Through all that pain and confusion I couldn't stop myself from grinning, showing him my bloodied teeth.

You are filled with evil and I'm going to get it out of you.

How will you do that?

By exorcising you, he replied softly. Then, drawing a metal crucifix out of his pocket he raised it dramatically up before him and started slowly moving towards me. He looked so comical as he approached me. One foot ahead of the other, carefully as if he was doing a balancing act like a trapeze artist on a rope high above the fires of hell. His eyes were fixed on the crucifix.

Careful you might miss your footing, I said with a smirk.

But he didn't respond and kept moving forward. I didn't budge an inch but sat there watching him. When he realised that I wasn't going to cower in fear or even try to get up and back away, he stopped, confused, wondering what was going to happen next. Then he closed his eyes and dropped the hand that held the crucifix to his side. With the other he made the sign of the cross and started bellowing:

I call upon you St. Michael the Archangel, you who are the greatest and most beautiful and powerful divine being, you who are the Prince of Heaven's armies, protect us against the rulers of the dark world and their wicked spirit armies. You Prince of Peace come and help us crush Satan beneath our feet. Come on, come on and help us grab hold of the dragon, the old serpent, which is the devil and Satan … tie him up and throw him into the pit that has no bottom so that he vanishes forever.

He stepped even closer, his cassock reeking of garlic and dried fish. He looked down at me and bending forward pressed the crucifix on my forehead and then quickly stepped back in case I decided to react. But I didn't. Instead I watched him. Locked eyes with him. He began mumbling again. Then stepping back a bit, raised the crucifix again and asked,

Tell me, who are you? Who? What is your name? Identify yourself. Identify yourself in the name of the Most High. When he got no response, he shouted shrilly, *I cast you out, unclean spirit, along with every satanic power of the enemy, every serpent from hell, and all your fallen companions; in the name of our Lord Jesus Christ. Be gone and stay far from this creature of God. For it is He who commands you, He who flung you headlong from the heights of heaven into the depths of hell. It is He who commands you, He who once stilled the sea and the wind and the storm. Hearken, therefore, and tremble in fear, Satan, you enemy of the faith, you foe of the human race, you begetter of death, you robber of life, you corrupter of justice, you root of all evil and vice; seducer of men, betrayer of the nations, instigator of envy, font of avarice, fomenter of discord, author of pain and sorrow. Fear Him, who in Isaac was offered in sacrifice, in Joseph sold into bondage, slain as the paschal lamb, crucified as man, yet triumphed over the powers of hell.* Then he rushed forward and marked three signs of the cross again on my forehead. *Be gone, then, in the name of the Father and of the Son, and of the Holy Spirit. Give place to the Holy Spirit by this sign of the holy cross of our Lord Jesus Christ, who lives and reigns with the Father and the Holy Spirit, God, forever and ever.*

He waited. Watching me.

For a moment, I didn't know what to think, what to say, what to feel. The courtyard outside was filled with people from the village, I could even hear babies crying and mothers trying valiantly to shut them up. A large bumble bee entered through the front door and buzzed around the room. The sound grew louder and louder until my own head began buzzing. Father Rozario stood with his back against the wall. There was fear in his eyes. I could hear him breathing. He whispered, *I can feel your presence Dark One, Viper of the Pit of Hell, Scorpion of Death and Destruction. Don't come any nearer, don't come any nearer.*

The bumble bee buzzed even louder and headed towards him, circling around in front of his face.

Outside, a fight exploded. Warren had turned up with a gang of fisherman who ploughed into the crowd and sent people scattering. Father Rozario, sensing that his own life was in peril ran into the bathroom and locked himself in. Warren entered with a couple of fellow warriors. *My God, look what they've done to you,* was all he could say. *Where's the frockman?*

In the bathroom.

What are we going to do with him? Kaka Koli, one of the fisherman asked.

Leave him there for a while, let him stink himself out. Warren wasn't in a forgiving mood. *What exactly happened Arnie? What got into them?*

It's been building up for some time. I knew something was going to happen but I didn't think it would be this. My head was throbbing and my ribs ached painfully. I could hardly think straight and kept spitting blood. I felt as if I had swallowed a couple of teeth. *Just let that man out of the bathroom and allow him to go in peace.*

Na, said Kaka Koli, *we'll give him the treatment.*

No, please, don't be like them, please. I didn't want anymore violence. I had had enough.

Warren sidled up to the bathroom door, tapping on it. *Are you enjoying yourself in there? Are you alone?*

Please let me out. I'll mind my own business if you let me go. Pleaded the priest. I'll get the lights and phone working again.

If you had minded your own business in the first place then you wouldn't have found yourself locked up in a bathroom. Warren seemed determined to teach the man a lesson. *This is not being Christian, that much I know. You're the worst example of a man of God that I have met. I can't believe holy people can do this. You're trying to exorcise him? He should be trying to exorcise you. But he's minding his own business. You aren't even allowed to do what you were trying to do. You know it and I know it. You have to get permission. I've seen it in the movies. That's what you are supposed to do. You can't just turn up here and start throwing the cross at this fellow. You're crazy man, crazy. This is not being a holy Christian fellow.*

Kaka Koli was of the opinion that Warren was wasting his time. *We will drag him out and tie him up and take him out to sea.*

Don't be foolish, Warren wasn't going to such an extent. *I think we should let the fellow go or there'll be trouble, they'll bring more people here and you will go off and bring even more people and we will never be peaceful neighbours after this. It will be them against you all.*

This is our chance to teach them a lesson once and for all. Kaka Koli raised his voice and jumping up, headed for the bathroom door. The others who had been quiet until then, jumped up and grabbed hold of Kaka. He shrugged them off, folded his lungi in half and tucked the hems into his waistband then heaved Warren out of the way and slammed his heavy body against the bathroom door.

Don't break down the door Kaka, I shouted. *Go around from the outside, you can get in through the window.*

The man and his friends rushed out and a moment later the bathroom door opened. *I think he's dead,* one of them said.

Aarey, he's not dead. He's just pretending to be knocked out. I've seen enough dead people to know that. The dead ones don't breathe. This one is breathing. Can you hear? Asked Kaka, *he's even making sounds.*

They brought him out and laid him on the rug. *Put some Orange Special down his throat and he'll be up,* Kaka called to one of his buddies who produced a bottle of country liquor. They forcibly opened his mouth and poured some raw stuff. The man struggled, almost choked and then sat up.

Go now, go, chul phoot, chul phoot, the fisherman chanted in chorus. And that's what the fellow did, scrambled up and staggered off. When they were sure he had left, they settled down to a drink. Warren had a sip or two then stood up and went off to put my bedroom into shape. Kaka found a towel and a bowl of water and cleaned me up. I was stripped and put into bed, covered with a sheet. The voices continued in the next room for a while and then I slipped into what seemed like a coma. Something, I don't remember what it was, brought me awake. I lay there, staring at the ceiling. Warren was sitting in a chair nearby. The lights had come on.

Arnie, are you awake? Arnie?

Yes. What's it?

Something strange going on here, something very strange. Seems like there's someone in the house.

Maybe one of Kaka's boys, I suggested.

A window banged.

You heard that? His voice was a bit shaky.

Must be the wind.

There's no wind. It's still out there. Arnie, it's still out there.

Then it must be someone trying to scare us. I had gone past caring why the window was banging. Warren got out of his chair quietly and leaping through the window, rushed off around the back of the house to check out what was going on. He came back white in the face.

There was no one there Arnie. I saw the window banging by itself.

Rubbish.

Yes. I saw the window banging by itself.

A little later, the window stopped banging and I slipped into sleep. The last thing I remember was Warren sitting upright in the chair with Mother's stout walking stick in his hands.

Changing Seasons

Winter was approaching and the air had got decidedly cooler. It's never really cold by the sea but then it's cooler than other times of the year. There were more locals on the beach and kids and young people brought the whole place alive. The sea was quieter and gulls wheeled everywhere, filling the air with their cries. I had enjoyed two weeks of bliss after that humiliating encounter with Father Rozario and the gang of ruffians. Of course, it was still on the front page of local gossip but no one harassed me. Neither did they speak with me. I mean, none of the Catholic lot spoke with me. I guess, if I was not a Catholic there would have been no problem at all. I'd be anyway headed for damnation because my God was different from theirs. But Kaka Koli and his lot didn't mind defending me, I had never imagined they would. But they did. Maybe it was their way of getting back at the cross-wallahs.

Anyway, winter was approaching and as usual I was out in the shade of the palms in Mother's deck chair watching activity on the beach. People were shouting and running back and forth. Then came a few cops striding officiously past as if the beach was theirs. Something was obviously in the wind. I walked out and enquired but didn't get a response. Someone said *murder* and someone else mentioned Princey's name. *Princey? Murdered? Not possible. Don't believe that*, I told myself as I walked in the general direction that everyone seemed to be going. Towards the far end of the beach, a large crowd had gathered. By the time I reached the cops were already shooing people away and cordoning the place off.

A body lay near the water's edge. There was no head. *Princey got his head taken off. The chap must have used a chopper,* an old woman said as she limped away from the scene.

More like the work of a sword or an axe, another added. *You know what I mean? Looks like the murderer came up from behind and whoosh—took his head off his shoulders in one swipe. Wonder why he did that.*

Ah, the one who limped went on, *nowadays people will kill even for a cigarette.*

This looks more like a crime of passion.

There wasn't any passion in Princey, he was just a nice guy. He talked too much and was a bit of a busybody.

I neared the cordon and took a good look. It was obviously Princey. He was wearing his favourite blue and white checked shirt and denims and looked as if he was sleeping. Everything was so relaxed. I wondered where his head was.

Jacinta stood on the other side behind the cordon, staring at me. *So you've come to enjoy the scene eh? This isn't a movie, it's real. The pasting never kept you away? Its people like you who killed him.*

Everyone turned to look at me.

Why would I want to kill your son? Does it look like I'm capable of doing it? I quickly replied.

Of course you are. You are capable of even killing your own mother. And you did. You sent her to a home.

That's none of your business. I wasn't going to let her say whatever she wanted. She decided to go on.

Expect us to believe that? She persisted.

I don't care what you believe and what you don't.

My poor Princey, without a head, he took away your head, my son, my only son. He took away your head. He'll be punished for this, he's not going to get away. A group clustered around her were sobbing and then they all started wailing. One of the policemen started waving his lathi, shouting at everyone to move back further.

Father Rozario turned up and pushed his way to the front and stood beside me without realising that he had done so. *He'll burn in hell,* he declared dramatically and accidentally pointed upwards. Everyone gasped. He suddenly realised what he had done and sheepishly brought his hand down to his side. *He was a man of God, this one,* he added.

The smell of garlic was overpowering. I tried to step back but my arm brushed his hand. He turned towards me and appeared as if he had seen a ghost. He backed away, his face going pale and his lips trembling. Jacinta yelled, *curse him Father, curse him.*

I walked away quickly, stumbling along the beach.

It's him, I could hear her shouting. *It's him. He killed my son.*

Yeh hai mundi, yeh hai mundi, a cop's voice rose from the mangrove clump. And there he stood holding up Princey's head by its hair.

The women began screaming and the crowd surged towards the cop. Soon he was surrounded by people who were clamouring for a closer look.

Hut, hut, get away, get away, the other cops intervened and got everyone to step back. Since their attention had turned away from me I didn't have to run so I returned at a slow trot.

Once home, I started shutting the doors and windows. Warren appeared almost out of nowhere. *Hey, don't do that. If you do that then they'll think you are guilty. Stop it.*

They're going to think I'm guilty anyway.

But you couldn't possibly have done that, he insisted.

Of course I didn't do it. But the way that woman's behaving, they'll all start saying that I've done it.

O come on, they won't have any proof. He tried his best to reassure me.

The cops have to crack the case quickly so they'll start picking up suspects. I'll surely be one of them. And you and Kaka Koli and the others …

But I insist–don't start locking yourself in. Just get on with your day. I mean try to be normal. His voice softened.

Can anyone possibly be normal in a place like this and in these times?

You're right, he agreed, patting me on the shoulder, *but try.*

I went into the kitchen and made coffee and we sat sipping the steaming brew at the table. Through the open door that led out into the veranda we had a view of the beach and watched as the crowd trouped back towards the village. An ambulance led the way. *There goes Princey and his head. Poor chap. I wonder who did that. Must have been really angry with the fellow. He was a good guy, Princey, well–an okay okay sort if not a good guy. Tried to be helpful. But something changed in him.* Warren shook his head. *Something, I don't know what.*

He changed with me for sure. After what happened with Rosie and admitting about Sarah. I stared into my empty mug.

That was a stupid thing for you to have done.

What? Have it off with Sarah?

No, that's your business and she wasn't a minor anyway.

Then what? I was curious.

Admitting it.

So you think I should have lied?

Yes, you fool. None of this would have happened.

Kaka Koli came in. *I'm going to Nala Sopara. My family's*

there just now. The others have nowhere to go and are waiting to be picked up.

Why are you running away, they'll suspect you even more? Warren grabbed him by the arm. *You sit down here. Sit.*

Leave my arm, Kaka was visibly agitated. *I don't want to get mixed up in all this. It's all because we came to help you.*

I'm sorry. There was nothing else that I could say.

He walked out.

After a moment's silence, *what do you honestly think is going to happen?* I asked.

They'll pick Kaka up when he tries to leave Gorai, they'll pick up the others, they'll pick me up and they'll pick you up. In a little while. He had hardly finished speaking when we heard the sound of a jeep. *There they are. Keep sitting. Let's hope for the best.*

There was no best only the inevitable. Four policemen entered the house. The Sub Inspector who led the posse ordered us to step out on to the veranda. Warren did a stupid thing. I don't know why he did it. He broke free and ran for his life. Two cops were sent after him. One of them remained with the Sub Inspector and searched the house for anything that they could use as evidence. An hour later, they tried to grill me for information, when I started crying they looked embarrassed. *Just tell us what you know and we'll try and make it a little easy for you.*

I don't know anything. I didn't kill the man nor do I know who did it.

The others returned, dragging Warren. They had managed to catch him and had beaten him up. *We're going to get a lot out of this one*, they said.

We were taken off to the Police Station and joined the others who had also been picked up. They looked like they were going to beat the hell out of me once they were free.

The questioning lasted seven hours and I was so exhausted and stressed out that I collapsed. When I surfaced I found myself in a locked room with the others, all of whom had bruises, black eyes and torn lips. No one spoke and the silence was deafening.

Late the next morning, an unexpected thing happened. We were told that we were free to go but were first invited to have something special to eat with the Sub Inspector. So we went into the Sub Inspector's office and joined him for a meal of parathas, dahi and achaar. When we were through, in came glasses of hot tea spiced with ginger.

We caught the fellow, said Sub Inspector Yadav, *actually someone has confessed. A Gurkha security guard from a big shot bungalow on the beach. He walked in here with a bundle of his own bloodstained clothes and the murder weapon–his kukri. And he told his story. Straight. I didn't have to hit him, I didn't have to kick him. He said straight. He signed his confession. You can go now. The jeep is waiting. I am not saying sorry because this is our job.*

It took a week for the real story to break. Princey, it turned out, had been accidentally beheaded when the security guard caught him in the premises of the bungalow. The man mistook him for a thief. And what was he doing there? He would service male guests. He'd have to scale the rear wall and get into the property because the owner didn't even want his security guards to know what was going on.

The information was first said to be false, fabricated to malign the victim and his family. That didn't stop other stories about Princey's secret life oozing out of the woodwork, the embarrassment was unbearable. But then, life has a way of mending itself, healing wounds and going on. I don't know why I felt guilty and rotten inside.

Nights became unusually chilly and I could swear I heard Princey's whistle somewhere in the dark on the beach.

Gorai sank into a peculiar type of inertia, as if so much of energy had been spent that there was nothing left inside. And with nothing left inside, everything lacked drive. The CCs and the PCs and all the 'others' (I mean the ones who don't get a chance to go to Heaven) were stuck in their usual groove like broken records. It was as if we were in a pause between seasons. Surely something had to change, be reborn, start afresh, take a new path, whatever.

Then a letter arrived from Chrissie.

My dear dear Arnie,
It's been such a long time since I last wrote to you. So much of my life has changed since then. Jason's passing away left me stranded like a whale in the desert. I never realised how much he meant to me, how much I depended on him, how much I drew from his steadiness, composure, balance. He gave me what my parents were never really able to give me. I wish I had realised this earlier, when he was still around to be more appreciative about it, to let him know.

Sorry Arnie, sorry for starting off on such a note. But this is all that's on my mind at the moment and I need to share it. I'm writing to you because I can now feel this huge emptiness in my life and need to fill it with sharing and meaning. I don't expect you, Arnie, to bend over backwards just to help me feel better. But I would like to keep a connection going between us. We are connected Arnie, connected.

I know that the circumstances under which we met weren't the best. I walked in on your life when you were trying to make sense of it and cope with your mother. At that time I do agree that I used you to fulfil a need I had. I didn't realise that

I would have to deal with your mother. And then she and I got caught in a tangle which we could never resolve. You were left behind. As for my Jason, he always said that he would have loved to be friends with you but somehow things didn't work out that way, his world and your world were poles apart.

Then you'll say in all this, *Chrissie, you have a son, don't you need to work on that relationship too?* Yes, sure I'm working on my relationship with Luke. He's a fine young man, dedicated to the business we're running. He manages our little resort. I like to call it a resort. It's in Colva. We've got twenty four rooms, a grove of coconut palms, a little restaurant and lots and lots of sun beds. Business is good. I depend on Luke because I need someone like him who knows how to deal with all sorts of people–the restaurant staff, housekeeping staff … and the guests, that's the main thing, the guests. I'm so proud of him.

Okay, let me come down to the point again, we must give our family ties another chance.

Waiting to hear from you,

Your sis,

Chrissie

Dear Chrissie,

Nice to hear from you.

Let me start by saying that I'm not the letter writing sort. I don't have your sort of focus to sit down and actually write about what's going on in my heart and in my head and then put it in an envelope and go to the post office and put a stamp on it and post it. It's like a safari for me. That doesn't mean that nothing's going on in there. A lot goes on in here but I can't get myself to write it down and I don't fancy walking through the village to the post office to post the letter. So please forgive me.

About Jason. You say he's no more? When did that happen? I'm sure he was a fine guy but I had to really struggle to have a conversation with him. I finally gave up. Maybe if I was his wife it would have been different.

About Luke, don't tie him to your apron strings like my mother did. Allow him to be himself. He shouldn't turn out a misfit like me.

And finally, about this family connection thing between you and me, I don't know how we're going to keep it going if I don't like writing.

Keep writing if you want and need to but I can't promise replies.

With affection

Arnie

My dear dear Arnie,

I was thrilled to see a letter from you in my post-box. I had quite forgotten how elegant your handwriting is. When I think back to the time when we were writing out the envelopes for my wedding invitation, I tell myself, *Arnie writes like he's stringing a necklace of pearls.*

To get down to answering you, Jason drowned. The sea took him. Can you imagine that? A merchant navy officer with years of experience at sea–drowning. Actually it was more of an accident, a stupid accident. We were out on a picnic with the Cordeiros and the Coutinos, remember them? Mathew Coutino was the guy who stammered and his wife Thelma was that wiry little woman who loved dancing alone? And the Cordeiros who looked like twins? I'm sure you'll remember, think. So we were out with them on a picnic and Mathew and Jason were tanked up with beer and a belly full of Thelma's Goa Sausage Biryani and went for a walk and a paddle. Once they got into the water, Mathew went for more than just a paddle and seemed to lose his bearings and started thrashing about in the water. Jason didn't realise that it was just a joke and went after him and got carried away by one of those big waves. It was quite a while before we got his body out. It turned up two days later far down the beach and you can imagine what it looked like. Now Luke saw it all. Saw the drowning and saw his body. He didn't speak for a month, not a single word. Nothing came out of his mouth, nothing it all. And that was quite a shock for all of us because he was such a talkative fellow. Since then I've been very protective of him. I don't want him to be hurt anymore. So if I'm tying him to my apron strings it's because of this. Yes, yes, I know what you are saying, it makes sense. But this is the big challenge for a mother.

On another note, are you saying that Jason got on better with women than men? Not true. He had a crowd of male friends. You saw them all at the wedding. But it's just that he needed time to get to know people and relate to them.

I don't want to write a long letter and challenge your patience. Just one more point–about staying in touch, I mean you and me. I'd be happy to visit you, if you like, as and when I can. And you can visit us whenever you want. We have lots of space here. You can stay with us in Panjim (that's where our little home is now) or at the Blue Mermaid, our resort. You can do whatever you please there, no one will disturb you. Luke will be delighted. Think about it.

I'll write off now,

A big hug,

Your sis,

Chrissie

Dear Chrissie,
Sorry for the delay in writing back to you. As I had said, I'm hopeless at this sort of thing. Besides that, I was getting the roof of the bungalow re-tiled and the windows and doors repaired. The fellows I hired to do the job were actually fishermen but have knowledge of roof repair because they mend their own roofs. I had to ply them with drink and food to keep them working. It's all done and the place is looking respectable. I've been throwing out all Mother's old stuff that's useless. So you are welcome to visit whenever you want. Luke too.

I don't know how to say this but believe me, I feel really bad about the way Jason went. That he went is bad enough, but the way he went ... such a cruel joke.

Goa? You are inviting me to Goa? Maybe, I'll turn up at your doorstep one day, who knows.

With affection
Arnie

My dear dear Arnie
I was getting a bit worried when I didn't hear from you for a while but then I told myself *Chrissie, he warned you didn't he?* Of course I'll visit you. And seriously, think about visiting us in Goa.

This is going to be a short letter because I'm off to look at a girl for Luke. She's from a good family they say. Who knows?

Lots of hugs
Your sis
Chrissie

Ps. I've enclosed some snaps of us and the resort.

Getting letters from Chrissie and writing back started

building an invisible bridge between us. It was somewhat of a 'family feeling' but not exactly one. There was a link, we shared the same father, but our reaching out to each other started becoming so real and sensitive that I began to realise that for the first time in my life I was forging a relationship of my own choice. I felt myself reaching out beyond the confines of my own solitary world. This affected me in more ways than one. It helped me feel less self-conscious, opened in me the need to communicate more deeply and made me feel–good. I mean positive. I looked forward to each new day and didn't just live each moment for the sake of living. I ate regularly, walked a lot, started a new kitchen garden, built bird boxes and feeders and sometimes walked into the village market just for the sake of it.

I had begun trying to find myself.

I looked forward to letters from Chrissie and even tried elaborating my own letters to her and filling them with more information and feeling that I dug from deep within my life. That got me into the habit of keeping a diary. And it didn't end there. I pulled out the trunk full of books that I had bought and never read because my life had overtaken me. Dragging the trunk out into the veranda I flipped back the latch and carefully emptied the contents. Dusted the books and lined them up against the wall. It was a bizarre collection including *The Count of Monte Cristo, The Man In The Iron Mask, The Hunchback of Notre Dame,* Mary Shelly's *Frankenstein,* Bram Stoker's *Dracula, Robinson Crusoe, Don Quixote, The Outsider, Heart of Darkness, Crime And Punishment, Lord Of The Flies* and others. Had I bought them because perhaps they reflected some aspect of my inner world or what I was going through at the time? Probably. Had I really journeyed out of that darkness or was that just a false dawn? I couldn't tell.

I threw away the trunk because it was falling apart and packed the books into neat bundles in the hope of disposing of them at some second hand bookshop if I got the chance.

Then the need to acquire a couple of farm creatures got hold of me and I considered buying fowls and ducks and a pig but gave up the idea because I didn't want to leave them in the care of anyone else in case I decided to travel. To Goa, for starters. Then maybe other places too. I bought myself a large map of India and spent hours browsing over its length and breadth with a magnifying glass, spotting the names of places, trying to imagine what they'd be like if I visited them. Pushkar, Bastar, Dhar, Pithoragarh, Gosaba, names and more names. The Andamans. I fancied going there.

I felt as if I had woken up from a deep sleep and was trying to find my bearings again in the waking world, all of life rushing at me at great speed. Like meteorites in space. Was it another season that would change and I'd find myself rudderless, buffeted by unseen waves and storms, no flash of a lighthouse visible?

Whatever it was, even if it was an illusion, I decided to stay with it and wrote to Chrissie that I wanted to visit her. She was over the moon so I found a caretaker, thanks to Warren, and caught an overnight bus for Panjim.

2 ON ANOTHER SHORE

On the Shore

Chrissie, how do you manage without a man? Living alone must be really difficult.

I'm not exactly alone Sabby, I replied, *got my boy and we're great friends and we have Blue Mermaid and that keeps us busy. And besides, the cherry on the cake is that Arnold is here.* My breakfast arrived on a tray. There was porridge, fruits, juice, a fried egg with the perfect face of the sun right in the middle, toast, marmalade and a side plate with sausages and bacon.

Call this a breakfast Sabby? It's a meal for a week. You don't have to be so generous with me. Just dropped in for a cup of tea.

It's breakfast time. And breakfast at Clementine is always a lip smacking affair.

What do you all serve at Blue Mermaid?

The usual, American, English, Continental and Indian. You've never visited.

It's like going on a safari getting to your mermaid place. I mean, you don't have a proper road from Colva Square, either there're too many sand dunes everywhere or open drains that stink to high heavens.

Thanks for the compliments. I didn't want to argue with him because I knew damned well that everyone was jealous of Blue Mermaid. So what if it is a bit difficult getting there from Colva Square? But once there it's a mini paradise. As you approach, the fence stretches on both sides of the beautiful bronze coloured iron gate that we fixed up there. And all along the fence there are rows of bougainvillea all heavy with blooms. Loy's done a good job looking after them, watering, trimming, feeding them fish manure and all sorts. Actually, coming to think of it, he's done a good job with the rest of the property too because as you enter you'll find large shrubs of hibiscus, leaves shining and flowers wide open, on either side and to the right on the seafront we have a lovely shady clump of coconut palms. In the middle there is our restaurant which is on a raised concrete platform, airy on three sides and you can sit there all day and do what you please. On the other side of the property, that is southwards, we have a small wood with old trees–mango, neem, some cashew and lots of others, even two jamun and one peepal tree. And in the middle of the wood there is a really large clearing. Actually there never was a clearing there, it was Luke who thought up the idea. *For bonfires,* he said and cleared up the place. The first few bonfires were disasters. A group of Russians partied around a fire till early in the morning and got so drunk that they started tossing liquor into the flames and ended up setting their own ground sheets on fire. Another tried fire walking and three were hospitalised with severe burns. Anyway, it had become all too complicated so Luke turned the area into a camping ground and set up tents for outdoor lovers. At the back of the property, westwards, are rows of tiled roofed rooms forming a 'W' and beyond–the land rises to a hillock on top of which we've built an exclusive bungalow with a small garden. Sometimes when it isn't occupied, Luke uses the place.

And after that, the land slopes down to a paddy field which has a café and day rest and lounging rooms, all part of a solid bamboo house on stilts. It's a great hit in the season. When paddy is out, we grow all types of other greens. That's all Loy

Mascarenhas' work. The paddy field and the rest of the trees and plants and flowers and creepers are looked after by him so well. He misfires sometimes and that leads to problems. Like the time he insisted that we should have small rockeries at different places in the property. It sounded so interesting that Luke and I decided to let him set them up. The guests were delighted when they saw the results. Loy got his fair share of pats on the back and a couple of bucks as tips when they checked out.

A few other resorts tried poaching him but he didn't rise to the bait because he knew that they would dump him when the season came to an end and the blistering summer and the monsoons took over, forcing all the seafront resorts to shut down. May to September end there'd be nothing for Loy to do if he had decided to accept their offer. But with us, he was part of our family and stayed in the little cottage at the corner of the property, getting his usual salary at the end of every month. He calls me Ma. Luke was uneasy with that at first but now he's got accustomed to it.

Then one dusk, when a couple of guests were sitting out on one of the small patches of lawn which sported a rockery, they saw a snake emerge from the pile and head towards them. It was the woman who we've nicknamed Mrs Australia who noticed it first. Apparently, she stopped talking mid-sentence and let out an awful yelp, jumped up and down in her chair till it toppled over backwards sending her legs into the air. Another guest tried clicking snaps of the snake whilst the others scattered, collecting Mrs Australia on their way out. She continued to scream and yell as if her bottom was on fire. Meanwhile other guests turned up and so did Luke and I. One of the guests, a writer fellow claimed he knew all about snakes. *That's a rat snake*, he declared, with authority. *In India we call it a Dhaman. Harmless. Non-poisonous. It feeds on rats and mice. We are lucky that he's here to keep away those rodents.* The group made sounds of approval. Mrs Australia returned with a stick. *Go on, go,* urged the writer fellow, who was one of those Indian types who imagines he's some sort of guru, *click as many pictures as you want, he's a beautiful fellow.* When the reptile had been photographed, it turned and made its way back through a gap in the pile of rocks.

The next day, Mrs Australia bustled her way into the office with her stick. *That was no rat snake we saw last evening, it was a Russels Viper. Jack took pictures of it and we went to town and checked out on the net and that's what they say: it's bite is deadly. It's painful getting a bite from one of those. You bleed like hell and start vomiting and your face swells up, maybe even your kidneys fail or you get septicaemia or your heart fails. What we saw was no rat snake. It was a deadly Russels Viper. I suggest that you clear up all those piles of rocks and keep the place safe.* She was gone before I could reply and went back to her room tapping the ground with her stick.

An hour or two later, we started clearing away the piles of rocks. Snakes of all sizes and colours slithered out and I'm sorry to say we had to kill them all and then burn them to ashes. We never found the Russels Viper. It probably found a hiding place somewhere near Mrs Australia's room.

But first things first. My Sunday morning breakfast with Sabby holding forth like he always does at Clementine. Once he is on a point, he doesn't let up. *I suppose, Chrissie, that must be good for you, a long lost brother dropping by and your son to share your everyday life with and pamper and all that. But you do need a man. Now I'm talking about a man. Someone who isn't a relative.* He lowered his voice and looked me straight in the eye. *Your man.*

Go on with you. I'm too old for all that. And even if I put myself up on the market. Just imagine me running around with a guy at this age. I mean a brand new guy. You seem to be having a problem with me being happy with my family.

Oh no, I'm not. But your 'brother' is passing through and will go back to wherever he's come from and as for your son, wait till the boy finds a real mermaid and you'll lose him forever.

Where'll he go? Blue Mermaid is his. He'll always be here.

'Always' is a dangerous word. Nothing lasts always. Certainly not children. Let them find their own lives and loves and they'll be gone, slip through the fingers like sand. Gone forever. And they never seem to forgive. Do your best and you get kicked in the teeth finally. Don't do your best and you'll still get kicked in the teeth anyway. My Xavier has kicked me in the teeth after all that I've done for him. He's waiting for me to pop off so he can sell Clementine and kick up his heels with his loose wristed friends.

He won't sell Clementine. I tried to reassure him. *You built that place up from nothing and now you have twelve rooms and a pretty decent bar and restaurant.*

But he doesn't want to spend his time looking after a place like Clementine. The life at sea has spoilt him. That's why I didn't want him to join the Merchant Navy. They can't stay still after that. So you see, I've written him off in my head. Now there's just me. Even among friends in Colva, I'm still alone. Oh well, I know I'm boring you. On another note–what the hell does that long lost brother of yours do all day long at Blue Mermaid? Hope he's not leaning over Luke's shoulder all the time. Doesn't he feel a bit lost? Send him along to my place and I'll get him into some action.

Why on earth should the fellow feel lost? I wanted to know. *But if you would like to meet him I'd be happy to do the introductions.*

I did meet the fellow a long long time back when you and Jason were hitching up.

The word's called married, Sabby, MARRIED. When we were getting married.

What are you losing your peck for? Knowing full well what I was reacting to.

So coming back to where you left off.

You mean where you butted in, is more like it. Sabby sighed. And when Sabby sighed it meant that he was getting restless.

Okay, you win, when I butted in. So you know him.

Just a wee bit. Slightly shy and kind of droopy when he's in a crowd but full of life when he's on his own.

When did you see him when he was alone? I was curious.

Walking down Colva main street, heading to the beach. There he was striding along and I think he was whistling.

Whistling?

Yep, whistling. It was like he seemed happy that he was by himself and didn't have to deal with anyone else. Yes, bring him over, I'd like to get to know him.

Okay Sabby, I'll follow up on that one. I had another cup of good strong Assam Tea and kissed him on the cheek and he tried to hug me but I got away. *Thanks for the super duper breakfast and of course the company.*

Always my pleasure. He puckered his lips and kissed the air.

I know Sabby fancies me no end. But I've had enough of men. Really. My life's complete at Blue Mermaid.

And so I walked back along the beach wondering how Arnold was doing. Already a week into his stay and he seemed to be getting along okay. Of course, that was because he was at the resort and Luke was there and everyone treated him with respect because he's a part of the family. If he had been anywhere else he would have crawled into his shell. Doesn't have the social edge, poor chap. But inside, deep inside, I know there's something special there. Who can see that something special? Who would want to befriend him? Sabby seems like he wants to try but who knows what his real intention is … maybe he just wants to get a bit closer to me. I hoped it wouldn't end up in a mess. I don't know why I was being so protective. After all, he had lived by himself and managed his own affairs. Granted he had got into all sorts of crazy situations like letting that woman into his home and ending up with half the village on his property and a priest trying to get the devil out of him.

In fact, when I first got to know that I had a brother it was by accident. I was a girl then and had just returned from school and found Mum and Dad tangled up in a crazy argument.

She was shouting her head off about how she had found out that he was married earlier and had left his wife and son in the lurch. *I want to walk out, I want to walk out on you idiot man,* she yelled, *see what you've done to me.*

He shouted back, *I've given you love, a beautiful daughter and a damned good life. So what are you complaining about? What's it to you if I was married before?*

Mum became hysterical. *What's it to me? What's it to me? You idiot man, it means everything to me because you have made me part of your crime. So I am also guilty.*

Dad tried pacifying her, *this is no crime,* he said softly, and I imagined him hugging her and stroking her hair. Mum had beautiful long hair.

She cried a bit and then she started shouting at the top of her voice, *this is no crime? Bloody hell, you are sounding like an innocent from Paradise who doesn't have a clue about what is acceptable and what is not. This is bigamy. Bigamy. And you didn't think of even talking about it to me? You have cheated me, let me down, how many more women have you done this to? How many half brothers and sisters does Chrissie have out there? How many?* Then Mum threw herself on the bed, I knew she had done that because I could hear her body hit the bed with a thud and her fists go thump, thump as she punched the mattress and then a tearing sound.

Dad's voice broke in, *why are you tearing up the pillows. Stop it will you.*

Puffs of cotton floated out of the room and soon flooded the room in which I stood, some even settled on my head. *I'm tearing the pillows,* Mum was sobbing, *because here is where you and I have spent beautiful times and now I don't want to remember it all. I don't. All this is sinful. Everything in this house is sinful. You have even tainted my precious little daughter.*

Our daughter, Dad snapped.

Half the world's children must be yours. But this is MINE.

Sit down, will you. Dad tried to put on a reasonable voice. *You will never know what a miserable life I had before I met you. I love you and I thought I could make a new life with you ...*

And so you married me and told me a lie that you were single. Oh God, what a fool I've been. I don't know how many other women you have out there.

So what do you want to do? Dad still tried sounding reasonable and that must have irritated Mum even more. *So you want to leave? Do you want me to leave? What do you want?*

You are a clever man you are, she responded. *You know that I'm madly in love with you and will never leave you. No, let this be now, let this be. I just feel cheated, I feel cheated and it's going to take a long time for me to get over this.*

There was a long silence in the room and suddenly Dad walked out and stood rooted at the door when he saw me. There was confusion on his face. Neither anger nor sadness, just confusion. I ran out and headed for my little playshed under the trees. Once inside I shut the door and stood with my back to it, keeping it closed as there was no latch.

I heard Dad approach the shed and rest his head against the door. He was breathing heavily. Neither of us said anything. We stayed like that for a long time and then he said softly, *dumpling, my own precious dumpling*. That was the line he always used when he was at his affectionate best. *I don't know whether you will ever forgive me. Will you?*

I didn't reply.

Dumpling? Are you there? Are you listening to me?

It was my turn to be confused. *How many brothers and sisters do I have?* I asked.

He didn't reply and I could hear him sobbing then he walked away.

It took us months to get over that difficult time and the only thing that stayed with me was the fact that he hadn't replied when I had asked him *how many brothers and sisters do I have?* That got my imagination going and I'd often lie in bed at night imagining that I had a whole brood of brothers and sisters and even gave them each a name. But I tried to push my real brother way to the back of my mind because he was real.

I was thirteen when Mum got pregger. Dad was out at sea and I'd spend evenings pampering her. It was good for me that Mum's big craze was lemon and honey pancakes, because I could make them. I turned them out hot from the kitchen in all shapes and sizes and stuffed her good and proper. I was happy that I was now going to have my own little brother or sister. Mum was sure it was going to be a girl because she'd often sneeze before she went to bed. *That's a sure sign you are going to have a little sis. Just wait and see.*

I watched her belly grow day by day and her face become brighter and brighter. She was glowing and I was so happy for her until the day it happened. We'd just finished dinner and she and I were there in the kitchen cleaning up when she suddenly staggered back and sat in a chair. She was moaning and a trickle of blood leaked out of her to the floor. I ran to the phone and got the neighbours and the doctor and we moved her to the hospital. She lost the baby that night and next morning I sat at her bedside, looking down at a strange pale face with dry lips and glazed eyes.

Dad arrived two days later and the house sank into silence like a ship sinks to the bottom of the ocean. She was sure that the baby she had lost was a girl and every night she prayed to God to keep her little girl safe. She even set up a shrine at the corner of the garden and lit candles every Sunday. A little plaque read, *IN LOVING MEMORY OF MY LITTLE GIRL.*

The walk back along the beach to Blue Mermaid seemed endless. I really don't know why. The wet sand oozed between my toes and the waves went lap lap. And memories circled around in my head like planets in a universe. I had been so stuck up in my thoughts that I hadn't realised that I had walked past the resort and was actually far ahead. Embarrassed, I turned around and walked back.

Such a long walk in the sun and no hat on your head. It was Arnie.

We had a lemonade in the café. Arnie said nothing but I must say that he looked relaxed.

Luke joined us later and after they had glugged a beer each, they walked back to the office, leaving me to my ownsome so that I could look back into my head at the planets floating around inside. I'm not good at this selective memory thing. I start with one and end up bumping into others as I go along and then I am surrounded by sights, sounds, smells, people, places and everything else. I remember kneeling and praying with Mum at the shrine and our words got lost in a rainy wind that had come swimming along the shore. We were drenched but Mum didn't want to get up until she had finished her prayers. We walked in soaking wet and Dad watched us go into our rooms and didn't say a word. All night the storm raged around us and I lay there thinking about the soul of my sister floating around somewhere. I finally decided that she was in Paradise and fell asleep.

And the next morning when the sun came up and there was light everywhere, I walked with Dad to the water's edge and got my ankles wet. I was really happy to be alive. Just imagine–I had a sister in Paradise, a brother somewhere on earth and myself. The three of us. All connected by Dad. So we were all at the water's edge. The frothy waves lapped at our feet and there was a flock of seagulls swirling about in the air.

Later that day when we were at the table drinking tea and eating Mum's delicious chicken sandwiches, she said, *maybe we should explain to Chrissie that she has a brother and also tell her what his name is, where he lives, his age and everything that's important about him. As much as it hurts me, she has a right to know. I don't want to brush this sort of thing under the carpet. So go on, tell her.*

There was a long and painful silence then Dad started, stumbling with his words at first and after that he continued as if he was making his confession. The three of us cried as he spoke. And there before my eyes I saw the big strong father I once knew turn into a cry baby.

That night when he thought I was asleep he came into my room, sat at the edge of my bed and looked down at me. I watched him through my almost closed eyelids. He was saying something to himself but I could not understand what it was, until of course he said *'Amen.'* What followed was quite clear. *Listen Chrissie, I want you to know how sorry I am for being such a trickster. I know you will never forgive me. I've had everything I've ever wanted from my life and now the time has come when I don't think that I have the right to want any more. Maybe when you are older you'll understand what I am trying to say.*

When he was leaving the room, I whispered, *I forgive you Dad.*

He stopped, sighed and left the room.

A few days later he left for sea. I was at school that day and when I returned Mum was arranging a small bunch of flowers at the shrine, singing quietly to herself. *He's gone, your father, gone to sea. There's something in your room for you.*

It was such a strange feeling standing there, alone, Dad gone to sea, Mum singing at the shrine of her lost baby. And there I was alive and wondering what for? Why? Why was I alive? Why? But I got no answer, not even in my head or my heart. On my bed lay a small hamper of goodies and a large packet in a pale blue envelope. He always put special things in large pale blue envelopes. I sat down on the bed and picking up the packet, stared at it, wondering what was inside. It was heavy, felt like some sort of album.

The Packet

Although I was really curious about what was in the packet, I was afraid to open it in case I discovered a truth that was too hard to stomach. So I did the next best thing–I put it away in my cupboard. I'd open it when I was ready. Mum was obviously curious and wanted to know what was in the packet. That night at dinner she asked, *you lucky bug, what did Dad leave for you this time?*

Just the usual, sweet tooth stuff, tee shirts and a little extra money.

That's it? Nothing else?

Yes. And some, I don't quite know, stationery and maybe a book I think…

Why don't you have a look?

I will.

Are you sure you haven't had a look? Mum's voice was a bit edgy.

I didn't answer.

There's just two of us here Chrissie. No point in keeping secrets. She was pushing.

Dad left those things in that packet for me. I'll open the packet when I choose to.

I just want to make sure that there's nothing in that packet that will get me worried.

Why would there be? He's left it for me. I realised that Mum was getting worked up and I'd have to say something that would pacify her. But I didn't know what to say so I left it at that. After that I was sure that Mum thought that there was some sort of conspiracy going on. Things were not the same between us. And then one day I decided to open the packet. Actually, it was a Sunday and I had said a good long prayer, quietly in my heart and in my head after holy communion. Yes, I had finally decided to open the packet.

Once I had taken the decision, I could hardly wait to get home. Mum of course took her time, which was odd. Usually she'd head straight out of church after Mass, on the way chitchatting a bit here and there. And then we'd walk home past the fish stalls and the fruit and veggie shops. But on that Sunday, her chitchatting led into conversations and it was ages before we finally reached home, in silence all the way. After breakfast I went into my room, took out the packet and placed it on the bed. *Mum, let's open this together*, I called.

Not really. That's your business. I've decided not to even ask.

Oh come on Mum, please.

She came to the door. *When I say no, I mean no.* Then she shut the door. I was now alone.

When I flipped the packet over to open it I noticed something. It had been opened and re-sealed with a fresh strip of tape. There were other signs on the packet that showed that it had been opened and hastily rewrapped. I felt cheated. Mum had opened it before me and had taken a look at its contents even before I had. And it was my packet. Dad had given it to me. It was for me. But then I calmed myself by thinking of my prayers at church that day. There was not going to be anymore bitterness between us. She was my Mum after all. If she had opened the packet, well, she had opened the packet because she was anxious. Once that was cleared in my head and heart I opened the packet.

There were a bundle of letters, a small photo album, his St. Christopher medal on a chain and a letter from him. It was pretty obvious that Mum had gone through everything with a fine tooth comb. But I quickly pushed that thought out of my heart and head and opened Dad's letter.

My darling daughter,
I had planned to write this letter to you a long time back but didn't because I thought that you wouldn't be ready for it. But then you overheard the argument between your mother and me and learnt what there was to learn in a very unfortunate way. I know that night you whispered that you had forgiven me and it was very generous of you but how could have forgiven me so easily? I haven't even forgiven myself. Besides that, neither has Mum forgiven me. I know you believe in the goodness in all of us because it helps you feel safe. How can you still feel safe when you know that your family is based on a lie? Chrissie, I have really let you down and feel so ashamed that I have done this. I am not fit to call myself your father. And I am not fit to call your mother my wife. How can I ever set things right?

I have nothing more to say. Only this, that you will remain my daughter, my child, borne from my love for your mother.

These letters and photographs are the only memories that I carried with me before I met your mother. They are yours now ... and will help you to understand what I once was, who I once was.

With love and God's blessings,

Dad

P.S. I've written your brother Arnold's address on the back of this sheet. Keep it safely. One day you may want to meet him.

I threw myself across my bed and cried with my face pressed hard against my pillow. Later, I sat up and went through the rest of the packet, starting with the photographs in the small album.

The first page had a few black and white pictures pasted on it. A very young and handsome Dad with a tall, slender beauty. They looked so happy to be with each other. The faded scrawl on a white slip below read, 'With Monica the day I proposed and she accepted.' The next was called 'The Big Day' and it had four or five pictures of the wedding which looked like it was a very lavish affair. The bride and groom were all decked up and the cake was enormous. Dad was glowing.

And as I turned page after page, his unknown life came alive. Monica pregnant, the arrival of Arnie, Monica and Arnie, family picnics, parties … and then none of all that, just pictures of the lovely old house surrounded by coconut palms, the beach, fishing boats and then several blank pages. The pictures pasted on them had been torn out. It seemed as if it had all started with a great big bang and then fizzled out. Just like our family.

As for the bundle of letters. Some envelopes had little coloured drawings by Arnie of a sailor on board a ship with red sails. In some the sailor was looking through a long telescope, in others he was waving a small blue flag or holding up a swordfish by its tail. The other envelopes contained loving letters from Monica. The last letter was from an unknown woman by the name of Peggy. 'Thanks for the wonderful night darling,' it read. I wondered if Dad had included that letter intentionally or was it there by accident. I would never know.

Why had Dad left that packet for me? Didn't he realise that it would only make it worse for me? Was it his way of making a complete confession? Strange way to do it. I would have liked for him to have told me a little about my half brother Arnold. Suddenly I got the feeling that I hadn't really known Dad. He was a stranger. Someone with a mysterious past. Someone who had brought me into the world and just walked away. I was fourteen and fatherless. Maybe that was for the good, finally. Maybe I would now be able to stop looking up to my father like some sort of hero and treat him just as a man ... with a bagful of insecurities.

I bolted my door, bathed and slept.

Mum and I began the next day in a new relationship. I began to understand her much better. And as we had just about settled in, the news of Dad's death arrived like a solitary crow cawing on the tree outside. We grieved, yes, we went through the long and the short of the procedures to get his body and bury it with whatever dignity we could accord it. I even wrote to Arnold and his mother but never got a response. Who knows? The letter may have gone astray.

And then life slipped back to its usual pattern. Just Mum and I and we worked out a rhythm that was good for both of us.

So that's the way it was. And after all those years there I was sitting in my own café which was part of my own resort, on my own property, running it with my son. And my brother with me. What more could I ask for? What more?

Later that day, Arnold popped a question, *I would like to stay on a bit longer here, is that okay with you two?*

Luke hugged him affectionately, *Sure thing Uncle Arnie, stay as long as you want to, isn't that so Mum?*

Of course, goes without saying.

And so we moved Arnie into a larger room which had its own veranda. It was private and gave him a little more elbow space. Besides that, it wasn't very far from the office–a place that he had started spending a lot of time in, playing standby for Luke whenever he was out. I was happy that he had adjusted so well. This definitely was a new side to him and I hoped that he'd give it a chance to develop. He did try, sure he did try but sometimes he couldn't control himself and flipped back into old familiar ways, would become moody and stayed away from us.

Usually when this happened I'd pretend I hadn't noticed and leave him to sort himself out and come back to the world when he was ready but it bothered Luke. *Uncle Arnie is in the dumps today. Can't figure out what I've done wrong.*

You haven't done anything wrong son, don't let it bother you.

But it does bother me, I can't help it. I was there with him in the office today and he helped me do all the filing then I left him for a while, just a while, say about half an hour and when I got back his expression had changed. He wouldn't even look at me, got up and left grunting, 'be back.' But he never came back. So I went over to his room and knocked on the door and he wouldn't open it when I knocked. Back at the office I sat there trying to work out what the hell had happened. I've been asking around to try and find out from the others.

I pitched in, *who?*

The waiters and any others who might have gone to the office. All they did was look strangely at each other, as if they were surprised that I should be asking. As if I should know.

Go on with you Luke, something or the other must have bothered him. When you get on a bit in years you'll start behaving that way. Even the littlest thing will set off a cracker.

I'm not that way at all Mum, I don't think I'll ever be that way. When you work with people you learn to adjust. I mean bend a little this way and that. It's the work I'm doing that has made me this way.

But look at it this way, son, he isn't working here. This is not his job, this is not his profession. He's just visiting and he doesn't know what to do with his time so what does he do? He visits you in the office and tries to help out and be around you a bit.

And he's definitely a help, Mum, he's good with figures, and he's even shown me a couple of ways I can keep a track of the House Keeping staff. Stuff I didn't learn at catering college.

So there you are, he's got his good side too. Not everyone's like you Luke. So don't start getting het up about his behaviour.

It's not that, I just hope I'm not the cause of it.

Why should you be the cause of it? How can you possibly be the cause of it? Stop blaming yourself Luke.

Suddenly I realised that Arnie had entered. *Sorry, don't mean to interrupt you two but there're two queers out there asking for a room. Do you give room to queers?*

Shsh, Uncle, Luke turned almost red in the face, *shsh, Uncle.*

What have I said wrong? Did I say something wrong Luke? Chrissie?

Luke took a deep breath, then breathed out, trying to calm himself. *You mean there are two persons out there who are gay.*

I don't know whether they are gay, they look more irritable to me then gay, but they sure are queer.

Uncle, actually that's none of our business what they are. That's their business. So long as they don't upset the other guests and they pay their bills, it's fine.

So you don't have a problem with what they'll be up to in their room? He went on.

No, as I said, it's none of our business. Anyway, how do you know that they are gay?

I just told you Luke, they are anything but gay. But they surely are queer.

Son, why don't you go ahead and sort it out. I suggested.

Luke left abruptly. Arnie stood there, confused. *I don't understand what's going on. First I come here and discover that you two are discussing me and my moods threadbare and then your son starts getting ratty with me. Aren't we all entitled to our moods Chrissie? And then to top it all he starts babbling about those two fellows out there being gay. They are anything but gay. They look so unhappy. Poor fellows.*

Don't worry about them Arnie, Luke will take care of them. About you catching us talking about your moods, Luke is struggling to understand you. He wants to understand you, he doesn't want to hurt you. In fact he's been talking about how he's learnt so much from you.

The young are in a hurry to get someplace, fast, and often miss the details. The small things. And then, before they realise it, they're slowing down and they're old. We have to travel through our whole lives to finally reach our own door and enter into our own home where we can be ourselves and feel safe. And this feeling safe is all so fragile. One little thing can crash it to pieces and we have to work to put it together again. The young will never be able to understand this Chrissie.

Luke respects you Arnie, believe me, he just wants to get it right. On another note, how about a beer?

A beer it shall be.

We sipped in silence, then he asked out of the blue, *are you happy with your life Chrissie? Are you?*

Yes, I suppose so.

Now don't suppose so. Say so.

Yes, I replied, *to be honest, somewhat.*

Don't you get lonely without a man?

How about you? All these years living by yourself Arnie …

I didn't live Chrissie, I didn't live. I just existed. I managed. I'm trying to start living now. Now. I hope I don't become a burden in the process Chrissie.

We're family, you are safe.

I went over to him and hugged him.

Luke walked in grinning. *Blondie is back, this time he's brought a sporty Australian with him.*

Who is Blondie? Arnie wanted to know.

One of the fellows you just met.

Ah, the ... the ... whatever fellows. Listen I've got a feeling I've crossed my wires on this. Think you'll have to clear it up for me Luke.

Some other time maybe.

We sat around saying nothing really. Luke got himself a beer. *You going back to Panjim tonight, Mum?*

Yes.

I think I'll stay back.

So he did, and I got to know later that he had sat up almost all night chatting with Arnie. To be honest, I had got a bit worried when Luke said that he was staying back. It's because I linked it up with the fact that Blondie and his new guy had arrived. I had all sort of niggling worries about him mixing up with them. True, I am worried about his future. Not about him earning a living. He'll have no problem about that. It's about his relationships. He does meet women, know women, has a few close women friends but nothing like him having a woman. I mean, his own woman. He doesn't talk about it at all, just shrugs it off. So when Sabby started off about his son and his loose wristed friends, that rang a bell somewhere at the back of my head. But I didn't want to start panicking. *Keep calm, Chrissie,* I said to myself, *keep calm, stop your wild imaginings. Luke doesn't have a loose wrist. He's a nice straightforward fellow who will grow into a perfectly okay person. Stop getting paranoid.*

But my other self, the self that brings all the bad news, asked, *what are you worrying about? So what if Luke has loose wrists? There's nothing you will be able to do about it. There's nothing he can do about it. It's not a disease that you can treat, it's his lot in life. It was your lot in life that you had parents whose marriage was a joke and you couldn't do anything about it. You have a half-brother who lived with a controlling mum and you couldn't do anything about it. You had a husband who the sea took away from you and you couldn't do anything about it. So what the hell are you getting so worried about people and things that you can't change? What's wrong with you? Just get on with living your life and stop all this nonsense.*

At one point I had even hoped that someone would tell me that Luke was having it off with some of the single women who stayed at Blue Mermaid. I was willing to go to any extent to prove all was well with him.

It wasn't long before I managed to get Arnie talking about that night. *Quite a son you have Chrissie. He's got an interesting head on those shoulders of his.*

Why do you say that?

He has a way with words.

You two haven't been discussing me have you?

A lot more.

That means you two have been discussing me?

Oh come on Chrissie, of course we talked about a lot of things, you included, but I'm not going to gossip about it all.

Gossip, about what? Listen here Arnie, is there something that I should be worried about?

When I said 'gossip' I meant that it was a conversation between Luke and I and he hasn't given me the permission to tell you or anyone else.

Christ Arnie, I'm not anyone else, I'm his mother and your half-sister. All I'm asking is whether there's anything that I should be worried about. Yes or no?

You are beginning to sound like my mother. Don't let's ruin this relationship.

That got my goat, he was comparing me to his mother. *How am I beginning to sound like your mother? How?*

You want to know everything, all the time.

I hope you aren't trying to drive a wedge between Luke and me.

Now where are you off to? Arnie sounded irritated.

I'm not off to anywhere, all I did was ask you a straight question.

He threw himself into a chair, *you seem to be thinking that there's some conspiracy going on behind your back. All we did was have a long chat.*

So what's wrong with me asking you what you talked about?

Why are you so insecure about your son? Or are you worried about your relationship with him?

I have a perfectly fine relationship with my son. I was getting uncomfortable with the way the conversation was going. I wanted to get out of it but didn't know how so I steamed ahead.

Finally, he got up, *seems like I'm getting you anxious. And this is your space and I have to follow your rules. Right. And Luke is your son. Well, he talked about his work here, his plans to add a lot more to this place, about the interesting people who've passed through here, he's in touch with some of them still, about relationships, his parents, wanted to know about mine …*

Does he have a woman in mind?

I wouldn't know.

How does he manage without a woman Arnie? Have you ever thought about that?

Didn't strike me as unusual. I've managed without women. He replied in a matter of fact way.

That's not exactly healthy, I insisted.

In that case, how about you? Why didn't you go off and find a man after Jason died?

How do you know I didn't?

Did you?

Yes, I did. I found fellows for relief, that's all.

Are you serious Chrissie?

Of course I am.

So then, how do you know Luke and I don't also find women now and then for relief?

You wouldn't.

Let's call this off, he finally said, sounding exasperated. *If I'm getting in the way of your relationship with your son, please tell me and I'll be happy to go home. I don't want to go through this whole damned mother-son thing again. A lot of my life I lived in Mother's shadow, had her telling me what I should eat, how I should live. You're doing the same damned thing Chrissie.*

I am not doing the same damned thing. I am just thinking about my son's wellbeing that's all. He doesn't seem to realise that nor do you. Sons will never ever bloody well realise that. Either way, their mothers are to blame.

Stop feeling sorry for yourself woman, you are sounding like my old woman. Seems like she is your old woman too.

That got my goat. *My old woman? Not a chance. She'll never ever be my old woman.*

Well, something is the same between you two.

What do you mean? I wanted to know. *I am a nurturing mother, a supportive mother.*

All mothers like to see themselves that way. Look what my mother did to me, look what you are doing to Luke.

Luke's done a lot more with his life so far than you did at his age.

Don't be surprised, he said quietly, *when he gets up one day and scoots.*

Luke will never scoot.

Have it your way, he said and walked out.

The Blue Mermaid

After my last face off with Arnie, he stayed away from me and so did Luke. It was damned frustrating. I didn't know what to think, what to do. Was something wrong with me? Was I a control freak? I was doing my best for my son and that seemed to be wrong. There was something about what was going on between Arnie and Luke that bothered me. My son was a straightforward fellow until this bloody brother of mine arrived. Was Arnie turning him into a womaniser?

I collared him. *Come here Luke. Sit down for a moment please. Just a moment, not more than that, I promise. Yes that's it. Right here. Now son, look me in the eye and tell me, do you have a girlfriend?*

This is getting out of hand, Mum. What's that got to do with you?

I'm concerned, worried. If you don't have a girlfriend then why don't you have a girlfriend?

What difference will it make to you whether I have a girlfriend or not?

What a silly question, Luke. Of course it makes a difference. I'll be comforted if I know that you have a girlfriend.

Comforted? Why? How about if I tell you that I don't have a girlfriend and don't believe in having a girlfriend–you won't feel comforted?

You're still quibbling with words. Think that's going to confuse me and shut me up? Stop treating me like a nincompoop. I was really losing my peck.

All this while you've never even mentioned the subject. What's with you now? How's it suddenly popped up?

He was really irritating me. There I was getting red in the face and he kept calm. I suddenly gave up. *Okay, have it your way. Girlfriend or no girlfriend.*

We sat there in silence. I must say I felt stupid about the way I had been behaving. How did all that suspicion come into our relationship? How? *I'm sorry* was all I could say.

You don't have to say that. He looked exasperated. *Just tell me simply–what is really worrying you? That I'm becoming friends with Uncle Arnie and leaving you out? Or that there's something wrong with me because I don't have a 'girlfriend'? Which one?*

I didn't say that there's anything wrong with you. I'm ... I'm ...

Okay, so you think ...

I didn't let him finish his sentence. *Listen, I want you to find a woman who is worthy of you, who appreciates the wonderful person you are. I want you to marry and have children and settle down. And wait, wait, don't interrupt me–and yes I feel left out because I think you are sharing stuff with Uncle Arnie that you don't want to share with me, that worries me.*

He walked out and returned the next morning.

That really got me worried. There was something that he was keeping from me, something that he was sure I wouldn't like and didn't want to tell me. So I told myself, *listen here Chrissie, you're not going to take this one lying down, Luke's your son and you have every right to know what's going on with him, whether he's running around with nappies or has someone in the closet. And when he doesn't tell you what's on his mind, you have every right to start getting worried. If you think he's loose wristed ask him straight off, ask him if he is and see what he has to say.*

My other self butted in at that point and said, *tell him he has to mend his ways. Tell him that he comes from a respectable family and can't footle around like this. You have to be gutsy, woman, you have to be gutsy. There's no other way out. Because if you're going to let him go on this way it will be disaster for you and all that you have tried to put together.*

That's the point at which I began thinking about what I had to face when I met Hilda's family. Now Hilda D'Costa is a sweet girl, soft spoken and intelligent. Has done her B.A. and a diploma course in Marketing. Would have made the right sort of partner for Luke. He wasn't warm to the idea of me going and talking to her parents. *We're just good friends Mum, why are you pushing it?* Anyway, I went and met them and was quite taken aback by their behaviour. They didn't like the idea of Luke as a son-in-law and even suggested that their daughter deserved a different sort of husband. *A big fella,* said Grandpa D'Costa, *don't mind me saying so but maybe Luke should build himself up much more, look more like a husband.* I felt awkward listening to him go on like that and then the conversation moved on and the sandwich stared sticking in my throat and my mouth went dry when the old bugger started talking about Dad and suggested that things weren't right with him and Mum. Really cruel fellow. Hilda's dad was a real bloody spineless chap. He never said a word and let his wife and dad do all the talking. And so I had to listen to them talk about how they wanted Hilda to marry a doctor or an engineer or even a civil servant. A real job, a secure job. They didn't feel too good about the sort of business that Luke was running. Fools, my boy could run circles around a hundred of them. They didn't deserve him. When the men had left the room and only Mini D'Costa and I were left facing each other I told myself, *go on and tell her that her daughter would really be happy with Luke, go.* And my other self muttered, *don't be stupid, cats don't drink wine, they drink milk. These are milk drinkers, what can you expect from them. Give her a piece of your mind, go on, give it to her.*

But instead, I found myself saying, *thanks for the tea and eats Mini, I think I'll be off.* And I did just that. I walked home. Choking. Now if the D'Costas thought that Luke isn't man enough, I wondered what other people were thinking.

Then the unexpected happened. Sabby rang up and invited himself over. I didn't believe my ears when I got his call. *You're pulling my leg, Sabby.*

Not at all.

Okay then, come for lunch.

And so Sabby turned up for lunch. All in white. I had never seen Sabby dressed in white. Linen. A straw hat tilted to one side, his enormous eyes shining. He looked happy.

How's Mrs Millionaire?

Fit as a fiddle.

And where's the beloved son and the dear brother?

The first one's finishing off some work and will be with us in a while. And the second will turn up sometime or the other.

So that leaves us to ourselves.

I took him on a small tour of Blue Mermaid and he was suitably impressed at the end of it all. *I'm thirsty. I'd like my beer iced cold.*

I'm aware you like it that way.

Stretching out at our family table under the palms, we relaxed. After the usual chit chat about this and that I asked, *what made you suddenly decide that you wanted to visit us?*

Visit you, to be precise.

You're flattering me.

Not really. He took a long, deep, glug and clearing his throat, smiled. *A proposal.*

Proposal? My heart skipped a beat. Was the fellow going to propose to me? *Or what sort of proposal?*

Actually, I don't know how to put it.

Try putting it simply.

Not now, will need a few more beers to start sounding simple.

We laughed and the topic moved on to Arnie. *When's this elusive brother of yours going to show up?* He asked suddenly.

Sometime soon, I suppose. But honestly I wasn't sure.

What does the fellow do with himself the whole day?

He walks, suns himself, reads, tries his hand in the kitchen, helps out in the office.

So you put the fellow to work as soon as he got here ... why don't you let him off the hook and send him down to Clementine for some wholesome company. He chuckled, leaving me a bit uneasy.

What do you mean by 'let him off the hook'? I wanted to know.

I mean controlling him. You women are great at that. Hasn't the fellow rebelled as yet?

I don't control him. Nor do I control Luke.

Hoho, you don't need to get sour Chrissie, it was just a joke ...

Suddenly, it seemed that we had nothing to say to one another and sat looking out at the sea. Blondie and the Australian sporty guy were jumping and splashing in the water. We watched them return. Blondie patted his partner on the bum and then on the head, dropping his hand to the man's shoulder. *That fellow is an embarrassment,* said Sabby. *He used to come to Clementine for breakfast and even tried to chat up one of Xavier's loose wristed friends and Xavier punched him. Wasn't a pleasant sight the way the fellow's cut lip bled and his shirt was splashed red and he kept saying, 'get out of the closet man.' And Xavier replied, 'there's no closet here, we're out in the open and I'm not taking any bullshit from you.' And then he started pushing him around till the fellow left the place. Later he came back with a big black guy and they sat down at a table right in the middle and the black guy thumped on the table, as if he was playing a tabla and this blond fellow whistled a tune and they called the waiter and ordered fried farts and onions. The waiter, Chop, you know Chop–the fellow with bug eyes and a huge double chin with lips that go flip flop when he talks–didn't know what to do so he came over to me in my office and asked, 'boss, those guys want fried farts and onions.' So I replied, 'it's not on the menu today.' So Chop went back and told them and returned with a black eye and a bruised jaw. And outside there, the black guy was throwing around tables and chairs and frightening away the guests. I rang for the cops and they turned up in a jiffy. Of course the blond fellow did the vanishing trick but it took three cops to pin down the black guy who was high on something or the other. He has never come there again. Is he a bother?*

Not really Sabby. He's okay. Doesn't trouble anyone here. The waiters don't like him here because he hardly tips them.

That's common. Particularly with the Russians. The commies really buggered up their brains. They bargain for everything, even a bloody cup of tea. Ask anyone in the area, they'll tell you.

Don't say that Sabby. All Russians aren't like that.

Most of them are. They go shopping with calculators. He looked around, *I don't see any here.*

That's because they didn't make it in time to bag a sun bed. The Indians got here before them today.

Shouldn't say this about my own people, Chrissie, but they're such brazen oglers. And they don't even realise it's not nice.

Anyway, on another note, I said, *what's this proposal you mentioned earlier? Come on Sabby, put me out of my misery.*

He stood up and stretched, *later. Where are the two men in your life?*

Just be back, I replied and set off to call them. Luke was still busy with guests in the office so I walked over to call Arnie. His door was shut. *Hey Arnie, Arnie, Sabby's been here a while and it's already time for lunch.* I knocked, once, twice and thrice.

I heard you Chrissie, coming in a moment.

I'm waiting.

You don't have to wait. I'll join you in a while.

Arnie, is something the matter?

He didn't reply. I heard another voice from in there. It sounded like a woman's voice. A loud whisper.

I walked away, back to the lounging Sabby.

Abandoned? He asked. *Don't trust men Chrissie, don't trust men. Believe me, they're all on their own trip.*

That would include you too? I enquired.

Sure. Come on, sit down and relax. Take it as it comes. Ask your guy for another iced beer.

A beer later we ate our lunch, topping it off with banana fritters.

Okay, he said, clearing his throat, *time for the proposal.*

I readied myself. *Okay, shoot.*

How'd you like to team up with me?

What's that mean? Can you put it even more simply? I asked.

A partnership. No, not exactly a partnership. A merger. Clementine and Blue Mermaid. You and I.

Are you proposing to me?

In a way, yes, I'm proposing that we merge our businesses and ourselves.

And what would it be called?

The Blue Mermaid of course. I'll drop our name. You and Luke are doing a great job of this place. I'm sure he'll be able to turn my place around too.

Are you serious?

Yes, of course.

So what about this 'you and I' thing?

Will you marry me?

I burst out laughing and ended up giggling.

What's so funny? He had turned red in the face. *I'm serious, I meant what I just said. Why are you laughing at me?*

I don't know what Luke will say to this, I went on, *he may find the merger thing interesting, but I don't know what he'll have to say about the you and I bit.*

But I'm not proposing to Luke, I'm proposing to you Chrissie. You.

What will everyone say? At this age?

So what?

Luke finally joined us. *Sorry,* he said, looking at Sabby, *was tied up.*

Ah I wouldn't worry if I were you, Sabby replied, *that's the lot of us guys, either we're tied up or we're set free. And when we're set free, we don't know what to do with our freedom. Before I forget, Melissa sends a hi.* Luke visibly blushed but Sabby continued. *She's in town and will be around for some time. So what should I tell her?* He seemed to be enjoying Luke's awkwardness.

Which Melissa is this? I wanted to know.

The German. Sabby was quick with his reply. *The dog lover. The one who stays at Clementine when she's in Goa. You know who I'm talking about Chrissie, the one who insists on taking Banjo for a walk whenever possible.*

Oh you mean that one. The really skinny one.

She's not skinny, you should see her now, everything in its rightful place and in abundance. He seemed to relish his words. All the while, Luke stood there not knowing what to do. But Sabby didn't let up. *This here son of yours, is quite a draw.*

Okay Sabby, you're embarrassing him.

I'm joking, he changed the tone of his voice. *I'm joking. But she did say hi.*

What's your problem? Luke suddenly asked, his voice hardening.

I just said, I'm joking.

You're making fun of me and you are doing it in front of my mother to embarrass me. I don't like being made fun of.

Now don't be rude Luke. He was just joking. I tried to straighten things out but realised that it was beyond my control. Sabby was on Luke's territory and was going to pay for being rude.

Luke sat down slowly and leaned forward, *shall we start having a chat about those two pet Ayurvedic massage women you have? And …*

That's enough son. He was only joking.

Come on boy, I'm happy to take it on the chin and shake hands after that.

Things got a bit out of hand until Arnie arrived and separated them. *Oh come on Luke,* he said, *why are you getting so worked up?*

Luke didn't reply and shoving back his chair, walked off.

So then, hello Arnie, Sabby tried to sound his genial best and my brother shook his hand spontaneously and they soon eased into each other's company. What a relief it was. I didn't want Sabby going away feeling insulted. Leaving them to get to know each other I went off to calm Luke down. I walked into the office just in time to see one of the female guests pat him on the bum. I backed out as noiselessly as ever and returned to the family table. Sabby was ready to leave and after a few pleasantries drove away.

We have a lot to talk about, you and I, I said to Arnie. *And I want explanations.*

Can't you just let the boy live his own life? He's twenty-eight and not a kid any more.

But I'm his mother.

Go on Chrissie, stop being controlling.

Who was that woman in your room?

Someone.

Who?

Oh stop prying. By the way, I think you are worried about Luke's preferences, don't be. He's into women, not men. We were talking about women that night. Okay? Now will you get off his back? Will you?

But I haven't seen him with a girlfriend.

Please Chrissie, stop thinking about girlfriends.

After the initial confusion, I felt relieved. I had a normal son. *Hope you don't spoil him Arnie*, was all I could say.

Promise.

The sense of relief passed after a few days and I started taking a second look at all the women who turned up at Blue Mermaid. Which of them was he making out with? What attracted them to him? His boyishness? When I got tired of thinking about all this I gave up. I decided to give him a little space, hoping against hope that he wouldn't do something foolish and end up falling in love with a woman from God alone knows where. He's a simple fellow, my Luke. I'm sure he thinks he's some sort of a stud and so what?

But back of it all there was that woman Melissa. I was never comfortable with her. Very pushy, loud, and she always seemed to get what she wanted. When she did not get it, she'd make it miserable for everyone. I remember the time she checked into Room 7, the corner room, and would sit out in her veranda and keep throwing scraps to our three dogs. She spoilt their eating habits doing that. We reminded her so many times but the stupid woman wouldn't listen. She just had to call out in a high pitched voice, *Come here Lolly, come Dingo, come Chindsy* and those stupid dogs would go running. Much as we stopped them they kept going to her. She had a way with dogs. Okay, okay, she had a way with dogs but then it didn't end there. She'd turn up in the kitchen and instruct the boys what to feed them and when to feed them and when she didn't think that they were being fed right she'd go off to the bloody market and bring chicken and mutton and get the boys to cook the stuff up. When they started objecting and reported the matter to Luke and he called her into the office and gave her a talking to, things settled down a bit but on her next trip she brought three ducks and gifted them to Blue Mermaid, suggesting that a little pen be made for them, with a pit in the middle with water in it. She made such a damned fuss over them that everyone started getting irritated. What took the cake was when she tried taking them for a walk to the water's edge. *Ducky ducky, ducky, ducky,* the boys on the beach would call out to her. The kitchen boys called her Duck Madam because they said she even walked like a duck with her rear sticking out a bit and her feet turning a bit outwards. One of them, Teki, the little Nepali chap with spiky hair and small bright eyes, made up a song and dance item inspired by her. It was called *Duckwallah Nach Gaana.* It went something like this,

Come Lolly
Come Dingo
Come Chindsy
Quack,
WhooHaa
WhooHaa
We go do swim swim
Come ducky
Quack

Then Blondie turned up with a reedy little guy and checked

in right next to Melissa's room. By the second day they were arguing over the ducks. Luke went over to sort it out and came back laughing his head off. *Blondie told her that the ducks are making too much noise and crapping all over the place. Besides, she shouldn't get attached to creatures meant for the pot. That got her goat and she said they aren't meant for the pot. And he said that they were fat enough for the pot and would make a good grill. Maybe she should sell them to the kitchen and go and buy herself some ducklings and start all over again. Then Mrs Australia joined the spat and suggested that Melissa should keep the ducks in her room if they meant so much to her. Mr and Mrs East German, two rooms away, sat with their feet up grunting as they read their books like two walruses.*

So what the hell did you do? I asked Luke.

I told her that she should keep her ducks in her room.

You said what?

I just told you. I told her to keep her ducks inside her room.

You didn't. Not possible that you'd say something as crazy as that Luke. They'll cause a mess.

I know, I know Mum. She knows that too and will take them off somewhere else.

And then she'll start off with our dogs again.

So do you want me to ask her to leave? She's using the AC room and is on a long stay. That's good money Mum. Let me handle it my way.

To add to the drama, the ducks disappeared one night and Melissa was inconsolable. So Luke handled her his way and calmed her down, only to discover that she returned the next day from the market with a pair of squirrels in a cage. She kept the cage on the table outside the room and would keep plying the rodents with bits and pieces of food and she'd talk to them and sing to them. She'd even read loudly from her book every afternoon. That would disturb Blondie who'd come out and snap, *please lower your voice. You're not in an ivory tower, there are other people inhabiting this place. Please lower your voice.* But she'd ignore him.

One day while trying to pet the creatures she slipped her hand into the cage and got bitten. The offending squirrel dug its teeth in and wouldn't let go. She ran out into the garden trying to shake it off but didn't succeed. Then she tried pulling it off but it didn't budge. Blood streamed down the side of her arm. *Someone do something, someone do something.*

The gallant Luke wasn't at the resort at that time but as soon as he returned he was informed and yelled to the kitchen boys to get the sharpest knife. Teki was in his element, he snatched up a meat chopper and rushed out. When she saw the weapon she nearly went into convulsions, *you think you are going to chop off my hand you little Nepali mountain boy? You'll do nothing of the sort, you hear me?*

A crowd of guests had surrounded her and even the beach sellers hawking fruits and sarongs rushed in to get a good look at the spectacle. Teki grinned gleefully and kept spitting on the blade of the chopper and wiping it on his apron. Finally someone snatched it from him and a few moments later there was a yelp. Melissa had fainted. The crowd moved back, staring down at the bloodied body of the headless rodent. And the head? Well, it was still stuck to her hand and they had to get Dr Braganza to get it off and give her a couple of stitches and a shot.

Gallant Luke hovered around her and settled her into her room and even fed the lone squirrel in the cage.

Everyone suggested that she return the animal to the place where she got it from. *It wasn't exactly a shop,* she said, *I got them from some boys who were busy torturing them. I actually rescued them and even paid for them. I'd rather set this one free.*

So she took the cage out to the clearing in the woods and set it down on the ground and sat down cross legged beside it. Then she held up the cage and looking at the squirrel said, *now I'm going to set you free. You better run off somewhere safe or the foxes will get you.*

There are no foxes here, jackals maybe, someone said.

Okay, let's say jackals may get you or a hawk or cat or dog or some creature. Now little one, run for your life. Then she laid the cage down on the ground again and opening the door said, *go on, off with you, off with you.* But the creature crouched shivering in one corner of the cage.

I think you should leave the cage open and let's all step back, I suggested.

She did just that. A few moments later it crept out, flicked its bushy tail up and down, called out shrilly and then bounced across the open ground, heading for a tall tree. We watched as it rushed up the trunk of the tree to its topmost branch. A kite swooped in and snatched it up in its claws and flew off. No one, not even Melissa, said a word. We walked back to our lives in silence.

Melissa checked out and appeared one evening walking down the beach with a large Boxer on a leash. *That's Xavier's dog Banjo*, said Luke.

So she's checked into Clementine, was all I said.

He didn't reply.

Melissa faded out of Blue Mermaid and was quickly replaced by a dozen other oddities. That was a season for oddities. There was the Israeli group who would sit around a table full of candles after dinner and lustily sing Jewish songs whilst a full moon hung up there in a Goan sky, then they'd run off straight into the sea chanting something or the other. Then the unforgettable Ukrainian couple, quite elderly, Luke and I called them Mr and Mrs Tomato because they'd returned from town one day with bags full of tomatoes, cucumbers, peppers, bananas and other fruit. That's all they lived on. On the evening before they left, they stood side by side facing the sunset, then walked down to the water's edge, scooped up some in their palms and poured it over their heads, did a Namaste to the sea and walked back.

That was the season too when we had Mr and Mrs Skinny (a really skinny couple, if they stood sideways they'd vanish) who played bowling with coconuts. A very competitive twosome who often ended up squabbling then sitting at different tables for dinner. Then there was Mrs Pink Hat who paraded around with a frilly pink hat and a tiny man by her side. Of course the hat got blown off one day and sailed down the beach. It landed just in time to be run over by a life guard's jeep. Much to everyone's surprise they buried the hat where it lay crushed.

Oh yes can't forget our storytellers. The *Gupshups*, that's what Loy called them. The fellow is an Indian with a strange kiwi accent and his wife is from Bangkok. She's really tiny and whenever he managed to catch hold of a willing listener he'd start rattling stories and every little while would stop and ask his wife, *isn't that the way it happened?* Or *isn't that so?* And she'd reply in a birdlike voice, *yes, absolutely.* He'd come up with stories about his adventures with sea snakes and river snakes and crocodiles ... the Andamans being his favourite haunt.

I'm wondering now, how many of the women who have come as guests to Blue Mermaid have been up to hanky panky with Luke. Melissa for sure. And how many women have had it off with Arnie. All this right under my nose. Well, what can I say, men will be men. I'm feeling like an old maid in the midst of all this.

I really started thinking about all of that good and hard. *Have I really given up on life? Here's Sabby offering himself to me on a platter and I'm behaving as if I'm a vegetarian. Huh, not a vegetarian, more like a vegan. Am I going to turn my back on life and keep growing older and older and Luke gets latched on to someone and goes off and has his own life. What will I have? Nothing. Why am I so afraid of admitting that I want a man? Is it that I feel I'm being disloyal to the loving memory of my Jason? Probably. Or maybe I'm scared to start all over again because something may go wrong again.*

Arnie's Plans and Chaos

I woke up one morning in Panjim with a start. *Good God, wonder what Arnie's plans are. Has he any clue about the state of his home in Gorai? Sure he can stay here for the rest of his life if he chooses but what about that property?*

When I caught up with him at Blue Mermaid, *hope your home in Gorai is safe. Any news from the person you kept there to look after the place?*

No, but it must be safe, can't go anywhere really.

You trust the person you left in charge. Right?

Yes of course. What a silly question. Would I leave my own house to a stranger?

Just checking, that's all Arnie.

Warren, a friend of mine fixed up someone to keep an eye on the place.

Have you called to find out if all's okay?

Are you sure there's no problem about me staying here? He asked. *You sound as if you would be happy if I left and stayed in my own home.*

Don't be foolish, you can stay here forever if you choose to. I'm worried about the safety of your property, that's all.

Are you sure?

Yes I'm sure Arnie. Now stop being stupid and call that friend of yours and check up if all's okay.

The fellow doesn't even have a telephone.

Then ring your own place.

The phone's always a problem. And don't start suggesting that I should go and take a look. I'm struggling to leave the bad times behind and trying to remake myself, Chrissie. It's been hard and I'm thankful you welcomed me in here ... he stood there, eyes all droopy, voice hesitant. *Be honest, if you think I should rent a place around here somewhere, say so.*

Cut the shit. You are my brother.

Half-brother or stepbrother.

Brother, Arnie, brother. I'm sorry if I was a bit ratty and bothered about what you and Luke were up to, that was just a mother's anxiety, nothing else. You are my brother and we are here for each other. Now coming down to brass tacks. Why don't we ask Loy to go down there and check out if everything is okay. If there are any bills to be paid or any other follow-up, we can ask him to do that. He's a real handyman not just a gardener and he loves travelling, we can also treat him to a day or two in Bombay. And while he's about it we can get him to ensure that the phone is working and fix up for the caretaker to be there in the house for a few hours every day so you can ring him up. Or he could ring you up.

You've got it all worked out Chrissie, I don't even have to think ... He hugged me. *Thanks.*

And so Loy set off for Gorai. A few days later we got a harassed call from him saying that the house had been occupied by three families and they wouldn't even let him into the property. *So I'll have to go and sort things out after all,* Arnie spat out the words, disgusted. *I thought Warren would have taken care of all that. Feel like selling the place off and shifting to Goa.*

Or turning the place into a mini resort, chipped in Luke, *or a restaurant or something. I've been checking up on Gorai and they say it's not a sleepy little fishing village anymore and after the amusement park opened the whole place has changed and there are restaurants and hotels there now. Didn't you notice them Uncle Arnie? And there was all that confusion about the garbage dump and the water pollution and so much of the fishing getting ruined.*

Really? I know about the amusement park, it's called Essel World. And of course the dump but I didn't realise there was all that pollution going on. And the other stuff–hotels and restaurants and all that? You must be joking. Arnie looked a wee bit confused.

I'm not joking, it's for real so let's get those people out and clear up the place and if you want we can start planning. I'll help you Uncle. Don't sell the place. You're sitting on a gold mine. We could even turn it into a Guest House. Keep someone there to manage it properly and you stay here in Goa. You can always drop in there as many times as you choose.

Great planning Luke, but I don't have that sort of energy anymore. I'm getting on in years.

Nonsense Uncle, you're not short on energy, you're impressive.

It's amazing how those words from Luke really pepped him up. His face broke into a big, broad smile. *That's very generous of you Luke, let's see what's the best we can do.*

We'll make it happen. Luke was all charged up.

That night Luke and Arnie sat up and worked through a doable plan and set off for Gorai a few days later. No one had a clue about what was waiting to happen.

The first call came late one night. It was Luke. *Mum, it's a real mess here, the families staying here have cops as relatives. In fact one family is a cop's family. We couldn't do a damned thing because they had emptied out all of Uncle's cupboards. Few of his belongings remain. It's so sad Mum. Uncle doesn't know what has hit him. We managed to move people out of his bedroom so we are using this space …*

Hello Luke, Luke can you hear me? Luke?

The line went dead. What an absolute mess it was. I was terrified that something would happen to them. I walked around Blue Mermaid like a zombie, trying my best to focus and get on with the work. The season was coming to an end and there was so much to be done–closing of accounts and rain proofing the place before shutting down. The last guests were still to leave and when the place was empty we'd start work in earnest. But I couldn't concentrate. I was worried. No news from Gorai.

Then, when I was about to leave someone in charge and head straight for Gorai, the call came. It was Luke again. *Managed to get them all out of the place, Mum, I'll give you the details when I'm back. They've ransacked everything. Fortunately Uncle's property papers were in his bank locker. If they had been left at home then anything could have happened. But the fencing to the property has been all pulled out and the boundary lines have been covered. There's a nexus operating here.*

What about Arnie's friend Warren?

He's in the lock-up. Seems he double crossed someone in this whole deal and they nailed him. It's all so damned complicated and I'm not getting much help from Uncle Arnie because the shock has packed him up and he doesn't seem like the same person anymore. You won't recognise him Mum. I'd really like to bring him back with me but I can't.

Why?

Because I can't trust anyone to take care of the property. Everyone's on the take here–the local dadas, the cops, the residents, party workers, everyone.

Can't you hire a security agency?

They won't last here. They have to be supervised all the time.

So you're going to leave Uncle Arnie in that state and come back here to your own secure home? Eh? Are you crazy?

What am I do? I can't leave you to do the shutting down. I have to help you. We are partners, remember?

Yes, I know we are partners son, but Uncle needs you.

Listen, we can do another thing, I can appoint a security agency to take care of the property so Uncle won't feel so insecure. And I can get hold of a Man Friday to help him around the house. I'll come back there, help you do the shutting down then come back here and take things from there. Okay?

That sounds a little more reasonable. How's Arnie's financial situation.

Excellent. He has more money than he knows what to do with. But he doesn't use it. It's taken me so much of effort to get him to go shopping to redo the house. We've also had carpenters and painters in. Will return soon Mum … Mum …

Yes?

Don't worry. We'll find a way around all this mess.

The picture was quite grim. I couldn't see a way around all the mess unless both Luke and I pitched in and helped Arnie out. He needed family support because he couldn't possibly do anything by himself. I wished he would decide to sell the property and get it over with. That place held too many memories for him. It suffocated him. Luke's idea of a Guest House or so called mini resort was a bad one. At least at the start.

Sabby called several times during that period of limbo and invited me over for a meal and a chat. I kept putting it off until it started sounding rude, so I went over to Clementine.

He tried to sound his peppy self but I noticed the stress beneath it all. *What's going on Sabby? Why does your face look so strained?*

Nothing major–business okay, just the son driving me crazy. And that woman Melissa has checked in and insists on taking care of Xavier's dog. And Xavier has this impression that there's something on between us and that she's trying to hook me because she wants this property. Now isn't that a joke?

Why should it be a joke. Quite possible.

Stupid. I'm not even interested in her that way. An okay person to talk to, but that's all. She's not here free, she pays for her room. No one can understand why she keeps checking out of one room and checking into another. She says it gives her the feeling that she's coming here for the first time, the touristy feeling. Anyway, Xavier wants me to sell this place or knock it down and build it up afresh with a proper lounge and disco and what not. I'm uncomfortable with that sort of thing. You know what I mean Chrissie, I'm old fashioned. I'd prefer to do something like what you and Luke are doing. That's why I suggested we merge. Did you talk to Luke about it?

Didn't really get a chance to. But let him get back and I'll mention it to him. That is when he gets back. He's out in Gorai, helping Arnie with some property problems.

So what about the other merger?

What other merger?

I proposed to you Chrissie and you didn't even respond. Yes or no.

There's too much happening in my life just now Sabby. I have hardly any space in my head to think.

That's the same with me, but we're never going to have much time or space to think. This is about feeling Chrissie, feeling. Not thinking. So what does your heart tell you?

You're a good man Sabby, a good and honourable man and I'd be a fool to say no. But I don't know whether I am coming in or going out at the moment. Let things settle down a bit and I promise you an answer.

Time is running out, as it always does and before we know what is happening and where we are, it's all over and done with and there's no more time to love or hate or do the things we always wanted to do.

I know. You are right.

Okay, for starters, let's meet a little more often, shall we? The season is over and you are shutting shop so you'll have a lot of time on your hands. Surely we can meet more often, can't we?

Okay, we will.

The meal ended hurriedly because an argument had broken out between Melissa and Xavier. Dirty words flew back and forth and ended with Xavier shouting, *you take Banjo into your room again Melissa and I'll throw you out.*

This is not even your place, how can you throw me out? I pay for my room, it's not free.

On that note, I got up to leave.

About the merger, Sabby said softly, *let's sort it out fast or this boy will poison me.*

When I got back, Luke had returned and was sitting out at the family table, sipping a beer. He looked like he had just got back from the *dhobi ghat* after being soaked and slammed and battered and dunked and squeezed and spread out on the line and dried but not steam pressed. I'd probably end up doing that.

We can talk later, I said, *you look a wreck.*

You should have gone there with him, not me. He's insufferable.

I thought you liked him and got on well with him and you two had your plans for a resort and all that. Now you discover that he's insufferable. I had to stop myself from being sarky.

I'm not sure where to start from, he took a deep glug from his mug and leaned back with glazed eyes. And when he did that I knew there was something big coming. That was a habit of his when he had gone through the wringer. He sniffed a couple of times. *Forget it, later.*

That's what I just said, we can talk later.

But I want to get it off my chest. I don't want to live a moment more with all this rubbish inside me.

Okay then, go ahead.

I don't know where to start from.

Start anywhere. It's easy when you start at the beginning.

Before he could respond, it happened. Suddenly and unexpectedly. Crows, clouds of crows. Now this is not an exaggeration; there *were* clouds of crows. They were everywhere, swooping and cawing. Like they had had enough of a hard life and had turned up for a holiday just when we were shutting for the season and they were cawing their heads off *don't you dare shut shop, we've arrived for a holiday, get out the food, food and more food* ... Luke dropped his mug in the sand and started thrashing his arms about as crows started swooping low. He fell off his chair and scrambled into the restaurant, making a bee-line for the kitchen. Once inside, he slammed the door shut. The black birds swirled above me but I didn't run. I sat there watching them flap and flutter, circle and caw. After a few moments a crowd of them settled all around me. They sat there very silent. The ones who were in the air stopped cawing. It was crazy. Was I imagining it all? *Have I turned deaf?* I asked myself and didn't know what to answer. I looked at the birds, I mean I looked at them straight in the eye and they seemed to be looking at me too. Trying to say something. They were afraid, really afraid and I didn't know why. A strange feeling filled me. It was eerie. As if I knew something that no one else did.

Hoi, hoi, I could hear the kitchen staff shouting, *they've got into the kitchen.* Loud thumping and thwacking followed and I realised that they were swatting the birds with whatever they managed to pick up.

I got out of my chair and left the flock of birds sitting there like little statues. A moment later they took to the air and flew around noiselessly. Before I could reach the kitchen, the door flew open and the injured birds were flung out. *Stop that, will you? Stop. They're frightened, they want protection. And you all are killing them. What's got into you?*

Come on, enough of that rubbish, Luke came out with a stick in hand, there were feathers stuck all over him and he had a crazed look in his eyes.

You've gone mad, son, mad.

What did I do wrong? They've been attacking us.

They're scared, that's all. They've done this before.

I don't remember.

When you were born. Don't you remember?

If I was small how the hell would I remember that they've done this before. Anyway, why did they do it then?

Some ugly soul poisoned them. A few hundred. Their bodies were scattered everywhere. We found out later, much later. What I didn't tell him was that we had such bad luck after that, it was horrible. First the storm then wild winds for a week that flattened hundreds of homes. Then a huge oil slick floated in and then oh God so much else. Some holiday makers drowned. And mind you, this happened after the damned monsoons when the new season had started and business along the beach was swinging along. What a mess. Fortunately we were not really in the business to this extent then. Now if I were to tell Luke all of that either he'd be shit scared or he'd make fun of me and say that I was spicing it all up.

When a calm fell we got to know that hundreds of birds had been poisoned and their bodies lay scattered everywhere. The air smelled of feathers. In the dark, I walked out into the open and looked around me. Not a bird in flight. They had all settled in the trees and were silent.

It was clear that Luke's hysterical reaction had little to do with the crows and more to do with all the stress that he was under. The sooner he got it off his chest the better. Maybe I shouldn't have said, *we can talk later.* Stupid of me. It would have been better if I had kept my bloody mouth shut.

We didn't go back home but remained in the resort. Luke fell into bed with his travelling clothes and shoes on. I didn't want to meddle with him so I just let him be. He got up the next evening. Bathed, changed his clothes, drank a couple of beers, stuffed his face with food and fell into bed again.

The Smiths and the Schmids

The season closing work was delayed as the last two couples the Smiths and the Schmids extended their stay a little longer. Even if the place was empty, I wasn't in a position to start work. Right on the edge of Hell. Thank God, at least not *in* Hell. But mind you, I could very well have fallen straight into Hell if I wasn't the tough person I was ... and am. I didn't really mind if guests decided to stay on a bit so long as that didn't eat into packing up time too much. Those two couples weren't that much of a bother most times. They were quite predictable so we more or less knew what it took to keep them happy. The Smiths had their morning tea at half past six. The 'Mister' of the two called it 'Chotaa Haazri.' I didn't know what the hell he was talking about until he explained that his grandfather Bertrand who had spent years in India as a 'businessman' learnt the local term for the first cup of morning tea. When it got a bit on my nerves I informed him that the Raj doesn't live here anymore. Pat came his reply, *Angrez chaley gaye aur puttar chhor diyey. The English have left but their offspring remain. Ha ha.*

I told him that I didn't think it was funny and he replied, almost under his breath, *Why are you bothered? You're Portuguese.* I chose to ignore the comment. Shouldn't argue with guests. They should feel they are right even when they are talking rubbish. Of course I wouldn't take it lying down if they start complaining about the food and the service. If they are right, well okay … but if they are wrong–I wouldn't keep my mouth shut. There was an American chap who checked in early one day, had a breakfast of toast and porridge and then an hour later got violently sick and vomited all over the place. The doctor in town said that he'd got food poisoning. When the man recovered he presented us a fat bill for all that he had shelled out for his treatment saying it was the steak he'd eaten at Blue Mermaid. My God, I really put up a fight and finally managed to get him to move. That didn't stop him from shooting his mouth. The story of the rotten steak did the rounds until it came back to me at a party. *I believe an unfortunate Swedish fellow got steak poisoning in a Colva resort.*

It was an American and he was a guest at the Blue Mermaid. We don't serve steaks. I let fly.

Then how did it happen?

Figure it out.

The man became a bit of a joke and earned the nickname 'Steak Mister.' He carefully avoided our place whenever he visited Colva and we'd see him march down the beach, eyes straight ahead.

Mister Smith wasn't obnoxious. All he had was a bad habit of putting anything Indian down. When they'd first arrive at the resort for their holiday, they'd sit out in the restaurant for a cup of tea. *So how's the new superpower doing?* He'd never fail to ask. Then under his breath he'd mutter, *bloody banana republic if you ask me.* We had all learnt to ignore his question and the comment that followed and tried our best not to react. Arnie didn't know that he was meant to keep his trap shut so when he heard Mister Smith shooting his mouth he asked, *then what are you doing here?*

I didn't get your question, the man looked a little surprised that the question had been thrown at him.

Simple. If you think this is a banana republic, what are you doing here?

I'm a tourist.

Then enjoy the confusion and stop complaining. Nowhere else is entertainment as cheap as here.

You can say that for human life too. Mister Smith continued to talk without even looking at the man who had challenged him. A kind of uppity way of treating someone he considered an inferior. His round blue eyes stared intensely out at the sea. *Dolphins*, he said to his wife, *there they are, dolphins. Just look at them. They're welcoming us Martha, they're welcoming us. That's what I like about this place, the sand, the sea, the sky, the fishing boats, the dolphins. I wouldn't mind dying here.*

It's a banana republic, remember? If you are buried, they'll steal your skeleton. Arnie asked for it.

Mister Smith turned around and looked at him in the eye. *Talking to me?*

Arnie nodded.

Are you a guest or are you staff?

What's the difference?

Makes all the difference. If you are a guest, I'd be happy to argue with you but if you are staff, you shouldn't be sitting around here arguing.

I'm family.

He glared at Arnie and then turned around to finish his tea.

Don't argue with guests Arnie, not allowed here. There are ground rules here and this one is important. Don't argue with guests. I kissed him on the cheek and straightened his collar.

Suit yourself. This is me.

The me doesn't work here. It's us. We.

But Arnie kept spoiling for an argument whenever he got a chance. Until the day they met each other on the beach in no man's land and got talking in a civil way and came back and had a beer. And that was that. I really don't know what happened.

Poor Arnie, in short while he was with us in Colva, he had become a new person and then in one shot he had been flung back into his pit in Gorai. Wonder what the two would say to each other if they met now. Anyway, the Smiths minded their own business. They usually did when it was at the tail end of their visit. They'd become quiet … as if they were already suspended between two worlds.

The Schmids. Hmmmm, they were another kettle of fish. Heinrich (his Mrs called him Henny) claimed to belong to a family of Black Forest clock makers. Not sure what that actually means. Sure he must have made clocks but a clock maker is a clock maker why Black Forest? The same Black Forest where the cake comes from? I asked his Mrs once whether she baked cakes and she replied softly that she only ate them. In fact she looked a bit surprised that I had asked her such a question. Who cares? When my curiosity starts getting my soles itchy I try to settle the matter. But that time around I gave up. Enough was enough. And anyway, never bothered to ask them because getting them to talk was such a tough business. He had this thin long head with a big nose and round beady eyes and delicate gold rimmed spectacles which he'd keep pushing up his nose every time they slipped down a bit. Then he'd clear his throat and quickly glance at his wife before he even opened his mouth to say anything. The man's face had no expression on it but his fingers played with each other when they were not caressing something he'd take out of his pocket. He did it so quietly and smoothly that sometimes I didn't even notice when he'd done it. But then suddenly there it was in his hands. I didn't want to embarrass the fellow by staring at his hands so I decided to ask Henrietta, his wife, about it.

I had been standing at the service counter one night during those last few days when I saw her walk in and sit at a table so I went over to her to let her know that service wouldn't be possible as it was already past ten. She said that her husband was asleep and all she needed was a coffee then she was going for a small walk and after that back to the room. And so I got her a coffee and we started chatting until I plucked up the courage to ask about Henny's *thing*.

It was as if I had unlocked some secret door and she had suddenly changed from being kind of straight-backed and stiff upper lipped to emotional.

Your husband plays with something. What is it? I asked.

She looked at me as if I was from another planet, *that's his thing, his personal thing. I have never touched it. He's had it from a boy. He says touching it makes him happy. That's his business you know.*

But what is it?

I don't know. His mother said he used to be a noisy and violent boy. Threw a stone at his cousin Gerard when he was angry and blinded the boy in one eye. And he used his fists too when he was in a rage. They tried tablets on him but they did no good. One day when the family was on a picnic in the forest they met a group of gypsy music players who performed for them and then they got talking and just before they left one of the women gave the boy Henny this thing. No one else saw it, just Anneliese, his mother; everyone else was busy having fun. But Anneliese saw the woman give her son this thing then whisper something in his ear. He put it in his pocket. It was magic. Real magic. The boy stopped talking and crying in his sleep, he became more calm. Everyone noticed it. But then he wasn't a bright fellow anymore. I mean the bright fellow that he used to be. Well you get something and you lose something. Henny is the simpleton of his family. Simple man but good man. Minds his own business. But believe me I worry about this thing of his. Worried that he may lose it one day. Then what will happen? He's got it in a little pouch and he doesn't show it to anyone, not even me …

All these years and you haven't seen it? You are his wife. Surely you have some idea about what it is and what it looks like?

No I don't, she blushed, *he is my man but I never cross the line. I never told anyone what I have told you now.*

Why?

Because these days I'm not feeling good. I feel something no good is going to happen. I may need help …

So you feel I can help you then?

Yes, maybe. I don't know. You are a kind person, that I know.

I was scared of what I was getting myself into. *Don't worry,* was all I could say, *think positive. Nothing's going to happen. I mean nothing bad.*

How wrong I was.

The next day began hysterically. Henrietta was at my door at six in the god dammed morning. *I don't know what to do.* She was distraught.

Come on in, I made her sit down and rushed off to get her a coffee. When I got back she had fallen off her chair and lay there on the rug babbling in German. Trying to get her up was no good so I let her lie there and gently placed a cushion under her head.

A while later she got up slowly and hauled herself into the chair. *It's his thing.*

What about his thing?

It's gone. Gone. He couldn't find it this morning and has locked himself in the toilet and is weeping in there and won't come out. Like a little boy. Henny, Henny.

When she had quietened down a bit, she finished her coffee and looked at me. I felt damned sorry for her. *Okay, let's see what I can do to get him out of there.*

He'll get violent. Be careful.

Don't be silly. You can't leave him in there. Don't know what he'll do to himself. I handed her a damp towel to wipe her face. She took the towel from me and stared at it, helpless. *Wipe your face and let's get him out of there.* When she didn't respond I wiped her face and she flopped back into the chair, her eyes wide open and staring into mine. They were large and blue and seemed to expand when I looked deeper. Couldn't get my eyes away from hers.

I am scared, so scared. What if he does something to himself?

Come on, no time to waste. I tore my eyes away from hers and pulling her out of her chair, called two waiters and walked across to their room. The bathroom door was still shut. We banged on it. *Mr Schmid will you please open the door.* No response. Not even a whimper. Nothing. *Mr Schmid, do you hear me? Open the door. If you don't we will have to knock it down. I don't want to do that because I will be damaging my own property. Mr Schmid, do you hear me?* One of the waiters went around the back from the outside, climbed on to a stool and managed to open the small window and peered in. Then he came back out of breath, saying he could see Henny crouched in one corner. When his wife heard that she stumbled out to take a look herself, tried to climb on to the stool and fell off, bruising the side of her face. That didn't stop her. She scrambled up and straightening the stool climbed on to it and looked in, talking quickly in German. From a soft whisper her voice rose and became really wild, like a witch screeching a curse.

Suddenly she tried to climb in through the window. The stool fell to one side and she hung there, clutching on to the ledge, legs thrashing about the place. We steadied her, put the stool back under her feet and tried to get her to come down but she started kicking us and shouting, *Mein Maan, Mein Maan.* Finally she toppled over onto one of the waiters. The other, Mendonza, a sturdy fellow, climbed on to the stool and got in through the window. There was chaos in there once he landed inside the bathroom.

He was like an animal, Mendonza said later. *When I got in there he was in the corner like a cat. I slowly went closer and reached out to hold his hand and help him up and he sprang at me, trying to get at my face with his fingers. See these scratches everywhere. He came at me, Madam, making hissing noises just like a cat. I am sorry I had to push him very hard and knock him down. That was the only way I could stop him from attacking me anymore. I'll pay for the stitches that he has got on his head.*

When they brought Henny back from the hospital he refused to speak a word, just lay in bed and stared blankly at the ceiling. A day or two later, we saw him sitting out on the veranda, with the same blank look on his face. *He won't talk,* Henrietta was inconsolable. *Another week and we'll be back home. What am I going to do with him there?*

Can't we search for his thing? Have you searched hard enough? I looked into her eyes again and this time they made me feel uneasy. They had become the same blue as the sea looked the day my Jason died. She didn't reply. *Have you?* I asked again. Still no reply. *Maybe we can all search. If you can get him out of the room and have him sit out we can get housekeeping to search when they are cleaning up. What's the colour of the little bag?*

What little bag?

The one in which …

The finger is?

Finger? I really got the heebie-jeebies. *You mean the thing is a finger? Precious Lord. A finger?*

I had stumped her. She looked at me confused. *Yes,* she said quietly. *Digitus V. Distal IP joint upwards.*

What the bloody hell does that mean?

She held up her hand and showed me the top part of her little finger.

You mean that's what it's called?

Yes.

How do you know that?

I studied Anatomy. Her voice had no expression in it. It was flat and cold.

We need to talk. I took her into my room. *What's going on here? Some sort of black magic? Whose finger?*

Someone's finger. That's not important. The little finger is very powerful. It stands for the soul or the spirit inside us. You know your Bible well? Check Romans 7:22; Ephesians 3:16; 2 Corinthians 4:16. You can even check 1 Peter 3:4, he says 'And it is the hidden person of the heart of the woman.'

I swallowed hard. Something was sticking in my throat and just wouldn't go down. *So did the gypsy woman give him that thing?*

You mean the finger.

Yes.

What gypsy woman?

The one you told me about. The musician woman who gave it to him and whispered something in his ear.

Where is that story from? His mother gave it to him. Got it specially for him. His mother had a way with magical things.

Then why did you tell me that cock and bull story about the gypsy woman? Come on Henrietta this is becoming a bit of a joke.

This is not about a cock and a bull. It is not a joke.

Ok, it's not. But I don't want any black magic going on here Henrietta.

Look here, let me clear up this thing story. There is no black magic in all this. None at all. This is a very special thing which his mother gave him. It's from her own finger. To protect him and calm him and help him through life.

So you know all about it. Why did you say that you didn't?

I wanted to keep his secret. It's a personal thing.

I found the pouch that evening. It was in the flowerbed close to their room. Only God knows how it got there. God or Henrietta. I carried it back to the room, shut and bolted the door and took it out. It was a small shrivelled thing, wrinkled to the touch. I held it in my palm and my hand and arm began tingling. I broke out in a cold sweat.

It looked like shutting down for that summer was going to take longer than usual. Every moment something new cropped up. So it wasn't just the damned crows but a magical little finger and a damned high tide which flooded out the resort and destroyed a lot of furniture and washed away Mendonza and after that came a motherless storm ... the whole bloody universe was busy throwing bad luck at us. When there was nothing left to throw, things settled down and we shut for the season. Mind you, I did the organising because most of the time Luke wasn't there. He was present of course but his brains were somewhere else. Then he left The Blue Mermaid and went back to Panjim leaving me to tackle things. And lo and behold, when I finally wrapped up the place and returned home, he wasn't there. No note, no telephone call. Nothing. I hadn't a clue where he had vanished to.

Most unlike Luke. Even if he was in a hurry, he'd leave a note. If he had a little more time he'd leave a letter. The boy had grown up writing notes and letters to me. All written in neat handwriting. Straight lines on blank sheets. They'd be left all over the place, sometimes stuck on my bedroom door or kept under my pillow where I usually keep my rosary. But this time–nothing. This was unlike the fellow. Not a squeak. Checked around with friends but no luck. Lodged a complaint at the cops station. They didn't take it seriously but said that they'd keep an eye out for him. But I didn't give up, checked out his old haunts in the north. No one had seen him for a long time.

Then one night I got so frantic that I yanked out his drawers, spilled the contents on the floor and rummaged around amongst the pile of stuff for a clue. Nothing. Threw open his almirah doors and hauled his clothes and other belongings out. The room looked like it had been bombed. I sat on his bed and looked teary eyed at the mess around me. It was if I was stranded on an island surrounded by the debris of a ship shattered by a storm.

The mattress, that was one place I hadn't searched. God, the mattress, how stupid of me. I hauled back his mattress and found his letter. Stupid fellow, leaving such an important letter under his mattress. Seems he wanted me to suffer in confusion before I found it.

He had stuffed a few carefully written sheets into an old envelope and tied it up with string. I had a long night ahead of me.

Dear Mum,
Sorry it had to come to this but there's no other way out. I have to leave. I don't want to stay on and become a mess like Uncle Arnie. I want to just get away, go far away, I don't know where. Anyway, it doesn't matter so long as I'm really far away from all of this. I can't take this anymore.

When Dad died my world ended. I died inside Mum. After that all I did was try to keep you happy. It was not me but 'your son' who was with you and he worked hard at being your son. Worked hard to help you feel that life has a meaning after all and that despite the storms and stresses and the loneliness, life had something to give you. But I'm a human being Mum, I can't go on with this pretence. Too much has happened to me, far too much. I didn't decide to do this earlier because I thought somehow I'd manage and find my own way and get on with my own life and this 'mother and son' thing would fall away like snake's skin.

Gorai was the last straw. I offered to help Uncle Arnie out and went down there, little knowing that I was walking straight into a deep dark smelling pit crowded out by ghosts. And amidst all of it, there he was–a frightened old man cowering in a corner, talking to his dead mother all night, vanishing on to the beach and returning hours later–eyes red, clothes full of sand and seaweed, going on and on about some woman named Brenda and a fellow called Princey who lost his head–and lots more. I realised that the poor man was struggling to clear out the ghosts inside him. He seemed to think that I was the person who was going to help him. But it was bad timing. There were ghosts all around us–I mean living ghosts who we couldn't get rid of. Whole families of them squatting in the house and turning it into a slum. They had either stolen or destroyed uncle's possessions and we couldn't do much to stop them and throw them out. In fact, slept in a small store room and spent the day out on the veranda. And we couldn't even use the bloody loo. We crapped and pissed under the trees.

The people in the village called him a mad man and treated me as if I was some young wheeler dealer who was trying to appropriate the place. Even the damned Parish Priest behaved weirdly. *When you stray off the path, son,* the fellow said, *this is what happens.*

The 'ghosts' in the house did everything in their power to keep us out, including pissing on the store room door and threatening us. Uncle got roughed up twice by some drunks and when I intervened they thrashed me silly. When I went to complain at the cop station, they kept me there for the night. Because I had not bathed for days, they made me strip and gave me a bucket of water to clean myself then didn't give me back my clothes. I lay there in a dingy room. I awoke to find two cops in my room and they stayed with me all night. I can't even begin to tell you what happened. The next morning they let me off.

I got back to find Uncle was missing. He returned much later tired and scared and looking like a beggar.

Anyway, we began to sort things out, you know all that, and I managed to get Uncle back his property. I'm not going into all those details, they're of no use here. This is about how I felt, how broken and useless and hollow I felt; how I now need to set myself free once and for all. And you need to know. I don't mean to hurt you but this is the truth and I'm sorry I have to share it with you.

Now you take care of yourself and be the brave one that you've always been. Let me go Mum, cut the cord and let me go.

Luke

I was really in a fix. I was in a mess up to my neck. Without Luke, managing The Blue Mermaid would be like struggling up Calvary with a cross on my back.

3 LUKE'S LETTERS ON THE RUN

Snowbound

I've been snowbound for a week and all I've done is drink hot black tea and stare out through the big glass window at the snow covered range of mountains that surrounds the town of Leh. Here a month, wondering where to go next. I keep asking myself *what's a Goa boy doing up here in the mountains, shivering in his chuds? What's a Goa boy who has grown up with the sun, the sand and the sea doing in the snow, feeling dizzy and pukey all the time? What's a Goa boy who is used to be surrounded by churches doing in a place crowded out by Buddhist Monasteries? I'm realising now that unless one really knows deep in one's heart WHY one is leaving home and what one is leaving home to do, one can never settle down anywhere. That's me. All I've done is get up and leave even before I've hardly arrived. I can't stop leaving.*

Dad would constantly sing a song that Mum couldn't stand,

'I got no bags and bags to slow me down

Well, I'm travelling so fast my feet ain't touching the ground

Travelling light, travelling light ...'

She couldn't stand Cliff Richards. *Most peculiar chocolaty voice. A man should sing like a man.*

But Dad's gone now, the sea got him. And Mum, well, Mum's around. She's around all the time. I can't get her out of my system. Her presence fills this room, fills every room I have tried to live in, every room I've tried to sleep in, every place I try to forget in, every moment I try to become myself.

But she is there and I'm her son, always, I'm HER son. I don't hate her or dislike her or anything of that sort. I love her as a son 'ought' to love a mother and respect her even more because she was both mother and father to me. She fought for me, worked for me, supported me. But damn it, she didn't give me a chance to grow up and become myself. I'm not blaming her, I'm blaming myself. I should have asserted myself much more than I did. I sailed along because there was always butter and bread on the table and I got what I wanted and did what I wanted … but all because of her and not because of me. Because of her pushing and not my trying, because of her dreaming and not my aspiring, because of her insistence and not my persistence. Because she wanted me to be someone not because I was ambitious.

I wonder what Mum would have done if she was in this room, I mean physically in this room. She'd definitely say, *it's like being in a fishbowl, glass all around, Luke, let's remove that glass and wall it up with wood panelling, good wood, dark brown and well polished. A room should be warm and private, that's why they have rooms and live in them or they might as well live out in the open in a tent like those wanderers who go from place to place with their cattle and sheep.* As for me, I lie here in bed and look up at the ceiling. Row upon row of poplar beams holding up a tiled roof, its belly latticed by willow rods. That's what the fellow of the house told me they are. Harvested them from his own woods.

I'm sick of this sweet black tea and plan to put on something really warm and set out to the market to find myself a drink. A proper drink. Rum maybe. Not brandy or whiskey. But neat rum that has a way of burning itself down the throat and heating up my insides in such a way that there's an oven going there.

Outside, the cold wind burns my face and the snow crunches as my feet sink in. I walk down the narrow lanes of

Changspa past closed shop fronts and enter the sleepy market warm with clusters of woolly folk. On one of the high lanes running parallel to the main street, I find what I am looking for and head back as a snowstorm starts. Apricot Lodge, that's the name of the place I'm staying in, is inviting with its warm interior. Tsering, the owner hands me a large thick woollen shawl. *Cover,* he says, *you'll die.* I cover and get warm by the time I reach the top floor. Another large pot of sweet black tea is waiting for me in the room.

I pour myself a stiff rum and tip it down, feeling the flames rush into my stomach. Sitting back on the bed I close my eyes as the warmth spreads. When it settles I take another slug and start the sensation all over again. The third and the fourth follow in quick succession. I'm on fire and I'm surprised my clothes aren't burning. I get out of bed and switch off the light then draw back the curtains and look out into the night. Streetlights with haloes around them form a necklace all the way down to the distant market. The fragrance of wood smoke fills the air and finds its way into the room. Street dogs are squabbling somewhere along the road.

I top two more rounds of rum with a couple of cups of cold tea and sink in among the quilts, covered with Tsering's mighty shawl. It's a pity I wasn't able to write my letter to Mum or anyone else today. But then it's a bit of a joke really because I'm not really writing the letters on paper but in my head. Each time I write them, I try to tear them up and throw them away but they don't get torn up and collect there in a bag. I really don't know what the hell I'm going to do with it because it's getting bigger and bigger. What am I going to do with them when the bag is full and can't take anymore? Will the bag ever get full?

LEAVING

Dear Mum,
I don't know where to begin. There is so much going around in my head and that's confused the hell out of me. I don't know how to explain to you that I am leaving not because of you but because of what I am going through. I need to be by myself and sort it all out for myself. I know this will come as a shock to you but what to do Mum? What to do? I don't see any other way out of this. I'm leaving. I'm leaving because this is the only way I can sort my head out.

Please don't crucify yourself because you think that you've failed. You haven't. You did your best.

God bless you Mum. I hope you'll have the courage to move on.

I love you.

Luke

BOMBAY

Dear Mum,
I'm not sure if I'll ever post this letter. Write it I will, to prove to myself that I still love you and care enough to share my experience with you and let you know what's going through my head. It's Bombay I've reached. Found a small guest house in Borivali East. They haven't even asked me for ID proof and don't seem to care so long as I pay in advance. And I'm paying them in cash anyway. Left my cards and cheque books and everything at home. All the cash I ever saved is with me. This is crazy, carrying around so much cash. As if I have robbed a bank. I really can't believe that I'm doing this, actually doing this. Have been stuffing myself with *kheema pav* and drinking

Irani tea and staying off the street for most of the day and coming out in the evening when the streets are crowded and people are too busy getting home that they have no time to notice. This is very irritating, I am already beginning to feel as if I am a thief. Maybe I am a thief. I stole your happiness Mum, no point in saying sorry because sorry would be meaningless. And why so? Because I'm a liar. If I really loved you I wouldn't have done this to you. I would have told you, *Mum I need a break because I'm cracking up inside and need to get away to mend myself.* Then gone away for a holiday. And maybe I'd have taken a woman. Or found a woman on the way. Mum I've had affairs with more women that you could ever imagine. All sorts of women. If I have to even begin to tell you, you'll get a heart attack. To be honest, most of them were not even affairs. We just did it, that's all. A few were affairs or little more than affairs. I'm sure if you had to read this letter you'd start asking me who the women or girls are. Yes Mum, there were girls too. You know the one you call Simpy who came on a temporary job? The one who assisted in housekeeping. I did it with her Mum. A number of times. And also with older women, white women. Now don't laugh at me–that German woman whose husband rubbed that thingy in his hand? She was one of them. And that Dog Woman? Her too. But I didn't think, and still don't think, that it was wrong. I'm an adult and there's nothing wrong. And anyway it was mutual. I didn't stalk her. Sorry Mum. Why am I going on so obsessively with this? Women are actually far from my mind. I'm just so damned full up with baggage that there's no place for simple joys anymore. That's true, women are simple joys. Men are scrambled balls of barbed wire. We don't know how to be simple. We are constantly trying to achieve something or the other and impress people and control. When some women become like that it's not because its coming from inside them … it's coming from us … we make them like that. Remember the time Mum when you thought I was having fun with guys, I mean that I was gay? I wanted to explain all this to you then ... about this being the reason why I can't be gay. It's NOT that choice of sex that I have a problem with, it's got to do with what goes with it, what it is a part of. The weather in Bombay is horrible. The heat before the rains is so uncomfortable that I can't manage it. At least in Goa, I had the sea. I'm a beach boy Mum and when a beach boy has to live away from the sea it's just like a mackerel living in an apartment.

I want to go on but I can't because I need to go out into the streets and walk among people and not sit here in this room and let my fears overtake me.

I love you Mum

Luke

FIRST RAIN

Dear Melissa,

It rained today. The first rain this season. A really heavy shower that went on for two hours and there's brown dirty water swelling out of the drains and the whole place is smelling and I wish I was back home by the sea walking along the beach, my whole body tingling with the lash of the rain and the wind and the sea rough as hell. I'm thinking of you even though I'm sure that you couldn't possibly be thinking of me. I remember every word you shared with me those afternoons when it rained. I remember that crooked smile of yours when you didn't believe what I was saying. I remember you asleep and me talking to you and you waking up later saying you were not asleep and guessing your way through what I had said. I remember it all as if it happened a while ago. I also remember me asking you several times what you thought of Uncle Arnie and you didn't reply but changed the topic. You were so good at changing the topic when it became uncomfortable. Why couldn't you have told me that you were sleeping with him? I would have felt a little awkward but it would have passed. After all Melissa I didn't own you, we were not in a relationship, you said you needed me and I needed you, you said you didn't find young men attractive enough, you said you preferred older men, I didn't mind you saying that. I accepted it, you could have told me about Uncle Arnie. I didn't know what to say when he told me. It wasn't a happy time for him when he mentioned what had happened between you two. That was a difficult time back in Gorai. His home was literally falling down around him, he was emotionally in a mess, I was trying to sort out his legal matters, we'd spend nights drinking and talking, often it was about you. I was sure he was in love with you. May be he still is. Melissa, what a pain love is. No, I'm not in love with you. I think it will be very difficult for someone to fall in love with you and if he does–he will find it even more difficult to stay in love with you. You are too real to love. By real I mean just too damned REAL. When I find better words I'll explain myself a little more clearly. At the moment I'm not able. Imagine if all women were like you Melissa, what a difficult life it would be. Men wouldn't know what to do with them. May be I did love you a bit–that is if one can love a bit. May be I loved you more than a bit. But was it love? Come to think of it, the truth is that I was quite hurt and confused when I found out that Uncle Arnie had been with you. God, Melissa, I can't believe that I am saying this to you.

I can't continue. It has started raining again so I am going for a walk. I want to get wet, soaking wet, I want to feel the rain lash at my body. I want to wash you out of me.

Luke

MOVING

Dear Mum,

This is to let you know that we've had no rain today so I think I should check out and leave the city. I know that if I am here when the rains start good and proper, I'm never going to leave and I'll end up returning to you. I don't want to be safe anymore. I want to take risks. I want to vanish and reappear somewhere else with my memory washed away.

Sorry.

Love

Luke.

ON A BUS

Dear Melissa,

I am learning what it means to move with the heart. That's what you said you did when you were travelling, moved with the heart. It's quite difficult to follow the heart because I've never really listened to the heart because I was busy getting on with my life with Mum. Organise. Organise. Organise. That's all both of us did. Plan this and plan that and plan the other. Everything predictable. We couldn't take risks. It was too tricky. There was too much at stake. When Mum used to tell me *why don't you go on and enjoy yourself, loosen up a bit son,* I couldn't do it. I couldn't loosen up because loosening up meant I'd have to relax and go off and start *being myself.*

Sorry, here I go again analysing myself. I really am unsure how you'd react if I really wrote this letter and sent it to you. All night in the bus I thought about the travel you did with that poet fellow in buses. You described it all so well. You were so good with details. I wonder if that is a *woman thing*. I find it tough getting into details and I think it's the same with a lot of men I've known. The big picture, yes, but not the little stuff. I'm in Ahmedabad, planning to catch another bus to Bhuj. Will do that tonight. For now, I'm in an AC three star just for the day. Washed up and plan to go for a walk after a damned good haircut and shave. Plan to shave off my hair and moustache and beard and redefine myself. May be one of these days I'm going to look into a mirror and find a stranger looking at me. Don't know what I'll say to him.

See you one day, hopefully,

Luke

KUTCHI KHANA

Dear Sabby,

I'm sure you'll be surprised to get this letter from me, considering we've not exactly been buddies. You're Mum's territory, Mum's property and about to team up and run a resort and a guest house cum restaurant together ... of which I don't want to be a part. From the way things were going when I split the scene, it's evident that you two are going to end up with rings on your fingers and cake cutting and all that sort of thing pretty soon. So good for you. Actually I'm writing to you because just a while ago I had a thali in a restaurant in Bhuj. Good Kutchi food. And while I was eating I remembered how you raved about a meal you once had in a

Kutchi person's home in Goa. I thought that you were going over the top that time but now I understand what you meant. And I understand why you wanted to do a Kutchi Night at Clementine to attract Gujjus in the season. Kutchi grub is tasty. Their khichdi with kadhi is worth killing for … then there's the khaman-dhokla, rotlas and chhas, shrikhand and puris and a lot else. Sure you get the same stuff in Bombay and places in Goa but this is authentic stuff. I could turn vegetarian for a year at this rate. Apart from all this, how's the 'tie-up' going? Any progress?

Luke

BHUJ RAIN

Dear Mum,

It rained the morning I reached Bhuj. So damned hard that it looked like the bottom of a sea had cracked open and all the water was pouring through. It seems that it hardly rains in these parts and that this was a freak downpour. Holy Jesus Christ, what a damned downpour. The whole town was upside down with chaos. Filthy water everywhere thick with garbage and overrun by pigs, goats, cows, cats, dogs, massive rats, camels and human beings of every shape and size. They were everywhere. Good for me that I found a place to stay pretty fast and lodged myself on the fourth floor. I shut the windows, put on the fan full blast, covered up and crashed out. What a solid snooze I had Mum. You'd have been proud of me. You were right. Sleep heals. I got up and bathed and asked for tea. Nothing to write home about. Very hot, thick, rich and sweet tea overflowing into the saucer. I miss your tea, the light one that you make with a few drops of milk in it and just a wee bit of sugar. The first cup in the morning always made me feel good and ready to face the day. The second got me ready to slay a dragon like St. George did. The third sent me off to work. Thanks to your teas, I became something. But then I must admit that it was more than just your teas that made me Mum, it was also your constant support and inspiration. You have the patience of Job. That's your special gift. I haven't inherited that from you, for sure. I've inherited little from you, what a pity. You have a restless son, Mum. A really restless fellow who has ants in his pants and can't sit still. God alone knows if he will ever manage to get the ants out of his pants. They rush around inside and bite him all over. He doesn't know what to do Mum. I'm sure that you feel cursed. Your husband died on you and your son ran away and now you are looking for refuge in another man's heart … not that I have a problem with that. It's your life Mum, your choices. You have to find your way like I have to find mine. Reminds me what I saw when I looked down from my balcony. Way down below I saw people and animals making their way through the water slush. Each found their own path to dry spaces. Just like our lives Mum … I wish I had the courage to actually write these letters and send them … I don't. I don't want to be found, I'm on the run … from myself.

Your Luke

WHAT'S THE RAIN LIKE IN GORAI?

Dear Uncle Arnie,
What's the rain like in Gorai? Does the wind blow as hard as the wind on the shores of Goa? What do you do when it rains? Sit inside, huddled up in your armchair, drinking? Or what? Do you still drink as much as you used to Uncle? Or have you turned over a new leaf? I can't imagine you turning

over anything. Instead I can believe everything turning you over. You are a cross between a child and a really tough and interesting full grown man. So I never knew when you changed from one to the other. Sometimes I was talking to one and it became the other or the other way around and it left me wondering. What did you and Melissa talk about? You remember Melissa don't you? You know who I am talking about? She is unforgettable. If you remember her, do you think about her much? I mean really THINK about her. One day Uncle Arnie, when I have hung, drawn and quartered the past and finished off all my ghosts and dumped my baggage in a gutter somewhere, I'll see you again. I still believe that you can turn that place into a wonderful boutique resort, a small one I mean. But exclusive. Did those investors from Bombay ever come back? I doubt they would have, considering the way you treated them. If I hadn't showed them your property and other papers they would have seen you as an illegal squatter. What did all this do to you? Who did all this to you Uncle Arnie? Was it that you didn't have a proper father and you had a mother who dominated you? I know what it is like not to have a proper father, I mean–to have a father for a short time and then not have him anymore. Okay in my case he died, right before my very eyes, he drowned. But you didn't know for a long time whether he was alive or dead. But anyway, both of us didn't have a father. We had a mother. From whatever I've heard I wouldn't have wanted to have a mother like the one you had. Why am I trying to dig out the entrails of the past when they do not exist anymore? I won't disturb you Uncle Arnie. Will write again when I have something to say.

Cheers

Luke

TO THE SEA AGAIN

Dear Mum,
I couldn't manage to stay very much longer in Bhuj because it's a Godforsaken place and everyone looks at me so strangely. I wonder if it's my bald head that's giving them some weird impression of me. Maybe I should grow my hair back so that I don't stand out in the crowd. Damn the crowd. Damn whether people stare at me or not. Damn everything. So I left Bhuj and travelled south towards the Gulf of Kutch and–the sea. The place is full of guest houses and finding one to stay in was easy and one facing the river Rukmavati was easier still. My window opens on to the waterfront and I have sat here for hours letting the smell of the river and the fragrance of the sea flow towards me, sometimes separate and sometimes mingling. I think I'm slowing down a little bit. Just a little. I can hardly feel the ants in my pants. A few bit me yesterday but not today. Today, I'm much calmer. If you were here in front of me, maybe we would have been able to actually have a chat and I could tell you what I really want to tell you face to face and not keep avoiding issues. When I am calm like this I start thinking about my pals and wonder what they are up to. Seen them around? Particularly Tony and Joey. Has Tony's leg mended? Must have by now and he must be out on his boat again. Joey was doing AA when I last saw him. Seen him? Heard of him? It's not a good feeling, this, constantly in a new place with no one to really talk to. Mum, it's getting really lonely. I haven't been on the road very long but I am already feeling like a needle in a haystack. Forget about anyone else finding me, even I can't find myself. I'm lost.

Luke

WALK ALONG THE YARD

Hi Tony,

What you up to man? You got your leg or you haven't got your leg? Joking man, joking. Hope your leg is good and you're back with your boat after silver. There are boats everywhere around me in Mandvi. Boats of every shape and size. Yep, some of them are really bloody big and they're making them by the dozen. Maybe one day you can come here and get a boat made, a really solid boat and sail it all the way back from the Gulf of Kutch down the coast to Goa. I wouldn't mind coming with you if it's a big boat. The smaller ones scare me. I don't want to get drowned at sea, you know what a funk I am. So man, what you doing with yourself? How's Elsie? Still with her? I hope you are. She's a good woman, I'd kill to have someone like her. Good looking, intelligent, got a good job, doesn't want to rush into marriage. I've asked you so many times to find me someone like her. But then I suppose love doesn't happen that way. I hope I can make it back there one day when I have finished my penance. Hah ha, it's not exactly penance, I'm just running away from myself. When will I have the courage to return? And you call yourself a friend. Why couldn't you do something, say something, advise me when I confided so much in you. All you said was that it was my business and you couldn't help because I am a stubborn chap and just won't listen until I'm fallen on my face and can't get up and shout for help. Boss, by the time that happens, you'll have got married and had babies and grand babies and won't recognise me or even hear my voice. Sorry I'm sounding so full of self pity. I'm screwed in the head and haven't a clue about what's coming next.

'You lock the door
And throw away the key
There's someone in my head but it's not me.'

Remember that song boss? Remember the night we sat on your boat on the beach and drank and sang to a moon that had turned dark amber? You have a good voice boss, so has Elsie. My voice always screwed up the song. I can't really SING because I can't let myself go. I'm always holding back. And that other time at your birthday party when we were kids ... remember the time your dad gently asked me not to shout when I was singing but to open my mouth and let my voice flow out. Your mum stopped him and took him away and I was so damned upset that I left the party early. And the next day you said sorry for your dad but he didn't. Yeah, but I let that pass. You're lucky that your mum and dad are still around even though you don't need them.

'And if your head explodes with dark forebodings too
I'll see you on the dark side of the moon'

I really hope I get to see you again and life goes on after that without any downs.

Cheers and don't drink hard.

Hugs for Elsie.

Luke.

TIME TO MOVE NORTH

Dear Mum,

I'm moving north because there's too much of nostalgia here. The water, the boats, the distant moaning of the sea, the air smelling of home, I can't stay here, I have to move on. If I stay here any longer I'll take root, I'll start making friends. There's a woman here who I fancy. I don't want to let anything develop. I have to move on. This is getting ridiculous. So that's it, your son is setting off again and soon he'll be up and away and following where his feet take him. More when I've reached somewhere. If I haven't then you won't hear from me. Why the bloody hell am I clutching on to your apron strings like a drowning man clutches at straws? Why? And you, you have no apron strings that you can clutch on to. You've got your man who you will be spending the rest of your life with. He will never really know how lucky he is. I wish I was there when you two tie the knot. I know you will want me there. The first time you married you had Uncle Arnie there. This time around you may not even have him there. And I won't be there. Mum, why have I messed up my life like this? Why Mum? I wonder what I'd do with my life if I got a chance to live it all over again? Knowing me, I'd probably mess it up.

So, I'm moving north, Mum,
Luke

STRANGE LANDS

Dear Mum,
I don't know why I'm putting myself through all this travelling. This isn't me. I'm not a traveller. I'm a beach boy. I'm dead without the sea. Dead. All night I rattled along in a bus that kept breaking down, out of Mandvi, heading northeast to Samakhaili carrying the fragrance of the sea with me, on to Palanpur, everything changed so fast–people, places. I got off at bus stations, found a place to bathe and change and move on.

By the time I crossed the border into Rajasthan, I was so tired that I fell asleep, finally, and awoke with the sun burning down on me and I found myself in a place called Sirohi crowded out with temples and ruins of fortresses, the past and the present all thrown together in one jolly heap. That wasn't a place for me to stop so I moved on through Pali to a place called Ajmer. At the bus station I found myself amongst crowds of backpackers all headed to Pushkar as if they were making a bee-line towards the Promised Land. Tons of Israelis among them. And Europeans in all shapes and sizes. So I joined the merry throng and got pulled into the temple town of Pushkar arranged around a so-called sacred lake. A bit of a touristy joke that started getting on my nerves so I spent a couple of days fooling around the narrow streets and moved out, heading towards Jaipur which was much too pompous with its royal imitations everywhere. Jesus Christ save my soul, I headed north this time, desperate to get out of Rajasthan. Crossing Haryana I landed up in Punjab. Phew, I found it much more interesting. In Amritsar, I spent more than a week, roaming the old walled city. There everyone was much more real. Sorry I'm saying this, but I found the Golden Temple much more beautiful and peaceful than a cathedral. A cathedral is made to make you feel small and be in awe of God. The Golden Temple makes you feel elevated, makes you feel good about yourself. Mum I really wish you make it there one day. If you do, you'll understand what I am talking about. I spent hours sitting quietly on the cool marble floor, staring out at the sacred lake and the temple in the middle. That was my last stop in Punjab and then I was out, heading into the mountains towards Dharamsala and McLeodgunj. Sorry Mum this must be sounding like Greek to you but I'm writing it all down before I forget and soon all of these faces and places will get muddled up into one awful mess then swept away. I've already forgotten the details of all these places and more, the feelings I felt, things that happened to me, my loneliness that kept washing over me even when I was in a crowd. I can't go on Mum, I can't go on.

I miss you Mum,

Love

Luke.

WHO AM I? WHERE AM I?

Dear Mum,

This is going to sound strange to you and may even surprise you but I'm finding it increasingly difficult to think that as a Christian I'm going to heaven and everyone else who is not a Christian is going to be left out. I've met a lot of good people on the way, Mum, people who helped me without even wanting to know my religion or where I am from. I grew up in a bubble and remained in there, unaware of the world outside the bubble. Now that bubble has burst, I have begun to look at everything with a new pair of eyes. In McLeodgunj I'd often take a walk along the beautiful wooded path around the main Buddhist temple and the home of the Dalai Lama. I felt so calm, so settled, so at rest, as I walked. I didn't have to be a Buddhist to feel that. I just felt it, as if the very path itself led me on towards the quietness in myself. I'm going back there one day. Moving out of McLeodgunj was difficult but I had to do it … head on towards Kullu, Manali and then along the high road to Leh. That will be my last stop. My place of rest. The place where I'll decide what to do with my life.

To the land of snow and ice.

Luke

Snow Storm

I've drawn the curtain back and sit and watch the snowstorm whirling outside. I can't go anywhere, I'm forced to be still, drink rum and feel it flow into me, spread inside and then move quietly deeper into me until it's in my blood. Why is it Jesus that you are so far away? You're not familiar anymore, you're not a part of me, you're not even on my lips like a curse. All I saw and experienced on the run from myself grew into a wave and washed you away. I need to pray but you aren't there, I need to ask *please help me* but it's no use because I know you aren't going to be there, you aren't going to respond, you can't respond, you can do nothing, nothing at all. I am left to myself.

But I'm not afraid of being by myself.

I have become so still that nothing affects me from the outside. I'm turning inwards, journeying inwards, there are untravelled paths in there that I never imagined existed, paths which lead me to places I have never seen, feelings I have never felt, thoughts I have never had, forgiveness I have never been generous enough to offer myself.

Outside the snowstorm goes on but inside the season has changed.

I will wait. I will give myself a chance to, think what I truly want to think, feel what I truly want to feel, become who

I truly am. I cannot rescue my past and straighten it all out the way I would want to. It's all gone, passed away, dissolved, washed away by the great wave.

When the snowstorm stops I find myself walking out, down Changspa and on towards the market, turn in to the temple courtyard and settle down to sit in peace. I don't understand the prayers that the robed ones chant but feel a warmth flowing from them. I look around me at gnarled fingers stroking beads and deeply wrinkled faces at peace in prayer. I am offered a bowl of butter tea and placing its rim between my lips–drink. Its rich, generous, thickness moves down my throat and into me, stilling me.

I have come far, throwing away my luggage and sit here now amongst the murmur of voices, lighter and quieter than I have ever been. I will never know what has driven me on and made me persist and stopped me from killing myself. Whatever it is, it seems to be good for me. I find myself smiling. The monk sitting across me is looking at me. His face blooms into a smile and the wrinkles at the corners of his mouth dance. Later, walking back, he catches up and walks alongside me in silence. Then once we have crossed Changspa he takes the left and I the right. A few minutes later I turn and look back at him. He's standing there, far out on the hump of the hill. I know he's watching me. I start walking towards him, I don't know why, looking down at the slippery path before me. When I look up again, he's gone. But I continue up the hill.

Once at the top I look at the undulating land all around and at the immense ranges of mountains standing around me. The blue-white sky stretches like a tent above me. I perch myself on a broken boundary wall and watch a local walk with three yaks, dragging their feet through the crunchy drifts of snow.

It's all gone now. I must go back and sleep and wait for the time to move on. Back to where I once lived? I'm not too sure about that. But at least I am willing now to forgive, even myself.

Something is glowing in me.

I sit up all night with the curtains pulled back, looking out at the dark outside and can almost see my whole life moving past–like people staring into this glass bowl where I swim like a gold fish. They are watching me and I am watching them. Then with all my strength I will them to dissolve and one at a time that's what they do. Dissolve. All that's left is me, as I used to be, walking along then stopping and peering in. I close my eyes and when I open them no one is there outside the fish bowl.

When dawn lights up the Himalayas I walk up the road to Shanti Stupa and watch the day unfold in beautiful shades of greys and browns and whites and creams, streaked with blue. I am on the way to healing.

4 CLEMENTINE

Good Night Irene

Sabby, I found a letter from Luke under his mattress. I don't know why the hell he kept it there of all places. Her voice was so strained and tired that I wanted to hold her in my arms and calm her down and tell her that everything will be okay. But Chrissie isn't the sort of person that calms down so easily. It's like she's walking on live coals all the time.

So what does the letter say?

I'll tell you about it when we meet. It's all too complicated.

Yes, mother and son relationships are always complicated, I responded, then regretted having said that, considering a father-son relationship is even crazier.

What do you know of a mother-son relationship? She snapped.

Sorry, I'm backing off. Just concerned about you. When can we meet? Should I come over if you aren't able to visit?

What are you going to do when you come over? Will you be able to get Luke back? No point trying to console me. She started sobbing and disconnected.

Luke had really gone and messed things up for Chrissie. The woman dotes on him and has done so much to help him along. I wonder what he could possibly hold against her. Where the bloody hell did he vamoose to? His crazy uncle in Gorai? I thought he had had enough of the man.

I suppose she now knows where he is. God, how far I went in my own way to trace him. I tried a couple of my seedy contacts … the ones who know the private parts of Goa like they fondle them every day. Jonsy the lame pusher, Birbal the bootlegger and his cousin Sashi known lovingly as Slash because of his skill with the sickle. And the other guys too. They had helped me find out where my two-timing wifey was slipping off to and even got me pictures of her having it off with her man. Of course they skinned me alive and emptied my pockets for loose change in the bargain but they did the job and I was happy to dish out. It wasn't the same this time around, they tried their best but turned up with nothing.

When I had suggested to her that maybe the chap had run off to his uncle in Gorai she smiled crookedly, *Gorai? Not a chance. That's the last place on earth he'll go to. The very last. He'd go to hell first before he got himself there, believe me. He's had his fill of his uncle. If you ask me he's probably in Timbuktoo, spitting sand in the eye of the sun.* Chrissie's got a colourful way with words, she has. That is if she wants to use them that way. She is a wise woman and a girl rolled into one. You never can tell which one she's going to be and when. Quite a character. Strong, soft, sharp, warm. I want her if she agrees. I really want every bit of her. I want to be beside her all the time, through thick and thin, in happiness and sadness, in sickness and in health, till death do us part. I don't know why I'm getting so dramatic. She hasn't even said yes but I'm sure she fancies me. Just imagine us being together-together, I mean really together-together, rings and all. And I get up every morning and she's there beside me and I go to sleep at night and she's there beside me. I really miss a warm body beside me. And once that's in place, I hope I don't start feeling that I don't have my own space any more. You know what I mean—my own space. And I start feeling that she's an intrusion. I've got so used to having my own space. I do things as I wish to do them. I throw my clothes where I wish, eat, sleep, get up, go for a walk, bathe, dress as I please. Even talk to myself in the mirror. I eat a whole lot of stuff that I'm not supposed to eat–pork vindaloo, sorpotel, fish curry that's so damned spicy that it blows a hole in the palate with every mouthful. She's not going to allow me to do all that. I mean, she'll tame me.

But before we get to that stage, there's this damned Luke who has to be brought back. I don't understand the fellow like I don't understand Xavier.

I really wish Xavier was different, not a shit like he is. If he was more responsible and not as crazy as he is, he'd be able to take care of this place and all the people who come and go from here. Instead, what does he do, leave his damned dog Banjo here to be taken care of and floats in and out as he pleases. Okay, let's say that it shouldn't be such a problem because we can easily get someone to take care of the creature. But no, it's not that easy. There's Melissa who stays here and does whatever she chooses with the dog. Like today, once again she has pushed off with Banjo and has been away all evening. That woman is up to all sorts of jiggeripokery. The other day she took him for a walk early morning along the beach and returned late afternoon and his tongue was hanging out of his head and he looked as if he was going to fall flat on his face and never get up again. And when I told her, *look here Melissa, if something happens to that dog then you'll be to blame.*

And you know what she replied? *Come on Sabby, if nothing has happened to me do you think anything will happen to him? Banjo's a tough guy. Certainly tougher than his boss. And anyway, this doggy will get even tougher with all the exercise I'm giving him.*

You're lucky Xavier isn't in town. If he was, he'd throw a fit.

Who says he's not in town? Of course he is. I saw him with his girls at the flea market. He showed me a finger.

Well, that's his business where he wants to be and whether he showed you a finger or not.

You just said that he's out of town.

Stop splitting hairs Melissa. You'd better order your meal soon. The kitchen is closing early today.

In a while, she said and sailed off.

I don't know what to do with this woman. She's decent business no doubt and is willing to stick it out in rooms that are far worse than other places in Colva because she says she likes it here and it's homely. And I don't want to spend on doing the place up. If the tie-up comes through with Blue Mermaid then maybe I'll have to spend even less than I'm spending now and get better returns.

Women. I'm no good at either understanding or handling women.

My ex was just the opposite of Chrissie. Irene was untidy, impetuous, expensive and in the face in everything that she said and did; she was so damned gutsy that she never spared a chance to challenge people around her with her openness. She went as far as challenging me to prove that she was going around with another guy. I mean, straight in the face that it left my nose bloodied. Not really bloodied but insulted and I couldn't do anything about it. Nothing at all. We'd go off to church and she'd never sit with me, at least not next to me. And after that she'd say she was off to meet someone or the other and I didn't probe too much because I didn't want her to feel that I was insecure. I just wanted her to feel that she was living with a very secure, confident fellow. I always like to give that image of myself to people. I don't want people to think I am the dependent sort. You know the winny-ninny sort who holds on to the one he loves like he's clutching at the last straw before he drowns … and asking all the time *where are you going? Who are you talking to on the phone? Where did you get that necklace from? Why don't you want to come to my bed tonight?* I'm the sort who likes to let people be. I suppose that's the problem. That's what happened with Irene. I just let her be. Didn't make demands on her … at least in the later years. Earlier I was all over her. *Irene this* and *Irene that* and *Irene you are my everything.* God, she was amazing when I first saw her. Waves of red-brown hair like her head was on fire. And at sixteen what a body. She won every damned race she cared to run, was easily the best dancer at socials and jam sessions and talked the hind legs off a donkey. A peculiar lilt in her voice– like up and down and up and down and then she'd sigh at the end of a sentence and wet her lips with the tip of her tongue and her eyes would twinkle. She had all the guys tripping all around her and babbling stupid, idiotic stuff, getting tongue tied whenever she looked at them. Can't forget the time when she had six guys tagging her one after the other at the last big school social. You, know the really big one.

Well, I landed her when she bounced off other affairs that she was having that turned sour. I landed her and held on to her until we were married. I was all over her and was forever babbling sweet nothings into her ears and giving her chocolates and flowers at the drop of a hat. And she obviously loved all of it. I gave her my all in bed and she enjoyed every bit of it. But then you know as well as me that beautiful people become ordinary when you see them over and over again, every breathing, living moment. They become like the beautiful house you live in which is great and makes you feel good and you try your best to maintain it and then one day you have other things to deal with in life and you start taking time off from appreciating the beauty of the house. And when you don't appreciate it, you don't maintain it. And when you don't maintain it, it slowly becomes ordinary. And it exists to keep you company. A habit. I suppose Irene became my long lasting habit. A habit I could never shrug off. Maybe I just saw a part of her and not others. So she continued to show that to me and became more and more ordinary. There was no colour left in our marriage. I didn't know what to do. I wanted to talk about it but she was never around. Served me right. Got news that she was seeing fellows. Actually I knew in my heart of hearts that she was seeing fellows and brushed it under the carpet but when everyone else started talking I felt pretty stupid and had to acknowledge it. Once I acknowledged it I said to myself, *look here Sabby, it's now or never. You got to decide. Either you stay with her or you don't. Then tell her straight off and get it over with.*

Huh, but I just couldn't do that and decided to win her back. And how the hell did I go about it? Simple. I started spending money on her–left, right and centre. But she turned out to be a bloody bottomless well. Everything I put in stayed in and got lost down there and whenever I peeped in to see if there was any water at the bottom of the well all I saw was a dark perfumed pit. She wanted to go shopping to Dubai so I sent her off, then she went to Kathmandu and Bangkok and off on a cruise. It was becoming a bit of a joke. I sold two of my properties so that I could keep funding her, abandoned a housing complex project and finally stripped myself bare–just for her. And of course finally I fell back on this place, Clementine. This place was down market for her. When I had started it a long time back she had thought it was a bad idea. *Cheap*, that's the word she used. *Cheap, a musty hole in the wall. Niche market you call it Sabby, bit of a damned joke. It's a sad, musty den where the old unwanted dregs swept up from all over the world collect. How can you live with all this oldness? Doesn't it smell of decay?*

How can you talk like that?

So you don't think this place is depressing?

Not exactly. I was reaching the end of my tether. *It's a bar and restaurant for older folk. What's wrong with that?*

Everything. Why older folk?

Why not?

Because it's so depressing. Walk in and you see older people slouched over their drinks or plates or singing along with ridiculous songs. It's like walking into the past.

You're scared of getting old Irene, accept that. We all get old and fall apart and vanish. That's life. You my dear think you are going to live on forever, so you don't want to be reminded about the truth. Haven't you learnt?

Learnt what?

If you live a happy accepting life, you'll grow old happy and contented.

Now you've turned into a philosopher. Dear God. When I first met you, you were a dashing fellow, you were everywhere–you danced, you sang, I was proud to be your wife. What happened to you? What happened to change you?

You. I was bitter. I let the words fall out of my mouth. *You were an amazing woman when I met you but all the paint got washed off and what I see now is a wooden doll.*

How dare you …

Scared of the truth Irene? Want to hear more?

She didn't and backed off. As the days and weeks and months rolled away, she lost herself in her old games, vanishing for days on end, returning washed out, tanking up and then vanishing again. Finally, Denzil D'Souza took her away from me. Ha, but I had the last laugh because we're Catholic and she couldn't divorce. So Denzil wore her out instead and passed her on to Tony Cordeiro. From there she moved from hand to hand, leaving a trail of sad stories behind each broken relationship. There were times when I was so overcome by pity for her that I actually felt like reaching out to her and bringing her home. I remember the many times that I'd drive up north to get a glimpse of her, just a glimpse. Finally I did. It was in one of those beach side shacks in Anjuna. She was at a table with a blond hunk with tattoos all the way along his arms, his neck and up to his temples. The fellow kept patting her on her cheeks till she brushed his hand away. Then she got up to leave and he followed her like an obedient poodle. She headed towards the exit, stopped at my table. *You following me Sabby? You following me to satisfy yourself that there's nothing left of me?*

This guy bothering you? Asked the hunk. Then he turned to me, *get off her back, you hear me? Get off her back.*

I ignored him.

You heard what I said? He persisted.

You talking to me? I wanted to know.

Sure thing man, I'm talking to you.

Do you know who she is?

She's my woman, he replied.

Now isn't that interesting? Because she's also my wife.

The fellow looked at her surprised. *You married to this thing?*

Was.

Is, I corrected her. *She is my wife.*

Leave me alone, Irene spat at me, *leave me alone.*

When I didn't respond she slapped me. I didn't move an inch just sat there smiling at her.

Stop haunting me Sabby, let me go, please.

So you can rot? Come home, I'll care for you, I'll give you whatever you want. Anything. Come home Irene.

Nothing there to come home to Sabby, a sad old café, a man who thinks he can buy love and a queer for a son.

What do you want Irene?

Nothing, she whispered and walked away, her poodle trailing behind.

She was found dead three months later, on the beach in Palolim, a heart attack, they said. I was duly informed and went over and identified her body in the morgue. I felt really bad when I saw her cold body lying there, exposed to strangers. We buried her in her favourite cemetery–the one where her granny lies. Xavier turned up briefly and then left, I didn't ask him to stay.

Back at Clementine, I got rid of whatever had belonged to her and reorganised my home in such a way that there was no sign that she had ever lived there. Then I did a whole makeover of myself–a new wardrobe, new car. Started smoking cigars and drinking mugs of beer. Tried to convince myself that I lived the good life.

All of this went on quite smoothly until one *Sing Your Song* night at Clementine when oldies are invited to sing their favourite songs, Jerry Butler, the geriatric took the mike and began to sing,

'Good night Irene,
Irene good night,
I'll see you in my dreams …'

It finished me off. I went home, stripped, stood under the shower and cried my heart out.

Threesome and More

Melissa returned late that evening with Banjo. I wasn't upset with her because both of them looked so happy and relaxed. Banjo trotted in, almost smiling and she greeted me with a faint grin. *So where have you two been?* I wanted to know, doing my best to be friendly.

No mood to do much walking today Sabby. Myself and Banjo sat around on the beach. He didn't want to chase dogs but shared my ice cream instead.

You're going to turn that dog into a human one of these days.

I'd prefer to turn humans into dogs.

I was curious, *so if you want to change me into a dog, what sort of a dog would I be?*

Personality or breed?

Let's start with personality, Melissa. Personality.

Okay. Trusting. Committed. Hard working. You …

I stopped her dead in her tracks. *That's enough on that front. How about the breed?*

Not sure.

Hmm. That a compliment?

This is not about compliments. You asked me about your personality and breed. I told you. So, you tell me. I'm going to ask you straight and I want a straight answer and no dancing around the tree.

You mean beating around the bush.

I mean dancing around the tree, Sabby. Dancing around the tree. Why do you keep correcting the way I speak English? I think I do a good job for a German. Most times people can't tell I'm German. That's because I've worked so hard on learning to speak and write English. It's like another mother tongue.

So they mistake you for a bloody Brit, right? Is that what you are saying?

Don't talk about my English. Talk about your own. Indian English. Sounds so cute. 'Like that only.'

I don't say that. I protested but she was getting carried away with her banter and didn't give me a chance. Not a single chance.

There, you are dancing around the tree. I have a question. A simple question. When will I have the chance to turn you into a Labrador?

Any time, I joked and she half smiled shrugging her strong broad shoulders.

Good show, do the Brits say that? Eh Sabby?

Yes, sometimes.

All these old ones who lie around here, the Brit ones, do they say that?

Yes. Sometimes, but what are you getting to?

Good show. I'm going to turn you into a Labrador right now. Good show.

I got an eerie feeling that something was about to happen, something really unexpected.

I can't turn you into a Labrador right here Sabby, but I can do it at your place.

Are you serious?

Aye aye Captain.

So now we're not in a kennel anymore but on board a ship. I joked nervously.

Yes, she replied, *and I'm going to help you sail her through rough waters, up and down, up and down.*

I really don't know what got into me. I broke out into goose bumps all over and my knees were slightly rubbery. Stupid damned feeling. The woman walked off. I wasn't sure what the hell I was expected to do. It had all happened so quickly that I was left confused. She wasn't playing mind-games, that was certain. She meant business and she went about it so brazenly. Either I chased the bait and lunged for it or let it pass so that someone else could do the honours. On impulse I decided to do the first.

When I reached the door of the apartment, she was standing there. *That was fast, no dancing around the tree I can see.*

No dancing around the tree, I stammered in response.

Once inside, she peeled away the years from me, leaving me reeking of perspiration, soaking wet, still tingling and unable to get up.

You panted like a Labrador, she said quietly, sipping a drink, lounging in an armchair looking down at me spread out on the carpet. *I bet that Chrissie woman won't be able to give you this my Labrador. Only I can because I have the secret mantra.* She stretched out one leg and trailed her big toe across my body.

I shut my eyes and when I opened them again I was lying in my bed. I tried to get up and out of bed but couldn't because something was tied around my neck. Good God, the woman had leashed me to the bedpost with my tie. My best tie at that.

It was morning, I found her in the kitchen making coffee. *What the bloody hell are you doing here?*

O so you don't want the whole world to know that I'm shacking up with you. It's too … what do the Brits say? Embarrassing. Yes? No bother Captain, I'm like that only. I'll go so that you can go out there alone and behave like you are this good decent guy. She left quickly, closing the door gently behind her.

I was in a hot stew. *Holy smoke,* I said to myself, *a real twist of events. That's what life has constantly thrown at me, unexpected things. People popping in and out of my life, new feelings. Okay it was nice but now what the hell am I going to do … leave it at the level of these quick mad moments and pretend to everyone else that nothing's happening. Or do I take her a wee bit more seriously … I mean like an affair or a relationship?*

I got no answer. Obviously. The old man up there pissed silence on me.

The whole day through she'd get on with her life and behave as if there was absolutely nothing between us other than the fact that she was a lodger in Clementine and I was the owner. She continued taking Banjo out for walks and fussing over him. In public, she was as indifferent to me as she always had been but when we were alone it was pure savage intimacy. I played along for as long as I could then gave up and collared her one evening. *Listen Melissa, I find this arrangement confusing. It's like living two different lives.*

What is?

This. Nothing between us through the day and at night we are like two wild animals having it out.

You are crude, eh?

I'm putting it mildly.

What's that mean?

Gently, in a civilised way.

You want me to stop? Eh? You want me to hang around your neck? What is the English word? Drape?

Yes.

So you want me to do that?

No, I mean the English word is drape.

She stood there with her hands on her hips. *Listen Sabby, do you like what's happened between us or not. Tell the truth.*

Yes, sort of.

What's 'sort of' eh? What's 'sort of' mean? Yes or no?

Yes.

That's it. So what's all the fuss about?

It's like living two lives.

We are all living two lives anyway. If you like something, enjoy it. What are you feeling guilty about? You like that Chrissie woman eh?

Where did that question come from?

From my mouth, where else?

Stop being stupid. I mean what's on your mind?

I know you like her in a different way from the way you like me. I hear also that you're going to do business with her, some kind of partnership.

And so she went from one thing to another trying to find out what's going on between Chrissie and me. Actually there is, in a more reliable way. We are heading towards marriage. No fireworks and great romantic moments but something wholesome. Something I can grow safely old in. But there's time before I get there. Marriage I mean. With Melissa, it's different. Quite different. She's a cracker. Excitement while it lasts. Can't get below the skin. Haven't tried but if I really did I wouldn't be able to understand her. A strong self contained woman who refuses to be soft and gentle. That's not a fault I suppose, it's a way of her surviving. She puts up this front which frightens people off. Tough white woman who treats little brown people like furniture

Yes Melissa, there's going to be some kind of partnership, let's see.

I hope I'm not messing things up.

Not at all.

She went off to her room leaving me to think about the strange situation that I was in. Wasn't long after, Xavier turned up with his friends. The idiot fellow just said hi and walked past me, towards a table at the far end. The sound boxes were rolling out some oldie stuff–Aker Bilk playing 'Stranger On The Shore' and 'I Can't Get Started' and Al Martino crooning 'Spanish Eyes' and 'Till The White Rose Blooms Again' and a lot of other stuff flowing over the tables. Old man Tommy Trilling was stuffing his mouth with chunks of grilled chicken and Baby Boyd sipped her beer and picked at her bowl of French Fries. As for the others, well they were at various stages of inebriation and mouth filling. Clementine was filling up for Friday night's Karaoke session. Lovely Linda and Brian Becoz, two yodellers from Palolim, got up to take the floor. The clatter of cutlery, clinking of glasses and chitter-chatter stopped. Then when the two reached the mikes, Xavier and his friends burst into a rowdy applause. They all stood up and flapped their arms and danced around, making babbling sounds. Sang their own version of 'Blue Moon,' coughing and spluttering as they went along. When they were through they bowed and sat down. Everyone was so taken aback that they sat there with their mouths open. *Go on Linda, go on Brian,* I called out.

They had hardly begun when Xavier and his friends jumped up again and started singing their version of Pink Floyd's 'Brain Damage.'

I walked over to their table. *What do you think you fellows are up to?*

Kirikokee, said Xavier and his friends giggled.

If you want to stay here, shut up, I snapped. *If you can't shut up then leave. Don't insult my guests.*

We aren't insulting YOUR GUESTS. Xavier snarled.

Of course you are, they've come here for an evening out and they are paying for it, they have every right to be left in peace.

You call this peace? It's the peace of the dead. RIP. This is supposed to be a restaurant and not a graveyard. You seem to get some unholy kick out of providing this waterhole for this lot. Why don't they go and die in their own country? I've had enough of you Pop. You live in a bubble which just doesn't seem to burst and you float around the place blissfully unaware of the world you are floating through. No wonder Mum went around the bend. You pushed her off the cliff and when she hit the water she was dead. Stone dead. And you … floating around in your bubble. He stared at me with confusion written all over his face. Then he fixed his gaze on me and looked straight into me, deep in. I tried to see something of the little boy I once knew in his eyes, something, anything, but I couldn't. There was anger, hurt and confusion.

He stood there swaying in front of me. Trying to say something. But no words came. Just spittle which trickled out and dripped down the side of his mouth. Then he collapsed in a heap, like a bundle of dirty clothes a dhobi dumps beside the water. His friends left hurried, none of them even bothered to pay the bill. We didn't remind them. Just let them go. I looked down at the fellow who was once my son. He was out for the count. I was sure that he wasn't just drunk, he had obviously been smoking some stuff. And booze and stuff thrown together cause havoc.

The waiters carried him off to his room. I stood there, dead centre of the restaurant, watched by my guests. What were they thinking? What? I couldn't tell. *I really am sorry for what has happened here this evening. I don't know what to say. Please don't pay your bill today. I am truly sorry.*

No one moved. They sat there looking at me. There was no anger or annoyance on their faces. Just a blank sadness.

Everyone paid their bill that night. On her way out Baby Boyd stopped by at the desk. *You're a brave man Sabby. If I was in your place I would have gone into a great big hole in the ground and refused to come out. But you've got your feet firmly on the ground.*

But it's another story inside, Baby.

Ah, we're all sailing in the same boat. Her wrinkles flowed into a smile and she rested her hand on my shoulder, *take care of yourself because there's no one else around who will do that for you.* She left.

Tommy Trilling gave me a hug and walked off without a word. Soon Clementine was empty, except for Linda and Brian. They sat a while, had their meal on the house and left, refusing to accept a wage because they said that they hadn't earned it.

From that day on, Clementine sailed on a sympathy wave with old fogies coming out of the woodwork and upping business like crazy. We laid on special rates and were streets ahead of other eateries considering the season was over and two and a half tourists rattled around in Colva. Our guests are residents in Goa, people who find themselves at home by the sea. They don't seem to bother about the fact that they are actually strangers on the shore, living on memories, cheap food and drink. What matters is the here and now. A lot of loners amongst them, of course, people who manage to live by themselves and have found a few brownies as friends and supporters, others are actually doing a heck of a lot for local causes, caring for stray animals, cleaning up the environment, spreading health awareness, running free food places and clinics. Then there are others who spend their time complaining about India–how everything is a bloody mess … the traffic, the garbage, casteism, classism, inequality, the rich and the poor living side by side, crime, no one is safe, they even rape babies who haven't been born, power cuts, corruption, the list is endless. Then why the hell are they here? Why? Obviously there's something here that's an attraction. Here they are someones but there? A face in the crowd. I know I shouldn't be saying all this, it's not fair. Getting old isn't easy. According to me, being a stranger in an alien land is far easier than being a stranger in your own land. At least in an alien land there's some vague possibility you can make new friends and start all over again … but in your own land new friends are hard to come by and starting all over again is a near impossibility particularly if you are living alone. It's difficult to accept that places you once knew as a child or a young person have changed, new people have come in, people dress differently, talk differently. You become a ghost from the past who cannot adjust to the present. The stories I've heard from some of my guests have left me really feeling bad.

Living in India is tough anyway, especially when one doesn't keep good health. Landing up in an Indian hospital is even worse. It's traumatic. So many of them haven't been able to manage and peter out, die in a ward somewhere one night amidst the smell of stale food and the whimpering and groaning of the grievously ill. Others die in their own homes or rented apartments often with no one beside them. And what do they leave behind? Nothing really, nothing of consequence. Quickly forgotten, other than *remember that old guy with droopy eyes and a pony tail? Died in his sleep and they found him locked in his bedroom by the landlord who had come to collect the rent.* Don't we all pass away some time or the other. Some sooner, some later. I wonder what Melissa will be like when she's old. And Chrissie?

But I just can't stop thinking of what will I be like when I'm really old and ready to go … what will I be like? Will I be alone?

Must get myself out of this ditch full of dark feelings.

Xavier. O God, Xavier. I keep wondering if he could get worse than what he was like that night and the days that followed. Just when I thought that I had seen the last of him, he surfaced again that night. His door was open when I passed to go to my apartment. *Hey you old bugger I want you to know something.* I kept walking. *You scared to face me eh? You scared to face me?* He shouted.

I'm not. I shot back and kept walking. *But no point talking to you. You're drunk and out of your mind. When you are sober, I'll be happy to talk. Maybe tomorrow morning.* Once inside my apartment, I slammed the door and bolted it. Stripped, went into the bathroom and stood under the shower and let the cold water flow over me.

There was a banging on the door, hard and furious. *Open up you old bugger.* It was Xavier. Then the banging continued. *Open the door.* By the time I reached the door to open it, two staffers had pushed past him and blocked the door. I opened it. He tried to push them aside but they wouldn't budge. Atul was taller and heftier than Xavier and shrugged off his efforts. *So you are scared of me?*

What do you want that can't wait till tomorrow morning?

I want to get out of here.

Then go, I replied. *I'm not stopping you.*

Ha, easy for you to say that. You'll get me out of your hair without any effort.

Okay then don't go.

You don't care a damned about me, you never did. It was Irene this and Irene that and Irene how's the good half of your brain?

Have some respect, you are talking about your mother.

She was hardly my mother when she was alive and now that she's dead, she really is of no use. But that's not the point I'm making

... when it wasn't about Irene it was all about yourself. I have always been a nobody in your world. You never knew what to do with me. You still don't ... because you don't care.

That's not true, you've never given me a chance. Never.

Where you're concerned, everyone else is wrong and you're the only one who is right.

So what is it that you want from me in the middle of the night? Can't it wait till tomorrow morning?

Why don't you tell those two bodyguards of yours to vanish so that we can settle this privately, just you and I?

I asked the two to leave. Babu walked away but Atul insisted on remaining. *Come on in,* I said to Xavier and he staggered towards me. When he reached Atul he stopped and stared at him, widened his eyes and said, *boo.* The man didn't even flinch, he stared back. It looked as if he was spoiling for a fight and was waiting for an opportunity to throw the first punch. But Xavier didn't allow him the pleasure and walked past him into the flat, slamming the door behind him.

He lurched around the apartment, refusing to sit down when I suggested he do so. *I'll do what I want to do. Don't you keep telling me how I should behave.*

I'm not telling you how you should behave. All I'm suggesting is that you should sit down. I stopped myself from losing my head. I had to deal with him calmly.

You want to know why I'm walking around and not sitting? You want to know? Yes or no?

Okay, why?

Because I'm taking a look at all this one last time ... to say goodbye. I didn't think I'd have to do this because I stupidly imagined that one day all this would be mine. All this. Even Clementine. God what a bloody name. Clementine. The whole world is moving forward and you are moving backwards. You're the laughing stock of Colva.

Get to the point Xavier and let's get it over with.

We'll go my pace, not your pace, you hear me? You hear me you old rat bag?

Yes, I hear you.

Okay. I was saying–I am saying bye to all this because I know now that it's not coming to me. You're going to live on and on and I'll have to wait for you to drop. But it's not that alone ... you now have a woman ... two women. That Chrissie woman and her closet son and this damned woman. The in-house polly taker. The kraut. The Nazi. The 'take me and give me' woman. Melissa. By the time these two women have finished, I'm not going to get anything. So I've decided to ask for my share now.

Share of what? I wanted to know.

Inheritance.

What inheritance? I'm not dead yet. I'm alive and kicking. This is my property. I earned it. I'll decide when I have to decide to share it with anyone. What's tickling you? You are thirty-three, have a good job on the ship. You are doing well for yourself. Why don't you just get on with your life instead of trying to snatch away what is not yours.

So you are saying that I'm not entitled to any of this? He stood there in front of me with his hands on his hips.

Not till I'm dead and that too not until you are mentioned in the Will. Till then, go about your own life Xavier, go about your own life. Support yourself.

But I'm your son. It's my right.

No it isn't. And don't you meddle with my personal life. Whether its Chrissie or Melissa, it still is none of your business. If you were not the way you are and lived a straightforward life and had good healthy friends, then maybe I'd be comfortable about the fact that you're going in the right direction ... then maybe I would give you something of this.

So that's the problem, is it? So you hate the idea that your son is 'queer' and abnormal and has 'queer and abnormal' friends? That's not respectable, is it? Who the bloody hell are you to judge me? This is my life and I'll live it the way I choose. This is sick. Your holier than thou frigging attitude is sick. He whipped out a kitchen knife, *I'm going to cut through this wrist of mine. I'm going to kill myself and you will be to blame because I've left a letter in my room and the police are going to read it and lock you up. You are done for Sabby. You are done for.*

Cut your hand off for all I care, I replied, sure that he wouldn't have the guts to do it.

I'm going to kill myself Sabby, I'm going to kill myself and you'll be to blame.

Atul burst in and lunged for Xavier who dodged him and slashed out with the knife which tore through his shirt and drew a bloody line across his chest. That didn't stop him and he continued to grapple till he dropped Xavier, knocked the knife out of his hand and pinned him down. Other staff rushed in and held him down. *You'll pay for this Sabby, you'll pay for this I promise.*

Let him go Atul. All of you leave the room. Take the knife away with you. Atul left with them. I sat in my armchair looking at him lying there on the ground. *So aren't you getting up? Or do you plan to sleep there tonight?*

He sat up, sighed then left. At the door, he turned and looked at me, *I didn't expect this of you.*

Neither did I.

I lay awake staring at the ceiling, wondering what on earth the future held for me. *All said and done he is my son and though to be honest I am very uncomfortable with him being a queer, he has the right to choose the way he wishes to live his life. Every right. But damn it, I have the right to feel what I am feeling and to react the way I am reacting. Every right.*

The next morning I discovered that someone had locked him in his room so I had it unlocked and knocked on the door. When there was no response, I banged on the door. *O God, o dear God I hope the fellow hasn't done something stupid. O God, no, please no.* We crashed the door open and found him lying face down on the floor. He had swallowed a fistful of pills, they said at the hospital and pumped it all out. I hushed it all up. Cost me a packet but I didn't care.

It took Xavier ten days to recover and when he did, he asked me whether he could invite his friends over for a 'bash.' I agreed unconditionally, determined not to interfere because I felt that that would get him off my back. When he next returned from sea, I'd give him a rent allowance and ask him to stay somewhere else.

That was the mother of all 'bashes' which scared away guests and turned Clementine into a drunken circus. The music was so loud that Melissa sent Atul down to lower the volume but he was chased away. Finally she went down herself. *What's going on here, eh fellows? What's going on here?* They ignored her. *I said what's going on here? Why so loud?* Still no response. So she went and turned down the volume.

When she left, someone turned it up again. So she returned and lowered the volume and left shouting, *I can't sleep, have some pity. Have some pity, you hear?*

But the volume shot up again but this time, she didn't return. Instead, Clementine was thrown into darkness. *Someone has switched off the mains,* shouted Xavier. People were stumbling and tripping over chairs and banging into tables. *We'll suffocate, open the windows. Where the hell are these slaves? Melissa, I'll fix you for this.*

The lights came on and the party staggered to its feet. When it was in full swing, the power went off again. Melissa played merry hell with them, turning the power on and off until, disgusted, the party fell on its face and passed out. Xavier left with his friends.

The next day when he returned, I informed him that I'd be happy to give him a good rent allowance so he could find a place to stay. *You are ruining my business, sorry, this can't go on.*

So you are throwing me out?

I'm relocating you. But you're welcome to eat and drink here, without your friends.

We'll see.

What will you see Xavier?

We'll see if you don't let them in.

If they pay they're welcome. Otherwise not. If they don't, I'll have them turned upside down and their money shaken out of them.

We'll see, was all he said. Then added after a while, *I'm taking Banjo. I don't want that Nazi mothering him.*

Okay. Suit yourself.

I got him a comfortable place in Benaulim and he quietly shifted in with Banjo.

But you can't send Banjo off like that Sabby, he can't even take care of himself how is he going to take care of the dog also?

Now don't start Melissa, Banjo is HIS dog, his pet. Banjo BELONGS to him. He can do whatever he wants to do with him. It is neither your business nor mine, please understand that.

What if he locks Banjo in the house and goes out? What will Banjo feel?

He won't do that, he has a damned garden there. Banjo can run free in the garden. Don't worry, I'm sure he loves the dog more than he loves me.

Yes, it is true Sabby, but loving an animal means feeding the animal, caring for the animal, taking the animal for a walk, being with the animal. Has Xavier been doing all this here? Who has been doing it? Who? Everyone here.

That's his pet Melissa. Now I've got him off my back I don't want to get on his back.

Fair enough. But that's not going to stop me visiting Banjo. I'm going to visit Banjo and keep an eye on him and take care of him when I can.

No you will not Melissa. For God's sake be reasonable.

Okay, I will give him some time but then I'll check on him. I'm going to check if Xavier loves Banjo or not.

Christ woman, don't complicate things. I ran my fingertips along her cheek.

Now don't be mushy Sabby or I'll eat you up in one go.

Life slipped into a calm for the next week. One week of bliss. I wasn't sure if it would last.

Battle for Banjo

With Xavier's departure, everything came together again and mended itself. Business picked up and we plugged in a Happy Hour. This brought returns. So did the arrival of voluptuous Peggy, a crooner. Nobody seemed to mind that she lisped because her mighty breasts and ample hips and hot lips compensated.

Melissa started feeling a little threatened so she quickly dug up a seedy piece of gossip about her and spread it around.

She was busted in the north peddling drugs, she said one day, secretively.

How did they let her out? I wanted to know.

They let her off because she has contacts. Before that she was in Bombay where she was thrown out of her job when they found that she was picking up guests. She had the big boss beaten up. And before that …

Come on Melissa, we all have pasts. So long as she's good at what she does who cares about her past.

True, but look at the way she wiggles her bum and hops up and down. She can't even sing straight.

Then why don't you show her?

You don't have to get angry Sabby. Look, and you're even getting red in the face. Something I should know?

Shhshh. Don't be silly.

So, just for that week, life took a huge u-turn and headed for the high road to good fortune. But by the end of the week the road disappeared and the first signs of problems to come showed up. *He's treating Banjo badly,* said Melissa.

How do you know?

The fellow was howling and howling his head off.

How do you know?

Why are you asking me the same question over and over again? Of course I know.

Melissa, I'm not stupid, I'm asking you–HOW do YOU know?

I saw him and I heard him. And he's looking so sad.

Why are you messing around at Xavier's place? I've had a tough time to get him to shift there and mind his own business and you go there and start meddling around. Why can't you leave him alone?

I love Banjo. He's my favourite.

Okay, fine. But why the hell are you turning up at Xavier's doorstep? That will irritate him and he'll land up here and the whole mess will start again. Why are you doing this? Why?

She walked off in a huff.

Two days later Xavier turned up. *So now you're sending that dog woman over to my place to spy on me.*

What are you talking about?

You know what I'm talking about. That dog woman climbed over the fence and came into my garden and took Banjo off the chain and started running around with him. Then the woman sees me and starts giving me a lecture that I shouldn't keep him tied up and I should take him for a walk and I should feed him this and that like a loud mouth dietician.

So what do you want me to do?

Tell her not to come near my property or I'll fix her good and proper.

Listen Xavier, this is between her and you. You tell her if you want to. Who am I to tell her?

She's your woman.

No she isn't.

O come on, cut out the crap. Warn her or I'll end up doing something which I will regret later.

You warn her, boy.

I'm not your boy so don't start that boy stuff with me. I may have been your boy a long long time ago in another life but not this.

Go and do what you want, leave me out of it.

And he did precisely that. Went up to Melissa's room and banged on the door, *come on out dog woman.*

What do you want? I heard her respond, almost as if she was talking to a child. The door opened. *Come on in.*

You come on out, he snapped. *I have something to say to you and I want everyone to hear. Come on out.*

There was a scuffle. *Don't you dare touch me, wait, what are you doing? Stop that.*

He dragged her out of her room and pushed her down the staircase. She stumbled out. *Now I'm telling you here in front of your man, you come into my home again and meddle with my dog and you've had it, you hear me? You've had it good and proper.*

I didn't meddle with your dog. I was just keeping him company. You chained him up and he was suffering.

Suffering? My big fat toe. There's nothing wrong with tying dogs up. Dogs should know who's the boss. Dogs should know their place. Dogs should …

Don't give me your stupid wisdom. Saying this, she gave him one hell of a punch that sent him sprawling over a table. *Come on, come on,* she taunted him.

He gathered himself up and walked out without turning back.

An hour later he came in with the cops. They took her off to the station and God only knows what happened there but she returned a couple of hours after that and went up to her room. The next day Xavier turned up again. *Banjo has disappeared. Gone. Where's the dog woman.*

Haven't a clue.

As if you'd tell me even if you knew.

Then why did you ask me?

He charged up and found a lock on the door. *The bird has fled the coop. I'm going to catch her and when I do I'll have her sent back to her own country on a one way ticket.*

As soon as he left, she returned. Sat at a table and ordered a beer.

So, where have you been? I wanted to know.

Out for a real good walk along the beach.

Did you take Banjo with you?

No.

Then where's Banjo?

How would I know? Ask Banjo's boss.

Well Banjo's boss was here and he was hopping mad because he said you had carried the dog away.

Stupid man.

For the next few days, there were no signs of Xavier. I rang him up. *Did you find your dog?*

Yes. He was here exactly where I had left him when I got back from Clementine. The damned animal keeps appearing and disappearing.

I suppose he keeps slinking off.

How can he slink off? He's tied up. How can a dog untie himself and walk off and then come back and tie himself up again?

Why don't YOU keep a watch on him?

You think I've nothing better to do?

Then pay someone to do it Xavier if you don't care.

You are Mr Money Bags. You do it. And he hung up on me.

I was pretty sure that Melissa was up to some tricks but I wasn't going to interfere. And then, surprise of surprises,

Xavier went off to sea. Alfred Mendez the owner of the place, informed me. He said Xavier had shifted out and left the dog with a friend. *I'll send the security deposit back to you.*

Melissa went bonkers trying to track Banjo down in Colva, up and down streets and by lanes, put up pictures of the animal and even went off and rustled up the help of an animal rights group who turned up at Clementine and held a pow wow around one of the tables. Part of their plan was to try and track down Xavier's friends and find out who had Banjo. One of them planted a garbled report about a stolen dog in the local newspapers.

But still no news of Banjo.

Melissa retreated to her room and the next thing I knew was that she had become so limp and lifeless that we thought she was going to pop off. Got the doctor in. *Nothing seems to be wrong with her. BP a bit low but that's all. We'll run some tests and see.*

So tests were run and nothing showed up. The doctor decided that it was stress and sedated her. That knocked Melissa out and sent her floating off into neverland.

As for me, I kept myself busy running the place. Peggy was a good distraction, quite a sense of humour and relaxing to be with. When things started warming up, Chrissie arrived on the scene and put an end to a potential cracker. It all happened so quickly that I didn't know how to respond. Of course, it was quite tempting to let myself in for a toss around with Peggy. It would definitely have taken my mind off all this Banjo business and the bitter taste that Xavier had left in my mouth. But it wasn't to be, not at that moment at least ... but there'd be time for it, later. Chrissie had arrived and I had to tend to her.

She was half her size, talked unusually softly and often stopped dead in the middle of her sentence and forgot what she was talking about. There was still no news of Luke and she hadn't heard from Arnie. Something in the stars I think, something that made life pretty uncertain for us.

I insisted that she stay for a few days and be fussed over. *What if he returns or tries to get in touch with me? How will I know?* She responded.

I think you should let me take care of you for a while Chrissie, you have no one else.

That's why I'm here, she whispered and dropped her face in her hands and cried like a child. *I'll have to go back and get some clothes and stuff.*

I'll drive you there and back. Just take it easy.

Later that day we were back at Clementine and I put her in the special room which had a view of the beach and the sea. It wasn't a great view but quite refreshing. *Now you don't start pottering around Chrissie, take it easy. Sleep, unwind. Ring the bell if you want anything and pick up the phone if you want me.*

Where's that Melissa woman? She asked out of the blue.

Right here. At Clementine. Been here all this while.

And Xavier? How is he?

At sea. Chaos on that front. We'll talk about that later.

Are you sure I'm not spoiling anything for you Sabby? You don't have to be so generous ... I'll stay a few a days and leave. I'm not destitute you know ... just that I'm so alone and vulnerable.

Come on Chrissie, cut out the explanations. Relax. Take one moment at a time. Everything will pan out. I kissed her on the forehead.

You're a dear, she said, settling into an armchair and closing her eyes. *And you've changed. For the better I think. There's a calmness in you that's reassuring.*

I'm surprised you're saying this considering how much I've gone through since we last met. We'll talk when you are feeling a little more adjusted.

We can talk now if you want.

No, later Chrissie. Have to get back to work and sort out a whole lot of things.

This Melissa woman, what does she do with herself all day?

When she was well, she'd be all over Colva.

You mean she's ill?

Yes, stress or something like that.

Crazy woman.

Hmmm. Now you rest a bit. I got to get back to work.

I left her huddled in an armchair, eyes half closed, breathing softly.

So now I had two unwell women on my hands. I had to figure out a way of getting them both on their feet again. And that damned dog Banjo … where the hell was he?

The days went by uncomfortably with the weather getting increasingly humid; frequent power cuts and water cuts made things worse. I really felt like pushing off to some place beautiful, calm, cool and unchallenging. I was sick of the smallness of Colva and Goa and everything that I had been living with. Probably that's why Luke left everything behind and walked away. Or did he? On the other hand, he may have found a more interesting life with more interesting people in a more interesting place where he could be himself. But he just vanished into the blue, leaving her unsure of whether he was dead or alive. Not that Xavier is any better. He's my son, sure, but he's definitely mental. And 'different' in his tastes. I have no problem with him being 'different' in his tastes but bloody hell he shouldn't be stuffing it in everyone's face. Xavier says that I am homophobic. No sir, I'm not homophobic. Of course a little uncomfortable with his sort of tastes but then I have a right to be. To choose to like or dislike something. What's wrong with that? What's wrong with a father being worried when he finds his son living a dangerous life … with AIDS and all that. What am I going on about? He has made a choice, it's his choice and I should make my choice.

And my choice so far has been doing what I'm doing. But am I really enjoying it? Am I? I just said, I'm tired of this small life. The same faces day in and day out, the same routine, the same damned sea, the same smell of the salt air, the same longing for something different, to be somewhere different and not having the courage to do anything about it. Damn. Damn.

Take it easy Sabby. Hold on by your back teeth, the hurdy-gurdy is turning. Don't let go or you'll plunge down and hit the ground with an almighty thud. Take a deep breath. Wait for the tide to turn and take you back to the shore, float, float along with the current. There's no option but to float. And the lighter you are, the better you float.

Talking to myself is my way of giving myself a pep talk.

Then finally a quietness came and I started feeling a little less restless. It was as if a pall of gloom had lifted like a rain cloud and moved away. Chrissie surfaced and started pottering around the place and ended up visiting Melissa and the two got talking and spending time together. She was good for Melissa and often sat by her bedside and listened to her babbling away in her own language. She even sang a few songs for her. Chrissie has a good voice and when she's in the mood she can really sound quite elevating. Sometimes sitting down there at the counter I'd hear her voice lofting gently over all the chaos, like an angel on its way to performing a miracle.

One late evening when the air was filled with the grating sound of the sea and heavy with mosquitoes and Peggy was busy making guests gooey with her crooning, Banjo returned. He sat there on the street outside the entrance as if waiting to be asked to come in. All skin and bones and large festering wounds on his flanks and thighs. When Atul saw him he started crying and rushed towards him. Afraid, Banjo turned and bolted and the two went streaking down to the square and on to the beach. Stray dogs followed them, barking hysterically.

Quite a while later they returned. Atul had made a leash out of a length of rope and hauled him in. He was taken up on to the terrace to his makeshift kennel, bathed in antiseptic water and fed. The next day, the vet took over and started the slow but sure process of healing. His arrival got Melissa out of her stupor and she took over from the vet. Of course she was far from her original self and could hardly focus on anything, often falling asleep at the drop of a hat.

She sometimes plucked up the courage to take him for a walk but was reluctant to go alone so she'd ask Atul to go along. A few hesitant sorties later she started moving around by herself … and in the days to come she became a little more communicative.

I found a note on my desk one evening. *There was nothing between us, please. I need to tell you something. When? M*

Tonight, I replied and returned the note to her.

I left the apartment door unlatched and she slipped in late night, closing the door after her. *Can I make us some coffee?*

Sure.

Later, settling down on the couch with her legs stretched out, *it wasn't just Banjo going away that messed me up. Also because of us.*

Us?

Yes, US. You and me. What happened between us. What I did to you and what you did to me.

Okay we did something, maybe we'll do it again. But it happened. It will happen. We are grown-ups Melissa. Unattached. These things happen. It's not the end of the world. Besides, I'm sure you've done it before with people you've hardly known.

Wait a minute, wait a minute. You are saying too much all together here, too much. As if you know everything. As if I agree with you. You are a man and I can't expect anything else from you.

Hold it, hold it. Let me start again. All I'm saying is we did something here and maybe we'll do it again. It will happen ...

Yes Sabby, we did something here but it's not going to happen again. You needed it and I needed it and we did it. But we aren't doing it again. Never. Why? Because you used me like a thing. I haven't meant anything to you other than something you can stick your thing into. No feeling came from you, nothing at all.

You must realise what I've been through Melissa.

What have you been through?

My marriage, my crazy wife, my crazy son.

So everyone is crazy but you. You are a real man Sabby, a real man, hiding behind your problems. We all have problems Sabby ...

What's the point you are making here?

There was only sex here, body to body. No feeling, mind to mind, heart to heart, spirit to spirit.

Yes. Sure. I agree. And as I just said we're grown-ups.

I am a grown-up Sabby, not you. You are a lost little boy. Maybe that's what attracted me to you. To turn the boy into a man. I felt that for once I had the chance to make someone into something. To be the teacher. I hope you understand what I am saying. Do you?

Yes, I think so.

So, you took what you wanted, had your fill and left it at that, coming back only when you needed to have me. Did you even for a moment think about what I needed? No, obviously not or you would have something to say now. And the other point–you used the word 'unattached'. Is marriage the only attachment? Is it? There isn't any such thing as 'commitment'? Tears filled her eyes. *And the last thing you said–I've done this before. You said it like as if you*

KNOW that, as if I go sleeping around the place making men stick their things into me. You Indians think all white women are an easy lay. Right?

For us ... I think you are going over the top Melissa. I didn't say that and I don't think that.

But you FEEL it.

No I don't.

Then why did you use me?

You are talking as if everything is over and that there's no way forward ...

Don't give me that bullshit. WAY FORWARD? YOUR WOMAN IS HERE. WAITING TO TAKE CHARGE. And you're talking about a way forward with me? Us?

What woman? Who woman?

Oh come on, don't give me that one. I live in the real world Sabby.

And I? Where the hell do you think I live?

In a bubble. A little soap bubble. Just as Xavier said. Wait till it suddenly bursts and see what will happen.

I wasn't going to take any more rubbish from her. She wanted to have it off with me, she turned me on, she USED me when she needed me. Now when Chrissie had arrived she was insecure and feeling left out. WOMEN. I should have run away from all this when the thought crossed my mind. Ha, as if I would have.

What do you want from me Melissa?

Nothing.

Then what's all this in aid of?

In AID OF? You don't know the REAL ME. You don't know me. You don't know that I have been only in abusive relationships. Starting from, O God, my grandfather. I've always been a THING.

Because you come on that way.

Damn you for saying that. Can't you THINK before you talk?

You're saying whatever comes into your head.

Okay, I'll keep my mouth shut. Speak.

I thought something could happen between us. I thought maybe we could …

I didn't let her finish her sentence. I didn't want her to finish her sentence. The conversation was rushing along to a place that I didn't want to visit. I just wanted to get on with my life and live it and not keep getting caught up in glitches. *Listen Melissa, I think we should call it day. I mean, it's late and we'll talk again. I am here and you are here …*

Now it was her turn to stop me from finishing my sentence. She came over and kissed me deep. *I want you Sabby. Just you, nobody else. Can I have you? Look at me Sabby, I'm talking to you. Can I have you?*

Since I couldn't answer her question I let her do whatever she chose to do with me. Then she made herself another coffee and sipped it in silence. I slipped into sleep and when I opened my eyes at four in the morning, she had left, leaving the door wide open. I shut it and throwing open the window stared out at the deserted square, the sound of the sea rising and falling like the snoring of an old man. The humid air streamed into the apartment and the smell of salt and weeds filled my lungs. *I can't go on like this, I really can't go on like this,* I told myself. *I have to settle my accounts, clear the deck, get on with my life in a peaceful way, not like this, no good this way. Always this sense of guilt, this sense of unfeeling, this sense of not wanting to commit. Commitment? What is commitment but a giving up of searching and questioning. This is all a joke. To the world outside me, I'm this settled fellow who has a good business … okay a crazy son and a crazy wife … who doesn't have something crazy tucked away in his closet? But they don't know ME.*

The smell pouring in from the sea started changing. It

became far cleaner, more purified, a fragrance from some far away land. The roar of the waves had also quietened. Down at the square, a gang of dogs had gathered, sniffing at each other, then as if as one they trotted off towards the beach.

There was someone at the door. I went out into the hall and stopping at the door, asked *who is there?*

Me. It was Melissa. I opened the door. She fell into my arms. *I couldn't sleep.* We walked back to the window and looked out at the sea crawling up the sand. *I'm sorry Sabby. I didn't want to hurt you. But you see I have feelings too. Not just for dogs.*

You don't come across that way.

How do I come across?

Tough, independent.

That's the way I have survived.

Was that true?

What?

About your grandfather?

Yes. He was my first. A hard man. But I learnt a lot from him. He taught me how to survive … to take life on and survive, never give up. Sabby?

Yes?

Are you going to marry Chrissie?

5 OTHER NESTS

The Linden Tree Nearby

When Sabby didn't answer my question *are you going to marry Chrissie*, I said to myself, *stupid woman, of all the guys you've met and thought about, you go and choose this fellow and he belongs to someone else. Now you have to admit you've made a mistake and un-choose him and get the hell out of the place … and don't stupidly make this mistake again. You are strong, you are wise … what happened here?*

I felt a little foolish so I kept to myself and avoided them. It was irritating the way Sabby would all the time make it a point to ask me how I'm feeling and be extra kind to me. He was pitying me for sure, feeling sorry. Also feeling guilty. And feeling a little scared in case I caused a scene. Now I wasn't going to tell the guy, *don't worry I won't cause a scene.* I wanted him to suffer a bit. I wanted to play with him as a cat plays with a mouse. Let him run and think he's free then trap him with my paw and then when he thinks he's going to be eaten up, set him free again. And do it over and over again until he's all messed up. But I stopped myself from doing that.

To be honest, the only thing that kept me in Clementine was Banjo. I was really attached to him. I felt as if I understood his soul. Animals have a soul. I believe that. And they treat their soul better than we humans do. We mess up our soul, scar it, tear it, drag it through the gutter, don't give it a chance to reach out to the stars. So what does the soul do? It shrinks into a stone and lies there inside us. Useless. The more you care for your soul and respect it and listen to it, the more it helps you. Animals, mainly dogs, have beautiful souls, real souls, souls that are always reaching out. We don't realise how much they help us.

When I was a girl of twelve living with Grandpa and Grandma I had a dog for a friend. Boz. A big fellow, all grey, with a white patch around one eye and a black patch around the other. He was a dog from the village. Nobody owned him but they said that he was once Herr Ludin's watchdog. Whenever they mentioned the master's name they said it softly as if they didn't want him to hear because they were frightened of him, even though he was already dead and gone. There was a story that late one evening a butcher cursed one of his customers, *just as mean as Herr Ludin.* And would you believe it? There was the dead man standing before him. The shock struck the man dumb for three months. When he got his voice back, he told his story. But that wasn't all. There were other stories too. More than a dozen of them. And so, people of the village learnt to speak softly every time they mentioned his name … and no one dared use it in a curse. When his master's estate was sold, they set Boz free and he'd spend his time roaming around in the nearby forest. Whenever he could not hunt food for himself he'd go from house to house begging for scraps. People gave him food because they were scared that if they didn't Herr Ludin would curse them. Boz rarely came to our house because it was set apart from the village and Grandpa had shooed him away a few times.

One day when Grandpa was asleep and Grandma was out gathering wild flowers, Boz turned up for food. He didn't come right up to the house but sat down under the Linden tree and watched me from there. I was a little scared of him because he looked so fierce with one black eye patch and one white eye patch and no smile on his face. Only looking and looking at me. So I went inside and had a good look at him from between the window curtains. And he knew I was there. The Linden tree was in flower and the wind blew some petals down on him. And I kept on looking and looking. All of a sudden I was not frightened anymore because I saw something which made me feel good. Really good. Everything was glowing. Even Boz's grey coat … as if there were little spots of light at the end of each hair. I quickly picked some bread and a piece of roast meat and went out to him. He stood up when I neared and wagged the tip of his tail gently.

He was such a dignified eater. He carefully ate morsel by morsel whilst I sat down beside him on a rock and ran my fingers through his thick soft coat. When he had finished he licked his mouth with his big pink tongue and then licked my hand.

Then I heard Grandpa shout, *get away from him, go on, get away from him. You'll get rabies or some dog sickness that will kill you. That's a dangerous dog, an evil dog, get away from him.*

It was such a special moment that I wasn't going to get up. *But I love him.*

Don't be foolish child, get away from him, I'm going to shoot, get away from him. He raised his catapult … I knew he had a lead ball in the leather piece and it would hurt so I got up and ran. A moment later I heard a thud and a squeal of pain and turned to see Boz limping away into the tall grass at the edge of the forest. *Come on inside. Come on child.*

I obeyed him. He was a kind man, Grandpa, at least I thought so then.

As the days passed, I'd often sit outside and wait for Boz to appear but he didn't. I felt he was somewhere out there watching me with his dark mysterious eyes, smiling at me as he did that day under the Linden tree. Seasons changed but not my need to see him again. Twice in the village when I had gone marketing with Grandma I thought I had seen him watching me from behind a parked car but didn't get a proper look at him. Who knows? It may have been him, it may not have. A lonely girl's imagination runs wild. Mine was everywhere. I saw him everywhere. Once I even saw him standing at my bedroom door, looking in at me.

Then one day I went with Grandma to gather wild flowers. We walked along the edge of the forest through the tall grass that was soft and feathery, gathering flowers growing between. I don't know what got into me but I decided to start walking towards the line of trees. When I reached them I felt a comforting warmth wrap gently around me and moved deeper. The fragrance of bark and roots and earth and flowering plants filled my little lungs until they were like the green lungs of the forest. The air was damp and moved about me ever so gently, parting and letting me pass through, then resting on my small shoulders, light like the wings of an angel.

I suddenly discovered that there were trees all around me. I was confused, looking around for a way out so that I could reach the grassy edge of the forest where Grandma gathered flowers. But there was no sign of a way out or even sight of the sunlit field. Light streamed down on me through the high branches of the trees. Then in the half light I saw him–Boz. He sat there among the roots of an old tree, watching me. I stood there wondering if it was my imagination or whether he was really there. Picking up courage I walked over to him. I reached out and he licked my hand and I sat down among the roots, near him. It felt so safe and secure. I didn't miss Grandpa and Grandma. I had Boz and that was enough.

Voices, I heard voices and there were people, many of them coming my way and calling my name. I wanted to hide so that they wouldn't be able to see me so I stood up and tried to hide behind the trunk of the tree. Too late, someone saw me and they came for me. When Boz tried to get away they spotted him and ran him down till he was tired and they beat him to death with sticks.

Grandpa was so angry with me that he locked me in my room and only opened the door to allow Grandma to bring in food. Then one night, he came in and sat down beside me, telling me that I shouldn't have gone into the forest and if they hadn't found me in time Boz would surely have harmed me, *my precious little one.* He gently trailed his fingers over my body under the soft quilt. I didn't mind it at first but then when he went on I started feeling uncomfortable and moved his hand away. He left but didn't give up. Night after night he returned to my bedside, making me feel strange sensations, frightening me.

Boz's passing really troubled me and I missed him terribly. More so because of what was happening to me at my grandparents' home. I began to feel as if I was a stranger there. It wasn't my home even though they were my grandparents. It was THEIR home. They were just saving me from my mama and dada's neglect. Since I was far too small to run away I decided to keep myself busy with *other* friends not humans. There were no stray dogs there like we find on Indian streets so the only choice I had was other people's dogs. And it was difficult making friends with other people's pets because their masters and mistresses were so possessive. Apart from that the people of the village considered my grandpa and grandma to be two strange old people. Except Leonie Eirich, a girl about my age. Everyone called her Le. We made friends one day at the market. Quite easily we started a conversation. Actually she started it, *I don't see that devilish dog around anymore.* I didn't know that she was talking to me until she repeated herself. *My father calls him Garmr. You, I'm talking to you.*

Me? I asked.

Yes, you. I said I don't see that devilish dog around anymore.

You mean Boz? He's dead.

Dead. Hmmm. Your favourite dog I've heard. You know who Garmr is? He is the guard dog at the gates of Hell. So in the day time he was Boz your favourite dog and at night he was Garmr guarding the gates of Hell. You scared?

No.

I was just joking. I'm Leonie, you can call me Le.

I'm Melissa.

I don't mind, we can be friends even though you are smaller than me.

That's how it all started. Le would sometimes come visiting. She wouldn't come in but stand under the Linden tree and call out to me and I'd join her and we'd go off gathering wild flowers just outside the fence of our garden. Sometimes she'd come in and we'd go around counting bird's nests tucked in the thicket of the hedge. We played other games too but the one I liked the best was when Le made up a story and we'd become characters in it. She was a good storyteller and enjoyed telling stories. *My mama learnt to tell stories from her mama and her mama from her mama. Same with my dada. But his stories are scary ones, he just can't be happy. Ever since he lost the use of one leg in an accident, he doesn't go out and work anymore. Reads books, lots of them. And all about long ago. We don't like him telling us stories but he doesn't care, tells them anyway.*

I've never seen your dada. Why do you call him dada?

He has some story about that too. He's stuck in his stories and doesn't like going out, sits among books all day. Up in the attic.

There are books and books and books. And he won't let anyone go up there … only sometimes when he brings back an old book from the library and wants us to look at the pictures in it. 'See here,' he says, 'here is what Frija looks like,' or 'Tiwaz' or 'Wotan.' Last week he had a really old book and it had a picture of the Goddess Hel and her terrible dog Garmr at the gates of Hell …

You're scaring me. I could feel the hair on the back of my neck standing up. *The attic must be a really spooky place.*

Yes but my mama makes up for it with her stories. And she tells them to me quietly when we are alone together … which is often because Bammy is always out.

Bammy? Who is that?

My big brother stupid.

How did he get a name like that?

The full name is Bamard. It means brave as a bear. Dada gave him that name. He says that a name makes a person. So give a person a name and it will enter his heart and his spirit and he will become that way.

So your father wants him to become brave as a bear?

I suppose so.

And your name? What does it mean?

Lioness.

Hmm. Your brother is a bear and you are a lioness. I wonder what I am.

Oh I already know. Dada found out and told me. You've got a Greek name it means honey bee. He says that long ago in Greece there was a nymph named Melissa, she was a sort of nurse who took care of one of the gods when he was a baby. Instead of giving him milk, she fed him honey. Bees carried the honey straight to his mouth. After that all the nymphs who took care of the baby God were called Melissa.

Na, that's a fairy tale.

We are all fairy tales, that's what mama says. Someone somewhere is telling a story and making new people all the time.

So you and I are made by different people?

Sometimes different, sometimes the same.

How do we know when we are made by the same person?

Best friends are made by the same person.

Can the same person also make animals and people?

Maybe.

In that case Boz and I have been made by the same person.

You and your Boz.

One night when Grandpa left my room, I lay there feeling very lonely and strange. I got out of bed and quietly went out into the hall. Through the windows all around I could see that the light outside was blue. When I opened the front door blue light flowed into the house. The Linden tree was glowing and beneath it stood Leonie with Boz beside her. Something stopped me from walking out and joining them so I sat down on the doorstep and looked at them. Drowsy I fell asleep … and when I opened my eyes, they had just turned away from me and were walking towards the forest. I knew that I would never see Leonie again.

News spread quickly the next day that Leonie had disappeared. Search parties went into the forest but returned empty handed. When the police reached a dead-end, they decided to take Egon Eirich and his son Bamard for questioning. Something, we don't know what, they said that made the police even more suspicious so they started searching the house, particularly the attic and Bamard's room. They found all sorts of feminine underclothes in her brother's closet and an old pair of Leonie's shoes filled with tiny pebbles in the attic, under Egon's bed. Neither of them could suitably explain the findings. So back they were taken to the police station for questioning. Angelika was left alone at home and spent a whole week crying and calling out to Leonie. Neighbours did their best to pretend that they hadn't heard her and never offered to help. After the first week, she lost her voice and fell silent. Two weeks later Egon and Bamard were let out but the case continued … so did the gossip. They found a part of her body in the forest a few months later. She had obviously met with a violent end.

Boz never visited me again but the Linden tree burst into flower that spring with such abandon that its branches seemed weighed down. Swarms of bees hummed around the flowers and birds flitted in and out of its thicket. A cuckoo took up residence one day and sent its clear call out into the clear air. I heard it float towards the village, then a wind rose and blew it back and it crossed over our farm and off towards the forest where it got tangled in the trees. Then another and another rose until the day was flooded with the call of the cuckoo.

Even Grandpa who seldom talked about birds and animals was struck by the cuckoo call and stood out in the garden looking at the Linden tree. Grandma joined him and after a long silence said, *that's the spirit of the Linden tree singing.*

What do you mean by that? He turned and looked at her, narrowing his eyes.

The cuckoo is the spirit of the Linden tree.

She had hardly finished her sentence when the bird flew out from amongst the flower laden branches. *There goes the Linden spirit,* he laughed.

Yes, there goes the Linden spirit, she repeated. Out into the world to spread peace and joy. It's spring. A time of birth. A time of new hopes …

You're a romantic, woman, a romantic. He went into the house. She didn't follow him but stood out there in the garden, me standing beside her. I thought of Boz. I thought of Leonie. I thought of the deep dark forest ... that was the day menstrual blood oozed from my body for the first time.

I hadn't learnt very much from the village school because most of the time Grandma found excuses why I shouldn't go to school and at other times, I found them. I didn't make friends because most of the time I was an outsider. Grandpa never let up on his nightly visits until the time came when I had got so used to him that I even missed him on the nights that he chose to sleep instead. I knew he had changed me from the inside so deeply and weirdly that as time passed I could hardly relate to people my own age and was attracted to people far older than me, like a tiny piece of iron to a magnet. Was I constantly looking for someone who was like Grandpa? I am sure that was it. I constantly needed to be with someone who was in command and in control, someone who in one way actually depended on me and in another way controlled me because he was older, more experienced and I could nestle into him.

Wandering Years

Drifting for a while after Father died in an asylum and Mother married again and gave me half his legacy, I became really afraid that someone was going to take it all away from me. So what did I do? I put it all away safely in a bank account that was a long term saving one and lived a meagre life, living in dormitories, shared apartments, in the shadows of city life, roaming from place to place, not knowing where I wanted to settle or what I wanted to do with my life. The border didn't stop, I always found a way of getting over to the other side and back ... one city to another ... Dresden and Wurzburg with their bombed out memories of war, Leipzig on the crossing of the ancient trade routes of Via Regia and Via Imperii, where nothing was ancient anymore, Erfurt with its old buildings and parks where people seemed to belong to another planet, Nuremberg, ah the misunderstood Nuremberg with its trials of war criminals … and I went on, drifting–sometimes with a companion and other times alone. Young fellows my own age bored me, desperately fumbling to get me into bed, others sang songs and composed poems, painted pictures, stole and lied … others were too serious for my liking, leaving me feeling an idiot. Women caught my fancy for a while–older women and sometimes much younger women who needed to be initiated. Yes, I got into the woman-woman thing but it made me feel like a misfit. That wasn't my scene so I said *damn, I want to do something that will help me feel good.* I always loved dancing so when I met the choreographer Peter Ullrich at a freak party I dug my claws deep into his amazing body. Fifty-five and flowing with life Peter had more than a dozen dancers who hung around him. All women around twenty who clung to every word he uttered. He was a radical spirit who spent his time experimenting with brief intense creations that moved from the perfect stillness of straight lines to the wild explosive energy of scattered curves. He leapt out of the shadow of Pina Bausch and rejected her work, presenting his own versions of Stravinky's *The Rites of Spring* and Brecht's *The Seven Deadly Sins.* His dancing women adored him more for it.

Peter came to me at the party as if he had sensed that I was in heat and we spent the next week together doing unimaginable things with each other. But before I could get him to agree to take me on and point my nose in the right direction so I could be a dancer, he left hurriedly, as if he was about to miss his train. But during that week I got to meet Joachim Muller, a Munich musician, who was older than Peter and even more of a rebel. He was busy at that time creating abstract music for the mysterious film maker Hans Speeger who was obsessed with India. Every three months he'd travel to some part of the country and return with dark images which he'd fiddle around with, overlay them with Joachim's tracks and produce short films then invite people for a viewing. The crazy composer took me along to three film experiences where we spent our time dropping stuff and losing ourselves in the darkness of another country.

When we were at the third viewing Hans made a pass at me and I responded. We saw each other a few times after that and he convinced me to travel to India with him. I hated the country–it confused me with its filth, confusion and primitive celebration of hundreds of gods and goddesses. I just couldn't understand why people should spend so much money and energy on worship of imaginary divinity. After a couple of weeks of experiencing the confusion I fled and went straight back to my old ways, obsessed with becoming a dancer. Time was running out for me and I got the terrible feeling that my body had lost its specialness. And once that feeling filled me I couldn't love my body the same way as before.

I wished I would be able to do a course, even a short course, at some academy or the other. Maybe someplace like the one Peter told me about, named after the place where Freyja, the goddess of beauty and love gathered her chosen dead people together and gave them a great time, you know–letting them do whatever they want to with her, offering them all the pleasures of life. So when they chose that name for the academy they hoped it would be a place where various forms of art got together as one.

That's where Peter's creativity was forged and set free. I wanted to go through the experience too. I really wanted to become myself, have an identity, go out and BE. But things don't happen that way in life. Just when you think you have a choice and are about to make it, the Universe steps in with a bang and throws you off your feet or gently turns your head in another direction, sometimes even throws a new person into your life.

Hans died suddenly in Delhi when he was on a trip to India. Joachim Muller brought the news, sharing the details with a solemn face. *Gone. We've lost Hans. Died on assignment.*

What assignment? I thought he never worked for anyone. Just peddled dope.

No, he had just been given a special assignment. To make a small film on unusual Germans living in the country. He shot more than he should have and got himself into trouble.

What do you mean?

You know what a freak Hans was. You saw the films the fellow made. Must have ended up meddling in someone's private life.

How did he die?

His body was found hanging down the side of an apartment block. It certainly wasn't suicide. It was murder. Imagine going all that way to die with no friends around you.

Is his body going to be sent back?

I'm going to cremate him there. What about you?

What do you mean by 'what about you'?

Will you come with me?

I don't know why I agreed. The very thought of going to India frightened me at that time. My earlier trip had been horrible and left me with nightmares which I couldn't get rid of for quite some time. The sickeningly rich and the pathetic poor rubbing shoulders shocked me. India was supposed to be a non-violent country but yet human beings were treated so badly and animals even worse. And the treatment of foreigners? I don't want to start talking about that. Every white skinned person was seen, and still is, as a walking piggy bank, waiting to be cracked open. I was washed over by a flood of relief when I went back to familiar shores. So then why did I readily agree? I don't know. There's a lot that I've done in my life that I cannot explain. So let's leave it at that.

Joachim and I landed in Delhi and were instantly thrown into the oceanic chaos of India. From the airport to the hotel stuck in a seedy part of the city, we drove through a desperate world crowded with high living and low living, mansions, gardens and buses belching vast swirls of black smoke. We settled for separate rooms which could be reached by climbing a dingy staircase that smelled of stale semen. It was Hans' last lodgings on earth. He had occupied the room on the roof.

That night I went up the last flight of stairs and reached the roof. The room was occupied by an Indian couple who sat out in the open, kissing and fondling. I tried not to notice them but when I did I found the guy was a huge dark skinned fellow who was more than twice the size of the woman who looked like she was only a little more than a girl. He reached over and lifted her out of her chair and slammed her down on his lap. She squeaked and then sighed. I tried not to listen and mind my own business and walked along the length of the roof which was strewn with broken chairs, a couple of toilet bowls, an old mattress and a lot else. Down below, a bizarre network of shops with blazing lights lined the narrow streets and cycle rickshaws pedalled their way between crowds of jostling people hurriedly going somewhere or the other. How and why did Hans choose that place? How did he survive the noise and confusion? What did he eat? Did he entertain Indian girls?

Mingled with the stench of smoke and poor living, was the fragrance of kebabs and curries, whirling and twirling upwards like angels who had nowhere to go. Something scared me about all that. I was overwhelmed by the loud music and strange languages that filled the air and began to feel nauseous. I turned away from the low wall and headed past the couple towards the descending stair. She was still sighing and squeaking. Back in my room I threw myself across my bed and slept, leaving the light on. I didn't want to wake up in the middle of the night in the dark with strange insects and feral creatures all around me.

The morning started at 5:00 am with the whole world around me coming alive–clanging and barking and shouting. I knocked on Joachim's door and when he opened it I realised that there was a woman in his bed. *So early eh? Are you crazy?* He looked like he could have hit me straight in the face but he didn't and instead slammed the door in my face and left me standing there staring at the number on the peeling woodwork in front of me. I walked down and into the streets searching for a tea shop. Found one easily and sat on a rickety stool and sipped hot sweet and milky tea from a cracked cup. After three teas, I was ready to face the world. That included the police station, the morgue, the embassy and everything else.

The police station was far easier to manage than we thought, the visit to the morgue made me piss involuntarily, the embassy was an unreal experience. What made it worse was the young German officer who kept asking me if I was alright. I finally told him in choice German only he would understand. *All's well, I've only rained in my pants.*

It was a relief when we finally got his ashes out of the electric crematorium and carried them away in two small clay bowls–one to be packed and taken back to Germany and the other to be poured into the Jamuna, one of India's sacred rivers. When I poured his remains into the water I whispered quietly to him, *I hope you don't mind the dirty water but they say it's sacred. And you always liked dark humour. Goodbye Hans.*

Joachim and I decided to part ways. I let him carry away the other clay bowl. After all he had known Hans better than me. As for me, I wasn't ready to go flying back to Germany, the counter shock would be too much for me. I wanted to go away and hide somewhere. Somewhere quiet. Somewhere undemanding. Up into the mountains? I wasn't sure.

In the days when I was trying to decide, I bumped into a small round guy with scraggly long hair and a beard that nearly reached his navel. *Greetings, many namastes and lots of shanti.* Looked distinctly Indian. Turned out to be Guyanese when we got talking and I had him say a bit about himself. A poet, so he said. Settled in Sweden. Married to a shrink. And much more. All in just twenty minutes maybe. And there was more to come in the hours that followed. He had come to India in search of his roots. *My ancestors were bricklayers in Benares. They were common folk, really common.*

So they belonged to Benaras? And where's that?

Those were two questions. Which one should I answer first?

The first.

They were from Benaras and went to Guyana as indentured labour.

So they had no one to lay bricks in Guyana? Come on, tell me another one.

He deflected my question. *Which part of Germany do you come from?*

I had no bloody inclination to talk about Germany. I was in India. *Where's Benares? Are there mountains there?*

He laughed and stroked his beard gently, *no mountains there but sacred temples and the holy river Ganges. The Hindus and Jains believe that it is the most precious of their seven sacred cities. If you die there you are sure to attain salvation. It's an ancient city. I'd be happy to take you there.*

Fast worker. Take me there, ha. *You mean take me to my salvation? There's no such state as salvation. It's our lot to live and die. What we do between the first cry and the last is entirely our business, your business and my business and each person's business, each person who lives on this damned planet. And do we get it right? Never. It's all trial and error. You try and you hit or you try and you don't hit. For example you are trying and not hitting, not as yet at least.*

It all boils down to Karma.

Bull crap, absolute bull crap. Looks like you're on a spiritual trip to mystic India. The India that you're looking for is not out there, it's in your head. It is all about what you WANT to see or LIKE to see, what you WANT to believe or LIKE to believe. I had no idea until then that I had even been thinking about all that. But there it was floating around in my head and when the time came, it all just came out. Like that worm that swims around in the bloodstream and pops part of its body out through a wound when it is in water, lays its eggs in the water and swims back down the red sticky river.

He had stopped stroking his beard in that pseudo-wise way and seemed to be leaning back in his chair, behaving as if I was about to attack him and he was getting ready to protect himself. *How do you answer for all the millions and millions of people in this country who share the same beliefs and go to the same sacred places? Surely there's something in all of this apart from personal will and personal desire. Surely there's something beyond.*

For you maybe, not for me. I was getting a bit irritated.

He took refuge behind his age. *I'm fit to be your father and I'm amazed how you can speak with such authority to me.*

No, you aren't fit to be my father. You are old enough to be my father.

Okay, okay, I get your point. I am old enough to be your father.

So I can't argue with you? Call yourself a poet? What's your name anyway?

Oh ho, someone's getting angry. Okay, if you want to know my name its Troy. Troy Tominto.

That's the name you were given when you were born?

Yes.

A Christian?

You must be a Christian too. Probably from Germany. And all this you are spouting is a reaction to a formal patriarchal society.

Your wife has trained you well. Yes, you are right, I am German. But I'm not Christian any more than you are. I'm Melissa.

How do you talk such relaxed English?

I learnt it well because I like the language. There is never an end to its many sides.

In school? In college?

No. I got myself special tuition. From a real English gentleman who was old enough to be my grandfather. Actually I found him very interesting. The English tuition was only an excuse.

You prefer oldies. Hmmm, how about me?

I didn't answer him, finished my coffee and asked for my bill.

You'll be in the country long? What brought you here?

You ask too many questions. And that too not one at a time.

Come on, stop sparring with me. You do the same. Can I see you again? He handed me a slip of paper. *That's where I'm staying.*

The man made me feel very uneasy. Strange in the stomach. I had the sickening feeling that I was going to see him again. It was his damned mouth that got to me. Couldn't see much of it because of all that hair around it. But whatever I saw, it disturbed me. The lips were fleshy and sensual and an almost canine tongue constantly flicked its tip over them. Gave me goose bumps.

In the Land of the Cowherd

Troy Tominto tracked me down to where I was staying and coaxed me into travelling with him to places around Delhi. We went to Agra to see the Taj. Magnificent shrine no doubt but what a waste. So much of money, so much of time, waste of human lives–all because some royal fellow wanted to remember his wife. Seems more like he wanted to be remembered by the shrine he had built for his wife. Couldn't stay there long and left telling my fellow traveller that I would be waiting outside. After more than two hours, he still hadn't come out so I returned to find him stripped to his underwear sitting cross legged facing the shrine. His eyes were closed and he mumbled some mumbo jumbo. A crowd of people had gathered and some of them were giggling. I had to get him out of there because it was becoming really embarrassing. *Get up Troy, that's enough now, you've proved your point. You don't have to whip a dead horse.*

Finally he hauled himself up and just before he was about to put on his clothes a gang of four fellows came up to him. They thought he was Indian by the way he looked and started babbling in some local language. *Hey man, what you trying to say? I don't understand a word. Not a single word. Talk English.*

They looked at each other, shrugged their shoulders and started pushing him around. *Making fun of Taj Mahal eh? Making fun of Taj Mahal?* Before he could respond, they hauled him out of the place.

I tried to block their way. *Listen there is some mistake. He is not making fun of the Taj Mahal. He is paying his respects, doing* namaste *and* shanti *and all. Let him go, let him go please.*

They brushed me aside. *He is trouble maker, we're taking him to station.*

Which station? I asked hurriedly, *bus station or train station?*

Police station madam. Please do not come. And they took him away.

I didn't know what to do. There I stood waving my arms about trying to explain to people around me that it was all a mistake but they stood there staring at me and half smiling. It was so damned irritating. *Stop staring at me, I haven't come from another planet, you hear me? I haven't come from another planet. Shoo, shoo.* They stepped back as I advanced and many of them walked away, leaving a few, mainly children and young people, to trail after me. I walked slowly first then stopped and turned around and they were there so I quickened my steps and started running. They did the same. And then before I knew what was happening others joined the group running behind me.

I tried to run across the road and nearly got knocked down by a big swanky car. The driver lowered the window glass and peered out. *What do you think you are doing woman?*

Turning around, I ran back straight into the crowd and they scattered. I took refuge in a betel leaf vendor's stall. *Hey hey, what you doing madam?*

Those people, they chasing me.

He shouted at the group and they dispersed. Then he turned to me, *which country?*

Germany.

You want change, I give you change. Local rupee.

No I don't want change.

Then what you want? He persisted.

Nothing.

Nothing? Every white one come and want something. Some change, some ganja, some other things, many other things. Madam, my good English, no? My good English, no?

I walked away quickly without turning around to see if anyone was following me.

I was tempted to go to the bus station and catch a bus to Delhi and leave Troy behind, that would have been the easiest thing to do. But I didn't. I had heard such terrible stories of people landing up in Indian prisons. So I decided to set off and try and get Troy out. But before that I had to locate the police station. There was only one way I could find out–ask some kind soul. *Excuse me, which way police station,* I asked a sedate, elegantly clad Indian.

Which country are you from? He asked in reply.

France, I lied.

You aren't from France, you're German.

Okay, suit yourself. But do you know where the police station is?

Straight down and hundred metres on your left.

So I followed his direction but there was no sign of the police station.

Every person I asked very helpfully sent me off in a different direction. Finally, when I was losing hope I found the place, in time to see a shaken Troy stumbling down the steps of the police station. A constable walked behind him.

Take care of this man. He needs help, lots of help, said the constable.

That's enough, Troy snapped at the man. *I'm a tourist and I bring this country business and this is the way you treat me?*

He needs a doctor, the fellow said to me and patted my fellow traveller on the shoulder.

You take your hands off me, you hear me?

I led Troy away. *What happened?* I wanted to know.

Everything happened. They first thought I was a mad Indian, then a Bangladeshi but when they saw my passport they started suspecting it was fake. While one lot were going through my bag, another lot was verifying if my passport was real and yet another was making life miserable for me by asking me all sorts of stupid questions. It all pointed to them wanting to skin some money off me. Then when they couldn't get anything, they claimed there was grass in my money pouch.

Was there?

Of course there was. They put it there. Now enough of bloody questions. Let's get out of here.

We went to the bus station and caught a bus to Mathura. *Please Troy,* I said to him in the bus, *please don't start doing crazy things again. When you are on your own you can do whatever you please but you are travelling with me …*

So I have to be on my best behaviour, is that it? I'm not telling you to do what I want you to do. Why are you expecting me to do what you want me to do?

He was getting on my nerves. *Now listen here Troy, all I am asking you is not to do something stupid again like taking off your clothes …*

He didn't let me complete my sentence and went at me. *Every second Indian walks around naked or near naked, Gandhi wore almost no clothes at all, all those rishis and holy guys sit naked on ice and meditate. What's the problem with me stripping to my briefs and meditating in front of the Taj? It defies logic to stop me.*

This is different.

How is it different? He wasn't going to give in. *Look at that beggar there,* he jabbed his finger out of the window, *he has no clothes on and no one is bothered about even stopping him. What do you say to that?*

Okay, suit yourself. I rested my head back and closed my eyes. We didn't say anything to each other for quite some time.

You want to hear some of my new poems. There's one about you here, he suddenly said.

Not in the bus, there are too many people around.

As if anyone would care.

They probably wouldn't but I would. That shut him up.

When we reached Mathura it was early evening and the air smelled of wood smoke. There were peacocks everywhere, trotting along, carrying their beautiful tails behind them or calling out, their voices full of longing. We headed for a devotees' rest house which they call a *dharamshala* and got ourselves a place to rest for the night. Troy insisted that we'd save our money if we shared a room. I agreed reluctantly, quickly dumped my bag, suggesting that we should go out.

Come on Melissa, you don't have to feel like a trapped bird. Why don't you go and freshen up then sit down, put your feet up and relax. I'm not going to eat you up.

I didn't listen to him and left him behind in the room, walking out into the courtyard and trying to get a feel of the place. At first the temple bells were quite soothing to listen to, particularly the ones that were far off but then the sound started coming at me in waves until I was drowning. Other sounds were added to the bells. They were the sounds of prayers and chants, human voices at such a pitch that they lashed at me. That wasn't religious devotion, it was chaos. I rushed back to the room and banged furiously on the door. *What's happened?* Troy raised his eyebrows, *had enough of the world.* There were tears in my eyes as I brushed past him and fell into a chair. *Do you want chai? Melissa, I'm talking to you, do you want* chai?

Okay, get me the damned chai. This is too much for me. I'm feeling nauseous. You didn't warn me Troy, that it was going to be like this.

Stop being so sensitive. Just rest. I'll get chai.

He was gone a long time. Meanwhile the skylight, high up near the ceiling lost the glow of light that had earlier filled it. A gecko started clicking on the wall to my right and another answered quickly. I flicked on the light and they fell silent. A few bats swooped in through the skylight and spun around the room. I kept talking to myself inside my head. *Of all the places on earth I had chosen to be here. Why? Why didn't I listen to my little voice of reason and refuse to take Troy's offer to travel a bit with him? Why didn't I set off for the mountains, just a small trip by myself and then return to my part of the world? My part of the world … a stupid way to put it. What is my part of the world?* Do *I really belong anywhere at all? I was born back there, right; I grew up there, right; I had friends and lovers there, right; but does only that make up for a feeling of belonging? Does it? No way. Then what makes up for a feeling of belonging? I don't really know because I have never really felt it. Could it be that actually no one really feels that they belong and that all they are doing is bluffing themselves? They throw themselves into the damned grind of everyday life and say at the end of the day this is my reason, this what I want to do, it gives me meaning, here is where I want to be because I belong here. They throw themselves into passionate make-believe loving which is actually a charade because they are trying to get away from their own sense of aloneness. They throw themselves into marrying and making families because it's a short cut to belonging. They throw themselves into religion because it's their mask of protection against themselves and they can happily be someone else. This is not me. I wouldn't do this if I had a choice. But I do have a choice. I am answerable to no one, neither family or friend. Then why don't I make my OWN choices? Why do I constantly allow someone else to make a choice for me? Is it because I can blame someone else if things go wrong? Maybe.*

Troy returned with chai, fruit and all sorts of savoury Indian snacks. We ate and drank in silence. *I'm going out,* he said, *for a walk. I'll get back to you later.*

I'm sorry, I said.

That's okay. We all have our own ways of dealing with new places, new faces, new feelings.

Why don't you read me a few of your poems.

Is that a serious request?

Yes. Please.

Okay, when I get back. And he was gone, leaving me to myself.

Troy returned the next morning, fell into bed beside me, slept for a few hours then got up, bathed and announced *we're going to do a lot of walking today. Are you up to it?*

Yes. Won't take long to get myself together. I kept my word and we set out into the world of pilgrims with the sun blasting the dusty air until each little grain seemed to glow. Down the narrow streets between the temples we went, Troy walked purposefully ahead of me as if he was on familiar ground. *Any reason why you are walking along so fast?* I asked but he didn't respond. Instead, he branched off down a narrow lane and we reached the banks of the river, flowing along brown and swirling. Descending the stone steps, we reached the waterside and sat in the shade of a spreading tree.

I brought you here first so you could see the big turtles. Look, look down there. I followed the line of his arm and finger and watched as the enormous shells of the creatures surfaced, hovered, then sank. Occasionally, they floated on the surface and jostled one another almost playfully. Then they'd disappear and reappear again upstream. *Let's visit a few temples and then cross over to the other side. There's a small village called Vishnugunj there. They say it's beautiful.*

I'm not up to visiting temples Troy, you're the one on a roots trip, not me.

Then what trip are you on?

No trip. I came to this country …

Yes I know, you came to this country to cremate a friend … sorry I should've remembered that. He smiled. *And you're killing a bit of time before going home.*

I have no home Troy.

Then what are you going back to?

Nothing.

In that case, why do you want to go back?

Where else do I go?

You've got the whole world to explore. You have money don't you?

Yes, more than I need; more than I know what to do with.

Then find a cheap country and spend your time discovering it. You can go on forever like that.

It's not as easy as all that. I brushed aside the matter, got up and walked off along the path that ran along the riverbank. Troy followed me. I slowed down so that he could catch up. *So then, what did you spend all last night doing?*

I met up with a Swedish group and we smoked and chatted. I would have invited you but I wasn't sure if you wanted to spend the night with Swedes. AND I wasn't sure if you smoke grass.

Sure I do. Sometimes. And thanks for saving me from the Swedes.

Ever had bhang*?* He asked.

What's that?

It's a paste made from the flowers and leaves of the female cannabis plant. You can put big dollops of the stuff in milk with almonds and other nuts or stir a lump of it into a glass of chai *and sip it. Gives a wholesome high. You feel good all over, nice and happy and high and tingly and its good for the digestion.*

Everything you eat in India seems to be good for the digestion. That's all I heard the first time I came to this country and on this trip too.

Come on, stop being so critical of the country all the time. You don't seem to have a kind word for anything here. Suddenly he turned and started running, as if he was chasing someone or something. It was a monkey swinging his camera by the strap and heading towards a tree. *Come back here you idiot.* But the creature had no intention of stopping and ran up the trunk of the tree and was lost in the branches above. Troy stood there with his hands on his hips glaring up at the animal, talking to it as if he was addressing a child. *Come on down at once or I'll come up there and teach you a lesson. That camera is worth a small fortune. Besides, you don't even know how to bloody well use a camera so what are you going to do with it? Tell me. Come on idiot, tell me.*

When he got no response, he started throwing stones at it. Two sadhus came out of the nearby temple and grabbed hold of him. The bigger of the two caught him by the collar and started shaking him up, yelling at him in the local tongue. *I don't know your language.*

You Indian, no? Asked one of them.

No no.

You Madraasi?

I tried to intervene. *Monkey got his camera. See see, click click, monkey got click click.*

That stopped them in their tracks and they looked up and saw the monkey swinging the camera by its strap. They called in a couple of boys and asked them to climb the tree and get the camera away from the animal. But the boys wouldn't go up until Troy assured them that he would pay them a reward. When they finally managed to get the camera back, Troy started bargaining with them to knock down the reward money. In the confusion, one of the boys ran off with the camera. Troy grabbed the other fellow and insisted that he would not let him go till the camera was returned. We waited in the sun for nearly two hours with the boy weeping loudly. Finally the camera was returned.

The day wasn't over because there was still a lot in store for us from a stolen wallet to an eatery rip-off. Finally, before evening, we crossed the river in a country boat and sprawled on the sandy embankment and watched the sun bleed over the holy city and listened to the clanging and tinkling of bells calling the faithful to prayer. At dusk we returned, making our way down the narrow streets, stopping for a *bhang* in chai … as if we were pub crawling. I floated back to the *dharamshala*, leaving Troy to continue his local explorations.

Even though I had begun to get irritated with his habit of getting into trouble at every twist and turn, I found my travelling companion to be an unusual fellow. He had an anecdote for almost every occasion to explain a point, defend himself or resolve a situation … and when he didn't have that, he'd bluster innocently through with a touch of exaggerated bravado. One morning, he launched into a long discussion which he claimed to have had with Samuel Beckett then ended his account saying that he'd one day win the Nobel Prize for his precious poetry. *Nobody, just nobody, today writes the way I do. Nobody bridges cultures and people and customs the way I do. No one uses words and images the way I do … This is precious stuff …*

I'm sure his work was precious stuff but he always chose to read me some of it at the wrong time. Once when I was half asleep, another time when I had a horrible headache and yet another time when I was so high on *bhang* in chai that I couldn't understand what he was saying. *What's up with you? Women will do anything to hear me read my work.*

I lost interest in his lips by the time we were back in Delhi and thrown straight into the arms of the communal riots of 1984 after the shooting of an Indian Prime Minister.

Fire in the Streets

The evening we arrived by bus in Delhi, the city vomited blood and fire in the streets. The driver raced the bus and wove it between bonfires of vehicles, tyres, furniture and human bodies. I was sure that we would ram into some other oncoming vehicle and topple over. What a way to die. Lying there bleeding in an alien country with memories flooding my brain in a fraction of a second before I blacked out forever. But that didn't happen. Instead, we raced on hysterically, horn blaring and every single person in the bus shrieking their heads off. A chorus of anxiety and horror.

Mobs streamed out of lanes like ants, dragging unfortunate victims and beating them into pulp then leaving them lifeless. Finally a massive crowd came pouring down the main road from in front of us and surrounded our bus like those giant African ants that swarm around a dying creature and strip it to the bone, like those piranha fish in the Amazon River that can reduce a body to a skeleton in a matter of minutes. Snap snap rip rip. *P-E-E-R-A-A-N-H-A* is the way my teacher Frau Hauptman pronounced the name in school. She had a very large mouth and opened it wide when she wanted to pronounce a word correctly. There were several gold teeth in that cavern and we all took turns in trying to counting the number.

So there I was thinking of Frau Hauptman's open mouth as the mob came closer. The driver waved his arms trying to scare them away. The conductor crouched down near our feet, covering his turban with his hands. I wondered why he did that but learnt later that Sikh people were being killed ruthlessly because Sikh guards had assassinated Indira Gandhi, the Prime Minister of the country. Even though I didn't know at the time why he was so terrified, I instinctively covered him with my shawl. The savages stormed in and ran down the aisle obviously looking for certain people. They caught two young Sikhs and dragged them out into the street, kicking and hitting them. *Phaasi, phaasi,* they were shouting, I didn't know exactly what that meant but I was sure it suggested a terrible end for the two men. One of the crowd caught sight of Troy and asked him where his turban was in a local language. Troy shook his head. Another grabbed hold of his collar and yanked him forward. *No, no,* he pleaded. *I'm a tourist from Sweden.*

No, no, they started mimicking him, *Tourist, tourist.*

Suddenly, they noticed that someone was hiding at our feet. *There's one here, there's one here.* They grabbed the conductor's feet and dragged him out on to the road. No one looked out of the window to see what was happening. A woman behind us stood up, screamed and began vomiting all over my head and back. I didn't have the courage to get up and move away.

Finally the ants left the bus and everyone seated inside started shouting at the driver to get him to start the bus. Once again, the driver took off at great speed, bashing smaller vehicles that came in the way, crunching over debris. Finally, the bus came to a halt and the driver jumped out and fled. For a few moments we were all paralysed and then we grabbed our bags and started shoving our way out of the bus. Everyone pushed and shoved and stamped and kicked. I fell but Troy yanked me up and heaved me forward. Once on the burning street we put our bags on our heads like refugees and started running, then seeing a violent mob beating people up ahead of us, we turned to the right and slipped down a narrow lane. I tripped over groaning bodies then picked myself up and carried on. When we came out on the other side, we saw an abandoned auto rickshaw. *Get in, get in, yelled Troy. I know how to ride this one.* And he did. I clutched the bags in the back seat, bouncing around as he took off like a rocket.

We zipped from street to street then ran out of petrol and abandoned the vehicle and started walking. It looked like there was a revolution going on. *This is supposed to be a land of non-violence and they shot the naked holy man and his granddaughter, now they are lynching people in the streets. I really can't believe my roots are here.*

By some stroke of luck we ended up near the railway station and raced our way down the familiar street which was lined with guest houses. Either some were overflowing with guests and had no place or others were bolted and barred from the inside. At some places tourists were asked to pay in foreign currency whilst in others they had to bid for rooms that were being auctioned. Over and above that they were expected to pay a fat deposit.

We couldn't get a room to ourselves but had to share one with three women from different countries talking different languages with a little English thrown in. There was Isabella a Spaniard with a loud voice who smoked like a chimney, Claudia a Frenchie who kept claiming that she had an Indian friend who was a journalist and he'd get her out of there and a really big built Canadian who turned out to be a real darling. Her name was Sabrina.

A meal? A snack? Ciggies? Drinking water? A joint? Beer? Sabrina had a way of getting all of that and more. She was the nurse, the shrink, the entertainer and the organiser.

Without her, we'd have all perished. And this is not an exaggeration. It's true. She had a special way about her that gave us all confidence. Isabella didn't like her and for the first two days avoided speaking to her. But one night she couldn't take the stress anymore and started crying uncontrollably and banging on the walls, *I wanta go out. It's dead in here. It's dead in here. I wanta go out. I wanta go home.* This got Claudia sobbing.

I can't believe I'm the only man in here, said Troy.

Aren't you lucky, I replied.

Sabrina started following Isabella around the room and the moment she began banging on the walls, she reached out and hugged her gently from behind. *Let go of me, no, no,* she cried and tried to wriggle out of the embrace. But Sabrina wouldn't let go.

You'll be okay. No one's going to hurt you my girl, no one's going to hurt you. They'll have to hurt me first, you hear? You hear?

Yes, came the little voice in reply.

Now you come and sit down there with me and I'll sing you a song. Saying this, the Canadian guided her to a corner of the room where a few cushions lay, making up a divan. Isabella curled up in her arms whilst she listened to her softly humming a lullaby. The lights went off and we sat there in the dark with the whole city going mad outside.

I don't want to die here, Claudia muttered, the tip of her cigarette glowing in the dark.

Ah, you won't, said Troy. *Worse things have happened in the world and people have survived. This is nothing.*

I just want to get out of here and go home. Home. Home.

Shsh, said Sabrina softly, *we all need to get some sleep.*

Anyway, continued Troy. *Once you die, you die. You're gone. It's the ultimate. When we are born we are already preparing to die.*

Shut up, Sabrina's voice was firmer this time. *Cut out the bravado. Everyone here wants to stay alive and you are already talking about dying.*

But it's true.

Okay it's true. No more please.

Have it your way, Troy sighed.

Later that night when we all realised that we couldn't sleep we crept out of the room and climbed the stairs to the roof. The darkness around us was lit up by bonfires and voices rose towards the night sky like dying angels. Sometimes the sound of sirens joined them and at other times voices on loudspeakers blasted the air, followed by the muffled rumble of trucks. *When will this end?* Claudia asked. *When?*

Never, replied Troy. *All this never ends. It goes on and on. I have a poem on guns.*

Not now Troy, it's not the time for poetry. That's what I said to him but he wouldn't listen.

Poetry is an island of sanity in an ...

I ran my fingers through his hair and tugged. That quietened him and he stood watching the city below him and around him, burning with sores. No one spoke after that. I felt as if the whole burning night pressed around forcing my own life and all that I had lived so far deeper into me. Pushing and pushing. I was inside the very heart of a black stone, unable to move, unable to say a word, unable to breathe. I could feel myself getting smaller and smaller. Above me the dark sky came down slowly and covered me. Nothing of who I was mattered anymore. All of it seemed so small, so useless, so helpless, so unnecessary. I sat down with my back resting against the low wall of the roof.

Troy began intoning a poem,

City of the dark night,
Floating on the death smoke of lost lives,
I cannot console your children stumbling in the alleyways
Of desperation,
I cannot console your women with dry eyes
Watching their men burnt at the stake, hung from lamp posts,
Quartered by hate,
I cannot console your men lost in the hollow sockets
Of their own eyes,
Lost in the sounds of their own heartbeats,
Lost in the somersaulting grief of their forefathers.

City of the dark night,
I want to kneel at your grave and say goodnight,
But cannot,
I want to whisper sweet nothings in your ears,
But I cannot,
I want to hold you in my arms,
But cannot,
I want to set you free from the earth where you are bound,
And watch you fly, light-winged,
Towards another dawn, another day.

City of the dark night,
You slip through my fingers,
Like thick black blood from an old wound
That refuses to heal.

One by one, everyone left, but I sat there on the roof all night, thinking about why I had chosen to remain in India and had not returned after Hans' cremation. Almost everything about the country had disturbed me, so what prompted me to hold on? Was I reluctant to go back because I had nothing and no one to go back to? Was I tired of feeling safe? Was I pushing myself out into the world so that I could experience more? Had I got infected by India and didn't even try to cure myself? What was it? I had an air ticket to return to Germany in a week but didn't want to. *What do I want? What?* I asked myself and got no answer.

I was twenty-six with no proper education, no career prospects, savings that were slowly seeping away, I couldn't stay still, I was a spirit gypsy, I was a stranger wherever I went. Now it's not that I felt out of place in Germany but just that I didn't FEEL German. I felt different. Without a culture, without a past, exploring the present, weaving my way between high seriousness and wanton free expression, between academic isolation and emotional adventure, between professional assuredness and wobbling unemployment, between radical reaction and mute acceptance. I walked through a landmine like a drunkard staggering across a speedway, oblivious of the fact that I could get knocked down at any moment.

India wasn't a way of escaping or a Utopia for low budget citizens. It was a whole new experience which was heavy like a sponge soaked in *bhang chai*. It was a way of being … a way one travelled down and lost oneself in and found oneself again in the eyes of strangers jostling down crowded streets or travelling in trains and buses or sitting in unkempt parks and cracking peanut shells. India terrified and confused me. India was like a lost child searching for her parents who had abandoned her in a temple complex teeming with pilgrims. India was a great big Mama with a million breasts. India was a glowing birthmark which appeared and disappeared on different parts of my body. India was the land where opposites met and merged then separated again, then attached themselves to each other like Siamese twins. India was the hour of forgetfulness floating between going and coming.

When the riots subsided like balloon with the air knocked out, we parted ways–each to a different destination, each to another home, another way of life. Troy leaked out of my life, leaving behind a sticky floor and a few stray lines of verse. I went back and restarted where I left off. Floating. The people I once knew were turning radical, Europe was in the throes of turmoil ... seething underneath the skin. We were all waiting for the final plague–the plague of change. It took a bit of time coming ... but when it did, the old died like flies and the new skipped through the debris.

The Wall came down.

I was there with a borrowed hammer and joined the heaving, sweating, drunken, dope-high thousands, slamming and shouting, slamming and shouting, calling in the angels of freedom and togetherness so that I could dance with them on ridges of concrete. It was a cold 9th of November in 1989 I remember. I was shouting, my voice joining the great chorus of kindred souls. Around me, slabs collapsed, scattered in shards, crowds crawled over them and poured past me, rivers of hopes and emotions were merging and forming a gigantic wave of humanity. Something was moving me, I don't know what. And then when I was exhausted and I couldn't lift a hammer any more, I peeled myself away because I was scared to start getting involved in all the so called reconciliation that flowed around me. It was intense whilst it lasted but it wasn't my battle, it wasn't my cause. I had to save myself from the times I lived in.

I inherited Grandpa's and Grandma's estate and stayed there for a while, trying to recover from the fervour of my experiences. There was a lot of work to be done on the house and it was a while before I managed to get it into shape. I worked on the garden with the help of some young fellows from the village and got it to look good … better than it ever had. The fence got repaired too and painted white. Outside, the Linden tree was in flower and a cuckoo called from its thicket.

One late afternoon I went out for a walk along the edge of the forest where sprays of wild flowers bloomed, thinking of all the times that had past–the times I'd gather flowers with Grandma, when I was lost and met Boz, the dreamscapes I lived in, all that and more. I tried my best to keep the memory of Grandpa out but he was still everywhere and I couldn't wish him away, as much as I had wanted to.

Late night I'd sit out in the garden wrapped in a shawl, eyes closed, letting the sounds of the dark seep into me and fill me till I was satiated then I'd turn indoors and lie awake in bed, my body trembling. I smelled him everywhere in the room. He hung in the air around me. He was under the bed and in the closet. He was trying to fill my life again and I resisted him with all the strength I had in my body and in my spirit.

I decided that I wasn't going to sell the estate. I was going to hold on to it and one day exorcise it of Grandpa by replacing him. Then I'd be willing to grow old there. But before that I wanted to travel some more.

In the days that followed I often walked into the village and did a bit of shopping and exploring. A lot had changed. Old shops had been demolished and new establishments had come up in their place. There were two new restaurants and a host of other small-time snack bars. Leonie's house was still very much there but only Angelika remained. Egon had hung himself in the forest and was found a month later, Bamard had left the country. Nobody quite knew where he had gone.

I carried a small hamper over to Angelika's place one morning. It took her a while to recognise me. *Do I know you? Do I?*

Yes you do, I'm Melissa, Leonie's friend. Remember?

No. I don't meet people nowadays. So I can't make any sense of faces. Leonie you said? I had a girl of the same name. She's in Berlin now, married. Can you believe it? Leonie married? She even has twins. Boys–Egon and Bamard.

I'm Melissa, of course you know who I am, of course you know me. How can you not know me? You lost Leonie in the forest a long time ago. Egon went too. Bamard is not here anymore.

Melissa, Melissa, look how big you've grown. I can hardly recognise you my little one. Come inside, why are you standing outside the gate. Come inside.

Inside, the house was musty and the stench of rancid cheese was everywhere as if a dozen labourers from the very heart of India had come visiting and had been sweating their hearts out.

Sit down Melissa dear, she insisted. I looked around the room and there really was nowhere to sit. The couches and chairs were overloaded with clothes and linen. An old fashioned lantern stood on the rug which had burn holes in it.

That's okay, I replied, *I'll manage.*

Sit down please Melissa, I don't like people standing around the house. I'm afraid that they'll end up doing something dangerous. And I can't have you do that here.

I left her babbling in the hall and went into what once was Leonie's room. It still was, where Angelika was concerned. Everything was spotlessly clean. Just as I remembered her room to be. I walked over to her closet and opened the doors. Leonie's clothes hung in neat rows and on a rack at the bottom was a line of her shoes.

Angelika walked into the room and stood at the door. *Time to eat Le, I've made your special supper. Come on, come on Le.* The table had been carefully set for two so I sat down and she did the same. But there was no food on the table. I looked at her and she looked at me.

Sometime later I got up, wished her well and left. She followed me out of the gate and on to the road. *I think you should go home now,* I said softly.

She shook her head sadly and replied, *Don't go away Le, I'll miss you terribly. Please stay.* I hugged her close and she cried. When I drew away we looked into each other's eyes. *I can't believe that I'll never see my Le again. Goodbye Melissa, take care of your life and when you are old come back. This is a place to die in.*

I walked quickly away and back at the house, sat out late and watched the Linden tree shiver in the breeze as moonlight washed its flowers and leaves.

There was a letter from Troy in reply to mine saying that he was planning to return to India and embrace Buddhism and sit at the blessed feet of the Dalai Lama. He enclosed a poem.

In the mountains sits the glow of the Buddha,
Stars around his head.
And at his feet the prayers of the faithful ones
Chanted on prayer beads.

Poor man, the burning streets of Delhi had really cleansed him good and proper. Good for him. But I didn't have those sorts of makings and smiled and put his letter in a drawer which I never opened again. It was a tiny drawer below Grandma's dressing mirror.

I knew my time at the estate was slipping through my fingers so I decided to prepare for my journey out again.

Before I left I sat down and wrote a letter to Grandpa.

Dear Grandpa,

It has taken me a long time to get the courage to tell you once and for all that you changed my life. You inspired me and you damaged me. I wonder what sort of person I would have been if you were not a part of my life and you were someone else's grandpa. I can't say and I won't say that I hate you. O God Grandpa I don't know what to say to you. After all this time and so much courage I don't know what to say to you. When I close my eyes I can see you sitting across the table from me, looking at me. You frighten me Grandpa, you frighten me. Please don't look at me like that. You aren't welcome anymore. You are the past and I won't let the past return under any circumstances. When I return, Grandpa, I will replace you so that there will be no room here for you anymore.

I'm leaving the house in good shape. The garden's better than the way you managed it and the fence looks good. Fresh and new and painted white.

I know you are very attached to this house but if you really care for me, please leave. Take your smell and leave. Everyone has their place in space and time.

Goodbye, I'm moving on.

Your Melli.

On the day I was to leave, I dug a pit in one corner of the garden, dropped the letter in and covered it with mud.

Journey to the Sea

My life's been one of journeys. Departing and arriving with no reason really other than wanting to constantly be in a new place each time, a place that expected nothing of me, a place that I had no attachments to, a place I could say goodbye and hullo to, a place where I roosted at and then caught the high winds at dawn. Apart from the Americas I travelled wherever my desire drove me. The Americas scared me with all their complexities, their demands, their securities and insecurities. I settled for South East Asia and travelled the usual circuits of Hong Kong and Bangkok, Vietnam, Singapore but it was far too exotic for me. They came at me with all their sights and smells and differentness. Of course Singapore stood apart from the rest but still I found it to be too different for me. Indonesia was a riot of opposites with Bali like a hidden eye, calm and beautiful when it opened, a place where even smiling was a ritual and stones and spaces were sacred. I almost fell passionately in love with the place but I awoke one morning and told myself, *this is not my kind of place, I can't be so damned polite and graceful all the time and* I left. I tried Australia but couldn't catch its rhythms. It was another world, another planet. Too much of everything.

The 90s wasn't the best time to be travelling in. The whole damned world was freaking out. The century went out with a bang … the reds in a fix with all that coldness becoming war,

Africa was cheering on its tribal wars and other simmering spectacles ... Somalia, Rwanda, the Congo, Algeria, Bosnia banged its head against crumbling walls till its brains started spilling out, the Middle East was one hell of a mess with Saddam Hussein trimming his moustaches whilst the Kurds burnt, there was Chechen too and India and Pakistan blasting away at each other, the Taliban was in Afghanistan and Los Angeles tried to fight off its riots. And so much more. Much more than I can remember. Every time I decided to travel somewhere someone or the other was busy making the place uninviting. It was as if some unseen being was reading my thoughts and then checkmating me. Damn. The whole universe was constantly hatching some sort of conspiracy.

And finally, after roaming around in circles, wondering what was awaiting me if I chose to get to the centre, I ended up on Palolim Beach in South Goa among people who the world had forgotten–dregs of society, drifters, adventurers, little families in search of Paradise, loners; everyone there in their makeshift shacks. Sitting on the biggest boulder in the area, I looked out to sea, blessing the new century as it dawned.

I made few friends and fewer lovers, seeking instead the companionship of stray dogs and other domesticated animals and birds, unable to understand why Indians who were supposedly a saintly lot treated other creatures so cruelly. They gave me a number of names such as Wild Lady, Dog Lady, White Bitch and Dobie. I accepted them gracefully and refused to be offended. When I tired of Palolim, I followed the shoreline and roosted in place after place until I reached Anjuna, then made my way back, settling finally for Colva and on to Blue Mermaid. God that was one hell of a place. Clementine was less intrusive. It suited me well so I decided not to look for another place but keep changing rooms instead.

Now you know what happened in Clementine, you know why I had to move away. Don't want to go through all that again so I headed off down the beach further south and found a quaint relaxed place where the owner looked always stoned, the waiters feather-brained and forgetful and every piece of furniture wobbly. But it was a pleasant location–a small grove of coconut palms, a line of sun beds, basic rooms facing the sea, a wholesome eatery and an ayurvedic masseur on call. On The Rocks, that's what it was called. The signboard that stood at the front entrance was a large metal cut-out of a trendy couple sitting under a colourful umbrella high up on a large rock. Their cocktail card had a long list of drinkables whose names ended with … On The Rocks. Every couple of months the names changed. Someone was obviously having a great time thinking up new ones.

The day I arrived and checked in, On The Rocks acquired four geese. They were happy looking birds and went flapping around the place. I took to tending them and ensuring that they were well fed and watered. I couldn't understand why everyone around me suddenly started getting hostile towards me, as if caring for the geese was some sort of a crime. So I went up to Ronny, a small skinny fellow who was the owner and asked him, *what's the problem? Do you have any objection to me taking care of your geese?*

Not at all, so long as they don't follow you around the place. Geese should be where geese should be and not where human beings should be. Guests don't like to have geese around them all the time. Everyone is not like you.

I'm doing nothing strange, I was getting a bit annoyed by the way he was going on, *all I'm doing is feeding your geese. I'm happy to take care of them.*

Okay, but don't bring them to where the other guests are, that's all.

So I kept them away from the other guests and stayed away myself. But the kitchen fellows still bothered me. They'd throw buckets full of leftovers and pieces of unwanted meat and bones into their feeding trough. *Why are you doing that? They won't eat that sort of food.*

Ha, Madam, Chimbu the kitchen assistant grinned, *it will make them fat and strong, they will even start talking and singing.*

You are being cruel Chimbu.

I am being clever Madam. Chimbu is clever. See Madam, they not your gooses. They hotel gooses. If they your gooses you do anything you want. But you can't do anything you want because they hotel gooses.

And so the battle for the geese went on and it started getting quite difficult for me to walk past the kitchen because if any of them saw me, they'd pass a remark that would make the others snigger. One evening Chimbu actually asked me, *Madam I have a goose too, you want to see it? It's a sweet goose.*

Suvarna Devi, the Indian yoga teacher who had brought a group of European learners for a course, called out to me when I passed her room, *hello Melissa, hello.*

I waved in acknowledgement.

Hello, hello, I want to say hello.

I waved again. But she didn't give up and jumping out of her chair scurried towards me. When she reached my side, *I thought maybe I should have a small chat with you.*

About what?

There's a lot of negative energy in this place and maybe you can help. Can we have a cup of tea later this evening?

I drink beer in the evening. We can have a beer.

I don't drink beer.

Very well then let's take a walk on the beach and have a chat about this negative energy that you want to talk about.

Actually it's my meditation time.

Another time then. I walked off, leaving her about to say something. I wasn't in the mood to listen to a solemn discourse on self-control and consideration. The woman had the irritating habit of launching out into a moralistic lecture on how to live a pure life. I knew very well that she was going to start off about my behaviour with the geese and I didn't want to insult her so I stayed out of her way.

Dutifully, every morning the geese would gather outside my door and honk away. They wouldn't stop until I opened the door and greeted them. and for the rest of the day they would shadow me. I had become the centre of unrest and there was little I could do about it. Suvarna kept trying to counsel me, the kitchen staff continued hassling me relentlessly and other guests behaved as if I was an alien who had dropped from another planet. Okay, I had disturbed the peace but they could see that all I was doing was trying to be kind.

If Bud hadn't arrived and checked in, they would surely have asked me to leave. Bud, dear Bud. Bud the enormous blob of fat. Bud, the ear to ear grinner. Bud, who didn't have a single ounce of malice in him. Bud, the quiet one. Bud, my bodyguard. Dear Bud from the deep Mid-West. We shared the same table a couple of times, got talking and I managed to get him to join me for a walk along the beach. He walked slowly, waddled like a goose and had to stop and rest a few times on the way. When we got back, he returned to his room and didn't come out till the next morning.

There were no geese at my door that morning, only a couple of bulbuls twittering on the dew-wet lawn. I opened the door, walked out and took a good look around but there was no sign of them. So I went reluctantly to the kitchen to enquire. I was just about to call out to the boys when I saw the garbage bin outside overflowing with white feathers. *They gone,* grinned Chimbu, *they gone, out, khaachaak. For eating.* I went back to my room.

There was a rattling at my door. Bud was outside. *So how are we this morning?*

Great, considering I just lost four friends.

What? Friends? Where? How?

The geese, Bud, the geese. They've been cut for the table.

O. Hmmmm. Are you coming for tea?

I joined him a little later and sat in silence sipping tea and watching dolphins bouncing through the water along the shore.

I know this is a stupid thing to say Melissa, but I don't think you are made for this world. Here people slaughter geese and serve them up on the table, they don't make friends with them. These people didn't buy those geese because they wanted to give them food and shelter and a lot of warmth and friendship. They bought them because they wanted to fatten them up and slaughter them. With you walking about the place with those geese following you around and constantly talking to them and feeding them, guests here started getting bothered. I've only been here a few days but I've heard them saying unpleasant things about you. Melissa, you aren't of this world. Neither am I. You because of the way you feel and I because of the way I look. So let's ... you and I ... start doing something about our loneliness and differentness. He reached out and patted me on the cheek with a podgy hand. *Wipe those eyes of yours and let's do something interesting today.*

Like?

Go to Anjuna. It's Flea Market Day.

It was a touristy thing to do but hopefully with Bud it would be different.

I was right. Being with him was both distracting and comforting. We roamed the Flea Market, bought a few silly things, chatted with strangers and drank beer till we were so bloated that we were ready to float off across the sea if a high wind came rushing along from inland. He told me nothing of his personal story and I told him nothing of mine. Occasionally he'd refer to people from his life as if I knew who they were. I never asked because he never gave me an opportunity to. To be honest, I didn't want to know anything about him and it looked like he didn't want to know anything about me. I think what I enjoyed most was the fact that I could take care of him. I had lost my geese but Bud stepped into the empty space that they had left behind.

He relished being taken care of, particularly when I made a public show of it … wiping drops of soup off his shirt, pouring water into his glass, helping him out of his chair, holding his hand as he staggered down the sandy steps to the beach, walking him back to his room with a torchlight. We needed each other.

I thought that the guests at On The Rocks were done with me because the geese had been slaughtered and eaten and wouldn't bother them anymore but I was sadly mistaken. Now they were having a reaction to Bud and I being together. We were oddities–man mountain and the blonde.

Come on Melissa, he said, *let's check out of here and I'll treat you to a really nice place. You in your room and me in mine. We'll get these people off our backs.*

Let it be Bud. Not worth it. Let's teach them a lesson. Let's stay right here.

That night I went over to his room with a bottle and when we had emptied it, climbed into his bed and spent the night lying in his arms, wrapped in rolls of fat. He snored loudly all night but it didn't disturb me. He was my great big teddy bear, my man mountain, my baby. If I could have breast fed him I would have.

I left him early the next morning and sat out in the café relishing the cool air streaming in from the sea. Fishermen were folding and stacking their nets and flocks of crows pecked at dead fish. Time passed as I sat there, sipping several cups of tea, waiting for Bud. When it was about eleven, I started getting a bit worried so I went across to his room. The folded piece of paper with which I had wedged the door shut when I left was still in place. *Bud? Bud? I'm coming in Bud.* No response … so I pushed the door open and stepped in. He lay in the same position that I had left him, on his right side, with his enormous belly spread out before him and the fat from his body hanging limp.

Bud? Bud? O no, Bud, please Bud, wake up, wake up. You can't do this to me. Bud. His eyes stared blankly, lifeless, his mouth was half open.

The police turned up along with the doctor and they shifted his body out. Two days later his wife and two sons arrived, claimed his belongings and paid his bills.

I had to leave, get out of the place and never return. That's what I did.

I moved from resort to resort, unable to settle in. Strangers moved in and out of my life. I found nothing common with them. Something had broken inside and it would be a while before I became again the person I once was.

It was a scary time because I had started hallucinating and I was unsure whether the people I met and the experiences I had were real or not. There was a fellow I called the Birdman who would walk along the beach with a large fish kite sitting on his shoulder. He held it in place with a string tied to its leg. He said his name was Bonzo and he worked as a Manager in a little resort down the beach called The Shack. He said that there was a bitch at the resort who had given birth to eight puppies. So I went to see them. They were beautiful, all pure black with little white patches all over their bodies. Every day I visited them there was one less. Then they were all gone, so was the bitch and the Birdman. There were other people and creatures too and they were all so real and yet so unreal. I was going crazy. I was cracking up. I returned to Clementine.

Sabby didn't appear to be surprised and welcomed me in. Banjo greeted me like a long lost friend. It seemed as if I had never gone away.

But I had changed inside. I was not the same any more.

Chrissie wasn't there. She was away in north India, following a lead that she hoped would help her find her son. But Sabby told me in a matter-of-fact way that they were getting married. Good for him and good for her and good that they were going to be a cosy little twosome.

I got back to the routine of walking with Banjo. This time I let him take the lead and we'd walk endlessly all evening and return in the dark. No one minded, least of all Xavier because he had moved out of Goa. But it was quite a struggle for me to build a relationship with Banjo again. I'd have to get a lot out of my system and out of my head to create space for him and start CARING for him.

What are your plans Melissa? Sabby asked over a beer.

I'm not sure really, was all I could say.

I mean are you planning to be here for a while?

Yes. I have nowhere else to go just now Sabby. I'm tired.

You're young and beautiful and you still have a lot to live for …

I'm fifty, Sabby. Please don't try cheering me up with those worn out lines.

So? I'm sixty-eight and I'm marrying again.

That's you Sabby. That's the way you are made. That's your culture.

I suppose so. Listen, I want to ask you something. A favour.

What do you want from me? I have nothing to offer.

You do … listen … when Chrissie returns from the north she plans to travel up to Bombay to meet her brother and bring him back here.

You mean Arnie.

Yes, Arnie. Now this is a long shot. A very long shot …

Go on Sabby, get to the point.

Will you go with her? You don't have to spend anything. We'll cover all that.

Money isn't my problem, I replied. *It never has been my problem. I'm curious to know why you think I'll be of any help. Isn't this a family matter? I'm not even a part of your family or Chrissie's family, why do you think I'll be of any use? Chrissie doesn't even like me … I don't think she'll want me to be part of this plan of hers. This is her family business. Anyway, what's wrong with that fellow Arnie? Why can't he come down?*

He may not be in any fit state.

So Chrissie wants me to go down there and be a nurse? Is that it?

It's not like that.

How does Chrissie know I'm here?

I've told her. She requested me to ask you.

If she wants help SHE should ask for it.

Sure, I'll let her know.

And so the conversation ended there and Arnie slipped into my head once again like a thief, stealthily. I didn't know it at that time but my life was about to take an unexpected turn …

6 THE RETURN

At Colva

I gave up on trying to find Luke and closed the chapter for a while. I knew I hadn't lost him for sure because something deep inside told me that he was alive and when he was ready he'd return to me. So back to Colva I went because I realised that I couldn't keep Sabby waiting any longer. I didn't want him to change his mind because I had got used to the idea that we were going to be partners. I looked forward to the days ahead. There was even a faint fluttering in my stomach. But in spite of that, at the back of my mind and heart there was a slight fear. Along with the marriage we were planning to bring our work together. That would mean that Blue Mermaid would not really be MINE anymore but OURS. It would become part of something larger. Luke and I had worked so hard to create our resort, brick by brick, idea by idea, we used all our charm, all our love, hard work and dreaming to make it happen and keep it alive. It had become a part of me. Without My Blue Mermaid, I would be Nobody. I suddenly realised that I didn't really want to lose it. The feeling grew so strong that it began to disturb my feelings for Sabby and took away the fluttering in my stomach.

He was quick to pick up on the change. *What's going on Chrissie? Why so distant?*

Just the strain of not having Luke here to help me manage Blue Mermaid, I lied, *nothing else.*

Don't worry, he reassured me, *we'll do it together soon. Better still, we'll get a damned good professional team and let them handle all of it and we'll go off for a long holiday.*

You must be joking.

I'm not, I'm serious. Don't you want to put your feet up Chrissie? What are you trying to prove by doing all this? And who are you trying to prove this to?

This is my baby. Do you want me to abandon my baby?

That scared him off for a couple of days. Then over dinner at Clementine, *something seems to have changed in you Chrissie, something bothering you? Someone said something about me, us?*

It's not about you or us Sabby, it's got to do with me and Blue Mermaid.

Are you worried that you are going to lose it?

It's not exactly that.

Then what is it Chrissie? I get the feeling that there's something you want to say and you don't know how to say it. Do you or don't you want the merger?

That's not the point, I was uneasy.

Maybe because Luke isn't here, you are feeling a bit alone in this. You'd like him to be in on all this.

Yes. But he isn't here.

Okay, there'll be a place for him in the arrangement. Let him manage everything. He'll be the CEO.

He isn't here, Sabby. Besides I would have liked to leave Blue Mermaid to him and left it to him to decide what he wants to do with it.

You want to wait? You want to change your mind?

Sabby, I said softly, *I'm beginning to feel pushed.*

Pushed? I'm not pushing.

Let's give it a rest. Please, can we talk about all this later?

That night, back at Blue Mermaid, I couldn't sleep and sat out alone in the moonlight, uneasy about the time ahead.

And then I heard his voice, *Mum*, it was Luke. I was sure it was him. I jumped up and looked around. Nothing, just the shifting shadows of trees in the moonlight. *Mum*, much clearer this time.

Luke, I can hear you son, I can hear you. Where are you? Can I see you?

This time, only the hiss and rustle of the palm leaves, nothing else. I knew then for certain, Luke was coming home.

I returned to my room and fell asleep, waking ever so often, listening for his voice but the night was filled with the sounds of the sea and the wind.

Three days later, I found Luke sitting outside my room at Blue Mermaid when I returned from lunch. He was a shadow of his former self. I didn't want people to start talking so I took him back to our place in Panjim and mothered him out of his mind. I didn't want to ask him any questions but let him be. Only thing I did was bathe him, dress him, feed him, play his favourite music and be there–present, with no expectations.

One morning he asked, *something's happened to Sabby?*

What do you mean?

Is he ill or something?

Not that I know of ... and I'd be the first to know.

Then why isn't he here?

He's not. He's over at Clementine.

Aren't you two married?

No Luke, not as yet.

That's good, he sighed, *because something's happened to him.*

A moment later there was a call from Melissa. *You better come soon Chrissie, I think we've lost Sabby.*

Yes, we had lost Sabby. Someone had taken his life quite brutally. There was blood everywhere in the hall where they had found his body with faint signs of life. By the time they got him to the hospital he was dead. So sudden, so tragic. The cops took over the place and combed it for clues. Everyone who worked for Clementine or were associated with Sabby were taken in for questioning but the cops drew blanks. Xavier who had been away in Portugal returned and presented himself, ready to take over Clementine but he was in for a rude shock when they took him in for questioning too. A couple of his seedy friends were hauled in after him and everything became rather messy. But the investigation lost direction and the matter settled down and then dissolved.

Through all the hassles, Melissa stood by me like a rock, organising, managing, being my backup at every twist and turn. I don't know how she managed it since she had been grieving her dear dog's mysterious disappearance. I think it was her peculiar sense of humour that pulled her through and lightened the burden. Everyone around her started treating her differently. That I suppose helped her along. She even went out of her way to try and help Luke feel better about himself and come back to earth and to himself. But she just couldn't get through to him. He seemed to be living in a bubble that refused to burst. We couldn't depend on him for anything. So we took care of him, hoping that he'd come back to himself one day. I didn't really mind when Melissa kept him with her for days on end because I knew she was trying her best. Hard not to be possessive but I managed somehow.

As for Xavier, well he was really out on a limb. He had just about got over the police investigation when he discovered that Sabby had left all his possessions to me. He was devastated and did his wickedest to make things miserable for me. It all started when he turned up one evening at Clementine, walked up to the desk and rapped it hard with the knuckles of his right hand. The heavy metal rings that he wore rattled the wooden surface, knocking over my glass of lemonade and spilling its contents on to my lap. Four of his buddies were with him. The black chap was there amongst them and he was standing just behind Xavier. *Don't think you'll get away with this you little Madame,* he hissed. The others added their two piece bits but the man in front of me didn't say a word. He slammed the desk top again and swept away everything on the surface. Then again and again till his knuckles were bloodied.

I decided to keep my cool. *Lost your tongue shippie?*

He's the owner of this place. He's Sabby's son. The black one said menacingly. *His own flesh and blood. And you … you have nothing to do with Sabby. You're not even his wife. The devil only knows what spell you cast on the fellow. You and that white bitch. Meeeeleeesaaa. Between the two of you.*

At that point, Melissa butted in. *What's your problem eh? What's your problem?*

I don't have a problem, the fellow said, *you have. And you are going to have a lot of problems bloody German.*

You wanking Nigerian with a pea sized brain, you won't get far.

What you call me?

A wanking Nigerian.

The man had hardly turned to face her when the waiters, the cooks and the cleaners stepped in and surrounded them. *I think you better leave,* I looked at Xavier straight in the face. *You better go or else it's going to be bad for you.*

He walked away with his little gang, heading for Colva Square, only to return a few days later and start trying to browbeat me. On his third visit he found Luke sitting in a corner nursing a beer. *Hello zombie. Any news from the other world? I mean give me some real news.* The black chap pinched his cheeks, *you heard what friend Xavy just asked, be a good boy and give him some good news ... like he's going to get this place and things like that.*

You're going to die, badly, Luke replied. *Soon.*

The black chap started laughing. *You talking to me eh?*

Yes, I'm talking to you.

There was a terrible silence. The black chap took a step back then kicked the table so hard that it sent Luke flying back with his chair, beer splashing in his face. *You think you can scare me? No, you don't scare me. Just because they're saying you can predict stuff you zombie, don't think I'm going to believe all that. I don't believe what you're saying.* But the man looked scared. He backed out of Clementine. *I'm going and I'll come back every day to show you I'm still alive.* When he left, Xavier shouted at me, *tell this son of yours that if he doesn't stop this rubbish stuff he's spouting, I'm going to deal with him.*

Time you left Xavier, who knows–you may be next.

You think this bullshit is going to worry me?

I'm not saying it will, my voice was low.

You better not. He left hurriedly with his goons.

God, that was another something to bother me. Luke's peculiar state. He rarely spoke, behaved like he was a walking dead man, said strange things to people. But he didn't stop eating and sleeping or anything of that sort, it's just that he behaved strangely. Took him to church, got the parish priest to talk to him, sent him to confession and communion but nothing mattered. Took him off to three shrinks but they couldn't make head or tail of him and kept prescribing all sorts of pills. But there were two things that he seemed to like–walking and spending time with Melissa.

When the news went around that the black chap had been knocked down and killed by a speeding holiday maker, word was spread by those who had heard Luke telling him that his death was around the corner. All Colva woke up overnight to the prospects of having a resident soothsayer. People started turning up at Clementine and Blue Mermaid to ask to meet him. They'd stop him in the street or follow him along the beach whenever he was out on a walk and pepper him with questions about birth, marriage, death, employment, going abroad, property and all sorts. He'd speak when he wanted to speak and kept silent at other times. Word went all the way up the coast to North Goa and then into the hinterland and before we knew what to do, Luke was besieged.

The parish priest was concerned, really concerned, about what was happening. *You need to get the boy away from here. Send him off somewhere closer to the Lord.*

What do you mean by that? I didn't like the way he was talking.

Maybe to some retreat. One of our fathers has a retreat place in Pachmari in Madhya Pradesh. He's healed a lot of people. Luke needs to be healed. If you want help on that, you can count on me.

Thanks father, I'll think about it.

When I told Melissa about it, she had a bit of a reaction. *None of his damned business. Send him off to be healed by some frock fellow somewhere God knows where and you'll drive him crazy. He's a bit different just now Chrissie, just let him be and he'll find himself. He's gone through all sorts. We are lucky he hasn't gone crazy.*

He's half crazy anyway.

What rubbish. He's more sane than all of us put together. There's nothing crazy about him.

Then what's all this prediction business that he's up to?

It's not 'prediction business' Chrissie, he's seen a lot and felt a lot and it's all inside him. You and I will never know what all this is doing to him. All we can see is the tip of the iceberg.

I can't handle too much right now. I can just about keep myself together and the business together. It would be great if Luke could take care of himself. But he can't.

Who says he can't? Melissa looked almost indignant. *Leave him be.*

But what are we going to do with all these people who land up here or catch him when he's out? How do we handle them?

Don't.

This is ridiculous Melissa. They're at him all the time. I have half a mind to make sure he remains at Blue Mermaid and have staff around him to keep people away.

Nothing was resolved. It was really frustrating. What added to the stressful situation was that a local newspaper put Luke on its front page. That got other papers and magazines into the act. Then television channels got wind of the story. PR agencies started hassling me. It was becoming a bloody joke. I hired two security guards and kept Luke at Blue Mermaid. Melissa and I managed to keep them all at bay ... and after some time, things began to settle down.

Then one day, when the three of us were having a quiet Sunday lunch, Luke stopped eating and said, *Arnie should be here. Arnie should be here. Where's Arnie?*

That finished us off. We started waiting, on the very edge of our chairs, for Arnie to suddenly turn up. *What do you think Melissa? Do you think he'll turn up? If he does, we'll have to deal with the two of them.*

But he's trying to tell us something. Melissa was serious.

What?

I don't know. He's definitely trying to tell us something. I don't think we should ignore him.

So what should we do about it? I had begun to feel uneasy.

Find out how he is. I don't know if you are aware of it but Sabby had once suggested that I go with you to bring Arnie here–for your wedding. He said that it was your idea.

But now I can't be marrying a dead man Melissa. What's the point? Besides, I'm tired, really tired. I want to sell all this off and go away. What would I do without you?

It was all going too far so that night I sat Luke down. *Look here Luke, something mighty fishy is going on. What's all this soothsaying about? First you vanish and abandon me to go it all alone and then you come back as if from another world and start talking like you know what's going to happen next. What's happening? Come on boy, what's happening. Can you explain this to me in simple terms?*

Explain what? My going away?

No, let that be, I've somewhat accepted that because you are back. You had your reasons and I've accepted all that, difficult to digest, but I've accepted it.

Then what do you want me to explain?

This fortune telling thing you are up to. I mean telling the future. When this one is going to pop off and when that one …

Wait a minute Mum, you are trivialising all of it. You are making it seem that it's all mumbo jumbo. It's not. It's real.

Real? Where has it all popped up from? I need to know because I am living with you. I want to know what I am living with.

I don't know myself. All I do know is that it came to me when I had emptied myself.

What do you mean by that?

Just that–emptied myself and everything inside me became clear. I was up there in the snow and ice with real people. But it's leaving me, I can feel it. It's leaving me as I slip back into life here and I get crowded out by everything. I can already feel that there's little space in there. I can feel it.

And you expect me to understand what the hell you are talking about? You expect me to believe it? I'm a Catholic.

I'm not expecting you to understand it or believe it. Just let it be, it'll go away. It's already going away.

As for Melissa, she had already made up her mind and a few days later announced that she was planning to make a trip to Gorai to meet Arnie.

What for? I wanted to know.

Are you jealous?

Her question took me by surprise. *No I'm not. Why should I be?* But she didn't reply, just booked her ticket and left for Bombay, leaving behind a vacuum which was difficult to fill. For a while I felt outnumbered, besieged. Nothing seemed right. Melissa had become an important part of my life. In that short while, her presence had grown on me and I had begun to appreciate her specialness. True, I had become jealous of the time she gave Luke and of course uneasy about the fact that she was going to be spending time with Arnie. And if she returned with Arnie she'd have them both. Where would I be? God, all my life I've been frightened of being alone and afraid to admit it.

I couldn't understand the strong feelings of dependency I had started having for Melissa. I wasn't uneasy about it but I nevertheless wanted to make some sense of it.

Her first call came one night.

It's crazy here.

What do you mean? Is Arnie okay? Is he with us?

What a stupid bloody question Chrissie, of course he's with us. But it's crazy here. I mean the situation he's got himself into. His house is now a Guesthouse run by someone else and he is living in his outhouse–the shed. It's all done up fine but that's not the point. If you think there's something wrong with your son … your brother beats him any day.

I listened to her rambling on about the mess that Arnie had got himself into and began to sense that beneath it all, Melissa was excited about being there–taking care of someone, sorting out his problems and finding a way out for him. That was the pathway to her heart.

Hullo, Chrissie, are you there? What's the silence for? Say something. Want to talk to Arnie?

When are you planning to return Melissa?

She didn't respond and hung up. Had she hung up or had the line got cut? I rang her back on her mobile but she didn't take the call. Sent her an SMS. *When do I expect you back? Lots to be done here. X*

Will be a while.

When can we talk?

Will get in touch. Lots to be done here.

I didn't call her again nor did I SMS her. It was scary being so dependent. *What's got into me? Something is going on inside me. It's disturbing. I can't handle it.*

I tried to distract myself by being busy, shuttling between Clementine and Blue Mermaid. Business was picking up again and we were sold out. The new managers I had hired were doing a damned good job and I made sure that I gave them, as well as the staff, attractive incentives.

But Melissa's silence unnerved me.

Inbox

Chrissie, don't know how to put this, but something strange is happening here. It's crazy but it's happening. Now where do I begin, it's all so complicated. Please be patient with me. When I got here it took me quite some time to find Arnie's place because there are so many guesthouses and hotels here and posh looking buildings and shops and touristy places and no one seemed to know who the hell Arnie is and where he lives. Anyway, I found his place. I couldn't believe that it is so tiny … until I discovered that he is living in his shed which has been done up. He rented the house and the compound to a fellow by the name of Brother Peter. What a strange name. But this Brother Peter fellow is a real crook. Charming but dangerous, just like a lot of Indians we know. Sorry I'm being racist. But this Brother Peter fellow can charm a hungry lion and take away its food and the lion will say 'you're welcome.' He took the place on rent from Arnie and stopped paying after some time. In exchange he did up the shed so Arnie would be 'comfortable.' That made Arnie 'grateful!' Can you beat that? Brother Peter has got everyone in his pocket and has already made a lot of money out of the place.

More soon, Melissa

Dear Melissa, what a relief to get some news from you. I've never been the internet type, except for work but I guess I'll have to change my ways if I want to be in touch with people a little more. Luke would do all that until his brain went soft. But I miss your presence here. You bring so much life into the place. You'll be surprised to know how many people really respect you now. I remember how they used to behave towards you and make fun of you and all that. They are singing a different song now. Melli Madam this and Melli Madam that. So when are you planning to return?

Waiting to hear from you, xx Chrissie

Chrissie, don't you want to know how your brother is? Strangely enough, he is not in as bad a shape as I thought he'd be. He's actually been 'dressing up' every evening and we go out for a drink and a meal. But from the way he talks about what he has been through, it's crazy … hallucinations, loss of memory, real damned harassment from the local people, thefts, murder, I know he's not telling me tall stories. But he's pulled through. And you know what did it? You'll never believe it. You'll never never believe it … walking therapy. He's up and out of the place at five-thirty in the morning and he walks along the beach and back. Does the same in the evening. I'm doing the same now. Remember he had a bit of stoop? Now it's gone and he's straight as a pine tree. He reads like anything and we've been to Bombay a few times.

More soon, Melissa

Yes of course I want to know how my brother is and I want to know how you are too. How are you coping? Are you staying somewhere near his place? How do you spend the rest of your time? I'm sure you must be finding it very stressful. I'll be here for you when you get back and you can put your feet up and take it easy.

Love, Chrissie

I'm staying with Arnie. It was his idea. His generosity. It's cramped but clean. A woman comes and cleans the place and cooks his food in his little kitchen. That's another story. The kitchen is in a small extension to the place. So is the bathroom. Arnie had to ask permission for that to be built! And the guy not only gave him the permission but built it for him. It's all so complicated. And don't worry about me, I'm enjoying the confusion.

More soon, Melissa

Hello Chrissie, no news from you. What's up? Is everything okay? I tried to get you on the line but you didn't take the call. The guys at Blue Mermaid and Clementine said you were busy and would call later. You seem upset. Why so quiet?

Waiting for news, Melissa

I'd just like to put it straight to you Melissa–is there something going on between you two?

Hello Chrissie. Something seems to be bothering you. What is it exactly? Arnie and I have had things going on in the past between us too. Maybe you weren't aware. And sorry to say, even Sabby and I in our lonely patches had a thing or two going on between us. But we are adults and these things happen. Have I upset you by saying that I'm staying with Arnie?

Please say something, Melissa

What am I to say? I don't know what to say.

Love you always, Chrissie

I'm so damned confused that I don't know what's going on in my head and in my heart. Why does Melissa mean so much to me? What is it about her that I can't do without her being with me? What's going on? All that and more went around in my head and I was well and truly in a mess. Though Luke had become more communicative and had actually started walking around the property and people weren't bothering him that much, he wasn't real company. And anyway, there was little feeling left. I really had a problem seeing him as my son. He was someone else's son.

And something else had begun to happen to me, I had started to let go of my past … all those memories of my childhood and growing up years and my dad and mum began to slip away, just like the water lapping the beach going away with the tide, slip away slowly … leaving just the sand and shells and a few crabs and then those too are gone. That's why I tried my best to look at what I had and what I could hold on to and feel happy about. Melissa was the centre of it all.

I didn't hear from her for quite a while after those emails. It really bothered me but I tried my best not to think about her too much and busied myself with work on Clementine as there was a lot to do. I renovated and spruced up the place quite a bit … replaced the furniture, made the bar a better place to sit at, got a new tandoor and added Thai and Tibetan food to the menu–that proved to be quite an attraction. Yes, and before I forget, got the whole frontage of Clementine done up super. That really attracted people. Though things were going really good, I was still quite worried about Xavier and his goons. I didn't know when he would land up with them again. He was hovering around somewhere in the shadows, waiting to strike when I least expected him to.

Then one morning I got a call from one of Sabby's old friends, Inspector Fernandes from Anjuna. *Sabby's son is in the box. He needs to be bailed out. Will you do it?*

What did he do?

There was a fight and they picked up someone else's car and drove off and bashed it up. All the others are in and nailed. I can let this one off lightly, but someone has to bail him out.

Doesn't he have his own contacts?

He's got nothing. You should see him now Chrissie, the man's really down and out. He's a mess.

I'm coming. Now.

I surprised myself.

At the police station I did whatever I had to and got him out. The fellow was smelling … it looked like he hadn't bathed or changed his clothes for god alone knows how long. He was in a real state. *I'll drop you home*, I said, knowing well that he had no home to be dropped to.

Okay. Drop me near the beach down that way.

Which way?

Damn, just drop me off here.

Listen Xavier, I know you haven't got anywhere to go. I'm taking you back.

Back where?

With me. You are Sabby's son–so you are coming home.

The man looked really confused. *Why are you doing this to me? Why?*

I'm not doing this to you, I'm doing this for you.

What's the difference?

Think about it.

Why are you doing this for me?

I didn't reply. He was embarrassed enough and I didn't want to start rubbing salt into his wounds.

We caused quite a stir when we turned up at Clementine. I ignored the stares and the whispers and told them to get one of the best rooms ready for him and packed someone off to pick up some night clothes. I was going to keep him in bed for as long as I could. I was pretty sure he was on something or the other and I didn't want him going off and getting any more of it.

What a dramatic turn of events. He wasn't exactly the prodigal son but he had returned home anyway and the challenge would be to keep him there. If Melissa had a 'project' I now had one too. I decided to send her a mail and let her know. A reply came almost immediately…

Good God woman, why did you do that? You should have left the fellow in the box. Let him get healed and he'll start making a nuisance of himself. How could you be so stupid? Believe me, once he settles in he'll start poking his nose in Clementine and then Blue Mermaid.

Next thing you know, he'll want his share of Clementine.

You've really got me worried, Melissa

I'm trying to put myself in Sabby's shoes and do what he would have done. If a time comes when Xavier wants his 'share' of Sabby's estate I'll give it to him. In fact, I think he deserves his share and you the other.

Love, Chrissie

You must be joking.

I'm not joking, I'm serious. Maybe you and Arnie could manage Clementine and we'll give Xavier all the other assets … that is, when I am convinced he'll do something with it.

What are you doing there so long darling? Come home. Chrissie

Looks like you are going to become like Artemis with many breasts. You love playing that role. This man has his roots dug in so deep that it will take a while to move him from here.

Melissa

Xavier

Xavier was my project and I was determined to make it work. So I started taking his food to his room and got the staff to take him his drink and cigarettes. He seemed a little awkward whenever he saw me but gradually settled into polite silence and avoided looking at me. Once when I took him his lunch I carried in a sandwich for myself. We ate together in silence. Then he said quite suddenly, *Is this some sort of house arrest?*

I smiled and he seemed visibly irritated.

This isn't a joke you know. Is this some sort of house arrest?

No, it's not. You are free to leave.

He finished his meal and then stood up, stretching his bony body, *time to go. No point hanging around when I'm free to go.*

So where will you go from here? I wanted to know.

Oh, there's a whole wide world out there.

Must be a great feeling to know there's a whole wide world out there and you don't have a rupee in your pocket and no home to go to. Why don't you stop being so proud Xavier? You are in your own home, try and be yourself. Sit down. Relax.

Shut up. You are sounding like my father. Relax. I hate that word. You say this is my home … I don't think so … I was thrown out of here. Humiliated. All because of my choices. I know that. All because of my choices.

I decided to push the discussion as far as I could. *What choices are you talking about?*

You know exactly what I'm talking about, woman.

You know my name, why don't you call me by my name? What's stopping you? I challenged him.

You know what I'm talking about Chrissie.

That's better.

Stop controlling me.

Why don't you get back to what you were just saying Xavier.

What was I just saying?

That I know what you are talking about. I don't. Tell me.

You are making fun of me.

Stop beating around the bush. Tell me for God's sake.

That I'm gay.

Okay, you are gay, so what?

And I prefer men, strong men.

Yes, so? That's your choice. I could see that he was feeling challenged but I wasn't going to stop. *I like strong men too but I don't mind strong women as well.*

What's this? Some sort of game, eh? He looked visibly uneasy.

No, it isn't a game. We're two adults having a conversation. Simple as that.

My father was ...

I stopped him dead in his tracks, didn't let him complete his sentence. *Your father was uneasy about you and your choices. But now he's dead and gone. There's just you and me ... and I don't have any problem with your choices.*

So what will happen if I brought my man in here ...

I won't take him away from you, he is yours.

I mean–you won't object?

No.

And the others in this place? He wanted to know.

I'm the boss Xavier.

He went into the toilet and leaving the door open–pissed.

Sighed loudly. Came out, stepped out of his night clothes and went back again, shut the door and bathed. I left.

Whenever I got the opportunity after that I had a chat with him and as the days passed he talked a lot more. Of course, he was still quite suspicious of me and my intentions and kept asking me if he was free to leave the room.

There's a hitch somewhere Chrissie.

Not at all. Try. Try just once. Come on out and we'll have a drink and a meal in the restaurant downstairs.

But he didn't budge. I don't know what stopped him. Was he afraid that something would happen to him when he got out? Was there someone out there waiting to get him? Was he just afraid of leaving the security of the room? OR was he too embarrassed to be seen by the staff and others in the restaurant? I couldn't tell. All I could tell was that he didn't want to leave the room.

Are you feeling uncomfortable here Xavier? Would you like to shift to the resort?

Stop being so damned kind and generous. This is all so unreal. 'Xavier this is your home. Xavier do what you like. Xavier nice nice.' Just shut up. This is all too damned sweet and suspicious for me. It's too sweet. You are expecting me to forget the past and pretend that the slate is clean and I can start all over again. I can't Chrissie.

Why can't you?

Because I have too much in there and it can't come out and unless I get it out I'm not going to be really free. And the sad thing is when I get free, I'll not be free anymore. Complicated, isn't it? Isn't it Chrissie?

Yes. But go on if you want.

Go on where?

Let it out.

I know why my father wanted to marry you.

Why?

Because you're so naive. But what he didn't know was that you are far from naive. You're like a spider in the way you lure people into your web. Just like one of my lovers. The black one. You know who that is. The one your Lukie polished off.

That was something that Luke said when he had half a brain …

Your Lukie has three brains if you ask me.

So do you want to move to the resort? I mean Blue Mermaid.

Yes. But not now. In a while if that is okay with you Chrissie.

That surprised me. *Sure.*

After that I stayed out of his way and got back to spending a little time with Luke who had started to recover even faster than before. In fact he had less and less of a memory of the peculiar phase that he had gone through. He spent a few hours in the office every day and even began to show up in the kitchen and housekeeping section. The staff rallied around and was supportive.

But there was a distance between us and it would take me time to come to terms with the fact that my son had changed. He had become someone else. I suppose it had to happen. It happens to all of us. We all change. I'm a good example–how scared and uneasy I used to be when confronted by people who were gay. I was terrified that Luke might have been gay. But there I was chatting with Xavier without fear or nausea or anything of the sort. I accepted him and his choices. Why? Was it that something in me had stirred and woken up? Something about my preferences that I myself was scared to admit and finally did? Had I really admitted to myself that I was a latent lesbian? Or was I just aware of it? Whatever it was, one thing was for sure, I had begun to allow myself to feel what I really wanted to feel.

We made Xavier comfortable in the same room that Arnie had once occupied. He liked the place because it was a little private and he could sit out whenever he wanted to. The staff made a special effort to help him feel comfortable and at home and he eased into the rhythms of Blue Mermaid. Almost all the guests were new so they minded their own business and got on with holidaying. Not that I had any problem with the old timers but it's just that they were getting under my skin with their advice. New guests are easier to cope with–most importantly because they didn't stay for very long, zipped in and zipped out and pushed off to see other places down south in the country.

Luke was a little upset because I hadn't discussed Xavier's situation with him. I wanted to but knowing him I had kept my mouth shut. If Luke knew too much in advance about anything or anyone he'd immediately start worrying and letting his imagination run riot. *Listen Mum, I have no problem with you bringing Xavier here and I don't want to know the background but it would have been nice if you had told me.*

If I had mentioned it to you, God knows–you would have run away or done something strange.

Why would I have done something strange?

Because you haven't been yourself and I was worried.

It doesn't look like you were in the least bit worried Mum because you brought him here and gave him a room. How do you think I feel when you've done this without even discussing it with me?

You are not yourself anymore Luke. You are someone else.

That's a stupid thing to say. I am myself, I am Luke, your son. Who else can I be?

I turned the conversation in another direction and he dragged it right back and started raising his voice. *If he is going to stay here however long, I expect him to be of some use.*

He's our guest. MY guest. He doesn't have to do anything.

Okay, suit yourself. Why don't you get guests like Melissa here instead of this thing?

Melissa is in Gorai with Arnie.

What's she doing there?

What do you think she's doing there Luke? She obviously likes the company of the man.

He'll wreck her so badly that she won't be able to put herself together again, believe me.

The conversation broke into little pieces of this and that and then dissolved in hot mugs of coffee. Then I said very quietly, *we're going to have lunch together tomorrow, Luke. You, Xavier and I. And I want you to be civil.*

Just once, he muttered and left.

The lunch turned out to be quite a disaster. Not the spread–that was gorgeous, delicious, lip-smacking. But a strong wind started up the beach and blew mouthfuls of sand at us. Xavier gulped his beer and left, Luke sat there pretending the sand hadn't disturbed him. *That's the problem with these city slickers,* he cursed.

That's okay. We all have our choices Luke.

Yes, I know, you should have said that to me a long time ago and I'd have been happy and so much wouldn't have happened.

So you are saying that I caused everything that happened to you?

Most of it Mum, most of it. If you had let me be, things would have been fine. No, but you wanted to control. You're a control freak. And you'll never ever change. Here's another good example. You're now trying to control Xavier. You are taking over his life, he's going to become your puppy dog.

Can't you be generous for once? I desperately tried to control my rising temper.

This property is as much mine.

Okay, it is as much yours. So?

So I want a say in whether Xavier stays or not ... and if he stays, how he's going to contribute. Well? What do you think generous Mum? He looked at me triumphantly.

Then I turned the tables around. *Why don't we decide right now, here and now. What's your opinion?*

My opinion? He can stay because you've invited him here. But if you plan to keep him here more than a few months, he's going to have to do some work. He'll have to earn his stay.

Why?

Why not? His voice was cold. Flat.

He's family.

Family? You call this man family? You call this criminal, family?

Yes Luke.

This is the man who harassed and humiliated you and me. He's no relative of ours. You weren't married to Sabby. You inherited his estate. That's the connection. Now you're feeling guilty that this fellow hasn't got anything.

I'm being Christian.

That's the joke of the season. Luke sniggered.

I don't think it's a joke. Xavier was standing at our table, his face expressionless. *I don't think it's a joke at all. Chrissie ...*

Luke didn't let him finish what he had set out to say, *Chrissie, hah ... now he's calling you 'Chrissie' ... next he'll be calling me 'son' and the staff 'boys' and 'girls.'*

Xavier ignored him. *I don't think this has anything to do with being Christian. Chrissie pulled me out of a shit hole and gave me shelter, asking for nothing in return. She drove down to that bloody cop-shop and got me out and gave me shelter. She fed me, was patient with me. She did everything that my parents didn't do for me ...*

Precisely, Luke butted in, *because she isn't 'your parent.' It's a lot easier to do unusual things for other people's children. But when it comes to your own ...*

The difference is, said Xavier, *that neither you nor I have been parents. We're someone else's children.*

So what's the point you're making? Luke had started to raise his voice.

The other remained calm. *So we will never be able to understand why they do and feel what they do and feel.*

Why don't you go and get married and find out, I'm challenging you.

Can we sit down please … and talk …

There was something in his voice that stopped Luke in his tracks. They sat down and fell into a long silence. Just when it had started to get uneasy for the three of us, Xavier started talking, *I want to say something. May I?*

I nodded.

Thanks Chrissie. Thanks for what you did for me. Sorry Luke, sorry for coming in here and causing so much of unhappiness. No I don't want to have anything to do with a resort or restaurant or guesthouse business. That's not my cup of tea. And yes, I do feel bad, really bad, that my father left me nothing in his will and that he left it all to Chrissie … I don't expect you Chrissie to give me a share of Clementine. I don't want to be accepted by your family. I want nothing. And you know why? I can't stand the burden of relationships any more. I don't want anymore strings pulling and tugging at me. I want to live my life my way. Every moment is precious to me. He left as suddenly as he had arrived. Luke looked visibly uneasy.

After that we didn't see him for days as he preferred to stay in his room.

Then I got thinking. *Why had he become such a recluse? Had he become more reflective? Remorseful? Something was not right. It bothered me.*

Three days later an intruder managed to get past the

security guards and tried to break into Xavier's room. He was caught but slipped away after a scuffle.

I knew this fellow would bring trouble with him. Luke sounded his self righteous best.

Why do you say that?

We haven't had a break-in in years. Suddenly it's happening now. And who is the target? Xavier. Why Xavier?

Because his room is secluded, that's why, I tried to explain.

That's not why, Luke was insistent. *There's some hanky panky here, isn't it obvious? This guy used someone to knock his father off, now the hit man is after him because he hasn't got his money or he's blackmailing him or some such filth.*

You seem to have become an expert on low life.

I haven't become an expert, Mum, any fool will tell you that. With a bent mind like his.

Enough of that Luke, this is disgusting.

When I talked to Xavier about the matter, he didn't have much of an explanation to offer, in fact, he seemed very edgy. *Something the matter Xavier? Something we haven't talked about? Something I should know?*

There's a lot you should know but I haven't told you because it would only scare you Chrissie.

Go on, try me.

I don't know where to start.

Start in the middle, go backwards or forwards or anything you like but tell me for Christ's sake.

I'm not going to tell you for Christ's sake, I'll tell you for your sake …

And then he told me everything … the drug ring he had been part of, stories of extortion, beatings, revenge … *But I had nothing to do with the death of my father, nothing at all. I think I know who did it and why.*

Why didn't you tell the cops?

You must be joking. They were people I knew. Why are you so damned naive?

I persisted. *So where are all these people now?*

Around, some in Goa.

Why are they after you?

You are asking me too many questions. I need to be in a safe place Chrissie, get me out of here.

You are going to have to answer me first. Did you have your father killed? Did you? Answer me?

It's too complicated. I can't explain.

Luke stepped in. *Fucking murderer.*

Watch your words, Xavier snapped.

There you are, I knew it. I knew it all along. I'm calling the cops.

No Luke you'll do nothing of the sort. We haven't heard the full story.

So you're going to cover-up for him and get him out of here?

Listen, Xavier butted in, *just get me out of here and I'll never bother you again. I did what I did …*

What did you do? I asked

I told them to frighten him out of the place but they killed him. Now they want me to pay them for killing him. And you know how much that costs?

You're sick. Was all I could say.

I told you, I knew it all along, Luke kept repeating.

Shut up, or I'll get you killed too. Xavier slipped his hand into his pocket and whipping out a flick knife went for Luke. I rammed a chair in the way and tripped him up. As he fell I lifted the small glass topped table and slammed it on his head. He shook his bleeding head and scrambled for his room. Before we could get to him he had locked himself in.

I'm calling the cops, said Luke frantically and ran to his office.

By the time we managed to break open the door, he had taken his own life.

The story was all over the local papers and our guests began quickly checking out. It was going to be a long time before Blue Mermaid got back to its feet.

I was at the very end of my tether when Melissa called.

How's your man doing, I asked.

Which man?

Arnie.

Can't change him darling. He's still with his mother, fighting her, loving her, afraid of her. What about your man?

My man?

Yes, Luke, your son.

Not very different from Arnie.

So that leaves just the two of us.

Yes, Melissa, just the two of us. We've all travelled so far, lived so much and have finally met on the shore. Come home.

I will.